Felicity Price is the author of four novels, *Dancing in the Wilderness* (2001), *No Angel* (2002), *Call of the Falcon* (2004) and *Split Time* (2005), and the best-selling biography *Dare to Dream: the John Britten Story* (2003). Felicity began her writing career at *The Press* in the 1970s before moving on to journalism at TVNZ, Radio New Zealand and *North and South*. Since 1987, Felicity has run an award-winning public relations company in partnership with her husband Chris Rennie. Felicity and Chris have two adult children.

A Sandwich Short of a Picnic

Felicity Price

A catalogue record for this book is available from the
National Library of New Zealand

A BLACK SWAN BOOK
published by
Random House New Zealand
18 Poland Road, Glenfield, Auckland, New Zealand
www.randomhouse.co.nz

Random House International
Random House
20 Vauxhall Bridge Road
London, SW1V 2SA
United Kingdom

Random House Australia (Pty) Ltd
20 Alfred Street, Milsons Point, Sydney
New South Wales 2061, Australia

Random House South Africa Pty Ltd
Isle of Houghton
Corner Boundary Road and Carse O'Gowrie
Houghton 2198, South Africa

Random House Publishers India Private Ltd
301 World Trade Tower, Hotel Intercontinental Grand Complex
Barakhamba Lane, New Delhi 110 001, India

First published 2008

ISBN 978 1 86941 949 3

Design: Elin Bruhn Termannsen
Cover illustrations: PurestockX
Cover design: Matthew Trbuhovic, Third Eye Design
Printed in Australia by Griffin Press

For Amelia and James, who taught me more about teenagers than I previously needed to know!

Chapter 1

I should have known things were going far too well; I should have known, dammit, that the rosy glow of contentment warming our family home was fuelled by the fires of hell building up to an almighty conflagration.

Even now, months later, when it looks like I might finally get even, I can't think of a single warning sign. And, believe me, I've plumbed the depths of my memory banks — as reliable as they can be with menopausal amnesia on the not-too-distant horizon. I've trawled through the days, the weeks beforehand, searching for any possible clues that my hitherto occasionally chaotic existence was about to become a complete full-time shambles.

That whole weekend had been unusually restful, apart from my daughter throwing up in the rose garden and the usual work dramas hanging over my head. Perhaps there was a clue in that? Should the alarm bells have rung at the first sign of Steve's apparent domesticity? Should the sight of him getting out the vacuum cleaner have warned me something was up? I'd thought he'd discovered yet another aerobic exercise. But maybe he was trying to warn me of an even bigger metamorphosis.

Or was it the shopping trip to buy him a couple of business shirts that triggered something? If it had been a cordless drill or a chainsaw we were buying, it would have been easy. But put him in a menswear store and he gets that possum-in-the-headlights look, a sure sign his retail patience has expired.

So what did I miss?

Search me! I've been over it again and again and I still can't work it out.

The weekend had started much the same as any other. I'd been to after-work drinks on Friday with the girls from the office — Ginny and Nicky, and Tracey, our joint PA. We all work together in the PR business Nicky and I started ten years ago.

Friday had been one of those days, with a restructuring announcement that was itself being restructured out of existence, a print job that had been folded before it had dried, resulting in several thousand unreadable brochures that looked like impressionist paintings, and a prospectus running well behind schedule. To make matters worse, Ginny was ratty after drinking too much Moët at the Tennis Open launch party she'd organised the night before and was ignoring my requests for a spare weekend pass to the tennis for my daughter Charlotte.

Just as I was finishing up at work, totally exhausted, Adam texted me that Charlotte had arrived home from a Year 13 end-of-term all-day party hopelessly drunk and was throwing up in the rose garden. Even allowing for his propensity to exaggerate, especially where his big sister is concerned, I guessed I'd be up to my elbows in Handy Andy when I got home.

The only thing that hadn't turned to custard was Mum's Alzheimer's.

I'd had a call from Dad at lunchtime gleefully announcing he'd just won the local Avery Villages bowls tournament with his mate Colin. After several traumatic months of trying to cope on his own at home with Mum as she became increasingly dotty, my older sister Stephanie and I had finally managed to persuade them to move into St Joan's retirement village (one of the Avery Group's numerous complexes around the country), where Mum could have proper care and they could still live together. Since then, Steph and I had paid for Mum to take Aropax, which was at least stopping the disease progressing for now and had stemmed her worst behaviour. This meant Dad could go back to his passion for bowls — and he was doing even better than he had when he'd belonged to the local bowling club. For him to win the tournament against teams from six other retirement villages was quite something.

Anyway, back to Friday night. The drinks session promised to continue until well after midnight. As usual, Ginny had forgotten to eat — not something I can relate to at all (I mean, I can forget where I've put my keys or what day it is, but I simply never, ever forget to eat) — and was coming back to life faster than Frankenstein's monster thanks to Nicky firing her up with apple martinis on top of an empty stomach. Tales of tennis pros' tantrums and hi-jinks were becoming more entertaining and less plausible as each cocktail hit the spot. After the hard slog to get everything sorted before 6 o'clock, I helped her finish off the bottle of Moët. Don't get me wrong — I'm not normally a soak. Well, not very often. It just seems to happen that by Friday, I'm so wrung out after a week of pampering and pummelling clients into shape that I need a decent dose of pinot — gris or noir, I'm not fussy. And if Ginny is shouting champagne, who am I to refuse her generosity?

If it hadn't been for Steve phoning me around 8pm to tell me he was on his way to pick up the fish and chips, I would have stayed on. But he sounded so tired and in need of a shoulder to collapse on that I excused myself and caught a taxi home.

Steve arrived with a big paper parcel of hot chips and had set three plates on the bench for me to dole them out. Adam was out doing his usual Friday night shift at McDonald's so wouldn't be wanting dinner, and it only took a few seconds of listening to the groans coming from the vicinity of the upstairs bathroom to realise that Charlotte wouldn't be up to eating for a while. I served out a generous helping of fish and fries for Steve and a smaller portion for me — a feeble attempt to keep the flab at bay — leaving the rest tightly bound in the slowly greasing wrapper. I suspected the parcel would remain untouched unless Tigger the spaniel managed to spirit it down to his level.

Tigger's ability to paw things down off the kitchen bench was becoming legendary. Despite his comparatively short stature, he managed to capture seemingly unobtainable prizes — a whole chicken carcass, a pottle of margarine, a loaf of bread, the best part of an expensive box of chocolates — even when they'd been pushed well back from the edge. Adam had reported once seeing the poor starving creature with one of his hind legs pushing on a bottom drawer handle while his front paw whisked a block of cheese sideways across the benchtop.

Such cunning, Adam felt, should be rewarded and he let Tigger claim the prize. (My reward was a pile of dog sick deposited neatly in the middle of Great-Grandma's heirloom rug the next morning.)

Needless to say, Tigger lay on the aforementioned rug drooling while Steve and I ate the fish and chips off our knees in the living room. Steve put some old Motown music on the CD and reminisced nostalgically about the BC days — Before Children — when we were free. I should have known then that something was up. I mean, Steve *never* gets nostalgic. But there he was pulling out the old photo album and poring over pictures of him and his friends arrayed around the bonnet of his souped-up car at the start of a rally; and an arty black and white print of him sitting cross-legged on the floor at his dilapidated flat he shared with two other commerce students. He chuckled away at the three of them, the only ones in their year to embrace the hippy culture. All the other students had been strait-laced, short haired and, bereft of women in their classes, enamoured of arguing economic theories and perfecting equations. Needless to say, they'd graduated with honours while Steve and his flatmates had scraped the C barrel empty.

'Look, Penny, the ball photos,' Steve cried, pointing at us, young and starry-eyed, red-eyed (either from the flash or having just consumed our first bottle of Cold Duck and therefore pie-eyed as well), among a group I could only just recall — fierce friends at the time who we'd long lost touch with.

'I'd forgotten how much fun we had back then. It seemed like one never-ending party.'

'I think it was,' Steve said. 'Pretty much everything I remember from those days was a gas. I don't remember much about the lectures.'

'I remember the exams,' I groaned.

'Oh God, weren't they the pits?' A funny look came over Steve's face. 'Isn't it weird how you forget about the bad things happening? Maybe I've got selective memory.'

'There are quite a few things I wish I could forget.'

'Like passing out at that fancy dress party?'

I laughed. The punch had tasted like lolly water but had apparently contained industrial-strength vodka. 'Not as bad as the time your old bomb broke down on the bridge and held up traffic for miles.'

Steve looked annoyed — that always was a sore point with him.

'Aha, but what about the time you walked right round the room with your skirt tucked into your knickers?'

I winced at the memory. I'd come out of the loo at a posh dinner party and managed to display myself to a roomful of horrified guests before one of them was kind enough to let me know.

'Don't remind me!' I wailed. It was still one of my worst nightmares.

I tried, but couldn't think of any episode in Steve's life that was quite as humiliating. Except the day I'd managed — or rather my friends managed — to expose and thereby successfully end his short but seemingly intense fling with Jacinta, the up-and-coming (in more ways than one, as it turned out) young accountant at his office. But it was hardly the time to bring that up now. Not when we'd just been on a trip along memory lane.

Unspoken, unwanted, the Jacinta thing suddenly churned the hot chips into a leaden, cold lump in the pit of my stomach. I'd done my best to put it right out of my mind for the past year, convinced that Steve had seen the error of his ways and wouldn't try to stray again. Besides, I'd learned the signs — the sneaky eyes behind the bold, smiling face when he came home late, the extra 'meetings' of the car club at night, the distracted look when we were out with any of his workmates and their partners. And he somehow looked and smelled better.

I'd not seen Jacinta since that time nor any evidence she was on his mind, let alone anywhere else on his body, and had no reason to expect their furtive flame would be rekindled. The sudden turnaround in his behaviour, the sudden absence of text messages and restaurant receipts in his pockets, the sudden end to late-night 'car club' meetings and 'working late' at the office. And the waft of expensive aftershave had disappeared along with his pride in his personal appearance. I was sure that the embarrassing 'outing' of the affair on radio had extinguished his ardour. He'd heard the announcer proclaiming their affair to everyone who knew them. He knew that I knew and that my friends knew, since it was my radio station friend Helen who'd engineered the 'ad lib' about them.

However, the reminder of that ghastly episode had darkened the rosy glow I'd been feeling. I stood and carried the greasy, sauce-smeared plates out to the kitchen, scraping the leftovers into Tigger's bowl. They were gone in an instant.

Adam arrived home from work, smelling of the deep fryer and full of questions: had anyone phoned? Were there any fish and chips left for him? And what was that disgusting smell in the hallway near the toilet?

I tried to catch Steve's eye, but he was in the kitchen showing Adam the still-warm fish and chip wrapper, so resignedly I tiptoed into the hallway, afraid of what I might find.

I didn't have to go far. Charlotte had obviously been sick again.

So much for dreaming of life After Children, I thought, as I headed back to the bathroom, arms now full of a bucket, disinfectant and scrubbing brush. It was some time before I could return to the lounge and by then, Steve had gone outside with Adam. I could just hear their muffled voices in the garage, along with the occasional thunk as they dissected one of the engines. The oily black mess they'd leave round the laundry sink afterwards would drive me crazy, but the thought of father and son sharing their mechanical passion cheered me in the meantime. The old British motorbike and Steve's classic Triumph Stag had been in pieces so many times I'd lost count, but it gave them a bond I'd never want broken.

• • •

The rest of the weekend was typical of any weekend in our house — Steve took the Stag out on a rally with his mates and was gone all day, returning home late after a pie and a pint at a country pub. Charlotte was understandably subdued, recovering in time though to take a friend to the tennis in the afternoon. And Adam went back to flip burgers after spending the morning at touch.

On Sunday afternoon, when Steve said he was going upstairs to clean out his drawers, I'd thought nothing of it. Okay, it did occur to me that it was a little out of the ordinary. He'd only been known to go through his wardrobe in any detail when he couldn't find his wallet or cellphone. Plus the time Charlotte told him his clothes were for fogeys and he dressed like her friend Melissa's boring old accountant father. That day he'd flung out a collection of old jerseys, ties and shoes that we were all glad to see the back of, although I'd drawn the line at his second-best suit. At over a thousand dollars, it still had to earn its keep, even though it was brown and three years old.

Preoccupied as I was with working out a project budget for a client, I didn't see Steve again until dinner time — with the exception of his short trip through the living room with the vacuum cleaner. That should have alerted me that something was up but, distracted as I was with figures (never my forté), I simply smiled and carried on wrestling with the calculator. The regular appearance after 5pm of Adam, with queries of 'What's for dinner, Mum?', interspersed with foraging in the cupboards to find something to snack on, alerted me it was time to abandon the budget and embrace the kitchen sink or Adam would eat the cupboards bare.

We ate dinner in the living room while Adam regaled us with tales from the exam front. His NCEA Level 1 mid-year exams were at last, thankfully, over. They had not been without their difficulties though, as Adam tended to put an effort into only the subjects he liked, like Science, and not much else. I'd heard from his friend Darren's mum, the redoubtable Louise Sidebottom ('See-day-bow-tom, please!'), that Adam had left his Maths exam very early, which didn't bode well for his results.

On the other hand, Adam told us over dinner, he thought he'd done pretty well in Biology last Tuesday. Since Biology was his passion — he'd wanted to be a marine biologist ever since going diving with his friend George last summer — this was somewhat cheering.

Charlotte talked excitedly of her plans for next year, going to uni with her friends if she passed her final year exams.

'You're getting very grown up,' her father said.

Charlotte looked at him as if to say, 'Duh! What did you expect?'

'I suppose you'll want to leave home soon. You'll be independent.'

'Not too independent, I hope. You'll always come back home,' I added.

'Like Josh,' Adam pouted. 'Bringing his washing home on Sundays and scoffing everything in the fridge.'

'Well, he can't do it any more, now he's in Europe,' I said. Josh had taken off on his OE as soon as he'd finished his History degree, looking for postgraduate work. However, he seemed to have got waylaid on a Contiki Tour of something like seventeen cities in seven days.

'Hasn't stopped him emailing for more money,' Adam threw back.

I'd suspected Adam had heard us talking about this; my suspicions were now confirmed. Steve and I had argued over it, Steve saying we should let Josh learn to live within his means; me countering that he'd earned a break away and it wouldn't hurt to give him something more to tide him over. Steve had scoffed at this, saying he'd just keep on asking for more and more until the Bank of Mum and Dad ran dry.

'That's none of your business,' Steve said to Adam. 'Besides, you wait 'til you're overseas. I'll bet you'll find it hard too.'

'No I won't.' Adam stuck his jaw out defensively. 'I'm not leaving New Zealand without a job to go to. I'm not interested in pub crawls around Europe.'

'Famous last words, son. I'll remind you of that in a few years' time.'

After dinner, Charlotte went up to her room to use the phone. Adam was upstairs too, studying Science. I was just about to make a cup of coffee and settle down in front of the TV when I heard someone clumping down the stairs, bumping something heavy along behind. The door into the hall was closed.

'What *are* you doing?' I called out.

No reply.

'Steve? Is that you?'

Still no reply.

Curious, I got up from the couch and opened the door.

Steve was walking through the open front door carrying two large suitcases, with a big sports bag slung over his shoulder. Rain was drenching the front path and blowing across the porch in wind gusts, catching the edge of his jacket.

'Steve?'

He put the cases down.

'That's a lot for the dump,' I said, laughing.

But Steve didn't even smile. In fact, there was a weird expression on his face, as if he was expecting a good telling-off for some transgression.

'Why, what's the matter, aren't they . . .?' Suddenly, I had a terrible premonition. I froze.

He stood there, staring, stammering, incomprehensible, his hands flapping by his sides as if trying to catch the words in mid-air.

'I'm . . . It's . . .' His arms continued to wade the air, his face a picture of betrayal.

'You're not . . .' I couldn't finish.

'I'm going to . . .' There was a dreadful silence I couldn't fill. 'I'm leaving you,' he said at last.

'You're leaving me?' I squeaked. 'Me and the kids?'

He nodded guiltily.

'But how can you . . . ? We just had dinner . . . We haven't even done the dishes.'

Dinner, the whole weekend in fact, had been so convivial. I couldn't fathom how the easy-going family man I thought I knew so well had suddenly gone upstairs and transformed himself into this callous, cold-blooded automaton with no apparent feelings for me or his offspring.

He just stood there, an alien, looking like another being had possessed his body. I soon found out who that being was.

'Why? Where are you going?'

He started stammering again. Finally, he came out with it: 'It's Jacinta. She and I . . .'

'Jacinta?' My voice cracked. I could hardly get the vile name out. 'But you . . . You've been . . .'

I didn't know what to say. I couldn't speak. I felt as if I'd been hit in the stomach with a clenched fist. My face felt numb, my brain even number. I doubled over, winded, feeling the tight grip around my middle, but forced myself to stand straight again.

Steve, my friend and lover for half my years on this earth, who had stood by me when I'd insisted on smoking cigarettes all those years before childbirth, who'd never complained during all those years of nappy changing and had managed the school run every morning without ever losing his temper at dilly-dallying children and lunches not yet made. Steve, who'd rescued me from certain insanity when Charlotte hit puberty, who'd managed to feed the children when I was late home again, and who'd been there almost always when I needed him. Steve the stalwart. Steve the sympathetic ear. Steve the cheerleader. Steve the support-wire to my knife-edge balancing act in our hitherto sheltered little world.

But not any more.

He'd transformed into Steve the slut, Steve the adulterer, Steve the sneak, Steve the traitor. He'd been cleaning out his drawers all right — cleaning them out permanently. The ties I'd chosen with care, the shirts we'd shopped for together that very weekend, the expensive suit we'd worried if we'd ever be able to afford. He'd been poring over them all afternoon, lovingly preparing them to take to *her*. Even his smelly gym shoes, the ones that Tigger got so excited about when he brought them home sweaty from his work-out; even his home handyman rough clothes — even they would be swept off the bed and into those two hulking suitcases, sitting like sentinels in the doorway. Sentinels of doom.

I must have been looking wild, because his guilty glare changed to grim defiance. He was guarding his suitcases as if I might snatch them away to prevent him going. It crossed my mind that might be a good idea.

He turned tail, gathering up the suitcases, one in each hand. He stood briefly in the porch, looking defiant and hard. All the sweet talk, the memory lane stuff, it had all been a sham, a softening up before the kill, a deliberate attempt on his part to get some sort of closure on our life together so he could start anew. And all the time I'd been thinking things were getting better between us, he'd been going through everything he owned, meticulously discarding clothes and belongings that *she* wouldn't approve of.

'I'll call you about the kids,' he said, and was gone.

He hadn't even told them!

I stood there in the hallway like a bumbling fool, staring through the open door at the driving rain, expecting the sound of his car returning up the driveway and nestling back into its space in the garage. I was sure it was all a mistake. But the minutes ticked by and he didn't come back.

The sound of the phone ringing brought me back to reality. I slammed the front door and ran up to Charlotte's room.

'Did you see your father just then?' I cried.

'No. Why? What's the matter? Where is he?' Charlotte

had picked up the phone and clearly had one of her friends hanging on the line. I didn't care.

I was in no state to think of the niceties of breaking the news gently.

'He just left.'

'Oh,' Charlotte said dismissively, and went to talk to her friend again.

But any thoughts she might have had about Steve just popping out for an hour were quickly dismissed when I wailed, 'No, not just left . . . he left for good.'

'What?' Charlotte stared at me for a moment, then picked up the phone and said, 'Becks, I've gotta go, I'll call you later,' pushed the off button, flung the phone back on the bed and rushed over to me. 'You're joking! Dad wouldn't do that!'

I could hardly believe it myself. It seemed like a bad dream.

My wails had penetrated to Adam's room; he arrived at Charlotte's doorway expectantly.

'What's Charlotte done?' he asked hopefully.

'Not me, stupid. It's Dad. He's gone.'

'So?' Adam didn't get it either.

'He's walked out. Vamoosed. Left home.'

'He can't have.' Adam stood rooted to the spot, his arms dangling at his sides awkwardly, his blue eyes startled.

'Well, he just has.' I plumped myself down on the side of the bed, dry-eyed, shocked.

Charlotte put her arm around me tentatively, for once speechless. I hugged her fiercely. Adam brought his fist down hard on Charlotte's dresser, making me jump, then he sat down beside me on the bed, nursing his hand. I freed one arm and hugged him too.

'But why?' Charlotte said eventually.

'He's having an affair.'

'No!' Charlotte was wide-eyed. 'Who with?'

'A woman in the office.'

'Dad wouldn't do that,' Charlotte said protectively.

'Well, he did, and he's gone to live with her. With *Jacinta*,' I spat the name out as if it were a worm in an apple.

'Wasn't she the woman who came to watch the touch finals?' Adam asked his sister.

Charlotte thought for a moment. 'Yes, that's right. That *was* her name. You were, like, working that weekend, Mum, and Dad turned up with someone from his office. She was really cool . . .' She broke off, realising her faux pas.

There was an awkward silence.

The touch finals had been months ago, which meant that Steve and Jacinta had been back on again for most of the year — which meant that the 'outing' that I'd fondly imagined had brought the affair to an end had only done the trick for a few months.

'The prick! Anything else he's taken her to when my back was turned?'

Adam looked guilty.

'What?' I demanded. 'Where?'

'Well . . . there were the car club meets. He brought this woman with him — the same one at the touch finals. But I didn't think anything of it. She seemed so nice . . . she was so young.'

Young! I was seething so much, I could hardly see. A red mist seemed to be rising over my eyes. I couldn't recall ever having felt so angry. I stood up.

'I'm just going to the bathroom for a minute.'

In the cool solitude of the upstairs toilet, with the door firmly locked, I tried to gather my wits. But instead I found myself sobbing uncontrollably while calling Steve the worst names I could think of. I got through several yards of toilet paper before I subsided enough to hear a timid knocking on the door.

It was Charlotte, offering to make some tea. She took her brother downstairs with her, no doubt relieved to escape. It was enough to bring me to my senses; I gave myself a severe talking-to. It was wrong to crack up in front of the kids, I knew that. Every book I'd ever read about child-rearing (although there hadn't been many — I'd been too busy trying to do it) told me that. Somehow, I'd have to pull myself together. I forced myself to leave the confined comfort of the toilet, stood at the bathroom basin and splashed cold water on my face until I felt able to look at myself in the mirror.

It was an appalling sight. My eyes, normally clear and blue, were pink and swollen, and my face was blotchy and pale, making the freckles stand out more than ever. My mascara had run sideways, accentuating the tiny crow's feet that had recently started marching towards my ears, and my usually obedient short blondish hair looked like a fright wig. I filled the basin, dunked my face in cold water (only briefly tempted to drown myself in it) and dragged a brush through the tangles.

But before I trekked downstairs for tea and as much sympathy as you could expect from self-absorbed teenagers, I checked out the bedroom to see what was left.

Nothing. Not even a stray sock or a dropped tie.

The family photos on the dresser had been raided; several were missing. But he'd thoughtfully left the one of him grinning happily next to me on our wedding day. I was so cross I hurled it at the wall, smashing the frame so that the picture fluttered to the floor amid a pile of broken glass.

Satisfied, I left it there and went to join the kids downstairs.

Adam was slumped over the breakfast bar, face in his hands, oblivious to the television blaring in the background and the stereo tuned to The Edge. I flicked them both off with the remote and went to sit beside him. Charlotte handed me the tea and deposited a hot chocolate in front of Adam — possibly the first time in history she'd made him anything. I smiled wanly for a moment, reflecting that it took a crisis to engender sibling affection.

I slurped the tea. It tasted metallic, but I didn't want to offend Charlotte so I drank it nonetheless. That's when I noticed she was drinking Steve's best whisky. There wasn't much left in the bottle — probably why he hadn't bothered taking it.

'Charlotte! You can't drink that!'

'Why not? Dad won't want it now,' she said bitterly.

'Because it's whisky, that's why.'

'But Gemma's Dad says it always makes you feel better.' She took another swig. 'Can't say it has yet. Maybe it takes two.' She slugged down the rest of the glass and poured another.

'No. One's more than enough,' I said and reached out to scoop it away from her. She swept the glass off the bench before I could get hold of it, spilling half on the floor.

I could see I was going to have to get a grip or we'd all be turning into alcoholics before the week was out.

By the time I'd settled the kids into bed it was well after midnight. I went to lock up and noticed the dining room door ajar. It only took a moment to realise why — there was a big gap on the wall where the Grahame Sydney had been. Steve must have taken it.

Our only big art investment, the Sydney had been my

refuge in times of stress, my inspiration, my muse. Whenever I felt down, I just had to look at those wide-open blue, blue skies and the smooth, bare brown hills and I found succour. Whenever the kids' demands grew too overwhelming, the Otago landscape calmed me.

I couldn't believe Steve would be so mean. It made me wonder what else he'd taken that I loved. I nearly flattened Tigger in my haste to find out.

Nothing else in the dining room had been removed. Great-Grandma's Sheffield silver cutlery was intact in its drawers; her silver tea set and bone china dinnerware were safe in the cupboards underneath.

In the lounge, the shelf of CDs was untouched; Great-Grandma's heirloom rug was still on the floor. He'd generously left me his Roy Orbison collection along with a stack of Dean Martin DVDs (mental note: second-hand store open tomorrow at 10am) and the pile of car magazines (mental note: recycling bin due out Thursday).

In the hall cupboard, his heavy coats and jackets were gone and his big golf bag with all the treasured clubs were missing, which was hardly surprising — they spent a lot of time in Steve's car boot.

He'd raided the wine cellar — a fancy name for a collection of boxes and old earthenware pipes that housed a jumble of reds and whites, some of the reds quite special. He'd taken all the good reds and left me all the crappy whites.

In the tiny back room off the garage I found he'd left his treadmill and weights machine — two recent additions to the household when he'd started his fitness frenzy. Probably about the time he started jumping on Jacinta, I thought sourly. I could just see him and Jacinta in their sterile apartment somewhere lifting weights and jogging in unison. I kicked his big blue exercise ball so venomously that it bounced off the weights machine and nearly knocked me over. (Mental note: sharp jab with meat skewer should fix it.)

Out in the garage, the big fat silver Ford had gone, of course. It was Steve's work car, leased by the firm; its grunty six cylinders and sprinty acceleration were a source of joy to a man who loved fast cars. The Stag, dirty from its back-roads adventure yesterday, sat mockingly in its corner, and the old Norton, in pieces still, took up most of Steve's workshop space. His tools, his greasy overalls, his old rally flags and banners — all remained in their place. (Mental note: charity rag collection due any day.)

I flew back inside and upstairs to the study — a fancy name for the fourth bedroom. It housed a jumble of family mementoes, piles of old magazines and half-read self-improvement books, and a stack of accounts needing payment piled next to an old computer connected to the internet.

Although he's a high-flying accountant, Steve's a bit like the interior decorator who never gets around to doing up their own house, or the plumber whose pipes are always blocking. A meticulous bean counter at work, Steve never handled the home accounts. I'm the one who has to carry out the monthly juggling act, working out which bills have to get paid before the phone gets cut off or the debt collector comes calling. So I would know, in an instant, if anything had been touched in our joint account — the one we use to pay for all the household expenses — or the savings account.

I dialled up the online bank statement. Both accounts were exactly the same as when I'd paid the weekly bills the day before he left.

I sat there for some time, at a loss.

Foolishly, I'd been convinced this would never happen to

me. It had always been other women in this situation; my role had been to join in singing 'I Will Survive' at their divorce parties. Sitting there in the darkened study, the desk lamp casting a pool of cold white light on the cluttered desktop, it seemed surreal.

I sank back into the chair and stared at the screen that Steve had spent the previous weekend taking to bits and then miraculously putting back together again, having fixed the fuzzy resolution.

Who would fix our computer problems now? I was hopeless with electronics. Anything further than plugging something in and switching it on was beyond me; I'd become complacent that Steve would always sort out what was wrong.

Like the time Adam had downloaded music from a website that had a virus, wiping out the family computer's hard drive. Steve had taken it as a personal challenge to fix it, though it had taken him over a month, grunting and swearing at it intermittently. He'd even coaxed the new printer into life long after I'd given up ever seeing a piece of paper with anything on it other than hieroglyphics and Martian squiggles. Steve was the sort of chap who would not be beaten by mere technology, and I'd been the beneficiary of his stubbornness many a time.

And what would I do next time my temperamental old Crackling Rosie decided to sulk? Rosie is a classic pinot red 1976 Jaguar XJS — sleek and low, and definitely high maintenance. Steve had made intimate acquaintance with her temperamental twelve-cylinder engine and had single-handedly kept the old girl on the road for the year since I'd bought it, refusing to accept friends' suggestions that we should pension it off, put it into storage and get something cheaper to run. After Steve's lavish attention Rosie had been on her best behaviour.

My reverie was interrupted by Tigger pawing me; I realised I was shivering with both cold and fear.

'Oh, Tigger, what am I going to do?'

There's nothing more self-affirming than talking to Tigger — he doesn't answer back and he never argues. In fact, I could swear he nods his head in agreement. He wasn't terribly forthcoming with a helpful answer this time, though. He nuzzled me again, so I stroked his ears, filtering my fingers through his soft, silky fur. As soon as I stopped fondling him, he pushed his nose up hard underneath my elbow, snuffling and whining.

Tigger's entire world revolves around food. Not for him the intricacies of relationships or possessions. He wasn't remotely interested in where Steve might be or whether he'd emptied out the cheque account. As long as there was enough money for Meaty-Bites and someone around to put them in his bowl, he was happy.

Thus ended the day from hell — with a whimper and a handful of Meaty-Bites.

Chapter 2

That cruel night has been imprinted on my memory ever since. Only now, now that I'm finally over it, now that the worm is turning, has the image started to fade.

Unlocking the side door to the garage and raising the big steel door with the remote, I approach the dusty Triumph Stag with a mix of excitement and apprehension. It looks so tiny next to my car — a stubby, bullet-nosed little midget beside a long, sleek concubine. I brush my fingers across the Stag's side panel and leave a clean patch amid the dirt and grime of eight months' neglect. The caked mud and road dust from that back-roads rally, the day before Steve packed his bags and departed, is still visible beneath another layer of wind-blown dirt that has seeped under the double door.

'Time for a clean up, old chap,' I say cheerfully and pat the Stag on his rump, before unlocking him and climbing inside.

It feels weird, sitting in Steve's seat behind the little, leather-bound wheel. I turn the key in the ignition and the lovingly maintained machine roars into life.

It feels even weirder driving his car onto the road, past the neighbours, past the shopping mall, waiting at the lights, hoping nobody recognises me. It's early, just before eight, but the roads are already jam-packed with people on their way to work.

The warm, almost-summer morning holds the promise of a great day for a catharsis.

It's quite a distance across town to where I have to go; but it's been a much longer and more tortuous journey to get to this point. I can't put it off any longer. The time has come.

• • •

Davina gave me the idea the day after he left.

She had arrived on my doorstep with baking. Charlotte had been unbelievably upbeat after school, convinced her father would be back home any moment, while Adam had slouched around the house communicating solely through grunts. For once he'd hardly touched his dinner and had retreated to his room as soon as he could escape. Charlotte had followed him upstairs, phone clamped to her ear.

'I heard the news,' Davina announced as she deposited chocolate fudge brownies on the bench, well back from the reach of Tigger's paw. She knew him well. 'Helen phoned me when I was having tea and told me. So I baked you some comfort food. Money talks, my dear, but chocolate sings. I hope it helps soothe your poor soul.'

Davina has lived next door as long as I can remember. She's well over seventy but far from frail. And she's almost like a mother to me. I made tea and while I ate almost all the chocolate brownies, we talked. Somehow I could tell her things I'd never admit to anyone else. Like how angry I felt.

'Don't get mad, get even,' she said, pushing the last two brownies towards me. Even I knew I'd had enough by then; I pushed them back. 'He deserves it, you know. If he wants to behave like a prick, he deserves to be treated like a prick. I've been lucky with Geoff. He's never shown any interest in straying. And look at your mother and father, together through thick and thin. Your father's a saint! But I know lots of young women who've had it happen to them. And the ones who've coped best have stuck up for themselves.'

'I know I should, but . . .'

'There must be something you can do. What about his clothes? Jo cut all her husband's suits and ties in half and dumped them in the driveway just before he was due to come and collect the rest of his belongings. Why don't you do that?'

I laughed hollowly. 'Nah, too late for that old cliché. Steve took every item of clothing with him.'

'Pity you can't get him back for a night and deal to him. I heard this priceless story of a woman who gave her husband a massage the night she found out he was having an affair. Very loving she was. Except she mixed hair-removal cream into the massage oil. He never suspected a thing until he woke up the next morning bald as a bandicoot — from head to toe. And while he was asleep she'd packed her bags and flown. She was on the other side of town by then. But she reckons she could hear him yelling with rage, despite the distance.'

'Too late for that now. But I admire her style.'

'Well, maybe there's something he left behind that's precious to him you can use to get your own back. What about his golf clubs? Beth managed to saw her traitorous husband's favourite putter in half, then taped it up and put it back in the bag as if nothing had happened. He didn't find out 'til he pulled it out in the middle of the green. His mates all thought it was hilarious.'

'No, his golf clubs are firmly locked in the boot of his car, and that's parked outside Jacinta's as we speak. There's only his stupid old Stag left behind.'

'Well, there you are then.'

'I couldn't cut the Stag in half, Davina, don't be crazy.'

'I'm not saying you have to cut it in half, Penny. You don't even have to touch it. But imagine if he never got to see it again?'

'Oh,' I said quietly.

'Change the locks on the garage, that's all. That's what Karen did. After her husband ran off with their shapely Australian nanny, she changed the locks on the shed where he kept his entire collection of Matchbox cars. He loved those silly things more than anything. It was ages before he managed to get them back, with Karen fighting it all the way through the courts.'

After Davina had gone, I phoned a twenty-four hour locksmith and agreed to pay a small fortune for a visit the next morning.

'Perhaps I should put a lock on you too!' I said to Tigger as he looked expectantly up at the bench where the two remaining brownies sat. 'You drive me crazy sometimes, but I couldn't imagine life without you.'

Not that it was likely that Steve would want a bumptious, greedy, grubby dog, I rationalised. Not enough to steal him, anyway.

The next morning, unbearably early, the locksmith greeted me glumly.

'Oh dear, oh deary me,' the white-haired beanpole of a man sighed. 'Hubbie's gone and you want to change the locks. Oh deary me.'

I'd made the mistake of explaining on the phone why I wanted the job done. I should have known I'd regret it.

'Er, yes. And can you do the garage first please.'

'Deary me, the garage.' He pushed open the door and looked inside. 'Hubbie had a bit of a thing about cars and bikes, did he?'

'Er, yes. No. Sort of.'

The overly familiar old geezer with his seen-it-all-before attitude was starting to get to me. I just wanted him to get on with it and cut the philosophy.

'Let me know when you've done that and I'll show you the locks in the house.' He nodded knowingly, produced an alarming array of tools from the back of his van parked in the middle of the drive and set to work. I took off inside and made some work calls to take my mind off the enormity of what he was — I was — doing.

An hour and a small mortgage later, I pocketed a set of shiny new keys, using one to open the garage side door. I felt like breaking into song: 'I am woman . . .' But I kept it in my head as I reversed the car out, scooted back in, pulled the manual door handle 'til the door closed, and switched off the automatic door-opener. The contents of the garage were secure.

And they stayed locked away for eight months.

Until now.

Our lawyers have agreed that it's time for me to return the old bike and the Stag. They're the last of his toys I've managed to hang onto.

Suzanne Cumberland, the high-flying divorce lawyer

my legal friend Liz put me onto, came up with the idea for holding onto his most treasured possessions — at least until I got what I wanted.

Mind you, Steve hadn't helped his case much by employing a phalanx of accountants to tot everything up — in his favour of course. It blew me away at first. Never one to bother with our own finances he became an overnight expert, presenting me with an array of financial statements and balance sheets that quite overwhelmed my limited grasp of such things. He'd not missed a thing — right down to his Dean Martin collection and my grandmother's jewellery. The only thing he'd forgotten was to put a price on the dog. Now why did that not surprise me? Once Steve had figured out the assets and liabilities, Tigger would definitely have come into the liability category.

My own calculations on all that sort of thing had followed the nine-tenths-of-the-law principle. My grip on fractions, however, had never been that good. These days, apparently, it was half of everything, straight down the middle — no matter that Steve had run off with the Grahame Sydney. Steve's valuation, I suspected, was way below market rates. But Ms Cumberland assured me I could get my own valuation and besides, when the divvy-up time came, they would take into account the value of everything else, most of which I had to admit I still had.

'You need to work out what it is you want most, and bargain for it,' she advised when I confessed about his toys being locked up in the garage where he couldn't get his hands on them. Steve had put them clearly on my side of the ledger as a debt owing to him. 'Use them as leverage. But not until you know exactly what you want in return. If they matter that much to him, you'll probably get it!'

So the redoubtable Ms Cumberland had let him know what I wanted in return for each precious item and he'd come back with his first offer. It wasn't great, but it was a start.

Consequently, in August I let him have his exercise equipment.

He'd been after it for ages. Weeks previously, the first time he'd asked to come and pick it up, he phoned just after Charlotte had come home in the depths of despair over a failed exam and Adam had prodded her into a full-blown row that had only just reached détente. The combatants had retreated to their rooms to sulk. Neither answered the phone, which showed just how bad things were. So I did.

After the usual pleasantries, during which I did not reveal that World War III was only temporarily in recess, he started to stammer, 'Uh . . . I, er . . .' There was a pause, which I was not going to fill for him. 'My, um . . .' I heard a woman's voice in the background — *her* voice, no doubt — urging him to get on with it, the Conniving Cow. 'We . . . er, I . . . I'd like my treadmill and the, er . . .'

'*We*?' I couldn't believe he'd said that. '*We*'d like it, would we?'

'I didn't mean . . .'

I'd been stunned into silence after that. Needless to say, he didn't get the treadmill. I'd found it hard at first, keeping it from him. If Suzanne Cumberland hadn't been so firm on it I probably would have crumbled the first time he asked and given it back. But the suggestion that '*We'd* like it' had riled me sufficiently to hold out a bit longer.

When I was finally ready, I phoned him at work and said he was welcome to take his precious treadmill.

He complained loudly about the length of time it had taken me to come to my senses and let him have his property back and about how heavily weighted the balance sheet was against me. I was only too well aware — he'd emailed it to me about a hundred times with increasingly caustic remarks. I ignored this further dig at the imbalance. After all, was it my fault he'd chosen to walk out of the family home?

'One small reward for one small step towards settlement,' I said. 'You want more? You want your old Triumph Stag? You'll have to do a bit better than that.'

He was lucky I was feeling so benign. Ginny had dared me to cut the belt drive on the treadmill before he came to pick it up.

'Just think of it,' she'd said. 'He'll be standing on it in his Lycra looking cool for the Conniving Cow and when he flicks the switch, pouf, nothing happens.'

I'd thought about it. I'd been hankering after revenge ever since he'd walked out. But tampering with his treadmill didn't seem to make a big enough statement. I needed something more than that, something that would hurt him almost as much as he'd hurt me.

• • •

I was offered lots of advice; I tried all sorts of remedies.

Retail therapy never failed to deliver a buzz — I could forget about Steve the whole time I was shopping. But the euphoria never seemed to last.

My first bout of it came right after my first visit to the divorce lawyer. Ms Cumberland was very nice, of course, but the shock of having to go to her, of finally realising that Steve wasn't coming back to me, sent me into the depths of despair. And we all know the golden rule: when the going gets tough, the tough go shopping.

It was not my proudest moment. But it sure made me feel a whole lot better — for a good thirty minutes, anyway.

I was walking back to the car from my first meeting with Suzanne Cumberland, my bag filled with damp tissues rolled into tight balls. The route passed several upmarket designer boutiques. So many shops, so little time for shelf control. Normally, I only ever window-shopped at these posh places. Not only were they expensive, but they rarely had anything larger than a size 12, and the shop assistants were all built like darning needles and never seemed to care about us pincushions who would never fit into their tight, skimpy clothes. I'd weakened once and tried on a gorgeous fantasy skirt and ended up looking like a multicoloured soufflé, with my tummy spilling over a waistband that threatened to cut my internal organs in half. I'd sworn never to return, and had been as good as my word.

But I'd made no similar promises about the designer shoe shop. My mind kept walking on by, but my feet had their own aspirations and headed straight through the door. Before I knew it, I was trying on the most divine pair of pale blue, soft green and pink stilettos with a price tag to match the height of the heels. They weren't exactly easy to walk in, but they looked fabulous. 'If the shoe fits, buy it,' I heard an inner voice saying. I ignored its suggestion to buy two pairs. Ms Cumberland had told me I could use the joint account for essentials. One pair: definitely essential. Two pairs: probably pushing my luck.

Another entry on my side of the debt ledger that Steve kept reminding me about, I thought, and hesitated. 'Good,' said a wicked voice in my head, wiping out any conscience I might have had. 'Go for it. Give him something to worry about when he tries to work out the depreciation.'

'They'll go with so many things in my wardrobe,' I told

the saleswoman as I produced my eftpos card and dialled in the pin number for the joint account. Whoever said money can't buy happiness didn't know where to shop.

Clutching the enormous designer carrybag, I all but collapsed on the nearest parking meter outside. I'd never spent so much on myself before. My most extravagant footwear to date had been a pair of winter boots costing just over $450 — and that had seemed bad enough at the time. Guilt set in and I scurried back to the office, trying to hide the conspicuous bag from Ginny as I edged through the door.

'Hey, you've been to my shoe shop at last,' she cried. I swear she has X-ray vision. 'What did you get?' So I showed her, setting her off in squeals of ecstasy.

'I shouldn't have really, they're so expensive,' I said as I obligingly tottered round the empty reception area.

'I hope Steve's paying for them, then.'

He did that time — or rather, we did, since it was a joint account.

Retail therapy wasn't the only remedy I tried. My friends at the Ladies' Philosophical Society had no end of suggestions, calling an impromptu meeting the week after Steve left. And last week, there was another get-together, to celebrate Helen's fiftieth.

The Philosophical Society — we call it the Philly for short — comprises me, Helen, Frances, Dianne and Liz, and we get together every three months or so. Sometimes there's a birthday to celebrate or departing husband to commiserate over (as happened within days of Steve's departure), but mostly we just schedule meetings when our diaries fit, and usually the only item on the agenda is champagne.

We met years ago through a women's business network, in the days when that sort of thing was a novelty. The network eventually died but the five of us clicked somehow and decided to keep on meeting occasionally, for lunch or after work, usually when the pressure demanded a release valve.

There's Helen, who has teenagers like me and who runs a group of radio stations; Fran, the CEO of a software company, who counters her bean-counter image by wearing short skirts and stilettos so sharp they could carve a Christmas turkey; Di, who runs a private hospital and, alone among us, is defiantly childless; and Liz, a partner in a tony law firm, who's a bit like the woman who lived in a shoe — she had more children than anyone else we knew, but it never seemed to faze her. She always looked like she'd stepped straight off the set of *Boston Legal*, yet never missed a sports event or birthday party, or failed to whip up a costume for a school play seemingly overnight. We'd long given up waiting for her to crack; like the Energizer Bunny, no matter how tough it got, no matter how many nights she'd been up with sick children, no matter how often she got hauled into the principal's office, she remained chirpy and ready for whatever life might throw at her next.

Helen had called the meeting — she was shouting, she said, to celebrate reaching mid-life without a crisis (unlike her husband, she said, who'd recently gone out and bought a pair of Ray-bans, leather driving gloves and a Porsche). Liz and Fran had promised to come but Di was in Wellington meeting with some government health official who apparently held all the cards for a subsidy they were threatening to withdraw.

I was a few minutes late, after driving round several blocks trying to find a park, while dabbing at my nose; I was coming down with another force five cold — even though winter was long gone. As I approached I could hear them talking about the tramping trip we're all planning together for January.

'Champagne!' Helen cried when we'd all sat down. The

only one among us to have been to a private school, silver-spoon Helen was born for champagne.

'Yes! The drink of love and lust. Bring it on!' Liz said dramatically.

'I can't, I've been taking cold pills all morning,' I said, sneezing at that precise moment.

'Oh, come on, Penny. A little numbing of the senses is just what the doctor would order,' Fran said.

'That's something coming from you — you don't even drink!'

Fran was a woman with a past — a past that none of us had managed to fully discover, but she freely admitted to going to AA meetings and wore her sobriety like a badge of honour.

'So? I still get vicarious pleasure from watching others getting stuck into it.'

I weighed up the temptation for a nanosecond and agreed that champagne would blunt the edge of my plight. Besides, the dull ache behind my sinuses could do with some anaesthetising.

We toasted the birthday girl and noisily sang 'Happy Birthday'.

'Isn't it great — the older you get, the less you care about what other people think about you?' I said. 'Ten years ago, we'd have been terrified of singing in a public place.'

'I'll drink to that,' Fran said, raising her ginger beer. 'I intend to grow old very disgracefully.'

'Well, at least we can celebrate reaching mid-life and all that goes with it,' Helen said. 'Men don't ever get past puberty!'

'To Helen!' Liz cried. 'Here's to another fifty!'

'To Helen!' we cried in unison.

'Life begins at fifty,' I added.

'I certainly hope so,' Helen said, raising her glass in response. 'James is going down to Otago next year, so I'm hoping that will herald a new chapter in my sex life.'

'I wouldn't count on it,' I interjected. 'Steve's idea of foreplay was prodding me to see if I was awake.'

'Yes. It's like the difference between a golf ball and a G spot,' Fran chuckled. We looked at her blankly. 'Men will always look for a golf ball!'

'Well, I'm hoping all that will change when the kids are gone,' Helen laughed.

'I can't wait for that day to come. Whoever dissed the empty nest syndrome never had to queue every morning for a bathroom occupied by a succession of teenagers,' Liz chuckled.

'Or wait for my elderly father,' Fran said. 'His bowels take forever to move, but he always manages to get there first. I'd get an extra bathroom, but since Jack's gone, I can't afford it.'

'I couldn't live without a second bathroom,' Helen said. 'It takes such a long time to put my face back together in the morning, and it seems to take longer every year that passes.'

'By the time I've put the Polyfilla into all the cracks, I've got the kids beating down the door,' Liz laughed.

'We never used to worry about bathrooms,' I said. 'Must be a sign of advancing years.'

'Tell me about it. Where did the years go?'

'Inside every middle-aged woman is a younger woman wondering what the hell happened.'

'Middle aged? We're not middle aged. I feel at least ten years younger than I am.'

'Oh yes, it's middle age all right. Someone told me I could

tell I'd hit fifty because all my houseplants were alive and I couldn't smoke any of them,' Fran said.

'I heard one of my favourite songs in an elevator the other day. How sad is that?'

'Fifty is when you finally get your head together and your body starts falling apart.'

'Hey, don't knock yourselves. We're getting younger every day,' Liz said. 'Fifty is the new forty for us baby boomers.'

'Try telling that to the guys I run into in the pub after work on Fridays,' Fran said. 'They've only got eyes for the chicky-babes. They're not remotely interested in anyone over forty.'

'That's because they're only capable of thinking with one part of their anatomy — and it isn't their head.'

'That's why there's a hole at the end of it — to let air into the brain.'

'And why they give it a name. They like to know who's making all the decisions.'

'Enough!' Liz cried, helpless with laughter. 'We always seem to plumb the depths.'

'That's because men give us such good material.'

'They really are stupid, aren't they? I mean, why else would they wear ties to work? Anyone who starts the day by tying a noose around their neck must be a total dummy.'

'And no fashion faux pas we make could ever rival the Speedo! Now that's really dumb.'

'Well, you know what happens when the doctor shines his little torch thing into a guy's ears?' We shook our heads. 'It lights up his eyes.'

'That explains it,' I cried. I've often wondered why so many smart women end up with a dumb guy. It's because that's all there is to choose from. They're all dumb.'

'No, they can think for themselves, but only about one thing at a time.'

'And some of them really are smart, sensitive, caring and good looking,' Helen said.

'Yes, but *they* already have boyfriends,' I added.

The waiter, who'd brought another bottle of bubbly, was trying to suppress a smirk, which of course only added to our collective mirth. As soon as we'd ordered lunch and he'd returned to the bar, we all burst out laughing.

'I'll bet he's heard it all before,' I said.

'I'll bet he's into dumb blonde jokes,' Liz said. 'He looks just the type.'

'Guys love blonde jokes because they're all one liners. That means they can understand them,' Helen said.

'I've never let blonde jokes get to me,' Fran said, tossing her blonde curls. 'I know I'm not dumb — and I'm not blonde either!'

'I don't expect any of us are still our natural colours,' Liz said.

We all shook our heads guiltily.

'That's another one of the joys of mid-life,' Helen said. 'The extra time you have to spend at the hairdresser.'

'And in front of the mirror extracting all those stray eyebrows that have started to appear on my chin,' I threw in.

'Not to mention the repair work on the face, the hands, the feet, the cellulite . . .'

'At least if we forget to shave for a day, it doesn't show all over our faces,' Fran said.

'And we can get dressed in the morning all by ourselves, without having to ask where everything is,' I added.

'And we don't have to fart loudly to amuse ourselves!' Fran said.

'We are undoubtedly the superior sex.'

'Speaking of superior sex, how's your love life, Penny? Have you met another man yet?'

'No, that's been the last thing on my mind. Though it hasn't stopped some of our friends — the people Steve and I used to see a lot when we were together — trying to set me up with the most appalling assortment of stray men.' I pulled a wry face. 'I know they were trying to help but . . .'

'You went out with them?'

'Well, not exactly. I'd find myself at a dinner part next to someone. It was so obvious. Besides, I didn't like to say no, even when I knew I was being set up. I didn't want them to think . . .'

'You don't want to worry about what people think,' Liz interjected, grinning. 'They don't do it very often.'

'Oh, come on Penny, a bit of a fling would do you the world of good,' Fran said. 'Show Steve you don't need him any more. Get your own back for what he did to you.'

'I don't think I'll need to find a fella to get back at him.'

'So you've got a plan?' Helen said.

'Do I detect the sweet smell of revenge in the air?' Fran said.

'You'll have to wait and see,' I laughed.

'If you need to broadcast anything, just let me know,' Helen said, referring to her public 'outing' of Steve last year.

'That was so cool,' Fran said. 'I'd love to do something like that again.'

'Not yet,' I said. 'But maybe soon. I'll let you know.'

'I hope you're not going to give him his toys back already,' Helen said.

I explained about his gym gear going back after his last offer, and how we might be getting close to a settlement.

'Well, he doesn't deserve it, the louse,' Helen said, looking lemon-lipped. Like the rest of the Philosophical Society, Helen had not held Steve in very high regard since his walk-out. 'Can't you drive his car off a cliff or something?'

'You should have done that the day he left you,' Fran said.

'Believe me, I thought about it often enough. With me still in it,' I laughed. 'But thankfully those dark days are long gone.'

'Amen to that!' Fran said, clinking her glass against mine. 'Just as well I already cancelled this afternoon's appointment.'

Fran had been through a hideous divorce after catching her husband having it off with the next-door neighbour. She had come home just on a year ago to find her husband of twenty years butt naked and bouncing around in the marital bed with the neighbour — a buxom, busty woman ten years his junior, who'd become bored since her youngest started primary school. Fran had been the only one in our little group in this unenviable position — until Steve decamped to Jacinta a few months later.

Fran had blamed herself for ages — probably still did, for all I knew. She was one of those incredibly striking women, not pretty or beautiful, but she made heads turn for a second look. However, she was convinced she was ugly and that was why Jack had strayed over the back fence. She just wouldn't believe that the thieving neighbour was plain and boring to boot.

'Amen!' Liz said, and we raised our glasses. 'Lucky my court case was adjourned this morning,' she added.

'And the ratings can go to hell for the rest of the day,' Helen sighed.

The meals arrived and the conversation turned once more

to the tramping trip we were planning early in the New Year on the Abel Tasman Track.

'So how are the kids?' Liz was sitting next to me and the others were engrossed in tramping talk.

'Much better, thank God,' I said. 'We seem to have got to the end of the school year without too many traumas. Charlotte's just sat her last exams. If she gets through, it's off to university next year. But she's got this fixation about her father coming to her prizegiving next week and the leavers' ball. It's the end of her schooldays, she says, and she really, really, really wants him there.'

'Do you think he'll come?'

'Who knows? I always hand the phone straight over to the kids when it's him. Charlie thinks he's going to come, and to the leavers' ball too. She wants me to buy her a new dress.'

'When's the ball?'

'Saturday night. I borrowed this ball dress from a friend. It looked just fine on Charlotte when she tried it on, but now she says it's hideous and she wants a new one.'

'Typical teenager.'

'Trouble is I can't really afford a new one. We're on a bit of a budget now that I have to be very careful with the joint account. And it won't be there at all once the papers are signed.'

'Men are so mean,' Fran cried. 'Have you noticed that whenever a guy ups and leaves his wife and kids, she always ends up much worse off while he romps away with fancy cars and pulls young chicks.'

'Tell me about it,' I sighed. 'He has endless funds to squire his squeeze the length and breadth of Australasia and yet he sends me constant reminders of how much I owe him. I always knew I was a liability, but I had no idea how bad I was.'

'Nonsense, he's the liability.'

'I'm going to have to sell the house at this rate.'

'Don't take any notice,' Liz said. 'It'll come right when you settle up, you'll see. And until then, you can still use the joint account for essentials for the kids.'

'True. I suppose it depends on your interpretation of essentials.'

'Exactly. And who's to say you shouldn't spoil the children occasionally? Especially when it's coming up to Christmas.' She gave me a subtle wink and finished her salad.

'Thanks Liz. I shouldn't be asking for free advice.'

'I'll send you a bill, sweetie,' Liz laughed.

As I demolished the last drops of bubbly in my glass, I looked at my watch and saw that it was after 3pm. But, unusually, I didn't care. Nor was I spurred to hurry.

We ordered coffee — to sober up, Helen said — and lingered over a second one before splitting the bill and going our separate ways. I walked the block and a half back to work with the usual feeling of euphoria that follows a Philly meeting.

I made a beeline for the kitchen for more black coffee. Ginny was in there; the coffee machine had just finished sputtering.

'Hey, you've got those Robert Clergerie shoes on. They're fab,' she said, pushing the button to make an extra one for me.

'I thought I'd show them off again at lunchtime,' I said, parading them in front of her.

'Steady on, girl, you're a bit wobbly on them.' Ginny grabbed my arm as I teetered, and sniffed my breath. 'Oooh! You've been at a boozy lunch. Good on you. If a girl's going to kick up her heels, she has to have heels that kick ass.'

I muttered agreement and slunk off to my office without coffee. Ginny was the one with the reputation for mainlining champagne, not me. Although she hardly ever showed it. Clearly, I did.

Ginny is one of our small but perfectly formed team of four at Project PR, and the only one among us who can combine the rare qualities of A-grade schmoozing and infinite attention to detail that make the perfect events organiser. Her hired marquees never blow down the night before a masked charity ball; her caterers never serve salmonella chicken; her champagne is never flat; her dancers never fall; her singers never miss a note; her bands never miss a beat.

Even her proportions fit the party-girl mould. Ginny is the archetypal tall, blonde bombshell, but beware of stereotyping her. She might look like a flawless fit with the long list of blonde jokes — a fashionista in full make-up, short skirts, high heels, fag in one hand, wine glass in the other — but she graduated BCom with straight As and you should see her mucking out the horsebox or handling her big bay mare over head-high jumps on her father's farm.

Then there's Nicky French, a non-flammable redhead, who comes up with clever ways of getting her client's products noticed and goes home to the delightful Dylan, who's just turned six. And Tracey Findlay, the backbone of the business, who is trim haired, trim figured despite three pregnancies, and always trimly attired, with never a sign of baby chuck or Marmite smears. Tracey disappears every day at three to switch her efficiency onto her *other* three hyperactive charges — her sons. Some mornings I've caught her remonstrating with us to tidy up the office kitchen or keep our timesheets up to date in the same voice she uses with the boys — a sort of cross between a sergeant major and an anxious mother hen.

The four of us have worked together for nearly ten years now — through childbirth and childrearing crises, through clients that are a delight and others that you could cheerfully murder, through campaigns that have been roaring successes and others that we'd rather forget. And in that time, we've worked out there are some things each of us is good at, and some things we shouldn't ever attempt again. Like the fund-raising antiquities auction I put together once that cost almost as much to stage as it raised; I've stayed well away from fund-raising and glitzy events since. Ginny learned the hard way that managing crisis communications is not her forté when her celebrity golf tournament ended up on the front page for all the wrong reasons. The adage that there's no such thing as bad publicity did not hold true on that occasion. Since then, when trouble has loomed, she's got me on the case right away.

Nicky, however, can handle pretty much anything — undoubtedly due in no small way to the work-out she's had every day bringing up young Dylan on her own since his scumbag father took off for Australia just months after their son was born.

'Here,' Ginny said a few moments later, depositing a strong black coffee and chocolate biscuit on my desk. 'Rich coffee and rich chocolate. All you need now is a rich man.'

'I wish,' I laughed. 'I'll settle for the coffee in the meantime. I'll be wide awake as well as trolleyed.'

I turned back to my laptop, which was just finishing its warm-up ritual. But when I clicked onto the email program, it refused to retrieve any new mail.

'Stupid thing,' I muttered, wrestling with the wireless mouse. I'd complained to Tracey before about its unreliability.

'What's the problem?' Ginny paused on her way out the door.

‘I’ve never liked this stupid wireless mouse thingy. It never connects properly through the remote and it’s always blinking its little red menacing eye at me.’

‘Penny, you can’t do that!’ she cried as I threw the mouse into the bin.

‘Bloody thing won’t work,’ I muttered.

‘Of course it won’t go, darling,’ she said, calmly retrieving the mouse from the bin and returning it to its place on my desk, where its red light happily resumed blinking at the mother ship. ‘But it’s not the harmless little mouse’s fault. Look.’ She held up a piece of cable. ‘You haven’t connected your laptop to the network.’

‘Oh.’ Ginny has about as much understanding of technology as a tuatara. I felt as small as the binned mouse.

‘You’ve had far too much to drink to be seriously trying to get any work done. You should drink your coffee and get a cab home.’

I was in no position to argue. Meekly I sipped the strong coffee, burning my tongue in the process, and bit into the chocolate biscuit.

‘The cab’s on its way,’ she called through from reception.

I stared at the screen, now connected to the network and filling with emails as they came through. They were a blur. I conceded defeat and closed it down.

Charlotte was on the phone when I arrived home. I left her to it. Adam was in the garage, immersed in a piece of his father’s old motorbike engine. He looked up, smiled half-heartedly at me and went back to his comfort zone. Superfluous to their needs, at least in the interim, I poured a glass of pinot noir and flopped in a chair on the outside deck, warming under the early summer sun. More wine, of course, was the last thing I needed. But I wasn’t listening to my rational self.

Charlotte woke me some time later, disgusted.

'Mum, you're drunk. Your breath smells foul,' she said with typical teenage tact. 'What are we going to do for dinner?'

'Well, I was hoping you'd cook us all something, honey,' I said, trying to look disarming. It didn't work. She rolled her eyes and pulled a face.

'I'll go and get McDonald's.' Adam offered, coming outside to join us. He never misses a trick when food is involved.

'It's all right, I've got something in the freezer.' I defrosted some frozen left-over dinners and set the table, making a show of being in command of at least some of my faculties.

'Mu-uum, you've set an extra place,' Adam complained when we carried our plates through to the dining room. 'There's only three of us now.'

Charlotte's face started to crumple.

'Damn, I forgot. Sorry.'

I quickly scooped up the fourth placemat and cutlery, hid it out of sight in the dresser, and carried on as if nothing had happened, talking quickly in the hope that Charlotte would be easily distracted. It didn't take long: I promised to take her shopping on Saturday for a new ball dress.

'Do you really mean it, Mum? It's not just the wine talking?'

'I really mean it, honey.' I scrawled a promissory note on a piece of paper and handed it over. Even I could tell my handwriting was suffering the effects of too much to drink; it was almost illegible. But Charlotte, bless her, was too excited at what the note was supposed to say to question its integrity.

'Thanks, Mum.' She gave me a hug and rushed off to text her friend Jenna.

With the effects of the wine wearing off, my dribbly nose had returned. By the time dinner was over, my nasal passages had started to resemble a small waterfall. There was only one remedy I knew that would be of any comfort: a hot toddy. With a good dose of brandy, lemon and sugar inside me, I slept like a baby.

The next morning, however, the waterworks didn't take long to reappear. I slugged back another cold pill and caught a ride into the city with Tracey.

'It's so infuriating. This is my second cold in a row,' I said as we idled in the traffic. 'Plus that awful flu Nicky gave me in the depths of winter. I've never had a year like it. Usually, I never get sick.'

Chapter 3

But there was no time to feel sorry for myself; no time to see the doctor; no time for anything more than popping another cold pill. I'd just have to soldier on.

Ginny had a big film premiere that night and she was in overdrive. Ginny never flaps, never loses her cool, never has a hair out of place or lipstick that fades. Her spray-on tan never mottles, her hemlines never drop, her heels never snap. And her events always run like clockwork. But there's something almost manic about the way she prepares for them. If I'm ever involved, I know to do what I'm told and leave the rest to her.

The locally made film had taken forever to finish, with budget over-runs, bad weather and a Hollywood star throwing tantrums. At last, it was to have its local premiere. But there was talk that there might be an animal rights protest over a horse that had been injured during filming. I'd spent the past week working with Ginny on media plans — one that included protesters and one that didn't — and spent a good part of the morning handling media calls.

I'd just finished going through a mock interview with her when Bill Bryant, one of the better-known lawyers about town, called. He'd just got off the phone from *ONE News* — one of his partners had apparently run off with the contents of an elderly client's trust fund, over which he had signing authority — and asked if I could help him fob off the media. 'That's the sort of thing you do, isn't it?'

'Sure, sometimes.'

He explained that his partner, Greg, had used the money over several months to pay for the sort of lifestyle he'd recently become accustomed to. 'I think most of it has disappeared into the coffers of the casino or at Partygirls.'

I stifled a gasp. Partygirls was a notorious sleaze bar and strip club, closely linked to the city's seedy underworld, where lap-dancing was just the beginning. It was not a name that would look good in juxtaposition with the upper-crust name of Soames, Bryant and Saville.

I shot round to Bill's office and drafted a statement for him to keep in his back pocket, in case *ONE News* had the facts already corroborated, and then worked out how to find out if the story was true. It would be foolish to come up with confirmation if they were only calling Bill's bluff and had nothing more than rumour to go on. But it only took two calls to confirm the worst — the partner was a Partygirls regular and was completely unrepentant. I drafted up some key messages for Bill and ran a quick media-training session with him before *ONE News* called back.

In between, Ginny phoned me a couple of times to ask

about the movie media, and Charlotte kept texting me about her father coming to the ball at the weekend. I texted Steve but there was no reply. In the end I turned the damn phone off so I could concentrate on the Partygirls problem.

I finally escaped from Bill's office at 2pm, having established that the TV news reporter didn't have enough for a story — especially a story about lawyers, who were likely to be (surprise!) litigious. No sooner had I turned my mobile back on in Bill's lift than it buzzed to tell me I had six messages.

The first one, from Ginny, said the protesters had arrived and she was using my media plan. 'The stuff-up fairy is back!' she concluded.

'Again!' I texted her back.

It's not that I don't love what I do. Believe me, I wouldn't swap my job for a solid-gold Boxster, but sometimes I wonder if I would have been better off with one of those nice nine-to-fivers where you turn up, push paper around, gossip about the boss in the tearoom, clock out on the dot and go home without having to take your work with you — not in your mind nor in your briefcase.

There's no way you can do that when you're in the business of PR. You're always on call, always thinking how you can do something better, or about what the media is saying about one of your clients. It's a thankless job on the whole; you spend hours making clients feel appreciated and adored but no one ever appreciates or adores you.

PR is a funny profession when you think about it — you spend most of your time on the phone or in front of a computer writing communication plans and press releases, and organising a hundred things at once. But everyone else thinks PR means party, party, party. And long lunches. I wish! The only long lunches I get are when I finally finish my sandwich at afternoon tea — that's if I've had time to go out and get a sandwich in the first place.

And despite what they say, it's not a licence to print money. I started out with nothing and I've still got most of it left.

Clients like Bill, though, don't help: they never tell you 'til the last minute they've got a problem; they expect you to wave your magic fairy dust over everything and solve it in an instant — make the media go away, make the problem go away, even — and only charge them for two hours' work. But in my opinion, the fairy dust is priceless.

I stood in Bill's lobby and dealt with two more messages then threw the phone in my bag, exhausted. After the last few hours, I needed major therapy. Retail therapy.

I paused in front of a shop window. The brightly coloured clothes it was famous for had often beckoned me inside but I'd always resisted. This time, I was drawn by an invisible hand into the brightly coloured Aladdin's cave where I soon found a frilly, floral-patterned furbelow to try on. And then another. And another.

The very first long fishtailed number I tried on looked fabulous — or at least it did in the darkened confines of the cubicle. I could just see myself at Charlotte's ball looking like Vivien Leigh in *Gone with the Wind*. Considering the state I was in, though, a flounced net curtain would have fooled me into thinking I was Scarlett O'Hara and forgetting my mother's frequent 'mutton dressed as lamb' epithet.

If the ruffles didn't put me off, the price should have. I nearly passed out when I read the dollars on the designer tag, but reality had buried itself under the lawyer's carpet and stayed there. Undeterred, I carried it up to the counter.

'I'll take it,' I said.

I was just about to produce my credit card when my

phone rang. Remembering all the messages I'd ignored, I answered guiltily. It was Tracey.

'I've been trying to get through to you, Penny,' she said. 'It's your mother. Apparently she's had a stroke.'

I dropped the frilly number on the counter and fled outside without even glancing at the shop assistant, who'd been scanning the label through the till.

'What? Where is she? How do you know?' I was in the middle of a busy pavement, buffeted by shoppers. I stepped back into the lee of the shop door.

'Slow down, Penny, it's okay. Sort of. She's in the hospital now. Your father called the ambulance and then called here looking for you. I've left messages all over.'

'Oh no, I've had my phone off. Oh God, I'm so sorry.'

I knew I should have checked those messages. I felt like crawling into the manhole under my feet.

'Did he say what happened? How is she?'

'She sort of passed out, he said. Just went all floppy and he couldn't get through to her. Before too long, though, she came round again, but still wasn't moving.'

I ran all the way to the parking building — well, most of the way; I had to slow down a couple of times to get my breath back — and raced over to the hospital, which was miles away of course, and every light was a red one. Then I couldn't find anywhere to park the car. After five minutes driving round the carpark I found a P10 space and took it.

Speed-walking to the emergency department, I looked at my watch: 2.35pm. I'd just have time to see Mum and have a talk to the doctor before my meeting at 4pm with a new client, an olive oil grower. Rumour had it that Panos Kerdemilidis made some of the best olive oil in the country and was looking to develop and promote a new brand for it. I'd been after his business for months and the thought of having to cancel sent me into a panic. I knew one of my rivals was also sniffing around and a late cancellation would surely drive Kerdemilidis straight to the opposition.

Just thinking about work at such a time made me feel like the daughter from hell, but I had to make a split-second decision — should I cancel the meeting, or would I be able to make it? Dithering with indecision, I was saved temporarily from making a call when my phone rang. I'd just arrived at the waiting room and the racket my phone was making as I rooted round in my bag trying to find it earned me disapproving stares from all around. I smiled apologetically as I checked the caller ID. It was Steve's mobile.

I vacillated. I knew I had to make sure he'd come to Charlotte's prizegiving, but this most definitely wasn't the time or place to cope with him — at least, not without getting into another row. I turned the phone off and dropped it back in my bag. The disapprovers looked less disapproving.

After waiting for what seemed an eternity, an aide finally took me to a curtained cubicle in the middle of a long, brightly lit room, scattered with beds on trolleys, each one bearing a patient, patiently waiting. I'd no idea so many people could be having some sort of medical emergency at 2.45 on a weekday afternoon. Some were clutching belongings; some had friends or relations at their side; some looked in a bad way, bleeding, coughing, crying, complaining; others scarcely moved.

In the comparative sanctuary of her cubicle, Mum was lying inert on top of a high, hard-looking bed on wheels. Her eyes were open, staring, unseeing. The sight made my heart stop. For a terrible moment I thought she'd passed away. But in that split second of terror and anguish, I noticed the almost imperceptible movement of her chest — in and out, in and out. I breathed a long sigh of relief.

Dad was sitting by her side, head in hands, elbows resting on the bed.

'Oh, Dad, I'm sorry. I should have been here earlier.'

He looked up, his eyes sad, his mouth forming a half smile of welcome.

'Colleen's not too good, I'm afraid, lassie.'

He stood and reached out to me. I hugged him hard, feeling his thinness. He'd lost so much weight since he'd taken on the job of full-time caregiver, he felt as frail as Mum was sturdy.

After a bit, he indicated that we should go to the corner of the cubicle, as far away from Mum as possible without going out into the busy room.

'The doctor says she might have had a stroke,' Dad whispered.

I knew that if Mum were okay, she'd hear every word. She always had her ears flapping, convinced we'd be talking about her — which, of course, we often were. I looked surreptitiously at her, expecting her to accuse us of plotting behind her back. But she hadn't moved.

'They're doing some tests to find out what the story is, whether there might be any damage.'

'You mean, like . . .'

I couldn't bring myself to say it: 'paralysed'. I could visualise Steve's Uncle Ross, who'd had a stroke and had been paralysed down one side. It had been ages before he could get about properly, and even then it had been a lopsided hobble. And he'd never got his speech back enough to make himself understood beyond a few garbled basics. With Alzheimer's to add to her burden, what chance did Mum have?

I hovered in the corridor to catch the doctor — a ponytailed woman who looked about seventeen — but didn't learn much more than what Dad had already told me. They were carrying out tests, she said. Mum would be admitted until they knew for sure what was wrong and what her prognosis might be. Then she took off on silent feet as her pager beeped insistently in her pocket.

Dad shooed me away after that.

'There's no point you waiting around, lassie. You go off and do what you have to. I'll get them to call you if anything changes. I'll be all right here.'

I traipsed down miles of corridors to find a cafeteria and bought Dad a sandwich and a piece of fudge. Apart from hospital tea, I discovered, he hadn't had anything since an early breakfast, so I sat with him while he ate, then took off with half an hour to spare before my meeting.

Nobody could say my life was dull and boring but right now a dose of dullness and boredom had big appeal.

There was a $40 ticket tucked under the wiper blades of the car. Cursing the totally inadequate hospital parking, I drove to the house on the outskirts of town where the olive oil baron had said he would meet me.

Panos, as I'd been warned, was extremely good looking. It took me a long time to pull myself together and focus on the task in hand: promoting his brand to the country's gourmet kitchens. And because more than half my mind was still on Mum and Dad, it took a good hour before I could extract myself. I promised him a costed proposal within a week and fled.

The long trip home across town in rush-hour traffic provided me with plenty of time to deal with phone messages. There were two from Steve. I saved a couple more until later then phoned the hospital and learned from the ward charge nurse that Mum had been admitted for observation. 'They are looking at her blood pressure. She seems fine now.' Then I returned Ginny's call to find out about the premiere. The protesters, having made the six o'clock news, had gone home and everything was now going to plan.

Thank God for the hands-free, I thought more than once as I manoeuvred the car through the heavy traffic. I swear I do some of my best work when I'm waiting at traffic lights or stuck in traffic. It was almost 6.15pm when I parked outside the garage.

'Mu-uum, you were supposed to be home ages ago,' Charlotte greeted me in the kitchen. 'It's Adam's prizegiving tonight. Had you forgotten? We won't have time for dinner.'

I was about to say she might have cooked something when I detected a comforting savoury odour coming from the oven. I nearly collapsed with surprise.

'Darling, you've made dinner. You're wonderful.'

Charlotte sniffed and tossed her ponytail.

'Wasn't me. Adam did it. He's made some random lasagne. From a packet.'

I didn't care if he'd made it from a tin of baked beans. To have dinner ready when I came home late from work and we all had to be out again within half an hour was such a joy that I almost cried.

'Hi, Mum.' Adam appeared in the kitchen and started fussing around the oven, checking his nicely bubbling dish and the timer. 'Five minutes to go.'

He pulled three plates out of the dresser then dived into the pantry cupboard, returning with the tomato sauce bottle.

'I fed Tigger,' he added.

'I wondered why he wasn't jumping all over me,' I said,

giving Adam a hug. 'Be down in a minute.' I dashed upstairs, did a quick change and arrived in the kitchen just as Adam was serving up.

'Charlotte,' he bellowed up the stairs. 'Dinner.'

Thanks to Adam's extraordinary bout of domesticity, we arrived at his prizegiving on time and, without having to worry about Steve being present — Adam had made sure he got the message he wasn't welcome — I settled down for the long haul of his school's end-of-year event, the day's frenetic activity going through my mind. I'd checked again on Mum's condition (comfortable) and told the kids in the car about the day's drama (leaving out the frilly temptation) before we left home.

Apart from Charlotte complaining every half hour or so about how boring the headmaster's speech was, and how unfair it was that she had to come ('Because Adam comes to yours every year, that's why'), the three and a half hours passed reasonably quickly. From the upstairs seating, I could see Adam down below sitting next to his friend Darren ('Fatty and Skinny', Charlotte called them mercilessly), seemingly engaged in some diversionary activity, engrossed in a small gadget in Darren's hand. By luck, or probably by design, they were seated a long way from the nearest teacher, and in little danger of discovery.

Adam always dissed the prizegiving, but it was compulsory. It was always a bit of a mission to get Steve along. He had failed to appear last year — probably because he was with the Conniving Cow. At the time, I'd believed his excuse about work. How naïve was that! So it wasn't a big deal to come on my own — lots of parents did, often taking it in turns to go through the annual agony of the lengthy performance. Unless, of course, your little darling was going to collect a prize. But that had never been a consideration for us. Adam was as likely to be awarded for academic excellence as an iguana. Apart from Science, he didn't even try. Charlotte, however, worked hard most of the year, but to her endless disappointment, her performance never catapulted her any further than middle of the class.

Adam's name wasn't called and neither, for the first time, was his friend Darren's. Their obvious joy after the ceremony, symbolising the end of school for another year and the beginning of the seemingly endless summer holidays, was to be heightened by a break-up party immediately afterwards at Darren's — the first time his mother had let him have one. I'd promised to come along and provide moral support.

Louise used to be the archetypal pearls-and-turned-up-collar poser, until her husband's abuse of her was finally outed backstage at the school play. But instead of hiding herself away, Louise had toughened up. Probably thinking she had nothing else to lose after her public humiliation, she came out fighting and left him, taking the kids with her. And now the pearls and pressed linen had been swapped for floaty florals, long swirly skirts and strappy sandals. She looked years younger.

• • •

Staying on at Louise's until most of the boys had gone home meant a late night, so I awoke the next morning feeling like I still needed a good night's sleep. But today was the day I'd promised to be up early to take Charlotte shopping for a new ballgown.

It started out as a pleasant mother-daughter bonding session. Charlotte's usual inability to make up her mind had been overtaken by a driving desperation to find something

— anything — that was better than the hand-me-down she had at home. So in an astonishingly short time we found both a dress, in deep Audrey Hepburn red, and some matching strappy shoes.

However, the smile on her face as we shared a coffee in the mall food court was quickly extinguished when her cell-phone buzzed loudly in her pocket. A couple of seconds later, she was close to tears.

She showed me the message. It was from Steve. He'd texted her from Melbourne, where he'd gone with Jacinta, saying he'd bought Charlotte something special there and he couldn't wait to get home for her to see it.

Typical! The fool of a man, preoccupied as he was with the Conniving Cow and their horizontal tango, had completely forgotten about his daughter's end-of-school ball and had skipped the country.

A great deal of comforting was required — then and for the rest of the day. The thrill of having her hair put up for the first time lost its shine; the fun of doing our make-up together wasn't such a laugh; the smile at the camera wasn't quite as bright.

Her partner, Miles — her high-school sweetheart who'd remained a friend long after they stopped going out together — did his best, turning up with a corsage. Charlotte had never seen one before — didn't even know what it was for — and then Davina arrived to take the family photos. Adam had gallantly stepped in to fill his father's shoes — and in my opinion was a much more attentive partner than Steve had been for many a year, though he danced like the proverbial frog in a blender, a dead ringer for his father.

Fortunately, the excitement of being dressed to the nines with all her friends and their boyfriends helped Charlotte get over the non-appearance of her father and, despite a late-night post-ball party, she was in fine form by Monday, the night of her school prizegiving.

Because it was going to be her last, the final hurrah, the farewell forever to schooldays, I'd virtually begged her father to be there. I'd phoned him on Sunday night, not long after he'd got home from Melbourne, and reminded him.

'Of course,' he said distractedly. 'I wouldn't miss it for the world.'

We'd agreed to meet him in the lobby of Charlotte's school hall. It was such a small space, Adam and I were jostled and shoved by families forging ahead to get a good seat. Charlotte had long ago joined her friends in their allotted seats to one side up the front, making me promise to sit next to her dad. I looked impatiently at my watch.

'Bloody hell, if he doesn't get here soon, we'll end up in the back row and won't be able to see a thing.'

'Don't worry, Mum. He'll be here soon. Besides, Charlotte's like me. She never gets a prize either. Doesn't matter where we sit.'

The crowd in the lobby was thinning. Apart from a few stragglers, everyone was now seated.

'Bugger him. I'm going in.'

Adam looked at his watch and sighed, as if he'd known this would happen all along. He took my arm and steered me through the double doors just as someone was starting to close them. I narrowly avoided being hit on the forehead by the polished veneer and ducked round the side to catch an apology.

I forced a smile and towed Adam to the only available seating for the two of us. There was a small space next to Adam should Steve deign to put in an appearance. But there was no sign of him.

'Bastard,' I thought, then realised by the look on Adam's face, and on the poor woman's next to me, that I'd actually said it out loud. I blushed and buried my head in the programme.

I thought back to the day Charlotte had first put on her uniform. Steve had taken so many photos of her as she left for school, she'd departed embarrassed while he was still snapping. She'd worked hard, mostly. With the exception of Year 10, when she'd behaved abominably for several months and got hauled in front of the principal almost weekly — as had Steve and I, to apologise for her behaviour — Charlotte had breezed through school, neither top of the class nor bottom, doing better in the creative subjects like Music and Photography, and taking part in everything she could find the time for: the school play, the choir (until it became uncool to sing in front of her peers), the hockey team — although one of the lower grades. God loves a trier, I thought fondly, smiling to myself at the memories: Charlotte in her hockey gear, long woolly socks, dirty knees, grubby shorts, grinning from ear to ear after scoring a winning goal; Charlotte bringing home her Photography portfolio and showing me the A+ mark in the corner (the montage of photos Steve had taken with him the day he left, I recalled with a pang); Charlotte crying over her Maths homework because she just couldn't get it; and Charlotte up on the school stage singing and dancing her way through the chorus line in *West Side Story*. I sighed. If only Steve were here for the last day as he was for the first, as he was for all those memorable moments in between.

'Mum, look!' Adam stuck his sharp elbow into my side, making me jump. I looked up, but couldn't work out what he was on about.

'It's Charlotte!'

I couldn't believe my eyes. My heart skipped a beat. It was indeed Charlotte, walking up on the stage, apparently to collect a prize.

'Good God! It's Charlotte.' My clapping was louder and more enthusiastic than anybody's; I felt like shouting and cat-calling. My daughter was at last getting a prize for something. On the last day of her last year at school. And her idiot father had missed it. I could have killed him. Except I didn't know where he was.

'What's it for?' I whispered to Adam.

'Photography and Drama,' Adam whispered back. 'Always knew she was a drama queen.'

Fortunately his remark was drowned by applause.

Charlotte smiled, accepted her envelope and skipped down the stairs off the stage, looking more pleased with herself than she had in a long time. She craned her neck, searching no doubt for us — and for her father.

Adam and I waited in the foyer afterwards while Charlotte hugged and re-hugged all her friends, as if she'd never see them again in this lifetime. Most of them, I knew, had planned to get together the following weekend, but tonight was a special night for all of them — a sort of rite of passage, when they officially stopped being schoolgirls and blossomed into young women, in theory anyway. I smiled at Adam as we watched from afar; he gave me an eye-roll in return. It was all too girly for him.

Charlotte's euphoria, however, disappeared the instant she came over to us and realised Steve wasn't there.

'Didn't Dad come?' she cried before I had time to congratulate her.

I shook my head.

'Nuh,' Adam said.

'But he promised!'

There was nothing I could say.

'That's so mean.' She walked over to a nearby settee and slumped down on it, a picture of desolation. 'He promised.'

'I'm sorry, honey,' I said, going over to her and resting my arm on her shoulder. 'I know you wanted him there. You won a prize. I'm so proud of you. Congratulations.' I gave her a hug, but she didn't respond. I could see she was blinking back the tears. 'You're the first in the family to win a prize at school. I'm so proud.' I deliberately refrained from mentioning Steve. I knew he'd be proud too, but there was no point rubbing salt in the wound.

Dejectedly, she walked to the car with us. She didn't say a thing on the way home, no matter how much I tried to coax something out of her. Even Adam was nice to her.

The minute I'd unlocked the front door she went straight up to her room, ignoring the joyous leaps of Tigger, and closed the door behind her.

I looked at Adam, who was watching her go. He shrugged. He was right. There wasn't much we could do. My hugs and congratulations weren't what she was looking for. It was Steve's praise she wanted.

I was halfway through making a cup of tea — after considering and rejecting something stronger — when I thought dammit, I'll phone the bastard and make him speak to her. The look on her face when she realised her father had missed her big moment haunted me still — I couldn't get it out of my mind. All the way home I'd been fuming quietly, building up a fine head of steam.

I punched Steve's mobile number on the phone pad and waited for it to ring. If it went to message service, I was ready to let him have it. But after three rings, he answered.

'Steve O'Neill speaking,' he said. There was quite a bit of noise in the background, like he was at a party or in a bar. My fury continued to mount.

'Hello, Steve. Penny here.'

'Oh. Hi, Penny.' He sounded slightly inebriated. He also sounded as if he didn't have a clue why I was phoning: not a trace of guilt.

'That's very noisy. Where are you?'

There was a bit of a pause. He was probably weighing up whether to tell me it was none of my business.

'At Puccini's. It's the new partners' party. Jacinta's just been made a partner.'

'Oh. That's nice,' I said between gritted teeth. Puccini's was one of the most expensive restaurants in town, where all the trendy people congregated.

'Yes, it is. So I'd better be going . . .' There was a pause. 'Was there something . . . ?'

'I was phoning to find out where you were tonight. You missed Charlotte's prizegiving.'

'Oh, damn, I forgot. Sorry, Penny.'

'It's Charlotte you need to apologise to. She's very upset. She won a prize.'

'She didn't! Damn, I should have been there. Can I speak to her?'

I forced aside my immediate inclination to tell him to go to hell and said, 'Sure.' I took the phone up to Charlotte, knocked on her door and handed it over to her without saying who it was, then left him to it. It was hard to tell, later, if it made any difference.

The whole episode, however, made me feel sick with fury. How could he be so selfish, so cavalier, so mean? My natural instinct to protect Charlotte from hurt and harm had been violated by none other than her father, who had been celebrating with his girlfriend instead of his daughter.

It was the last straw. I was so angry I could cheerfully have taken out a contract on him.

Charlotte's despair was the turning point; I'd now reached the point of no return.

• • •

From: Penny Rushmore
To: Elizabeth.oconnor@cavendishmacintyre.co.nz; DJones@healthcaremz.co.nz; francesd@datasave.com; Helen@radionet.co.nz
Subject: The time has come

I promised I'd let you know when I'd decided to let Steve have the rest of his toys back. I'll be returning the Stag to him in all its glory a few days before Christmas — a fitting Christmas present for him, after all this time. But I couldn't hold onto it any longer. As Liz will appreciate, you can only use these things for leverage for so long. Once you get what you want in return, the time comes to hand them over. I'll let you know how it goes.

Penny

From: helen@radionet.co.nz
To: penny@projectpr.co.nz
Subject: RE: The time has come

If you would like me to spread the word about your

generous Christmas present just give me the nod. It would be nice for such a deserving recipient to get a bit of publicity once again!

Helen

From: Penny Rushmore
To: helen@radionet.co.nz
Subject: RE: The time has come

Who am I to stand in the way of the fourth estate? I'll let you know the delivery details nearer the time.

Penny

Chapter 4

Birthdays are usually a cause for celebration in our house. When the kids were little birthdays meant cheerios, fairy bread, gooey chocolate cakes covered in lollies and shaped like trains and fairy castles, total chaos around the house and garden while they ran riot, and treats for Tigger's predecessor, busy vacuuming the floor. Then there was the age of the sleep-over — or rather the awakeathon. I'll never forget the night six over-hyped pre-pubescent girls giggled and squealed their way through endless repeats of the *Titanic* video and Spice Girls' songs, despite my hourly mad-dog acts to get them to go to sleep.

Of late, the kids' parties are decidedly adolescent. Giggles have given way to sniggers and snogging behind the camellia bushes. Sugar sprinkles and lollies have been exchanged for Speight's and Archers. But the cheerios still get scoffed, along with the pizza and sausage rolls. And instead of being kept up all night by the noise they make at home, I lie awake worrying if they're actually coming home.

But this year it was *my* birthday that gave me the glums. I wanted to keep it quiet. There was no point in having a party because there was absolutely nothing to celebrate; I was going to be even older than the Conniving Cow and even further removed from Steve. I had every reason to believe I could get away without a fuss. Falling just a week before Christmas, my birthday is often forgotten or, more usually, bundled up with Christmas presents — when one package fits all.

Steve had never been the most domesticated of men, nor the most romantic. But he had always been good at remembering birthdays — although admittedly my annual habit of marking it on the kitchen calendar may have had something to do with it. A cup of tea, a book voucher tucked inside a birthday card, the paper in bed before the day had time to come crowding in on me, Tigger nestled in a ball at my feet and the kids crashing around the house getting ready for school without needing me: it was pure heaven.

This morning, however, there was no cup of tea in bed, no gift, no Steve. The kids had forgotten, of course. There was no way Mum would remember in her befuddled state, Dad had never been strong on birthdays, and my sister was at the other end of the country absorbed in the proofs for her stupid book.

Stephanie had finally finished writing a sort of semi-fictionalised account of our great-grandmother, Annie Jane Morrison, who'd been an enthusiastic suffragette, tirelessly gathering signatures for their petition to Parliament to get women the vote in 1893. In one of her better moments, just before she and Dad moved into St Joan's, Mum had produced

Annie Jane's letters to her sister — the editor of the ladies' page of a provincial newspaper — and Stephanie had squirreled them away. A year later and, hey presto, Annie Jane's letters have been turned into a historical romance written by none other than my beloved sister. I didn't approve — I felt family history was personal and should be preserved as such, not flossied up to catch the chick lit market — but I had yet to communicate that to Steph. I was biding my time.

My birthday fell on a Monday and I thought it had escaped notice at first. The kids hadn't mentioned it and nobody said a thing at the office. But at morning tea, Tracey brought in a cake with enough candles to create a small conflagration, while Ginny and Nicky followed with strong coffee and prettily wrapped presents.

'Happy birthday, boss,' Tracey said as I blew out the candles. It took more than one breath.

'Goodness, there are enough candles here for an octogenarian,' I laughed.

'Just Ginny's little joke.' I looked at Ginny, who shrugged innocently.

'I would never dream of guessing how old you are,' she said.

'I'd rather not remember.'

'Nonsense. A woman never forgets her age . . . once she decides what that is!'

'Way to go!' Nicky laughed. 'I think I'll decide I'm twenty-nine.'

'Funny, I thought you were,' Ginny threw in.

'It's all very well for you, you're ageless,' I said. 'You're probably pushing ninety, under all that make-up and Botox.'

'Now that's not fair. I don't wear that much make-up.'

Further jibes about Ginny trying to hold back the clock

helped dispel my earlier self pity. And Ginny's card, as always, made me smile: 'Take the lead from Zsa Zsa Gabor,' she wrote. 'Become a great housekeeper. Every time you split up with a man, you keep the house.'

'So far, so good,' I laughed. 'I've still got the house. But sometimes I'd rather have the man.'

Tracey raised an eyebrow quizzically.

'Only sometimes. He was by no means perfect, but he was much better at coping with warring teenagers than me. In fact, they never seemed to fight so much when Steve was around.'

'Tell me about it,' Tracey said. 'Ever since Tom turned thirteen, he seems to have undergone a personality change, teasing his brothers until they're rolling round on the floor fighting. Yet the minute Gerry comes home from work, they're angels.'

'I don't know how you cope with three boys.'

'Neither do I sometimes.' She smiled wryly. 'It was okay when Mum could take them off my hands, but now that Dad needs such a lot of looking after, I can't rely on her like I used to. In fact, I seem to be spending more time helping her pick Dad up off the floor when he slips out of his wheelchair. By the time I get the boys in the car and get round there, the afternoon's gone and the dinner isn't even started.'

'Welcome to the Sandwich Generation.' I gave her a hug.

'Sandwich Generation? What are you talking about?'

'You know, women our age — or thereabouts,' I added, acknowledging that Tracey was almost ten years younger than me. 'We're sandwiched between teenagers and elderly parents, each side causing us grief.'

'Really? I didn't know there was a name for it. I'll

remember that next time I've got Dad in a fireman's lift and the boys are helping themselves to their nana's cake tins.'

'I had no idea your dad was in such a bad way.'

'It's come on quite suddenly since his stroke. I think we're going to have to look at some sort of care.'

'Well, I can certainly help you out with that one,' I said, pulling a face. 'I must have researched every nursing-care agency and rest home in town these past couple of years.'

Work carried on as normal. Apart from a phone call from my irrepressible client Jim Stephens (a toilet paper magnate who briefly caught my fancy a year ago when I'd just discovered Steve was having an affair) offering to sweep me off my feet and take me to lunch (politely declined), the day passed in much the same hectic rush as usual. At 3pm I got a text from Charlotte wishing me a happy birthday — she must have arrived home and remembered — and there were lots of cheery emails from friends and from the fabulous Philly four suggesting a half-hour meeting at 5pm.

This seemed like just the right antidote to the single-sheila blues that were threatening to overwhelm me during the afternoon. However, I was sitting in my office waxing lyrical to Nicky and Ginny about growing a year older when my mobile rang. I recognised the number.

'Hi Dad,' I said, trying to sound cheerful. 'What's up?' I covered the mouthpiece. 'Won't be long,' I mouthed to the others. Tactfully, they disappeared out the door.

'Ah, lassie, there you are,' he said. 'How are you getting on?'

'Fine, Dad. How are you both?'

'Well, your mother's not so good right now. I need to ask you a wee favour. She's asking for Stephanie again. I wondered if you . . .'

'Sure Dad, I'll pop round. But she's not likely to be fooled. It's usually only Stephanie she knows.'

'I know, lassie. But it's worth a try. It's very good of you, thank you.' There was a pause. 'You know, she's been different since that mini-stroke.'

'Yes. I noticed it too. But that's what happens, apparently, with Alzheimer's. A stroke can move it on a step or two.'

'That's what I was worried about.'

Our brief moment of being able to talk without Mum listening in was over. I could hear her voice in the background.

'Don't worry, Dad. I'll be round shortly.'

Further emails from the Ladies' Philosophical Society membership cast doubt on whether we would be able to gather a quorum and, with the need to go round to see Mum and Dad and a text from Charlotte insistent that I be home in plenty of time for dinner, we decided to postpone it.

From: Penny Rushmore
To: Elizabeth.oconnor@cavendishmacintyre.co.nz; DJones@healthcaremz.co.nz; francesd@datasave.com; Helen@radionet.co.nz
Subject: Birthday/Christmas celebrations

I agree with Di's email — we're just far too overcommitted for our own good. Our get-together will have to be in the New Year.
Horrors! Another year has almost flown by. Isn't it weird — the older we get, the faster the years seem to fly.
I promised to let you know: Steve's car is being delivered to his office carpark on Thursday afternoon at 4.30pm — just in time for the commencement of his office Christmas drinks

in the first floor cafeteria, which coincidentally overlooks the carpark.

It's going to take a lot of Dutch courage to get through the next 24 hours.

Penny

• • •

With just over an hour to spare before I needed to be home, I detoured via St Joan's retirement village and nosed Rosie up the narrow driveway to Mum and Dad's pale primrose plaster-coated villa. Dad greeted me looking drawn and unusually sad.

'I'm sorry to take up your time, lassie,' he said quietly as we stood at the open doorway, 'but she's taken a turn for the worse since she came back home from hospital. It's almost like the old days, before we got her on the Aropax.'

'What's that you're saying about me?' Mum called from the lounge. 'I can hear, you know.'

'It's all right, Colleen,' Dad called back. 'It's Penny. She's come to see you.'

'Who?' My heart sank. I hadn't seen Mum for over a week now and it sounded as if she'd had a relapse and forgotten who I was again.

'Penny. Your daughter.'

'I know she's my daughter. I'm not stupid, you know.'

Dad raised an eyebrow at me and smiled wryly. 'You can never be sure, these days,' he whispered.

He led me inside, where the sun was streaming in the lounge window. The cream and taupe striped wallpaper, dotted with their treasured paintings, the favourite mahogany pieces covered with framed family photos atop cream lace doilies, the cornflower blue and cream patterned curtains, the treasured trinkets arranged across the windowsill — the room was a picture of domestic tranquillity. But Mum was far from tranquil. She got up from her chair the moment I walked through the door.

'Where've you been all this time?' she demanded. 'You haven't been to see me for months.'

I'd heard her like this before and knew how to handle it. There was certainly no point in denying it — she wouldn't remember my last visit, or the one before that.

'I'm sorry, Mum. But I'm here now.'

I guided her over to her chair opposite the television and encouraged her to sit in it.

'Hmmph,' she expostulated as she sat down again. 'I was hoping for Stephanie. She's much better at coming to see me.'

This was definitely not true. Stephanie remained safe in her southern hideaway and hadn't been up our way for months. Mum often confused me with her.

'Stephanie's coming up for Christmas. You'll see her then.'

I sat down beside her and held her hand. She withdrew it immediately.

'Of course she'll be here for Christmas,' she sniffed and turned back to *Neighbours* at twice the comfortable volume.

I watched her, wanting to reach out to her, to give her a big hug, but knowing from past experience I'd be rebuffed. Rock of my life for so many years, my resilient, stocky little mum was always the cheery homebody, greeting me and Steph after school with hot chocolate and biscuits she'd baked herself. At night, she helped us with homework while Dad worked all hours at his service station. She was there for me, always — when I broke my wrist at netball, she got a taxi (Dad had the car at work and taxis were a luxury seldom indulged) to come and get me and take me to the hospital; when I came down with chickenpox, she nursed me back to health, bringing me homemade soups and raspberryade in bed; when my heart was broken for the first time, she took me to the movies and bought me popcorn and ice cream. (I'd been able to taunt Stephanie about it for months. Mum never bought *her* popcorn.) And now Mum hardly knew me. Our lives were topsy turvy — I was the nursemaid now. It was a role I'd gradually assumed as she'd become increasingly difficult.

For a long time, there was nothing you could really put your finger on, nothing that shouted 'Alzheimer's' — not that we knew much about it then, anyway. She'd get cranky for no reason, arguing with Dad if he put the tea caddy back in the wrong place, picking fault with things that never bothered her before. When she and Dad came over for dinner, the children were always too noisy, too rude, too disrespectful, too spoilt. True, they were all of these things at times, but until then she'd never remarked on it. She'd complain about the meal — too hot, too cold, too spicy, not as good as she would have made it. And she'd get restless — wanting to be off soon after she'd arrived. Sometimes, she'd worry that her friends were ganging up on her, were gossiping about her behind her back, were having afternoon teas without inviting her.

With hindsight, of course, it all added up. She was gradually losing her mind. Her brain was showing the first signs of shrinking, the first signs of the debilitating disease of dementia. But at the time, we couldn't work it out and, being the only one of her children in the same town, it had fallen to me to make excuses for her, cover up for her, and try to protect her from the ridicule and odd looks she was earning. The worse she got, the more I took on the role of protector and comforter; I became a sort of mother to my mother.

And after decades of being looked after by her, of having all his meals cooked, his clothes washed and all traces of engine oil obliterated, his home always clean and tidy, Dad had to learn housewifely duties, pretty much from scratch. My Dad, who'd spent something like seventy or eighty hours a week happily pumping gas, mending leaky radiators and replacing faulty carburettors, had to swap engine grease for elbow grease and work out how to boil an egg.

Mum refused to hand over her domain without a tussle, however: she'd insist on baking scones and biscuits, covering the bench with the contents of the pantry without having a clue what she was putting in the bowl. One time I arrived to find her breaking a dozen eggs into the waste disposal, counting them one by one. Dad had been hanging out the washing at the time. And if you tried to stop her, she got indignant and defensive. He tried to keep her out of the kitchen by diverting her with the television and photo albums, but old habits die hard with her — her kitchen is her castle.

It made me so sad, looking at her, a passive and pathetic shadow of her former self. The twinkle had long gone from her eye. The feisty, fun woman I had come to love after I'd left home and realised just how terrific she was had become an anxious, cantankerous, difficult old woman — old before her time and diminishing with her memory.

Dad, who'd been hovering in the background, went to the kitchen and put the jug on. I followed him, hoping to have a catch-up while Mum was absorbed in *Neighbours*. It always struck me as ironic that she didn't have any difficulty in keeping up with the antics of Bree and the Kinskis, but when it came to her own family, she was thoroughly confused. In fact, she sometimes talked about *Neighbours* and

Coro characters as if they *were* her family.

While Dad was getting out the cups, I heated the teapot then spooned the orange pekoe into it.

'Mum doesn't seem *too* bad at the moment,' I said.

'It comes and goes, lassie.' He rubbed his forehead distractedly. 'I don't know what to do. If I get the doctor, he'll no doubt want her to go into the dementia unit, and I just couldn't bear that.'

'I know, Dad. I know. But we've got to think about your health too. You can't go on wearing yourself out every day looking after her twenty-four-seven. It's too much for you. Your heart . . .'

'My heart's fine, lassie. Don't you worry about me, I'm right as rain.'

He busied himself with the tea tray and the subject of Mum's care seemed closed. I decided to make the most of Mum's absorption in the telly.

'I'm giving Steve back the Triumph Stag this week.'

'Oh, is that right, lassie? I wondered when you might be doing that.'

'The time has come, my lawyer says, to meet halfway. And the Stag is part of the deal.'

'Well, I guess that's for the best, then,' he said tactfully. 'Steve always was a bit soft over that car.'

'I know. Believe me, I've felt pretty bad about hanging onto it for so long, knowing he would give his eye teeth to have it back. But you know how lawyers are.'

Dad looked at me briefly — long enough for me to see that he had no idea how lawyers actually are.

'Well, anyway,' I said brightly, 'I've been generous and given it a good clean-up and a decent paint job before I send it back to him. It's something he's always wanted, but the mechanical stuff always took precedence. It seemed the least I could do.'

Dad looked at me quizzically again. The colour of a car was as unimportant to him as the state of the carburettor was to me.

'That's nice, dear.' He looked unimpressed.

'Yes.' I figured I'd given him as much information as he needed. If I told him the whole story, his heart would really go into overdrive or he'd suffer apoplexy. 'I'm picking it up on Thursday. He'll get it just in time for Christmas.'

'That's nice, dear,' Dad said again.

'Who's getting what in time for Christmas?' Mum arrived in the kitchen. 'Who are you talking about?'

'Steve is getting his old car back for Christmas,' I explained.

'Can't see what's so exciting about that,' she sniffed. 'He's had that old car for donkey's years and it never seems to be going. I can't understand what he sees in the ugly beast.'

It was a rare moment of lucidity from Mum. I was inclined to agree with her, but thought better of it in front of Dad.

'I'll find the biscuits, lassie,' he said, opening the pantry.

Mum elbowed him out of the way. 'Here you are, Ron,' she said, fishing out several porridge sachets and putting them on the tray. 'Here's the shortbread.'

I carried the tray, along with the porridge sachets, into the lounge and Dad managed to beat her to pour the tea. The last time she'd done it when I was there, she'd poured it into the sugar bowl and couldn't understand what all the fuss was about when Dad whipped it away to the kitchen.

'What have you brought these in for?' she queried, picking up a porridge packet. 'You can't eat these. Where are the biscuits, Ron?'

He scuttled off to fetch them, giving me a conspiratorial smile.

Neighbours had finished, so while Dad chatted about how he and Colin won the bowls tournament, I diverted Mum to the photo album to stop her interrupting.

While Dad recounted his winning bowl, my eyes scanned the photos as Mum flicked over the pages — Stephanie and me in lumpy, loose bathing suits at the beach, smiling at the camera in between fighting over who was going to put the shells on the sandcastle; Stephanie flashing her legs in those ridiculous hotpants she'd insisted on wearing long after they'd gone out of fashion, just to show off her enviable long legs; Stephanie like a pearl nestled in oyster satin on her wedding day; Stephanie with Seraya, the perfect child who'd never had a teenage tantrum nor exhibited the faintest signs of rebellion. These painfully drawn out admiration sessions inevitably brought out the green-eyed monster in me. I'd always been jealous of my big sister, she who could do no wrong, the tall, slim, golden girl who never got zits or puppy fat, who was never the wallflower at the school dance. But trawling through photos of Stephanie was the quickest way to calm Mum down and get her as close to reality as possible.

When I finally extricated myself from Mum, who had managed to waffle on about Stephanie ad infinitum in between Dad trying to talk about his big day, I drove home with thoughts of hot lemon toddies and a warm bed. My throat was sore again; it hurt to swallow — which, of course, made me want to swallow all the time. I was so sick of getting colds and the flu. But I didn't have time to go to the doctor, not with Christmas so close.

• • •

I arrived home while the news was on, just in time for dinner — prepared by Charlotte.

'It's your birthday, Mum. I want to make it special,' she said.

Knowing Charlotte's cooking, I feared it would indeed be special, but I let her pour me a glass of wine and usher me into the lounge.

'Happy birthday,' she said, giving me a kiss on the cheek and handing me a Paperplus parcel (she never bothered with fancy wrapping or ribbons). It was a *Vanity Fair* magazine.

'Hey, Charlie, you remembered! It's my favourite indulgence.'

Dinner was almost edible. A chicken arrangement, baked with apricots, nuts, breadcrumbs and an awful lot of garlic, it smelled divine and looked absolutely beautiful on the plate, surrounded with rice and snips of herbs from the garden. It was a triumph of style over substance. Charlotte was good at the presentation, copying the pictures in the recipe books, but she wasn't so good at the content, favouring short cuts and substitutions when she couldn't find the necessary ingredients in the pantry. I made appreciative noises while I wrestled with the rubber chicken; Adam, bless him, wolfed it down without seeming to notice.

Charlotte poured me another glass of wine and made Adam clear up while she watched *Shortland Street*.

'I hope you won't be offended if I take my wine into the study,' I said to her as I stood to go. But she didn't hear.

'Hang on, Mum. Don't go yet,' Adam called from the kitchen.

Suddenly the lights went out and he appeared with a piece of the divine pineapple cake they have down at the deli-café on the corner. The cake was topped with a single candle.

I grabbed the camera from the cupboard next to the TV.

'I want to record this for posterity,' I said. 'This really is special, Adam. Thank you.'

He cleared his throat a few times and mumbled something I couldn't hear, putting the little cake and its saucer on the coffee table and allowing me to hug him, albeit briefly. Out of the corner of my eye, I saw Tigger making a speedy dive for the cake, flaming candle and all, and managed to sweep it away from his grasp.

'You appalling dog,' Charlotte said, throwing a rolled-up magazine after him. He curled up on the floor just beyond the danger zone, his big brown eyes feigning total innocence.

I blew out the candle and wished for happiness for Adam and Charlotte — as usual. But the candle wouldn't go out, no matter how hard I blew. Adam chuckled.

'Gotcha!' he said, wetting his fingers and holding the wick until it stayed lifeless. He looked so pleased with himself, I laughed.

I spooned up a piece of cake and offered some to the kids, but they turned it down. If it had been chocolate, it would have been a different story, which is why it was all the more special — Adam had actually bought me something to eat that he didn't want himself. He went back to the kitchen and returned with a cup of tea, lukewarm from waiting, but hey, what does a small thing like that matter when I didn't have to make it myself?

I'd just sunk back into the sofa with the tea and *Vanity Fair* when the phone started ringing somewhere nearby. I scrabbled around the cushions trying to find it. The kids were always leaving it somewhere invisible and the only way to find it was to track down where the ringing was coming from.

'Where's the phone?' Charlotte cried, banging down the

stairs and coming back into the lounge.

'Found it!' I cried triumphantly, locating it underneath the sofa. 'Hello,' I answered, slightly out of breath.

'Hi, Penny.' It was Steve. 'How's things?'

'Okay, I guess,' I said guardedly. Maybe he had remembered my birthday after all, but I didn't want to get my hopes up too high only to have them dashed again. He'd become an expert at that these past few months.

'Can I speak to Charlotte please?'

'Sure.' I handed the hope-dasher over to his daughter who was waiting expectantly behind me. There is usually a fair chance that when the phone rings these days, it's for her. She disappeared with the phone up to her room for a few minutes then came bounding down again. She bounced over to me, plumping herself down on the other sofa, phone in one hand, the other hand covering the mouthpiece.

'Dad's going to the Coromandel on Boxing Day and has asked me if I'd like to come too, as a reward for winning those two prizes. I told him yes, but he asked me to check with you first. I can go, can't I Mum?'

'But you're going to Australia with him at the end of January, honey. You and Adam.'

'Yes, but this is special, just for me. Please, Mum. Please.'

'No. It's just not possible. We've got Stephanie and Seraya and Marcus coming up for Christmas and they'll want to do things with us on Boxing Day and the day after. They'll be expecting you to be there.'

'But Mu-uum. That's so unfair.' She looked at me pleadingly.

'No, Charlotte, I'm sorry, but no. Your father can't expect to change all our Christmas plans with just a few days' notice. Anyway, I thought he was having a party on Christmas night.'

'Yes, he is. They're going the next day, and they want me to come too. Please, Mum.'

'No, it's too much, Charlotte. You're going with him at the end of January. That's plenty.'

It seemed totally over the top to me, but then why did that surprise me? Steve seemed to have an endless supply of money these days to squire Jacinta to all the best places. I could feel the bitter taste of jealousy.

Charlotte flounced off, dejectedly imparting my refusal to her father as she went. I didn't hear the rest of the conversation, thankfully, as she disappeared up the stairs and out of earshot.

The phone rang again a few minutes later. I guessed it would be Charlotte's friend Jenna but Charlotte appeared and grumpily handed over the phone.

'It's Aunt Stephanie,' she said.

Steph had phoned to remind me yet again that she'd be up soon and to make sure I was going to meet her at the airport. She also wanted to talk about her book and how excited the publisher was about its sales potential.

'She thinks it'll go down really well with the baby boomer market, with the heritage and family tree stuff,' Stephanie bubbled. 'She thinks it'll be a bestseller.'

I could feel the old sibling jealousy rising again and had to fight with myself not to say something catty. Everything Stephanie did seemed to be a winner. Her books were bestsellers, her home was featured in *NZ House and Garden*, her husband and daughter were faultless, and the household income must be astronomical.

'That's nice,' I said, suppressing the urge to seethe.

I uttered a few more hyperboles and was happy to end the call when she finished her little rave. I did sometimes wonder if Steph irritated her friends as much as she did me with her endless fascination with herself. I managed to get in a few words about Dad needing more help with Mum, but if it wasn't about her, Steph wasn't interested, I thought meanly.

I flicked on the TV but couldn't concentrate, not even on the low-attention-span stuff that was running. Charlotte came through the lounge on her way to the kitchen, shooting me a hurt look. Adam, having done his bit with the birthday cake, had retreated to his room to race street cars. Tigger was asleep in his basket, twitching as he dreamed, no doubt, of bucket-loads of food suddenly appearing in his bowl.

I went to the fridge to pour another wine but I'd already emptied the bottle — it was sitting mournfully on the bench with just a few dregs in the bottom. The so-called wine cellar was empty. I'd forgotten taking the last bottle out when Davina was round for dinner last week, and I hadn't bought any more at the supermarket. The house was dry!

No it wasn't, a little voice told me. There were still a few drops of liqueur left.

I picked up the bottles and inspected them one by one, wondering if perhaps Charlotte or Adam had been raiding the liquor cupboard one night with their friends. Only the Baileys had more than a few millimetres in it.

I poured one, straight, and swallowed it in one. It hardly touched the sides, so I poured another.

Don't get me wrong, now. I'm not one to get stuck into the liqueurs as a rule. In fact, I don't even really like them. At dinner parties, I always pass on the port and Cointreau.

But tonight, I didn't care. Tonight, I couldn't taste a thing. Tonight, I wanted to bring on the sort of oblivion that a few swigs of Baileys could allow. I wanted a good wallow. It's my pity party and I'll cry if I want to.

The little voice that had pointed me towards the Baileys forgot to tell me that drinking alone is for losers, that my self-pity was entirely undeserved. Instead, I couldn't get it out of my mind that Steve and Stephanie and Mum and Uncle Tom Cobley, no doubt, were all deliberately making life impossible for me. It was as if all the pain that Steve had heaped upon me, all the achievements Stephanie had lauded over me, all the indifference Mum had shown me, had built up to a monumental wall of shame and hurt that was overpowering and disempowering me.

I forgot all about the good things — as you do when you're determined to feel sorry for yourself. I forgot about Charlotte's dinner and Adam's cake; I forgot about my Dad and how understanding and kind he was; I forgot about the clients who are a joy to work for; I forgot about the Philly girls; and I forgot about the silly old Stag being given its shiny new coat of paint. I could have saved myself a lot of trouble if I'd stopped to think.

I don't know how many little shot glasses I poured. And I threw the bottle out without looking at it the next morning, so I'll never know.

I remember in the middle of it all I found my way to the study and opened up the drawer with all the household accounts, insurance policies and bank statements in it. I remember being very purposeful about this, determined to find something, to look something up. But I've no idea what or why. I don't think I found it either. The next morning the papers were scattered everywhere. I'd highlighted our joint account balance in fluorescent pink for some strange reason, and then scrawled the pink highlighter across the page as well as across several others.

Some time about then, I'd phoned Steve on his mobile. I

have a feeling he was in a noisy bar, probably with Jacinta. It pains me greatly to recall the names I called him. I also know I cried. And I might have shouted a bit too, because he hung up. Even in my Baileys haze I knew I'd been a fool. I'd thrown the cordless down and flung myself on the sofa, pouring another shot to obliterate my stupidity.

'Mu-uum, what *are* you doing?'

There's nothing like the horrified wail of a teenage daughter to bring you back to reality. But even that didn't work.

'I'm having a nightcap,' I said. Or at least that's what I thought I said. Charlotte didn't seem to understand me. She picked the phone up off the floor and waved it at me.

'Mum, you're drunk again.'

'I am not!' I stood up, but didn't quite make it and collapsed back on the couch. 'Oops.'

She must have enlisted Adam's help to get me upstairs and into bed, because I woke up on top of the duvet with half my clothes on, the *Anvil Chorus* ringing in my head and a thirst that could have swallowed an entire bathtub. The house was ominously silent. I lifted my head high enough to see the red numbers on the alarm clock: 9.03. The *Anvil Chorus* moved up a few decibels to triple forte.

Damn! In misguided kindness, Charlotte had turned off the alarm and I was so late I was ready for interment.

As I stood under the hot shower, I let the force of the water pound against my throbbing temples and run down my body, stiff from lying in an awkward position all night but gradually flexing back to life under the warm stream. Soaping myself with Charlotte's favourite bodywash, I thought I noticed a small lump on the side of my right breast, not far from my armpit, but dismissed it. I was in no state to cope with that sort of thing. If it hadn't been for a brief voice of reason in my head, I would have left it at that. But before I got out of the shower, I touched it again, tentatively, terrified it might be real. I couldn't be sure, but it felt sort of superficial, sort of moveable. Which meant there was nothing to worry about.

Relieved, I towelled my hair, dressed and got ready for work, drinking coffee and answering an increasing number of calls on my mobile as the tasks I'd carefully planned for today turned, one by one, to custard. What made it worse was it was nobody's fault but my own. I wasn't exactly bright-eyed and bushy-tailed and I was late, very late. Without me there to okay the colour pass, the presses had failed to start rolling and the funeral firm's sponsored summer fun-run stickers, flyers and posters wouldn't be done before the printer closed for the summer holidays. Without me to check the final draft against the client's changes, the press release and photos promoting the luxury lodge's summer spa treatments wouldn't get to the travel magazines before their February issue deadline. Without me to brief the photographer and pick up the permit from the hospital management, the children's ward Christmas party photos wouldn't be taken.

I drove too fast to work and collected a speed camera fine. Damn! I saw the light flash as I passed. Despite the Berocca, the painkillers, several gallons of water and a hearty breakfast, my head still throbbed and I felt ill. I realised I was probably still marginally over the legal limit and slowed right down.

In the cold light of day, my reasons for going on a bender seemed totally pathetic. I had no one to blame but myself, I thought as I decided to stop rather than run another orange light. Today was shaping up to be one of those days when everything, even the traffic lights, was against you.

• • •

I'd like to say that I managed to salvage the situation at work by pulling myself together, but it was Nicky who saved the day and stepped in for me.

'I knew you were having a few issues when I phoned your mobile and got that weird message,' she said when I stumbled into reception and leaned heavily on Tracey's high counter.

'Weird message? What weird message?'

'You know, the one about the Conniving Cow.'

I was thunderstruck. I had no idea what she was talking about, but it didn't sound good. I let my laptop, umbrella and voluminous handbag slip to the floor, fished out the cellphone and dialled the voicemail number.

'You have eight new messages,' it told me.

'I know that, you stupid thing,' I growled at it and threw it on the leather couch.

'What are you trying to do?' Tracey asked in the tones of a patient teacher trying to help a recalcitrant child.

'Listen to this weird message, of course,' I pouted.

'Well, you won't hear it that way,' she said even more patiently. Suddenly, my mobile sprang to life. I jumped to answer it, struggling with the cushions under which it had disappeared.

'No, leave it, don't touch it!' Tracey put her handset down and leapt over to me. 'Here, come with me.' She led me to her phone and calmly put the receiver up to my ear.

'My phone's ringing,' I said, aware even in my haze that I was stating the bleeding obvious.

'Wait a second.'

It stopped and I heard a badly distorted, almost incomprehensible voice: 'Hi. This is Penny Rushmore.' Good God! Who was impersonating me? The strange voice went on: 'I'm not answering your call right now because I'm getting stuck into the Baileys.' I gasped in horror. This couldn't be me. It didn't even sound like me. Someone had got hold of my phone and sabotaged it! But how did they know about the Baileys?

'I'm out of my mind right now but feel free to leave a message.' There was a pause and I was about to hang up when I heard a loud sniff and the voice continued: 'And if it's you, Steve, you can go . . .' I slammed down the phone. I'd heard enough. It *was* me. A very drunk and maudlin me.

Nicky approached, holding up my mobile and smiling sympathetically.

'There's a special message for your sister too, but you probably don't want to hear that one. Might be a good idea to record a new one?' she said.

I groaned and buried my head in my hands. 'How embarrassing.'

'Be good if Steve had phoned though, wouldn't it?' Nicky chuckled. 'He'd have got the message.'

'Oh God, don't.' The thought appalled me. 'He'll get the message I got written off.'

That's when I had a vague recollection of phoning him in the midst of my pity party. I groaned again. It was so embarrassing I didn't want to mention it.

'Here, you'd better change it before anyone else hears it.' Nicky thrust the phone at me again.

'Oh, no!' It finally dawned on me that anyone could have heard it. I picked up my stuff and fled into my office, quickly recording over my appalling indiscretion. Then, before I could chicken out, I dialled up my messages to hear the worst:

'Hi Penny. This is your loving sister. Sounds like you're a sandwich short of a picnic right now. You don't sound too happy with me either. Just as well I'm arriving next week to knock you back into shape. I'll call you later when you've sobered up. Bye.'

Damn! Steph had heard whatever ghastly message I'd left and would never let me forget it. Plus she'd be here in just a few days and I still hadn't cleaned out the spare room, let alone spring-cleaned the entire house to pass her intense scrutiny.

I deleted the message quickly. The next was from the printer, trying to hide his mirth, reminding me we were running out of time, then one from Stuart the photographer, also sounding like he was suppressing laughter, anxious we should meet. Then there was my funeral director client, chortling openly:

'By the time you get this message, Penny, you'll be feeling the effects of all those Baileys. I've got some hot sausage rolls and pastries left over from this morning's wake if you need a pick-me-up! Oh, and by the way, how are the posters coming along?'

I smiled, despite myself. Andy had a legendary capacity for red wine and had been known to devour an entire funeral reception's savouries and cream cakes in one morning to raise his blood-sugar levels after a night on the town. One of the office girls had to rush out and buy up the high-cholesterol contents of the corner bakery to compensate while Andy and his colleagues attended to the funeral.

The thought of a fat-laden sausage roll suddenly seemed very appealing.

I listened to the remaining four messages, including a second reminder from Stuart that he needed to see me urgently. Ashamed, I made a note of them and decided it would be a lot easier to deal with everything after I'd had something to eat.

'Sticky buns are on me,' I called through the door to Tracey.

'Don't be silly,' she said, appearing at the door. 'You couldn't organise a tea bag let alone a whole morning tea. I'll sort it. Petty cash can pay. What would you like? A cream doughnut? Or a hot pie?'

Tracey knew me well.

'Both,' I said.

'Go for it,' she said. 'Calories don't count when you've got a hangover.'

'I wish. Don't you hate it when a five hundred gram block of chocolate can make you gain as much as two kilos?'

'One of life's biggest mysteries.' She grinned. 'Oh, and by the way, Ginny phoned in from the farm to say she's running late, but to tell you there is nothing more vengeful than the wrath of grapes!'

'And she would know!' I'd heard her make that feeble pun every time she'd come in with bloodshot eyes. Ginny rarely admitted to a hangover, but you could always tell when she'd been on the Moët from the early morning sunglasses that stayed on even when she went to the loo. I couldn't even *find* the sunglasses this morning.

I made a few urgent calls and shot to the loo for about the fourth time — the result of all the water. My face in the mirror stared back like a ghostly apparition. I'd applied far too much mascara and had forgotten the foundation and blusher. But I was in no condition to fix that now. The mascara had been hard enough to handle, involving several attempts and as many removals, and now I could see each one had left behind tiny blots resembling a series of squished ants.

I tugged at the toilet roll, wet a chunk of paper under the tap and dabbed at the bags that had suddenly appeared under my eyes. Inevitably, this only smudged the squished ants further afield, so that I now resembled an emo.

Defeated, I retreated to my desk just in time to meet Tracey returning with handfuls of brown paper bags. She took one look at me and fled to the kitchen, where I heard an outbreak of guffaws and whispers as she imparted my state to Nicky.

Back in the safety of my office, I retrieved my make-up purse from my handbag and had another go at repairing my face with one of those wet towel things I'd saved from a plane trip eons ago. It stung, but it did the trick. I gathered up what little dignity I could muster, stood up straight and strode into the kitchen determined to retrieve at least some of my reputation. Nicky turned from scoffing her chocolate muffin and looked at me guiltily, trying to hide a smirk.

'Very funny,' I said sarcastically. 'Just you wait until you're under the weather.'

'I wish. I never get the time to write myself off. Mind you, it's just as well. The few times I've overindulged, Dylan has been absolutely merciless the next morning. I swear he can tell. The last time, he arrived in the bedroom blowing on that dreadful rugby hooter his father sent him from Australia. Typical! He never sends money or anything that might be remotely useful for giving his son an education or the necessities of life. But a bloody great noisy thing like that he manages to wrap and post, no problem. I know he did it to annoy me. He knew damn well Dylan would use it all round the house.'

The pie and doughnut had the desired effect. My stomach felt a lot better and a second dose of painkillers improved my head. I was in a much better condition to face the day and catch up with everything I'd missed, with no time to dwell on my indiscretions.

I caught up on emails, checked the media alert list, and got the final okay on the luxury lodge news release and photo while Tracey drove to the hospital and got signed permission to take pictures in the ward. Next I checked the printer's colour proof and got Nicky to double check it for me, then called the printer to come and pick it up, grovelling suitably about the lateness of the okay. By the time I'd got Tracey to help me dispatch the lodge's press release and dealt with the myriad other mini-crises that arose, it was way past home-time.

Nobody was there, I realised when I walked through the front door to a silent house, save for the pitter-pat of tiny spaniel feet on their way to find me. Adam was flipping burgers and Charlotte had started work on Monday at a bridal boutique and wasn't home yet.

I'd fallen about laughing, of course, when Charlie came home and announced she was to be sucking up to potential Bridezillas. She'd never in her life shown any interest in the bride business — if anything, she'd rubbished the fairytale extravagance of it all. But she'd taken my mockery very calmly and had proved me wrong, probably just to spite me.

She'd entertained us with tales that would match the reality shows on television of young women who could never make up their minds and of mothers who would never be satisfied. Charlotte seemed to take them in her stride, enjoyed it even, listening to their bickering and sometimes full-blown rows, waiting for them to finish or — as had happened more than once — storm out of the shop, returning later to begin all over again.

I was secretly amazed that she'd put up with it. Comparatively volatile at home, she seemed to exhibit an astonishing patience when faced with challenging customers.

With no one to cook for, I pulled a carton of leftover beef casserole and cheese-sauce potatoes out of the freezer and looked forward to some much-needed comfort food. Needless to say, I avoided alcohol. All day, feeling absolutely vile, I'd promised myself I'd never drink again. But as I downed a glass of water — about my twentieth that day — reality got the better of me. Of course you'll want to have a drink occasionally, but just make sure it's occasional, I told myself sternly. You've been getting far too attached to the vino since Steve left and it's time to pull back. You need to cut down on the drinking — cut down significantly.

As I waited for the meal to heat up, I seriously thought of displaying the offending Baileys bottle on top of the fridge as a sort of beacon, warning me of the danger that lies within, reminding me of my never-to-be-repeated night of shame. But I couldn't face fishing about in the recycling bin to find it. Or even the thought of looking at it. My binge-drinking days were definitely over.

I checked the home phone for messages. There was just one. The Stag would be ready on Thursday.

Chapter 5

I arose early on Thursday after a troubled night's sleep, waking several times in a hot sweat with a dose of the guilts, worrying I'd overstepped the mark. My conscience hurt — the rest of me felt just fine. There was no going back now.

During the usual morning mayhem, when both kids happened to be in the kitchen at the same time, I told them I was giving Steve back his car today.

'Where's it been all this time then?' Adam asked. 'I thought you must have given it back to Dad ages ago, when it disappeared from the garage.'

'No, it's been at the paint shop. Steve always wanted a professional paint job for the Stag, so I've been getting it done as a special treat before he gets it back.'

'Oh.' Adam's interest in cars was in the engine.

'Can I have a car now, Mum? Now there's some room in

the garage?' I might have known Charlotte would turn the Stag's disappearance into an opportunity for herself.

'Maybe next year. I'll talk it over with your father.'

'What about for Christmas? It would be a cool Christmas present.'

'We'll see,' I said. I had no intention of getting her a car for Christmas and no funds to pay for one. That would be up to Steve — he seemed to have no end of funds these days, although you'd never know it from the lopsided balance sheet he kept reminding me about, which made it look like I had accumulated vast wealth while poor little Steve had nothing.

I dropped her off at the bridal salon on my way into work. I had some work to do with Bill and his legal defalcator, the fun run T-shirts to drop off at the funeral home (I was expecting much hilarity over the 'See you at the finish' tagline) and another meeting with Panos and his marketing man: the olive oilers. I had to take them through the communications plan for next year and I was secretly looking forward to seeing Panos again. The very appearance of him could calm my jitters.

I knew I had an hour and three quarters before I was due to pick up the Stag and a half hour after that before I'd told Helen I was dropping it off at Steve's office. So I went with the flow, taking as much time as Panos wanted to talk through what we were going to do; he had a reputation for being scathing if he didn't approve of something.

I had enough time after we were through to zip back to the office via the motorway and leave the car there, catching a taxi to the paint shop. My tummy was filled with butterflies by now; I was petrified. But I needn't have worried about one thing: the paint work was a triumph — most appropriate for a Triumph Stag. It positively gleamed.

I wanted to laugh out loud, to punch the air for joy, but managed to restrain myself because Trevor, the chap who'd spent the last few weeks lovingly sanding and adding each coat, was standing beside me, glowing with pride.

'It's been a pleasure,' he said when I thanked him. 'You don't often get to go all-out on a job.' He brushed away a fleck of dust with his chamois. 'The boys over the road were real envious.'

I took a photo of him standing beside the car, which made him even happier, then wrote out a cheque for a very large amount of money from the soon-to-be-extinguished joint account. It was, I rationalised, a joint expense.

With Trevor preoccupied on paperwork, I found myself alone in the cavernous workshop and returned to the car for a closer inspection.

The body of the low-slung Stag was bright yellow. It was so bright it was almost iridescent. And coming out from the front wheel well were long swirly tongues of stylised red flames, straight from the hell that hath no fury like a woman scorned.

I walked round the other side — more flames, just as breathtaking. And on the wheels, the bright red feathery BBS rims Adam had told me about, snaking out from the hub.

'Pity you didn't let me do the spoiler or the neons,' Trevor said as he came over with the keys.

'I think we've done plenty for now,' I smiled. In fact, I couldn't stop smiling. I thanked him and got into the driver's seat.

It started with a throaty roar. I hadn't asked for anything other than the paintwork, but I swear it sounded like it had been souped up, maybe with the nitrous I'd read about in Adam's street-racer game. Another little delight in store for

Steve, I thought, as I slipped it into gear and drove carefully out the workshop door onto the street.

To say it was conspicuous would be an understatement. It seemed as if everyone was squinting at me as I drove the few kilometres to Steve's office. I waved gaily back, starting to enjoy myself. The guilt was gone. The taste of revenge was sweet.

I nosed the Stag into the visitor's park at Steve's office, near the middle of town, eased out of the driver's seat, closed the door behind me and locked it, slipping the keys into the envelope in my bag. It had Steve's name on it and a cryptic note inside: 'Happy Christmas, darling. You deserve this. The joke's on me. Penny.'

With the butterflies twirling round in my tummy again, I caught the lift up to Steve's reception, dropped the envelope off for him and scuttled out of the office and the building before I could be spotted and, worse, caught in the act.

There was already a small cluster around the car when I crossed the carpark to the street but I looked the other way; I didn't want to attract any attention. Once safely over the road I found anonymity in the corner café, taking a table near the window with an excellent view of Steve's office and the gleaming gift waiting for him outside.

I didn't have to wait long. My coffee had only just arrived when Steve strode purposefully out of the front door, waving his keys and the envelope I'd left them in. He drew abreast of the little gathering around his car and the crowd parted for him to see the object of their attention.

As he slowly approached the car, he stopped dead, dropping his keys and an armful of papers on the ground where they scattered in the wind. He didn't even attempt to pick them up. Moments later his face went bright red and he started shouting. It looked like the words weren't very polite.

The Conniving Cow arrived and did an obvious double take, standing behind him, her arms flapping ineffectually, her mouth wide open. Then gradually, all around him, Steve's workmates started to laugh, pointing at the car and then at Steve. One even slapped him on the back in a comforting gesture, which seemed to enrage him all the more because he turned on the unfortunate fellow and punched him hard — missing, luckily, by a mile.

By now, even Jacinta was finding it impossible not to laugh and was trying to hide her mirth by turning the other way. Steve went over to her and pulled her round to face him, revealing the full force of her mirth. Disgusted, he turned back to the car, approaching it cautiously. He reached out and touched it in disbelief, as if hoping it was just a bad dream, then ran his hand over the swirling flames, over the feathery rims, over the racing stripe up the bonnet.

'Yup, Steve, it's all real,' I said quietly. 'Isn't it funny?'

'It's quite a joke you've played on him. You did well,' a voice said behind me. I turned. It was Helen, beaming widely. 'VJ is on his way.'

I gulped. 'Oh.'

We both turned back to the show across the road.

Steve was beating a retreat back into the office building; the crowd remained gathered around the car. If I didn't know them better, I'd have guessed they were admiring it, but I could tell from the inane grins on the faces of his workmates that this was a joke they would re-live in the cafeteria and over the water cooler many times.

No sooner had Steve disappeared than three big black SUVs pulled up and parked behind the luminous Stag.

'Here,' Helen said grinning. 'Listen to this.' She passed

me her MP3 player and I plugged one of the earphones into my ear while watching the three drivers approach the car.

'. . . crossing live now to VJ and the Black Blunders,' the radio host was saying.

'Hi, this is VJ reporting downtown outside Gardener's, the big accountancy firm,' a perennially chirpy male voice said. 'You've gotta see this to believe it. Talk about "Pimp my ride!" There's this amazing old seventies sports car down here and you should see the paintwork. Wow, it's something else.' There was a cackling laugh in the background and he continued, 'Someone's had the bright idea to paint it up like a street-racer car. It's so wicked. Bright yellow, with these big red flames coming out of the front wheels and real hot rims. Wow. I wonder whose car it can be? I'll keep you posted.'

That was the end of VJ's report. I sat there shaking — whether from suppressed laughter or hysteria I couldn't tell. I pulled out the earphone and looked over at Helen, who was still grinning.

'Did it go all right? What did he say?' she asked.

I started to laugh. 'Yes,' was all I could say before I became so helpless with laughter I simply couldn't talk.

'I think we'd better have some champagne,' I heard Helen ask the waitress as I wiped my eyes. 'We've got some celebrating to do.'

'What's going on over the road?' the waitress asked her.

'Looks like a new boy racer's arrived at the accountancy firm.'

'Yeah? They don't look like the types.' She indicated the conservatively dressed bean counters gathered round the car talking to the three radio guys.

'Appearances can be deceiving,' Helen said, suppressing a guffaw as the waitress returned to the bar to get our order.

'Well, you're quite a gal. I didn't think you had it in you.'

'Neither did I. And I almost pulled the plug on it more than once.'

'Wherever did you get the idea from?'

'It was all Adam's fault,' I said. 'I popped in on him the night after Charlotte's prizegiving. I was still mad as hell with Steve for going off with Jacinta and forgetting to come, even though Charlotte had virtually begged him to.'

Helen nodded.

'Well, Adam was on his computer, playing one of those car games. I watched him steer these really brightly painted, neon-strobing cars through their street race. There was something about the cars that set me thinking. I asked him how it all worked. Of course he couldn't believe I was really interested but then he gradually warmed up and showed me how it's done.

'He cut out of the game and brought up a picture of a hunky, grunty-looking car sitting in the middle of a big empty garage. He showed me how you choose your car, then you choose the wheels and find the sort of look you want — different coloured rims in different spikes and shapes, things called spinners that make the wheel rim look like concentric circles spinning in opposite directions, "roof scoops", a thing above the windscreen that looks like a truck horn, neons under the bodywork that shine a blue light on the road, aerofoils sticking out the back, and vinyls — different coloured painted flames that shoot out from the front wheels.

'Honestly, Helen, there's a whole other world out there you and I have no idea exists. I mean, when I took the car in to get its paint job, you should have seen the queue of cars there waiting for some of those things to be done to them. I didn't know it was such a cult.'

'Neither did Steve, until now,' she said with a wry smile. She looked across the road then handed me the MP3 player again. 'Here, put the 'phones back in,' Helen urged. 'Looks like there's some more action.'

VJ was on air again, making a phone call.

'I'm calling up Steve O'Neil, he's the owner of the hot car we told you about earlier. All his mates from work are crowding round the car and have given us his number.' There was the sound of a mobile phone ringing. It went to answerphone. VJ left a message: 'Yeah, gidday Steve. This is VJ, and you're live on Extreme Radio. We've been admiring that car of yours parked outside the office. The one with the yellow bodywork and the cool flame vinyls. All you need are neons and a spoiler and you'll be the coolest street car cruising the town.' There was further cackling in the background and VJ ended the call.

'Well, I think that about wraps it up,' I said, raising my glass to Helen. She clinked hers against mine.

'You've earned that,' she said. 'It's about time you took a stand. You've let him walk all over you for too long.'

I took a swig. My mobile started to ring. I looked at the display: it was Steve.

'Hi, Steve,' I answered brightly, buoyed up by the bubbly and Helen's support.

'You evil, ignorant woman,' he exploded. 'How could you do that to the Stag? You've completely ruined it. That was a terrible thing to do.'

'Yes,' I said. 'It was.'

'So . . . It's . . .' He seemed lost for words.

'You got my note?' I asked.

'Yes. It was . . . I can't understand . . .' he sputtered.

'It's my Christmas present to you,' I said sweetly. 'It's the least I could do after all you've done to me.'

'Oh, you're impossible!' he shouted, and hung up.

'Yes!' I cried, punching the air.

'You did it!' Helen said.

'You provided the icing on the cake,' I said.

We drained our glasses, relishing the sweet taste of revenge.

'Look, there he goes again.'

The departure of the Black Blunders and the ensuing loss of interest by Steve's workmates had left a gap for him to return unobserved. He approached the car again, unlocked the door, swivelled his body into the seat and started it up. It came to life with such a loud throaty roar that windows opened in the offices above and heads poked out. Everyone pointed and laughed as Steve drove off down the road, a shot of colour and noise in the usually quiet, grey office block.

Helen and I looked at each other and grinned.

'Yes, there he goes,' I agreed happily. 'You can't miss him now.'

'Wherever he goes, heads will turn — for all the wrong reasons,' Helen laughed.

'Maybe he'll attract the attention of a few cops while he's about it.'

'They'll never believe an old guy driving a car like that.'

'I wonder if Jacinta will deign to get into it.'

'Can't see it myself. He'll be on his own.'

We watched it idling at the lights then take off around the corner and out of sight.

'Party's over. I'd better get back to work,' I sighed. We stood to go.

'Let me get it, my treat,' Helen said, going up to the counter to pay. I gave her a hug, thanked her for 'outing'

Steve for a second time and we parted.

Back at the office, I headed for the kitchen to make tea. I needed a soothing cuppa.

'You all right?' Nicky asked me as I poured water into the cup.

'Sure. Why do you ask?'

'You've just put a teaspoonful of chicken soup powder on top of the teabag and stirred it all up. I don't think it'll taste very nice.'

'Oh, God. You're right. I'm a bit distracted.' I tipped it out and started again.

'Wanna tell me about it?'

I shook my head. 'It's a bit complicated. I'll tell you later.'

I went back to my room, turned the radio on to Helen's station and tried to focus on my laptop screen. A few minutes later VJ was cackling again about the hot street car he'd seen outside Gardener's and the old guy that had been seen driving off in it.

'You've been up to something, haven't you?' Nicky appeared at the door.

'You heard that?'

'Of course I did. It's up so loud, the whole office probably did. What've you been up to?'

I confessed. She roared with laughter.

'Serves him right. He's been asking for his comeuppance for some time.'

'You don't think I've overstepped the mark?'

'Probably, but hell, it's about time you did. You can't be a doormat all your life.'

'Me? A doormat?'

'Yeah, you've let him walk all over you while he's been having a high old time with that fashion plate from his office.

He's got what's coming to him, that's what I reckon.'

She returned to her office and I returned to my laptop, but I still couldn't focus.

I switched the radio off and grinned. Maybe Nicky and Helen and the others were right.

• • •

I didn't hear from Steve again after that — at least not until Christmas, when he came to pick up the kids. Meanwhile, I had to clean the house from top to bottom — including Charlotte's room which Seraya would be sharing — and try to keep it clean despite the frequent forays Adam and Charlotte made into the kitchen and living room, not to mention the dog hairs Tigger shed daily. My sister had never been the type to tolerate mess and the mere suggestion of animal fur on her immaculately pressed clothes would send her into hysterics. She was due in the morning at 9am. The willowy Seraya and her father Marcus were arriving on Christmas Eve, thankfully. I could only cope with all three of them in very small doses.

Stephanie arrived in a flurry of Louis Vuitton and instructions, determined that I was cracking up and she was going to sort me out in the short time she was here. She sailed along beside me through the airport in ridiculously high-heeled sandals (Ginny would have called them shag-me shoes), pipe-thin designer jeans and a cropped velvet jacket that must have cost a fortune, with a frilly white shirt that plunged almost to her tummy button. Her bronzed neck was hung with enough chains and chunky necklaces to harness an entire kennel and from her ears dangled enormous hoop earrings. Whatever look she'd been trying to achieve, she'd failed.

While Steph fired a volley of questions about the kids, Steve, the Conniving Cow, Mum's dementia and Helen's radio station (no doubt sizing up her chances of free publicity), I gazed in awe at the get-up, wondering what had come over her. My sister usually favours beige and white linen, classics, understatement. This was quite a transformation.

On the way in from the airport, Steph talked non-stop, mostly about her book and how much the publisher, the editor, the publicist and even the old lady across the road, for heaven's sake, loved and adored it and were all convinced it would be a runaway bestseller. She seemed to think I was dying to read it. I made a vague promise to have a look as soon as I had a spare minute (as if!) and detoured to visit Mum and Dad, thinking I might as well start her off with a reality check. If Mum was at all with it, she'd dredge out her 'mutton dressed as lamb' epithet.

I should have known: Ms Goody Two Shoes opted to stay with them and sent me off (damn, I'd miss Mum being the fashion police), telling me to pick her up after lunch. It was almost 10am. That meant I could whip home and power-clean the kitchen, which I'd had to leave strewn with dishes and toast crumbs to make the airport in time, while making the backlog of calls to the printer, the funeral director and the myriad other clients I needed to talk to before the Christmas break. But first, I decided to detour to the supermarket. The cupboards were bare — a statement Adam made every Monday after he'd hoovered up the contents of the fridge and pantry over the weekend — and Stephanie's family were notoriously picky about what they would and wouldn't eat. Organic this and free-range that — all very well when you didn't have to worry about blowing the weekly budget. And there was still the Christmas turkey to pick up at the butcher's

— organic and thankfully ordered ages ago.

The mall carpark was, of course, full and I had to park miles away, in the rain. I knew I'd been desperately short of exercise lately. It was over a week since I'd been out walking with Davina and the sprint through the puddles to the mall had me panting. This was followed by a further sprint around the shops to buy Charlotte's present (an expensive bikini she'd been coveting for weeks, which I'd asked them to put aside), Adam's pxt-capable cellphone (also extremely expensive), a book of old photographs and mementoes of the part of the city that Mum grew up in (extremely hard to find), Dad's Jim Reeves CD (extremely yukky) and the aforementioned turkey (extremely heavy). I had no idea what to get Steph and her lot (extremely picky): that would have to wait until she'd been around a day or two to give me a clue.

However, an armful of bags and an overweight bird didn't deter me from popping into Harvey's to see if there might be a little designer number to compete with whatever Steph might produce on Christmas Day. Fielding phone calls while stripped to my bra and pants and wobbling on one foot while I fixed the cellphone to my ear and stepped into yet another whimsy, I managed to find a skirt with enough red and green to be Christmassy, and a flattering bright red tank top to go with it. I produced my credit card; the days of accessing the joint account were over.

I flew into the supermarket, dumped the bird in the bottom of the trolley and whipped round in no time, tossing organic delicacies onto a mounting array of extravagances and calorie-laden treats: plum duff and brandy sauce for Mum and Dad, chips and ice cream for beanpole Adam, Greek yoghurt, raspberries and cantaloupe for peas-in-a-pod Stephanie and Seraya, French beans, new potatoes — all twice the price in the organic section.

By the time I'd loaded everything in to the car, sped home and packed it all away it was after 2pm. I had to get to the office before Tracey left — it would be the last time I'd see her until she came back from her summer camping holiday in three weeks. Steph would just have to wait.

Feeling only a tiny amount of guilt — after all, Steph escaped coping with Mum at least three hundred and sixty days of the year — I returned to the office instead of picking her up, phoning Dad on the way to explain.

'I wouldn't worry about your sister, lassie, she's fine. Your mother's as happy as a sandboy now she's here.'

'I'll bet,' I said jealously after I'd hung up.

However, I quickly forgot all about Steph when I got to the office. Predictably for the last day before the Christmas holidays, all hell had broken loose. The print job had come unstuck — the posters and flyers hadn't dried yet and there was only a short time before they closed; and the media was on the phone about my toilet paper client, Jim Stephens. Someone had claimed one of his promotional puppies had bitten a little girl at a shopping mall appearance.

Jim was one of the crankiest, biggest mood-swinging clients I'd ever known. He could be sweet as pie one minute and a vindictive demon the next. I'd been glad to get rid of him a couple of years ago when he complained interminably that he wasn't getting enough media coverage for his brand of toilet paper the puppies were supposed to be promoting. But in a moment of weakness, when business was quiet, I'd taken him on again and, predictably, had had a bumpy ride. The annual promotional tour had only just finished, later than usual because we'd had to wait for the litter to be old enough (the breeder managed to produce a new lot each year, and each time they were just as cute and cuddly), but with a reasonable amount of community-paper coverage, thanks to Ginny's charms on tour. That was one of the things she did really well — schmoozing the locals so that crowds turned up for whatever it was she was promoting and the community papers turned up to photograph it. This afternoon, not surprisingly, Ginny was nowhere to be seen. The Christmas party season was her big time of year. She'd promised to shoot in before we broke up but, knowing her, that could be anytime or no time.

Nicky was flat-out dealing with her own end-of-year crises, but the unflappable Tracey, bless her, agreed to stay on for another hour to help me out with the printing problems. I hugged her gratefully as she left to drive over to the printer's and got on the phone to Jim.

It turned out the little girl had just about pulled the puppy's leg off and it had indeed bitten her. Jim said it was a tiny puncture and he'd already paid the doctor's bill and the cost of the tetanus injection. He'd just spoken to some young whippersnapper from the Sunday paper, he said, and given them a piece of his mind.

'Jim, you know you shouldn't have done that,' I remonstrated. 'I've told you, when the media phone, put them off for a bit and don't say anything else until you've spoken to me.'

Jim doesn't like being told off. I held the receiver away from my ear as he related, in no uncertain terms, what he thought of the Sunday papers and the media in general and how it was about time someone told them the truth.

'Yes, Jim,' I said when his rant ran out of steam. 'But you don't need to make it worse for your brand by making them cross with you, do you? Now, let's talk about what we're going to do to set matters right.'

He calmed down a bit when I started talking about the brand and how we should move forward.

It's typical, isn't it — the media always leave it until the eleventh hour before you go on holiday to come up with some trumped-up tragedy and you have to drop everything to handle it. The last time this happened, Steve and I and the kids were about to fly out to the Sunshine Coast for a long-planned midwinter break. I'd ended up dashing to the airport with a suitcase full of inappropriate gear tossed in at the last minute and almost missing the plane, while Steve and the kids waited at the departure gate convinced I wasn't going to make it. Just what on earth I thought I was going to do with my polar fleece in the twenty-six degree heat I don't know. And I'd had to buy jandals and a swimsuit at the mall because I'd left them behind. But at least I was there.

This time, I didn't have to get anywhere exotic — just pick up my sister before Mum drove her completely round the bend.

I told Jim it was a simple matter of correcting the misinformation, putting it in writing and insisting the paper print the truth about the damn puppy, no matter what else they might claim. I knew from bitter experience that once reporters have made up their mind about a story, once they've been captured by someone with an axe to grind, it doesn't matter what you say, they're not going to change their point of view. All you can do is make it very clear to them, in words of one syllable or in a letter with a QC's imprint, that they are on very thin ice if they hold you or your product up to ridicule and contempt by printing something they have been told is completely untrue.

However, all this took time and, as usual, time wasn't on my side. I needed to see the statement from the puppy's owner and trainer, who was there at the time and, if it really was a storm in a dogbowl, I needed a shot across the bows from a friendly QC. Luckily, my media-minded QC hadn't closed down for the holidays yet. Luckily, Jim promised to shut up if any more media phoned and refer them to me. Luckily, the owner/trainer was able to put the story into a better perspective — and provide evidence in the form of a bystander who was prepared to attest that the child had been hurting the puppy at the time and had come close to breaking one of its little legs by yanking it so hard.

Among the numerous calls I took, one was from Charlotte, wanting to know where her Aunt Stephanie was and why wasn't I home with her.

'Long story, darling. She's at Granddad's. And I'm dealing with a bit of a crisis right now. Can you wait 'til I get home?

There was an audible sigh at the other end. 'Okay. Becks is here. Can we go to the movies?'

I looked at my watch. 5pm. 'Sure. Why not?' She'd probably get herself some popcorn and wouldn't mind a late meal. Adam was flipping burgers all night so would undoubtedly feed himself there.

It was just as well Charlie and Becks went out, because it was 7pm before I got home with Stephanie. Tigger leapt all over her, threatening the designer pants.

'I don't understand why you let this dreadful dog get away with such bad behaviour,' Steph said, shooing him away.

'Listen, when you have teenagers you need a dog so there's someone who's happy to see you when you get home.'

Stephanie looked blank; she didn't get it but then why should she? Seraya probably fawned all over her nightly.

Steph had been showing Mum the novel about great-grandma Annie Jane Morrison and Mum, of course, had been enthralled. Living in the past is Mum's forte: her poor shrunken brain finds it a lot easier to remember what happened fifty years ago than what she had for lunch.

'You're going to love the novel too,' Steph had said assuredly when I'd picked her up, tapping the inch-thick manuscript held together by two large rubber bands.

'Yeah,' I said, summoning up as much enthusiasm as I could. 'I'm looking forward to it.'

My bluff was called, however, on Saturday afternoon after the shops shut. I'd managed to glean from Steph that she'd like to own one of those naff crystal things you hang in a sunny window so that it casts colourful prisms around the room, so I'd swallowed my pride and gone into an airy-fairy trinket shop to buy one for her. Seraya was easy after Charlotte told me she liked opera ('Eee-eww, that's what old people listen to,' Charlotte opined). Steph provided the necessary clue about Marcus when she reminded me about his obsession with Japanese art. Other last-minute purchases kept me in the mall until much later than I'd intended, so I was knackered by the time I negotiated the traffic and parked up the drive.

'Here, put your feet up,' Steph greeted me. She was carrying two glasses of cranberry soda and beckoned me to the terrace, where she'd set the table with flowers. 'You take on far too much. You deserve a break.' Gratefully, I dumped the bags upstairs where she couldn't see the goodies I'd bought, changed into something casual and followed her outside.

'Mum and Dad are fine. The girls are still down at the mall, I'm surprised you didn't run into them,' she said, 'and Adam is still at work. Oh, by the way, his father rang and said he'd take him out shopping tomorrow.'

'Oh.' I sat down and put my feet up on the neighbouring chair. 'I'm glad you didn't offer me a wine,' I said and explained how I'd made a vow to cut back after that awful night she'd heard the strange message on the phone. Steph grinned sympathetically.

'Funny, isn't it?' I said. 'In all the time we've had the kids, Steve's never once thought about what they might like for Christmas or birthdays. I've always had do to the running around. And now he's not here any more, he's falling over himself to get them something. He's been on at me lately about spending too much on the kids. But I bet he buys Adam the most expensive gadget he can find. Guilt can be very costly.'

'As no doubt Steve found out when you returned his little car to him.'

'You heard about that?'

'The whole town seems to know. Charlotte told me. She thought it was very cool, what you'd done.'

'She did?' I didn't even know that Charlotte knew anything more than that her father was finally getting his car back. She'd never mentioned it and I certainly wasn't going to tell her the whole story.

'You go, girl!' Steph said, grinning. 'It's the gutsiest, funniest, best thing you've done in a long time. I wish I'd been there to see the look on his face.'

'It was priceless!' I started to laugh and then couldn't stop myself.

'There's no need to go into hysterics over the whole thing,' Steph said, giving me a sobering slap on the back. 'It's not that funny.'

'I suppose I'm relieved it's all over. I've been beating myself up all month wondering if I was over-reacting.'

'Course not. Any woman would do it given the opportunity. Don't knock yourself about just because your husband is having a mid-life crisis. He's the jerk. Not you.'

'Thanks Steph. I thought you'd be mad at me. I thought

you had a soft spot for Steve.'

'Maybe I did once. But it vanished the day he left you.' She took another sip of her wine, put the glass down on the outdoor table and gave me a piercing look. 'You know, you've come through pretty well for a baby sister. I was a bit worried about you there for a while. You didn't seem to be handling it at all well. Maybe painting his car canary yellow wasn't the most mature way to show your feelings, but it was pretty effective. He deserved it and I'm proud of you.'

I stared at her, incredulous. This didn't sound like my big sister, the sister who used to pull my ponytail, steal my one and only doll and hide her just to upset me, blame me for the broken vase/Coke on the carpet/smell of cigarettes after she and her friend Susie had sneaked a smoke in the back shed. And of course, Mum had always believed her because she was the favoured one.

'There's nothing like vengeance to settle old scores and free you up to get on with your life. Go for it.'

I hugged her back and smiled.

'I will.'

We talked until Steph announced she was going to order a pizza delivery. She returned with the phone and her weighty manuscript.

'Here, I'd really like you to start on this while I phone Marcus and make sure he's got the right flight time for Sunday,' she said, handing over the page proofs. 'I don't want to publish it if you don't agree with it.'

'Really?' I hadn't expected that. 'But what if I don't like it? I don't believe you wouldn't go ahead with it just because of me.'

'Let's wait and see what you think.'

It felt like I'd only just started reading when Becks and

Charlotte came back from the mall, arguing over Charlotte's inability to make up her mind about a purchase.

'She had about five things on hold in different shops. We must have gone back to them at least twice and she still couldn't decide,' Becks moaned.

'I have to be extra careful. I can't afford to make any mistakes,' Charlotte said defensively.

They took the shopping discussion inside to get a drink and outside again where they stretched out in the late sun with their diet sodas nearby. The racket was too distracting to concentrate on Annie Jane so I carried the heavy manuscript upstairs, hugging it close to my chest, feeling a surprising empathy with our gutsy great-grandmother. I had to hand it to her: a woman suddenly alone in the late nineteenth century with a meagre income and argumentative offspring to manage, she'd managed to cope a hell of a lot better than I had.

Chapter 6

At Steph's insistence, we all went to church on Christmas morning — to the family service, no less, which meant putting the hard word on the kids.

'But Mu-uum, it's so *gay*,' Adam protested when I broached the subject again.

I'd warned them several times on Christmas Eve that Stephanie had her heart set on it.

'Look, Penny, this could be the last time we're all together,' she'd said. 'You can see for yourself Mum's not going to be with us much longer — certainly not in her mind and possibly not in person either.'

'But she'll be impossible in church,' I'd replied.

'But at least she'll *be* there. I don't think she'll make it next year.'

I could see it was an argument I wasn't going to win. Most

arguments were like that with Stephanie. She'd always been able to boss me around.

'Well, you can sit next to her and keep her under control,' I'd finished weakly and returned to the kitchen to get dinner for the cast of thousands.

Marcus and Seraya had arrived late the previous afternoon, looking like something off the plane from Hollywood rather than down south, and suddenly our four-bedroom house was bursting through the weatherboards. It helped me last several hours without even noticing Steve wasn't there.

So far, Charlotte and Seraya were sharing a room amicably. I knew, however, the comparative peace wouldn't last — it never did with those two. They had very little in common — Charlotte had just finished school while Seraya had completed her first year at university studying architecture and would undoubtedly be even more self-assured and grown up. On top of that, the unspoken competition between Steph and me had filtered down a generation and inevitably spilled out.

Adam and Charlotte weren't giving in so easily to the church thing as I was. After telling me it was gay several times over and refusing to go, Adam huffed off to his room and slammed the door.

Charlotte's excuse was Grandma: 'She'll be so embarrassing.'

She had a point there that I couldn't argue with. We rarely took Mum out these days. She'd become incredibly querulous, complaining about the weirdest things, so that on the rare occasions we persuaded her to leave the safe haven of St Joan's, people would look at us as if we were into elder abuse.

So it was with two mutinous teenagers that Marcus, impeccable in a fuchsia pink silk tie and a dark Armani suit, and the equally narcissistic Seraya, in a ruffly wrap dress revealing every minuscule curve of her body, walked to St Mark's while Steph drove me in Marcus' rental car to pick up Mum and Dad (who would never have been able to squeeze into Crackling Rosie's tiny dickie seat). We'd left in plenty of time, which was just as well, because Mum was still in her dressing gown and was refusing to go anywhere.

'I'm sorry, lassies,' Dad greeted us. He looked beat. 'Your mother's not so great this morning.'

She perked up at the sight of Steph though.

'I should have come early,' Steph wailed as she led a suddenly compliant Mum into the bathroom to help her get ready.

'That girl is plotting against me,' I heard Mum say to Steph in a loud stage whisper out in the hall. 'She's trying to steal my silver.'

I smiled to myself at Mum's inventiveness, hoping that Steph understood enough about Mum's condition by now to know she was imagining it.

Steph ushered Mum back into the lounge fifteen minutes later, looking flushed and flustered, which was most unlike my usually unflustered sister. She flashed me a look of affectionate exasperation and kept her arm under Mum's elbow to stop her from getting sidetracked.

'What are you waiting for? We're ready,' Mum said, giving Dad a hurry-along. 'I don't want to be late. I do like a good sing at Christmastime.'

I raised an eyebrow at Steph and gave her an approving smile. Somehow she'd managed not only to get Mum looking quite presentable — almost as smartly turned out as she used to be in her pre-Alzheimer's days — *and* get it through to her that it was Christmas Day and she was going to church. This was no mean feat in Mum's befuddled state.

She got into the car without a single protest, thanks to Steph's firm reassurance, and we took off for church. We arrived just as the last stragglers were cramming into the back pews. I scanned the crowd and saw Panos, of all people, in his Sunday best, then noticed Marcus waving discreetly from a side aisle. Marcus hated anything that might cause a fuss or be construed as ill mannered, so it was hardly surprising he couldn't completely hide the understandable panic he was feeling at the approach of his unruly in-laws.

'Down here,' I told Steph. 'Marcus has saved our seats.'

I smiled nervously at Panos as I passed then slid into our pew. It was a bit of a squash, since Marcus had only managed to save enough room for two — hoping, no doubt, we'd find somewhere else to hide Mum. There was a bit more space further down the pew, but Charlotte and Adam were deliberately ignoring my gestures to move, trying to avoid having their Grandma anywhere near them. If it weren't for Marcus pushing against Seraya, who edged into Charlotte, knocking her into Adam (and causing a look on Charlotte's face that would have withered a lesser person than Seraya), Steph and I would have had to retreat to the back row.

'Who's that?' Mum said loudly as she was manoeuvred into the row between Steph and Dad. Fortunately, the organ was playing some sort of fugue thing before the service was due to start and Mum's voice was drowned out. Marcus couldn't stop a pained look crossing his face when Mum spoke.

'It's my husband, Marcus,' Steph said. 'You remember, Mum, he's in the wedding photo we were looking at yesterday.'

Whether Mum remembered or not was debatable, but Steph's reassurance seemed to be all she needed. I was beginning to think my fears were groundless. I'd tossed and turned all night worrying about today — about whether I'd get up in time to stuff the turkey and get it in the oven before we left for church (achieved), whether I had the right presents for everyone (unlikely to be achieved), whether Mum would behave in a public place (also unlikely), and whether we'd manage to get through the day without any major rows or disasters (even more unlikely).

It was the sermon that got Mum going.

'Who's that imposter?' she demanded when the vicar climbed the dais to the lectern.

'That's Mr Brown, the vicar,' Stephanie whispered. 'You know, Mum, he comes to see you at St Joan's sometimes.'

'Humph!' Mum said. Several people turned around to stare. 'That's not the vicar. He was a nice young man with glasses.'

'That was a long time ago, Mum. Mr Brown's the vicar now.'

Miraculously, that seemed to satisfy her sufficiently to keep quiet. She stared disapprovingly at the poor man, who had clearly heard his credentials being questioned by a cranky parishioner.

Mr Brown read a piece of scripture and started off on his annual homily about the significance of the birth of Jesus.

'What utter tosh!' Mum cried out when he came to the bit about the Virgin Mary. 'We all know that isn't true.'

I winced. Steph looked across at me and rolled her eyes.

'Mum, don't,' I whispered. 'You're in church. You can't just call out like that.'

'There's no need to patronise me, young lady. That man needs putting in his place. He's talking nonsense.'

It seemed every head was now turned to face us. The vicar paused then continued. I could feel myself going red.

Steph took Mum's hand and tried to get her to look her way, but to no avail. Mum had some sort of fixation on Mary and I had no idea where it was coming from.

'Vicar!' she called out with piercing clarity. 'You're behind the times.'

She paused for effect, as if waiting for everyone to agree with her. But everyone, myself included, was too dumbstruck to utter a word. Unfortunately, she hadn't finished.

'You should know by now, Vicar, that the mother of Jesus was an ordinary wife and mother, and that Jesus himself married Mary Magdalene.'

There was a further stunned silence from the pulpit.

'Oh no,' I groaned, then realised I too would have been heard by almost the entire congregation — Panos included. I didn't dare look up. The sound of tittering behind me was enough.

Thankfully, the Rev. Brown searched through his notes to find his place and continued the sermon.

'She's gone back to *The Da Vinci Code*,' I whispered to Stephanie, who appeared entranced in the vicar's utterings, as if nothing had happened. Marcus was also studiously looking the other way.

Mum had become an ardent Dan Brown theorist not long after his book had made him a household name. She'd followed all the theories and arguments almost fanatically for just over a year until the Alzheimer's had knocked it out of her. And now, for some inexplicable reason, the mention of Mary had brought some of it back.

'I think we should take her out,' I added, in case Stephanie hadn't heard.

'She'll make an even bigger fuss,' she hissed back, still appearing unflustered by it all. She started rooting round in her bag under the pew and emerged with a small silver photo frame, which she waved at Mum to distract her attention. But to no avail.

'Excuse me!' Mum called out to the pulpit, but the vicar continued with determination. 'You ought to know . . .' There was no acknowledgement this time, not even a raised eyebrow from behind the lectern. Without even glancing in her direction, the vicar kept sermonising, raising his voice several decibels. The tittering spread.

'How rude!' Mum said loudly. 'He's just not prepared to listen to reason.'

'No, Mum.' Stephanie had another go at distracting Mum with the photo. This time, thank God, she saw it.

'Oh, look at you. You look so nice in your swimsuit.'

Fortunately, at that moment, a baby two rows in front of us started bawling, which set off a toddler across the aisle, so Mum's quieter mutterings about the photo were hardly audible past our row. I looked down the other end of the pew: the three teens were staring determinedly in the other direction, no doubt pretending they had nothing to do with us. But I could tell from their faces there would be a fuss later.

When the service ended, I scuttled out with my head down, terrified of seeing Panos.

'Mu-uum, that was so heinous,' Adam said as soon as we'd got out the door.

'I'm never going to church with you again,' Charlotte added, including all her family in the sweep of her eyes. 'I told you it would be embarrassing.'

'What's that, dear?' Mum said.

Charlotte didn't miss a beat. 'You were very naughty, Grandma, calling out to the vicar like that. Everybody was staring at us.'

'But he was wrong, dear. Somebody had to tell him.' Mum looked very pleased with herself. I could have slugged her — and Steph for dragging us all along.

But Steph was unrepentant. She burst out laughing.

'It'll certainly be a Christmas we'll all remember,' she said.

'Aye, lassie, it will at that.' Dad started to chuckle and put his arm around Mum. For once she didn't bridle at the show of affection. In fact, despite her unexpected outburst, she seemed quite perky. I wouldn't go so far as to say she was with it, but at least she seemed to recognise some of us and had sung all the words to the hymns. The service seemed to have cheered her out of her usual edginess. I hadn't heard a single complaint from her all morning — apart from the very public one about the vicar, of course. I started to see the funny side.

'It sure was memorable,' I laughed.

'It was a nightmare,' Charlotte said, scowling. 'Don't laugh, Mum. It's not funny at all.'

Seraya was standing a few feet away, disowning us. Charlotte and Adam went to join her.

'Come on, Mum, let's go home,' Steph said and started to guide Mum towards the car.

'Yes, I'd like that.' Mum followed meekly.

The kids all walked with Marcus, happy to continue the dissociation, while we drove the short distance home.

We were greeted at the door by the comforting aroma of roasting turkey and a wildly excited Tigger, who loved family get-togethers. For him, they meant lots of food from people who were a soft touch when fixed by his pleading brown eyes.

'What are we doing here?' Mum demanded as Steph guided her through the front door.

'This is your daughter Penelope's house,' she explained. 'We're here for Christmas dinner.

I could see it was going to be an exercise in patience for all of us and offered a silent prayer that the kids would be up to it. I headed for the kitchen, leaving Steph to cope with Mum, without a moment's hesitation — after all, where was Stephanie the rest of the year to wave her magic wand and get Mum to more or less behave?

After tying the apron over my new Christmassy skirt — which was already starting to strain at the seams — I removed the lid from the roasting pan, flipped the pan juices over the bird and put the minted new potatoes on to boil. The kids had, after some persuasion, shelled the peas before church and all was ready to go. I just had to make sure I didn't get distracted and lose track of everything. Steph was such a good cook, I felt like I was on trial.

After scraping the store-bought cranberry sauce out of its jar into my best jug, I carried it through to the dining room along with the water pitcher. The table that Charlotte had helped me set earlier looked lovely — the white Iceberg roses surrounded by gold ribbon and tinsel glowing in the soft filtered sunlight atop the traditional red and gold Christmas tablecloth. I'd seen Steph's Christmas table decorations and knew there was no way I'd match her elegant splendour — she thought nothing of buying armfuls of white roses, lilies and freesias to match her pale green and white dinner-set; her marble fire surround was lavishly draped with pine garlands and flowers; her gold-rimmed crystal was unchipped; her expensive imported Christmas tree sported decorations in a different colour theme every year. Seraya and Marcus were well trained — they never broke the Villeroy and Bosch by shoving it haphazardly into the dishwasher; they never spilled tomato sauce or Coca-Cola on the Aubusson rug; they didn't own a dog that made a nightly habit of snuffling under the Christmas tree in search of beautifully wrapped gifts containing anything edible.

Tigger had only yesterday brought our entire Christmas tree — blinking lights and all — down on the floor in the middle of the night in search of food. By the time I'd leapt out of bed and rushed downstairs, he'd wolfed down most of the highly placed chocolates, with torn chocolate box, wrapping paper and card shredded around him. All that remained were a few wrapped in foil, and he was starting on them too.

Tigger is just so dumb when it comes to his stomach. He never reads the stories that tell you how dangerous it is for dogs to eat chocolate. Luckily this time it was only a small box he'd demolished, or it would have meant a trip to the vet again — and on Christmas Day, that would have required a small mortgage. The last time Tigger devoured a whole box of chocolates I'd had to rush him to the vet to have his stomach pumped. So it was a double whammy — a forty-dollar box of chocolates nobody got to eat plus an eighty-dollar stomach ache.

Marcus obligingly opened the Lindauer and poured everyone a glass. I quickly intercepted Mum's before she noticed — she reacted badly to alcohol — and exchanged the wine for sparkling grape juice. I knew from past experience she couldn't tell the difference.

'Happy Christmas!' we all said, raising our glasses. Even Mum joined in.

Then it was time for opening presents. Tigger was banned outside with his Christmas treat bone and we enjoyed the usual family exchange of things you don't need for things they don't want, while everyone smiled and tried to look as if their particular pair of socks, scented candle, book or hand cream was the answer to their dreams.

Mum remained bewildered throughout but happily accepted the bounty given her, eventually getting lost — as I'd hoped she would — in the picture book I gave her about the small country town where she'd grown up. Once on the outskirts of the city, it had since been absorbed by metropolitan sprawl. Stephanie had been exempted from any kitchen duty on the understanding that she would keep tabs on Mum, which was just as well because the kids were steering well clear of her. Adam went outside to play with his cellphone; Charlotte disappeared to her room with Seraya to text/phone/email friends who were no doubt over Christmas by now too; I returned to the kitchen to put on the peas and carrots, check the potatoes, make the gravy, baste the turkey and heat the dishes.

It wasn't until I carried the turkey through to the dining room and set it up ready for carving that I missed Steve. There simply hadn't been time all morning to notice his absence — the house was so full, the activity level so demanding. But carving the turkey had always been Steve's domain. He'd make such a performance about sharpening the knife, slicing the bird just so, extracting the stuffing in neat segments and arranging it all precisely on the platter.

'Would you like me to help you with that?' I turned around; it was Marcus.

'Er, yes please. That would be good.'

'I don't want to presume, but . . .'

'No, it's okay. Someone's got to do it. Thank you. Just don't let it out of your sight, or you'll find the dog will have devoured it.'

Marcus laughed. 'I remember one year he ate those

biscuits under the tree. Don't worry. I'll guard the turkey with my life.'

I left him to it while I rounded everyone up from around the house and garden. A quick tally revealed Mum and Stephanie had both disappeared so I conducted a wider search and found Mum in the laundry piling the clean towels into the washing machine.

'Here, let me help you,' I said, trying to divert her. But she wasn't to be deterred.

'It's all right, thank you,' she said stiffly. 'I'm perfectly capable of doing my own laundry.'

'Have you seen Stephanie?'

'Who?'

'Oh, never mind.'

In the brief silence that followed, I heard Steph's voice outside the back door; she seemed to be talking to herself.

I left Mum fumbling with the knobs on the machine, hoping they would baffle her for a bit longer, opened the door and was about to call out to Stephanie, but there was something secretive about the way she was hiding behind the hydrangeas and bending over the phone that made me stop.

I could hear snatches of what she was saying: 'I can't talk long . . . Marcus would be furious . . . much rather be with you . . . kiss, kiss . . . Tiger Tim.' There was a bit more I couldn't hear, then I saw her shut the phone. I ducked back inside, wondering what my hitherto perfectly behaved sister was up to.

Mum was still fiddling with the knobs and I could hear water rushing in on top of the already laundered towels. Seconds later, Stephanie came in through the open door.

'Mum, you don't need to do that today,' she said patiently, levering Mum away from the machine, 'It's Christmas Day, you deserve a break.'

Mum smiled and happily let Stephanie steer her back through the kitchen.

'Dinner's ready,' I said brightly, trying not to look like the guilty eavesdropper I was. Steph shot me a piercing look like she suspected I'd heard. I just kept on smiling.

'It's not what you think,' she hissed as she passed me.

I kept the smile frozen on my face; I couldn't think of anything mitigating to say.

On the way through the kitchen, Steph fetched Mum another grape juice and poured herself a Lindauer.

'Hey, that's the second bottle and it's empty now too,' she cried out, shaking it upside down to extract the last drops. 'Have you been slugging it back out here, Penny? I wouldn't blame you!' she chuckled.

'No, it's not me. I hope it's not one of the kids.' As soon as I said it, I realised it probably was. And probably one of mine. I couldn't see Seraya doing anything without perfect decorum.

'Well, it's Christmas, I suppose,' Steph said. 'And they're not going anywhere. They'll be okay.'

'Hmmm,' I said. I wasn't so confident.

It didn't take long for me to work out it was Charlotte who'd been getting stuck into the bubbly. She came into the dining room looking decidedly wobbly, crashed into the side of the table, tipping over the carefully arranged candelabra with its carefully draped gold ribbons, which caught fire, singeing the tablecloth and a nearby napkin.

The subsequent flurry of activity to douse the flames and set the table to rights again caused great mirth from Adam, who arrived in time to see it all unfold.

'Charlotte's drunk again!' He pointed at her and gleefully slapped her on the back, knocking her against her grandmother's chair. 'Charlotte's trolleyed.'

'I am not!' she cried, whacking him on the arm.

'Owww!'

'Serves you right,' I said to Adam. 'Now stop it both of you. It's Christmas Day.'

'What's the matter with her?' Mum asked Stephanie, straightening her chair after Charlotte's battering.

'She's happy it's Christmas Day,' Steph said, laying on the sarcasm. 'She'll be all right.'

'Please sit down, Charlotte. Adam,' I indicated an empty chair in between me and Mum, 'you too.'

Charlotte looked mutinously at her brother. Seraya arrived at that moment, texting, oblivious to the drama. Charlie took one look at her and plumped herself in the one remaining chair, at the opposite end of the table to Mum, sighing loudly. Adam reluctantly sat next to his grandmother and me.

'Seraya, please put that phone away and turn it off. It's Christmas Day.'

Seraya glared at her father, turned the phone off and slung it on the sideboard, where its blue light faded to black. 'Now, we're all here. Good.' Steph smiled serenely at us as if nothing had happened.

I passed the plates round as Marcus dished out the turkey and stuffing — cut quite haphazardly, Steve would not have approved — and encouraged everyone to help themselves to the vegetables and sauce. Adam ignored the vegetables, piled his plate with new potatoes and smothered them in butter. Charlotte and Seraya ignored the potatoes and made a great show of giving themselves lots of beans and carrots. Steph had about as much food on her plate as a fussy sparrow would eat, while Marcus and I helped ourselves to generous amounts of everything, earning Marcus a disapproving glare from his wife.

'Dad, would you like to say grace?'

Dad smiled happily and held Mum's hand. My heart went out to him — he so rarely got to be with his family now, and he was clearly enjoying himself, despite Charlotte's shenanigans. Even Mum's behaviour in church hadn't seemed to faze him. He bowed his head and said the Scottish grace he'd said so often when presiding over the big oak table at home, with us kids giggling and poking each other to cause trouble.

'Some hae meat and canna eat and some wad eat that want it,

'But we hae meat and we can eat and sae the Lord be thankit.'

He opened his eyes and looked around at his family, smiling.

'Aye, it's good to be here, lassies. Thank you both for all you have done to get your mother and me here.' He looked at Mum and took her hand again. 'Ah, Colleen, it's Christmas. I'm so glad we're here together.'

'Of course we're here together, you old fool,' Mum said kindly, smiling too. It was hard to tell if she was in the same space as the rest of us sometimes, but she seemed remarkably with it as she looked into his eyes and kissed him on the cheek.

'The Lord be praised,' Dad said and kissed her back.

It was such a long time since I'd seen Mum show any genuine affection for Dad, I could feel my eyes prickling. Even Steph was getting a bit emotional, though whether it was from Mum's apparent sudden sanity or some dark secret that was stirring her emotions I couldn't be sure.

'Happy Christmas, everyone!' I said, raising my glass. 'Now, let's eat.'

'Happy Christmas,' Charlie said after everyone else had

finished, and promptly got the hiccups. 'Oops.' She picked up her wine glass and tried drinking from the opposite side.

'Not with the bubbly, Charlie,' I said. 'That's what's caused the problem in the first place. Here, it's water you need.' I handed her the full tumbler beside her place setting. She stood up and bent over, but couldn't quite manage to get the water into her mouth. Realising the impossibility of completing the difficult manoeuvre in her condition, I was about to intervene when she knocked the table again, spilling the remains of her Lindauer on the carpet.

Tigger was underneath in an instant, licking, while Charlotte dived under the table, dabbing at the floor with her Christmas napkin.

'Tigger!' she protested as the dog transferred his tongue from the spilt wine and carpet to her face.

'Look, Mum. Charlotte's drunk Tigger under the table,' Adam crowed.

'Very funny. That's enough,' I warned, trying to look severe. But I was coming close to cracking up, though whether from despair, desperation or impending madness I didn't know. The day was turning into a farce.

There was a sudden jolt to the table as Charlotte tried to stand up and cracked her head on the edge. 'Owww!' she wailed loudly, then started to cry. 'Owww, it hurts.'

'Come on, lassie, come on.' Dad was beside her in a flash, helping her up and consoling her. She leant into his lean, firm shoulder and started to cry.

'I wish Dad was here,' she sobbed. I got up and went to comfort her, but she drew back and fled the room. Seconds later I heard the sound of her thumping up the stairs to her room. Seraya looked at her mother and excused herself from the table.

'I'll see if I can calm her down and get her to come back to the table,' she said as she followed Charlotte upstairs.

We started to eat our meal in silence. Steph was the only one to say anything, and only to Mum as she helped her eat the meal.

After a few minutes, the silence was interrupted by the sound of a door slamming. Seraya came back to the table, seemingly unfazed, shrugging her shoulders.

'She says she'll come down later. She wants to be alone for a bit.'

'Sorry, Seraya. She's a bit upset.'

Seraya shrugged again and started to eat her turkey.

'Would you like me to heat it up?' I offered, but she shook her head.

'No, it's fine.'

After dinner, Steph and Seraya helped me clear the table while Mum chatted happily about an incident from her childhood. I'd heard it many times — in fact Marcus was the only one it was new to. I covered Charlotte's uneaten Christmas dinner with clingfilm and put it in the fridge, pulling out the fresh berries and yoghurt. The microwave quickly dealt to the steamed pud, as well as the brandy sauce, and dessert was served.

Steph promised to serve it while I popped up to see if I could reason with Charlotte and persuade her to come back down. But there was no response to my hesitant tapping. Tentatively, half expecting to have a teddy bear or heavier missile launched at me, I peeked round the door. She was spreadeagled across the bed, sound asleep, snoring. There was no point in trying to raise her; much more sensible to let her sleep it off until Steve came to collect her and Adam at 5.30pm. I looked at my watch: just over two hours to go. With

Charlotte out of the picture, I suspected the family gathering would proceed in a much more orderly fashion.

I was right.

Adam, Mum, Dad and Marcus opted for the plum duff, though Adam helped himself to ice cream from the freezer in place of the brandy sauce ('Ee-eeww, yuk,' he pronounced when he tried it); the rest of us had the berries and Greek yoghurt. And I couldn't even finish that, I was so full.

Mum didn't like the plum pudding though.

'I used to put threepenny bits into the plum pud for you,' she said. 'Where are they?'

'It's not nearly as good as the one you used to make, Mum. But I just didn't have time to make one. It's from the supermarket, I'm afraid.'

That set her tut-tutting about how young people didn't bake things any more.

'It's such a shame,' she said. 'All those recipes I taught you both. You were so good at it, Stephanie, surely you bake for your family now?'

'Sometimes, Mum.' Stephanie knew how to fob her off. 'But I have to watch my figure you know.'

'Oh tsk, you do not, dear. You've always been nice and trim. Not like poor Penny. She always was on the tubby side.'

'Thanks, Mum,' I said. She always liked to point that out to me. Stephanie was the golden-haired girl, slim and trim and Little Miss Perfect. I was the ugly duckling — shorter, fat and naughty. I couldn't do much about being short, but I'd long suspected the weight problem and the tendency to misbehave were deliberate reactions to the regular comparisons by Mum. Like a sort of self-fulfilling prophecy.

The afternoon was incredibly quiet and incident free.

Charlotte stayed sleeping; Adam helped stack the dishwasher then retreated upstairs to chat to his friends on MSN; Steph kept Mum happy down memory lane; Dad chuckled along to the afternoon Christmas television offerings; and Marcus and Seraya took the decidedly tubbier Tigger for a much-needed walk in the park. On my part, I have to confess I fell asleep in front of the television, which is why I've no idea what Dad was watching.

My moment of peace was, however, brutally broken by the sound of a battering ram at the front door. Bleary-eyed, I looked around. Only Mum, Dad and Steph were in evidence and all three were engrossed. I struggled out of my departed dream world and answered the door. It was Steve.

'Er, um . . . hi,' I said lamely. I'd fully intended to be prepared for this moment, to have my hair just so, my make-up refreshed, my eyes bright and my demeanour breezy. Instead I was still groggy with sleep, my mouth was dry and tasted sour from too much Christmas joy, my eyes were puffy, my hair a mess. For all I knew, I could have a line of dribble down the side of my mouth and a crease in my cheek where, in the instant I awoke, I could feel my grandmother's engagement ring had pressed. I'd abandoned my own rings about the time I took the car to the paintshop, but grandma's pearl and diamond ring stayed firmly on my right hand.

'I, er . . . the kids . . .' Steve seemed as unsure of his ground as me.

'Yes. I'll get them.' I turned and fled upstairs, leaving Steve standing in the doorway. There was no way I was inviting him in.

'Charlotte . . . Charlie, wake up.' I shook her gently. 'Your father's here. Wake up, honey.'

She looked at me through half-opened eyes with a child-like dependency that reminded me of her babyhood.

'Dad?'

'Yes. It's after 5.30. It's time for you and Adam to go with him.'

'Oh. I'll get ready.'

The moment was gone. I went to fetch Adam next.

He was engrossed in his computer screen, which resembled the view through a cockpit windscreen. He was about to land on a virtual runway so I had to wait while he completed the manoeuvre and taxied to the terminal building.

'Come on, your father's waiting,' I said when I was finally able to get through to him. He didn't move. 'Come on, honey. It's well after 5.30. Have you got your bag? Your father's present? Your PJs?'

'Don't fuss, Mum.'

He stood and picked up his sports bag. It seemed remarkably limp and empty.

'Are you sure?' I pointed at it.

'Don't fuss. I'm fine.'

I gave up and went back down to Steve. 'They're coming.'

'Good.' He stood with his arms folded and looked angrily at me. 'That was appalling, what you did to my Stag, Penny. I couldn't believe you'd do something so downright mean.' He leant against the door and stuck his face closer to mine. 'It cost an absolute fortune for you to have your wee joke, and it's going to cost another bundle to fix it up. And you can pay for it. I'm bloody well not going to.'

'But Steve, I thought you wanted the Stag to have a paint job,' I said as innocently as I could. 'It just seemed appropriate, somehow — you know, to fit your new image.'

'That's not funny,' he spluttered. 'You think you're being

smart, don't you, you and your friends. I bet you all cooked this up over a vat of cheap Lindauer one night. I can just see you all rolling around with laughter like the witches of Endor, plotting how to get back at me. Well, you've had your little joke, and it's going to cost you big time.'

I ignored that. Suzanne Cumberland could sort that one out. And if I did end up paying, I figured it would be worth it.

The whole time he was yelling, I was visualising duct tape across his mouth and wishing the kids would hurry up so he would stop shouting at me and his aftershave would stop overpowering me. He'd always been fond of slapping it on in the morning, but now it smelled like he was marinating in it — presumably to impress the Conniving Cow.

'I'm sorry you didn't like it. I thought it was a beautiful paint job. Just right for the car — and for your newly acquired laddish status. I can't understand why you don't like it.'

His face went so red I thought he was about to have an apoplectic fit. 'That's typical . . .' he bellowed.

'Hi, Dad!' Charlotte flung herself at him and his expression changed in an instant. Adam wasn't far behind her.

He flung me a look of complete disgust as he disappeared down the drive with the kids. I stood there for a moment, clutching the door frame, sensing deliverance, feeling at last some sort of closure. For better or worse, I'd done it. I rested my case and was more than ready to move on.

Back inside, Mum was reaching the end of her tether. And so was Stephanie. I could tell from the pained way she was explaining to Mum that Julie Andrews wasn't really marrying that nice handsome man; that it was just a movie. Mum's appreciation of the difference between fantasy and reality was totally topsy-turvy. I wished mine was too.

'Come on, Mum, Dad, I'll take you home now.'

Stephanie flashed a grateful smile and offered to drive them instead.

'No, really, I need to get out of the house for a bit. I'll take them.'

After I'd helped Mum into the car I went back for Tigger and his lead. He'd already had a walk, but this time it was me needing a run off the chain.

I don't know whether it was Stephanie's benign influence or the effects of too much Christmas pud, but Mum was almost normal on the way home. She chatted about the afternoon, about Stephanie; she didn't even mind Tigger bouncing around behind her; and she happily let Dad guide her out of the car and into their house without a single protest — quite unusual for her these days. I helped him settle her down but left soon after. Dad seemed quite keen for them to be on their own.

'She's in a bonny way today, lassie. I'll be fine now, don't you worry about me.'

I drove home wondering how the kids were getting on with Steve and the Conniving Cow. I pictured how it would be, in some pristine high-rise apartment above empty city streets, perched nervously on white leather sofas, carefully cradling their glasses so as not to spill anything on the pale grey plush pile carpet. The Conniving Cow would have beautifully wrapped parcels to rival an origami master; the gifts would be so cool they would make hell freeze; and for the first time in his life, Steve would have actually managed to find his way to the shop to buy something for them too. And no doubt it would be just as cool as *her* presents and ten times as expensive as anything I'd tried to impress them with.

I could see her offering them tiny canapés, fashioned

by hands used to creating dainty dishes, hands that never had to wrestle with dirty nappies or dog sick, hands with all the time in the world to create works of art in the kitchen without having to worry about the aforementioned art being wolfed down in a nanosecond by a starving teenage boy with hollow legs. No doubt on his best behaviour for her, Adam was refraining from seizing more than one morsel at a time. I hoped, for the carpet's sake, Steve didn't give Charlotte or Adam much to drink. Unlike his father, Adam had yet to grow accustomed to alcohol, and Charlotte had had quite enough for one day. The last thing she needed was a top up.

I could just see them. But it didn't bother me. Unlike a few months ago, I didn't feel angry or upset or excluded. I didn't want to be there. I was, as Adam would say, 'over it'.

Chapter 7

Steph was waiting for me when I got home, nervous, on edge. Marcus and Seraya had gone to see Marcus' nephew on the other side of town, so there was just the two of us, Steph said with a meaningful look.

'Oh,' I said, wondering what was coming next.

'Tea?'

'Yes, please.'

She fussed around my kitchen, making tea in the pot and taking infinitesimal care over every step, as was her way, while going through the events of the day. When we finally sat down outside in the cloudy, clingy humidity, she said: 'I suppose I'd better tell you what's going on.'

'Oh?'

'You know, when I was on the phone before. When you were listening?'

'I didn't mean . . .'

'Yeah, yeah. I know. But I meant to tell you anyway.' She looked around the garden, her face riddled with angst. 'I've been having a bit of a fling with Tim Sayers.' I nearly choked on my Twinings.

'Tim Sayers?' I squeaked. 'But he's . . .'

'I know.' She had the grace to look slightly repentant. Tim Sayers — no doubt the 'Tiger Tim' I'd heard her refer to — was a minor celebrity on the rugby league circuit and he was, if I wasn't too mistaken, somewhere around sixteen. Well, maybe that's a slight exaggeration, but all the photos I'd seen of him made him look no more than thirty — if that! And, what's more, he was extremely good-looking, with long, dark, curly hair, which he wore tied back during games, an engaging grin and a cute bum.

'Stephanie! I never picked you for chasing stray talent, let alone a cradle snatcher.' I was gobsmacked. I couldn't believe Ms Perfect would do something like that. 'And what about Marcus?' I added. 'I thought you two were the happy couple.'

Despite myself, I could feel a few pangs of jealousy creep up on me. How unfair was that? Here I was, abandoned and alone, and there she was with not one but two men dancing attendance on her, both of them handsome and seemingly house-trained, and one of them young enough to be her son — well, almost. On the other hand, though, I had a momentary flash of delight that Steph wasn't as faultless as she appeared. I did my best to suppress it, with only some success.

'Things are never what they seem,' she said obliquely. 'Look, Penny, I can't explain it. I don't know myself why I've got into this mess. But it's a whole lot of fun, believe me.'

'Fun? But what if Marcus finds out? That won't be much

fun, I would have thought.'

'I don't want to think about it. I *can't* think about it. Besides, he's not going to find out. We're very discreet.'

'Yeah, like talking on your mobile outside my back door. Very discreet indeed.'

'I might have known you'd be listening in.' She shot me one of those looks she used to give me when I was a kid and I'd caught her sneaking in the back door after a secret rendezvous with her boyfriend. I'd always been the spoil-sport, while she'd always pushed the boundaries and got away with it. Mum had never found out and Steph had retained her favoured-child status. I would never have dared tell on her; it would have been more than my life was worth.

'Plus ça change . . .' I said, smiling ruefully at the memory.

Unusually for her, Steph was flushed and shifting uneasily, sipping the tea and fiddling with the teapot. Suddenly changing the subject, she said, 'So, what did you think of my book?'

I gulped. 'Er, I . . . uh. What are you doing to me? Do you like watching me squirm or something?'

'Squirm? Reading my book shouldn't make you squirm!'

'Well, it's . . . uh, it's very good, so far.'

'Oh Pen, you can do better than that. What do you mean, "Very good"? You didn't like it, did you?'

'Actually, yes, I did. I did like it.'

'So, what's the problem?'

'No problem, Steph. You're so touchy about these things. I quite liked it.'

'Well, that's a surprise.'

'It is?'

'Yes. I didn't think you would.'

'You didn't?'

'No. I didn't think you'd like me making things up. Like what they said, how they felt. And I thought you'd react badly to the uncanny likeness you bear to Annie Jane.'

'Me?'

'Yes, of course. Can't you see it? You have so much in common with her — and you both cope in similar ways.'

'But she was so gutsy, so brave.'

'That's right.' Steph looked at me as if to say 'duh!'

'Can't say I can see it myself. I mean, I was an absolute mess there for a while.'

'So? You might have lost your usual vim and vigour, but it wasn't for very long. And you coped incredibly well with those kids and with Steve being such a total dick, not to mention with Mum. You were strong, just like Annie Jane.'

'There you go, exaggerating again. I'm sorry, but you just can't make me fit your visions of the family coming full circle.'

'There *you* go, putting yourself down again. I wish I could make you get it. You're the glue that's holding them all together — Mum and Dad, the kids, and probably your business as well.'

'The glue? The only thing I'm holding together is the seam on my skirt, and then only just. I feel more like the meat in the sandwich, and it's falling apart.'

'Okay, have it your way. The meat in the sandwich. The lynchpin. The hub on the wheel. We all revolve round you, you know. None of us could do without you. Thank you for being so strong for all of us.' She put down her cup, stood up and gave me a hug.

'Hmmm. Well, it's nice of you to say that.' I patted her on

the back affectionately. 'I'd better find out for myself about Annie Jane and read the rest of your book.' I paused while I weighed up the implications of what I was thinking. Steph grinned at me. 'I honestly didn't think I would want to read it,' I continued, taking a deep breath. 'But it wasn't as bad as I feared.'

'Not as bad! Talk about damning with faint praise!'

'Oh, for heaven's sake, Stephanie, give me a chance. I've only read a little bit. And I liked it. Now please . . .'

'Okay, okay. I get the picture. I suppose I should be thankful for small mercies.' She sniffed.

'You're so defensive about your writing. Is it any wonder I'm scared to say anything?'

'I know. Marcus says that too. But I get so bound up in it, after all that time poring over a word processor and all that research in dusty libraries and museums. One minute you think you've created something so riveting, so special that everybody will want to read it. And the next minute you think it's utter garbage. So when you actually give it to someone else to read, for the very first time, you feel as if you've handed them a part of your life to open up and examine and make a judgement on. And that really is terrifying.'

I smiled. 'I sort of understand. It's like when I write something at work and a client emails me back to say this was wrong and that was wrong. You never completely become immune to it.'

• • •

'Anyone home?' It sounded like Adam, downstairs. I pulled my head out of Stephanie's book and looked at my watch. It was just after midday on Boxing Day and I'd gone back to bed after delivering Stephanie, Seraya and Marcus to the airport, via Mum and Dad's to say goodbye. I'd been revelling in the peace and quiet.

'Hi, honey. I'm up here.'

Moments later, Adam trudged into the bedroom and flopped down on the edge of the bed.

'Hi.'

Tigger bounded in behind him and leapt on the duvet, before being shoved back onto the floor by Adam. Not to be suppressed, Tigger then jumped on him, tail wagging, tongue licking.

'Don't.' Adam sounded cross. Normally he would have rolled on the floor and teased Tigger, making him rush around barking madly.

'You okay?'

'Yeah.' He turned from Tigger and looked at me, scowling. 'It was stink, Mum. I hated it.'

'What was stink, honey?'

'Last night. With Dad. Well, not Dad. He was okay. Well sort of. It was stink.'

'Why, what happened?'

'Ask Charlotte. She'll tell you. She thought it was great. She was stink too.'

He sloped off, shoulders slumped, feet dragging. He didn't look back. It was clear I wouldn't be getting much more out of him for a while.

I wondered why I hadn't heard Charlotte come in. Perhaps, since she thought it was great, she was still there? Then the back door banged and I heard her familiar pounding up the stairs followed by the slam of the bathroom door. Moments later, the shower started running.

Reluctantly, I abandoned Great-Grandma's increasingly

engrossing story, got out of bed and dressed.

My desultory tidying of the lounge, picking up stray bits of wrapping and ribbon, putting cards on the dresser, thinking about what a weird sort of day it had been, was interrupted by a booming on the stereo — Charlotte had arrived downstairs, wet-haired, surprisingly bright-eyed and cheerful.

'Hi, Mum,' she said breezily. 'Wassup?'

'Hi, honey. Good to see you. Have a good night?'

'Yes!' she said enthusiastically. 'It was the best. Dad and Jacinta had this really cool party, all these really cool people, like you know, that chick you see on the news sometimes, that reporter with the mad hair, and that guy off *Shortland Street*, and all these people from their work. It was just the coolest thing.' She looked at me for approval, which I felt compelled to give, despite feeling like reaching for the sick bucket.

'I didn't have anything to wear, just jeans and an old top, so Jacinta lent me this amazing outfit — a wrap dress from World, and these sandals with little heels, you just wouldn't believe.' Charlotte was on a roll the like of which I hadn't seen in a long time. She was positively fizzing at the bung with remembered excitement. 'She's the same dress size as me. Her feet are bigger, but it didn't matter with the sandals. And she helped me with my make-up. She just knows so many things like that.'

I ignored the implied 'and you don't.'

'That's great, honey, I'm glad you had a good time.'

'Yeah. I got to talk to that *Shortland Street* guy, and he was so nice to me. He said I was very sophisticated for my age; he didn't believe I'd just finished school.' She smiled wistfully.

'Sounds great.'

'Yeah.' She went into the kitchen and started rooting around in the refrigerator. 'Where's all the yoghurt gone?

And the trim milk — who's drunk it all? I want to make a smoothie. There's nothing for lunch.'

'Sorry, the supermarket's shut. You'll just have to make do. There's the light blue milk, and lots of fruit. And Vogel's.'

She wrinkled up her nose. 'I want a cleansing day today. No gluten. No fat.' She started to cut up apples and pears. 'I had so much to eat yesterday. And the cocktails last night were just wicked.'

'Cocktails?'

'Yes. Daktaris they were called. They were lethal.'

'Daiquiris,' I corrected. 'You liked them?'

'Well, not at first, but by the third, it was good.'

'The third?'

'Oh, Mum, don't be such a party pooper. I wasn't driving, I wasn't out on the town. I was safe at Dad's place.'

'Hmmm,' I muttered.

'And there was a lot to eat. Lovely bite-sized things. Canopies, I think they were called. And a big ham, and salads, and a whole salmon. Wow, it was awesome.' She finished making a fruit salad and took it to the breakfast bar to eat, along with a large glass of water.

I refrained from making the numerous sarcastic remarks that sprang to mind and occupied myself with making coffee as she continued her litany of luxury living.

'Coffee?' I asked her.

'No-oooo. I told you, I'm cleansing. No caffeine.'

Adam arrived in the kitchen at that point, fossicking for food. Like Charlotte, he opened the fridge, wrinkled up his nose, turned to the pantry with the same result, and said, 'What's for lunch, Mum?'

'Left-over salmon and caviar,' I said, before I could help myself.

'Ha ha, very funny.' Adam returned to the fridge, pulled out the plate of turkey remains and started to make a fist-sized sandwich. 'You should've seen Charlotte last night. She was all over Jacinta's friends, she was *so* embarrassing.'

'I was not!'

'You were. You sucked.'

'I was not.'

'That guy from *Shortland Street* couldn't get rid of you. You wouldn't leave him alone. And you kept falling off those disgusting shoes all the time, trying to be like *her*. You looked so pathetic.'

'Yeah? What would you know? You looked such a dork in those shorts and sneakers. *You* were the embarrassment.'

'At least I didn't try to pretend to be old and up myself. I don't know how you could grease up to those wankers like that.'

'Dad said he was proud of me being so grown up.'

'Well he would, wouldn't he? With you trying to copy *her* all the time.' He pulled a face. "Yes, Jacinta. No, Jacinta. Can I wear your clothes, Jacinta? Can I be just like you, Jacinta?" You were *so* shallow and stupid.'

'That's *so* untrue!'

'You should have seen yourself in the mirror. You'd be ashamed.'

'You should have seen *yourself* in the mirror, you big baby!'

'I didn't make a big dick of myself in front of all Dad's friends.'

'Adam! Charlotte! That's enough, both of you.' I stood between them and held my hands up. 'Enough!' I repeated when they looked like spitting at each other again.

Charlotte picked up her fruit salad and took it off outside

in a huff. Adam, unperturbed, continued slathering butter, turkey and cranberry sauce on his sandwich.

'She really went over the top, Mum. You should have seen her.'

'I'm glad I didn't. But I think we should let it drop now, don't you? I think we've heard enough about last night.'

• • •

The pair of them fought like that throughout the summer holidays, driving me insane. I couldn't even escape to the office for the first two weeks after Christmas because it was closed. And even when we reopened, things were pretty quiet. By the time I'd cleared the trickle of emails and messages, made a few phone calls and filled the best part of a day cleaning out the files, kitchen, reception and anything else to occupy me, I had no alternative but to return home and face the warring teenagers.

Peace only reigned when one or both of them were at their father's. Charlotte increasingly absented herself from home to 'suck up to Jacinta', as Adam put it. The Stag went back in for a fix-up paint job — not to the same paintshop, funnily enough — so Adam visited his father as seldom as possible; without the shared passion for old engines to preoccupy them, they had no apparent desire to be together. Steve returned to work soon after Christmas to get everything done before he and Jacinta took the kids on their planned holiday to the Gold Coast and was, according to Charlotte, often home late.

I have to confess that this piece of intelligence pleased me immensely, causing me to wonder if he were now taking *Jacinta* for granted too.

By the third week in January, the pre-Christmas routine

was back — Charlotte left to catch the bus into town to work at the bridal salon just after eight every morning and didn't return until dinner time; Adam slept late, ate his way through the fridge and pantry then walked down the road to flip burgers at Maccas until late; Mum had lapsed back into dottiness straight after Christmas Day and continued to drive us all spare; and for me, work had regained most of its frantic pace, with clients thankfully giving me plenty to keep me busy — and pay the Christmas bills.

I'd given myself a severe talking to after eating more than my fair share of Christmas cake and other temptations over the holidays and had gone on a diet, which had made me slightly crabby. There's nothing like acute starvation to fray the temper and I have to confess to more than a couple of rows with the ever unflappable Tracey, who fortunately took it all in her stride.

'On your post-Christmas diet again, I see,' she sighed when I bit her head off over something really minor for the second time that week.

'Yeah — eat less, get fit, die anyway,' I said grumpily.

My temper was not improved when the clanking sounds coming from under Crackling Rosie's enormous bonnet became increasingly ominous. I was driving home from work on a Friday in the pouring rain when the old girl started to sound like an only slightly muted traction engine. With a dramatic shudder, she finally gave up the ghost and stopped in the middle of the motorway, just before an offramp, effectively holding up two tootingly furious lanes of traffic.

I got out and opened up the bonnet — more for effect than any practical reason, as I had absolutely no idea what to look for — and within seconds was soaked to the skin, my thin summer shirt clinging embarrassingly to my bra.

I hurried back into the car and reached for my mobile, instinctively bringing up Steve's number out of the contact list. It wasn't until I heard his voicemail that I realised I couldn't ask for his help. He was no longer my personal home and car fix-it man. I hung up quickly.

I recalled Ginny's mantra: 'If it has tyres and testicles, it's going to be trouble.' She was right — and I had earned double trouble.

'Damn!' I shouted at the windscreen. 'Rosie, how could you do this to me?'

Nobody stopped to help. On the right, cars whizzed by. Behind me, those still stuck continued to blow their horns. The windscreen immediately started to fog. I reached for the tissues in the glovebox, behind the AA book. It wasn't until I shoved the book back in that I realised it could save me. I'd become so used to having Steve available to rescue me from breakdowns and fix things for me when they wouldn't go that I hadn't even thought of the AA.

I dialled the number. Someone would be here within ten minutes, they promised.

What the hell was I going to do for ten minutes with all these outraged drivers behind me? The answer came with sickening speed in the form of a red and blue light flashing up beside me; the police car pulled up and stopped in front.

He was very nice, considering I was blocking one lane and considering I looked like a drowned rat, trying to cover up my now-obvious nipples protesting against the wet and cold. However, he was more interested in the car than my nipples. The old Jag, fortunately, was the sort of old car the cop liked: his father had had one, he said, and treated it like one of the family.

Deftly, despite the frightening stream of traffic, he set up his hazard triangle, managed to direct all the stranded cars behind me into the free lane and helped me push the old girl onto the shoulder of the road, waiting with me until the AA man arrived.

The AA man poked around under the bonnet, muttered about crank shafts and bearings and big ends, looked very concerned and said he'd have to get a tow truck to come and take her away. It was beginning to dawn on me that not only was I going to be carless for some time, but getting her fixed was going to cost a small fortune.

The tow truckie, a burly salt-of-the-earth guy, arrived from nowhere and in no time the forlorn-looking Rosie was hoisted on the flat-deck and towed away. I let the kind AA man give me a ride off the motorway to the nearest taxi stand where, in a daze of annoyance, I caught a cab home.

Charlotte and Adam were both round at their father's for the weekend, so the house was empty, the dog was crazed with hunger, having had to wait over two hours longer than normal, and there was a litter of teenage grazing all over the kitchen bench and halfway into the lounge. I didn't have the strength to do anything about it.

I was stuck at home, with no car, no kids, and no plans to do anything or see anyone. I'd been so busy all week, the weekend hadn't featured. And now I wouldn't even be able to get to the supermarket or round to see Mum and Dad, unless I felt like trying out public transport for the first time in decades. I didn't even know if there *was* a bus to the supermarket, but I was damned sure there wasn't one over to St Joan's.

'Damn!' I said once again, this time to the empty room, taking a swig of sauvignon blanc. It tasted more of lemons than melons. I started to shiver. I was still wet through.

When everything turns pear-shaped, I told myself, there's

nothing like a good wallow in a hot bath. So I went upstairs, turned on the taps, poured in copious quantities of bubble bath and let the foam rise. But even hot, soapy immersion couldn't restore my equanimity.

I tried to find comfort in food. Ignoring the mess in the kitchen, I pulled the last of the Christmas cake out of the highest cupboard where I'd hidden it and ate the lot. Then I started on a tub of cookies and cream ice cream until I started to feel sick — literally and emotionally. I had ruined all the good I'd done by sticking to the diet all week and I felt no better than when I started — worse, in fact.

For the first time in ages, I took myself off to bed at eight o'clock, sans book, sans TV, sans anything. Stephanie had taken her new book home with her, I didn't feel like flicking through the travel book Liz had given me for Christmas, I didn't want to talk to anyone on the phone or even blob out in front of the telly. So I lay down, closed my eyes and hoped for sleep.

Tigger jumped on the bed and curled up at my feet; I couldn't be bothered turfing him off. The rain continued to beat down, drumming on the tin roof, a sound I usually found comforting; tonight it made me feel lonely. I lay there, my mind turning over and over, going nowhere useful, worrying about the kids, about me, about money, about that lump I'd found ages ago that I still hadn't checked out, about all those infinitesimal things that suddenly take on major proportions when all you want to do is fall asleep, while dusk turned slowly to dark.

The next morning, faced with finding a garage to fix the car, and pig-headedly refusing to consult Steve at any stage, I looked up the Yellow Pages and found the one I'd heard Steve commend to his mates as being knowledgeable about classic cars. Luckily, the ad said they provided loan cars for a small fee. With the Philosophicals' tramping trip coming up in two weeks I figured that I needed something with four wheels to see me through, even if it was a rent-a-dent.

When the mechanic heard my unscientific description on the phone of what had happened to the elderly Jaguar and the various phrases the AA man had used, I suspect he knew immediately that he was a) talking to a mechanical bimbo and b) about to earn a vast sum from the mechanical bimbo. I gave him the name of the tow-truck company and left him to make the necessary arrangements. He promised to call me Monday with an estimate; I made a note in my diary for Monday to warn me I'd need a lot of strong coffee and sudden access to a lot of money. I had absolutely no idea how I would fund this unnatural disaster, but at least in the meantime I'd have something to drive.

• • •

Rent-a-dent indeed it was. But I was in no position to argue with the overly genial giant who greeted me Monday lunchtime when Tracey gave me a lift to the mechanics'.

I'd spent the weekend close to home, walking to the supermarket — which necessitated an extremely small weekly shop so I could cart it home without the plastic-bag handles cutting off circulation to my fingers — walking to the movie theatre to wallow in a weepie, and refusing to answer the phone so I didn't have to own up to Rosie's temporary demise. The kids, of course, had no sympathy.

'But how will I get over to rock climbing next weekend? I'm supposed to take Jenna,' Charlotte wailed.

And Adam's world was apparently going to end if he

couldn't get dropped off at the wharf on the other side of town to go diving with Darren.

The sight of the battered old rent-a-dent, I knew, would not delight them.

The mechanic, built like an All Black on steroids, greeted me warmly, which was understandable, since I was about to keep him and his entire extended family in the style to which they'd always wanted to become accustomed. He explained what had happened to the car's engine using terminology that meant very little to me. Her big end had, apparently, seized and would need replacing.

'I wouldn't mind having a replacement big end too,' I joked, patting my backside.

He didn't seem to think this was at all funny.

'Oh, your starter motor has broken too, and I see your tyres almost need replacing.'

'In that case, you'd better fix the starter and almost replace the tyres.'

He didn't think that was funny either. And I must confess my sense of humour was fast disappearing too as his repair list got longer and longer. He went on describing the mechanical disaster that had occurred, wiping his hands on an oily cloth as he did so.

'Did you not notice a red light on the dashboard that wasn't usually there?' he asked, looking at me as if I were a naughty schoolgirl.

'Er, no. Can't say that I did.'

He put the cloth down on a nearby workbench and, with a look of exaggerated patience, said, 'That little red light is telling you that you have run out of oil.'

'Oh,' I said, trying to look wise.

'Yes, it's telling you there's no oil in the engine, and that's a very bad thing. Because, you see, without any oil, the engine seizes up and it won't go.'

'Oh.' Even I could see that was a problem.

'Did it ever occur to you to check the oil when you fill up with petrol?'

'Er, well . . . no,' I said lamely. I'd seen Steve fiddle about under the bonnet sometimes, but had left it to him to sort out. The practicalities of the internal combustion engine had always been completely beyond me.

He picked the cloth up as I was speaking and started to twist it into a tight ball. He seemed to be containing some sort of explosion, whether of mirth or anger or disbelief I couldn't tell.

By now I was feeling about one-foot-two tall and wishing I was somewhere else. Even back on the motorway, soaking wet, dealing with policemen and tow-truck drivers seemed preferable.

'Well, bugger me!' He was looking incredulous, scratching his head again. 'Er, pardon my French,' he added.

He indicated to me to follow him over to the car, where he lifted up the bonnet and gesticulated at the conglomeration of circles, squares and tubes. He leant over and pointed at a big circular container with a piece out the side, a bit like a silver snail's shell.

'Under that air filter, you see, is a twelve-cylinder engine.' He looked at me to see if I was paying attention. I put my head under the bonnet, pretending it all made perfect sense, and nodded sagely. 'It's in a V-shape, you see. V-twelve?'

I nodded again. What did he think I was — dumb or something? The answer came to me quickly: yes! And I deserved it.

'Now, inside those twelve cylinders are twelve pistons

that go up and down. And each of those pistons has a little bearing attaching it to the crankshaft at the bottom of the V, you see. And they need oil, or they're not going to keep going up and down, you see?'

'Yes.' I couldn't see a thing, of course. No pistons, no cylinders; just a mass of rubber hoses snaking everywhere and an awful lot of metal.

'And when they run out of oil, they seize up, you see? Just like here.'

He pointed in the direction of a whole lot more coiled rubber and metal and messy stuff.

'And when they seize up, kaput! They won't ever go again. You have to replace the whole engine.' He paused to see if this was sinking in. I nodded. I understood the implications of that last bit only too well: it was going to cost *both* arms and legs.

'And with this old model, a new engine could take a bit of finding.'

'Ah.'

I was right. It wasn't just about money. It was going to take forever to fix.

'Or I could get one of the lads here to rebuild it instead.' He got out a biro covered in grease marks and jotted down a few figures, scratched his head and came up with a sum that made me gasp. I was beginning to wish I'd called Steve after all. It would have been humiliating, but here I was getting the humiliation *and* the bill. For the first time in a very long time, it looked as though I was going to have to budget.

I drove the little rent-a-dent home, searching the dashboard for red oil lights and trying to get used to the manual gearshift and clutch. I'd already made a tit of myself driving out of the garage, crunching the gears twice before I remembered to push the clutch with my foot — I could just see Mr Grease Monkey folding his arms, rolling his eyes and looking like he expected nothing less.

I couldn't stop thinking about how much it was all going to cost and how I was going to afford it. It was just as well, I realised, that I'd already paid for the tramping trip, which wasn't cheap either, since we were having all our gear carried and our meals delivered pre-packaged nightly along with our packs and sleeping bags. It had seemed like a good idea at the time — now I wasn't so sure. Maybe I should have been more budget-conscious.

• • •

But by the time I met the girls at the airport I'd forgotten my financial collywobbles and was glad I'd opted for the pampered package. I was so exhausted from getting all my work sorted for the week away, and from getting the kids packed and off to their father's for ten days on the Gold Coast, that I could hardly lift my borrowed pack into the taxi let alone cart it up and down precipitous hills, across tidal flats and through soft sand day after day.

Adam had kept asking if he could stay home by himself. 'No, you can't,' was my repeated answer. 'Your father's paid for everything and it's non-refundable.' Steve, ever the bean counter, had bought a cheap package off the internet. I looked forward to reports of how the Conniving Cow would greet her economy-class accommodation.

Charlotte, on the other hand, was beside herself with excitement at the thought of ten days with Miss Fashion Plate and all the shopping she'd be able to con her father into paying for. She packed and unpacked her hot pink suitcase about a hundred times — even as her father was knocking at the door to pick them up — in between texting her friends and calling Jenna to ask, one more time, if she could borrow another bikini/top/pair of shorts or item of make-up.

No sooner had they gone than I had to rush Tigger off to the kennels. It was miles in the country but Tigger always knew, the minute we turned into the driveway, that he was approaching the doghouse and was about to be abandoned. As usual, he had to be dragged out from under the back seat where he'd retreated to tremble.

Alarmed when he first put on this pathetic show, I'd checked out the kennels. They seemed perfectly pleasant; all the other dogs seemed quite contented. The owner told me Tigger was always fine the minute I disappeared down the drive, so I had concluded that it was simply a ploy to make me feel sorry for him and take him back home — a bit like the kids used to do when they were little and I dropped them off at pre-school.

Peace had settled on the house when I returned, though sadly I wasn't there long enough to enjoy it. I had to drop off the rent-a-dent and finish my packing — stashing almost everything into plastic bags as instructed by Helen and Liz, the only two experienced trampers in our group — then catch a taxi to the airport, with no time for anything to eat and nothing in the fridge anyway, since I'd cleared it out and dropped the left-overs round to Dad.

Helen was looking as flustered as I felt when I found her waiting at the back of the check-in area, where we'd all agreed to meet.

'Hi, Penny,' she greeted me with an air kiss. 'We're the first to arrive. Di texted me before to say she was running late. Apparently the cleaning contractors are having staffing issues and there's no one to clean the hospital tonight. But knowing her, she'll get it sorted in time to get away. I'm surprised to see *you* here already. You're usually cutting it pretty fine.'

I laughed. 'I know. Truth is, the empty house was a bit unsettling. I was glad to leave.'

Di arrived at check-in puffing and flushed, her usual composure well and truly ruffled. 'I'll tell you later,' she explained, waving her hand dismissively. 'It's been a nightmare.'

The five of us checked our bags through to Nelson just as check-in was closing and edged slowly through security and the boarding queue to slump gratefully in our seats.

• • •

'This is the life,' Helen exclaimed as, drink in hand, she sat back in the plush leather chair in the Nelson boutique hotel's lounge and stared appreciatively out the panoramic window across the harbour. The sun had not long set behind the far-off hills and there wasn't a cloud in the star-studded sky.

'Fair suck of the sav!' That was Helen's favourite toast to a good sauvignon blanc.

'I'll drink to that,' I said.

'Me too,' they chorused.

'What a year!' Liz added.

'Tell me about it,' I agreed.

'And it's only just begun.'

'And I've broken all my New Year's resolutions alrea chuckled Helen. 'I've put on weight instead of losing it, drunk wine during the week and I've spent up large i January sales.'

'Welcome to the club,' said Di. 'I swore I'd stay ou

shoe shops, and I've bought three pairs already.'

'The fickle finger of fashion,' said Liz. 'I couldn't resist the summer sales either.'

'I've managed to avoid the sales,' I said. 'But only because I can't fit into anything any more. I put on so much weight over Christmas, it's a disgrace.'

'You haven't,' Fran said. 'You look just fine.'

'You're very kind, Fran, but the scales tell a different story.'

'I'm a great believer in a balanced diet,' I said. 'A cup cake in each hand. You can tell it works!' I patted my thighs.

'Hey, enough!' Helen cried. 'Enough dissing ourselves. Let's look on the bright side.'

'Yes. Look at us. A bunch of successful career women who've shown the world you can have it all.'

'You speak for yourself Liz, you're a shining example of success on all fronts. You've got your kids organised to run the house for you and a husband who's patience incarnate.'

'Some of us don't even have a husband,' Fran added. 'Mind you, I don't really need one with the dog growling in the morning, the answerphone telling me things I don't want to know when I come home after work and the cat staying out all night.'

'That's one thing that's made life easier since Steve left,' I said. 'At least I don't have to wait up any longer and worry when he'll be home.'

'You hate them when they're out and wish they'd come home, then you hate 'em when they're home and wish they'd go out again,' said Fran. 'I haven't missed that feeling at all.'

'A man's gotta do what a man's gotta do, and we have to do everything else,' laughed Di.

'Tell me about it!' Helen said. 'Sam's idea of helping with

the housework is dropping his clothes where I can pick them up. And his contribution to making the bed is getting out of it. I wish I could motivate him to do something round the house.'

'Don't hold your breath,' Fran said. 'Men are like the weather. No matter what you do, you can't change them.'

'Try hiding the remote control,' I said. 'Men are lost without Sky Sports.'

'Or put the remote under the duster. Then he might get the message,' Fran chuckled.

'I don't think he'd recognise a duster. The only thing he recognises next to the remote is small and tubular and has the word Speight's written on it.'

'I wish someone would invent a remote for doing the laundry,' I sighed.

'It'd have to be a woman that thought of it. The laundry is a foreign country to Sam.'

'I know. I hid Graeme's birthday present in the washing basket for a week because I knew that'd be the last place he'd go,' Liz said.

'Probably doesn't even know it exists.'

'A gizmo for cleaning the toilet would be the thing,' Fran said.

'An electronic toilet duck — now you're talking. If you can find them something electronic and none of their mates have got one, they'll use it.'

'I've worked out how to get Graeme to sweep the path,' Liz added. 'I bought him a gadget to suck the leaves up and now he wants to play with it every weekend.'

'It's the same with Evan,' Di chuckled. 'Ever since he got that water blaster he's been washing down everything in sight — the house, the car, the driveway. I reckon he'd hose down the cat if he could.'

'Bring on the ride-on vacuum cleaner,' I laughed.

'Just the same, despite all their foibles, we couldn't do without them,' Liz said.

'Oh, I don't know,' Fran said, patting her spare tyre. 'A world without men would be full of fat, happy women.'

The passing waiter managed to restrain his smirks and brought us another glass of very fine Nelson wine — pinot noir for Liz and Di, a mightily impressive gewürztraminer for me and a pinot gris and Helen — while Fran stuck to bitters and tonic. Liz sensibly ordered tapas and garlic bread. With all that on board, it wasn't long before we crashed into bed.

Chapter 8

A small bus picked us up early the next morning, along with a half dozen others on the same trip, and whisked us away across the Waimea Plain to the Abel Tasman National Park, dropping us off at Marahau with our day packs, packed lunch and water bottle.

We all said 'Hi' to the other group members but continued to keep to our own small enclaves over a cappuccino while we received a journey briefing. It seemed simple enough: over a few small hills while enjoying spectacular coastal views of golden sand beaches, seals frolicking round the rocks, kayakers to wave at as they laboured by and, at the end of it, good company, fine wine, a gourmet meal we only had to heat to eat, and a good night's sleep at a lodge in a sheltered bay known as Anchorage.

None of us were gym bunnies — we simply didn't have

the time — but we all figured we'd be fit enough to cope with an eleven kilometre walk carrying nothing more than a day pack and a spare tyre or two. And indeed we were fine for most of it, despite the sandflies and heat. It wasn't until the track left the coast and climbed a small mountain seemingly several times over that the idyll came to an abrupt end. The weather, hitherto balmy, suddenly turned to complete crap. Clouds scudding up from the south should have warned us that something untoward was on its way, but we were facing north and didn't notice them until the sun disappeared behind a rearing cloud-bank that grew thicker and blacker by the minute.

Big splodges of rain started to plop down through the bush. We stopped, pulled parkas out of packs and quickly donned them. From then on, the going got tougher, the hills steeper and increasingly slippery, while torrential rain ran in rivulets along the track and dripped down my back. My parka, which hadn't seen the light of day for several years, wasn't as waterproof as I thought.

We slogged on. Conversation petered out as we concentrated on putting one foot in front of the other without falling flat in the mud. Needless to say, I slipped and slithered regularly, covering my hands and legs with dirty brown clay and grazing my knees on more than one occasion. Tramping, I was quickly realising, was like climbing a precipitous staircase under a mud shower with all your clothes on.

At last, atop yet another hill, a view of yachts anchored in a cove was cause for elation: we only had to negotiate our way down there and we'd find shelter.

The 'tourist lodge' at Anchorage turned out to be a rudimentary tramping hut. We stopped and splashed cold water from the outside tap on our hands, legs and faces, so wet already that a bit more didn't matter, then sheltered under the wide verandah and looked around as the rain continued to pelt down. The bay looked gloomily grey, with a collection of yachts and motor boats hunkered down against the weather. There wasn't a soul in sight on the beach or on the decks of any of the boats.

There were, however, several cheerful-looking trampers gathered under the verandah, drinking from water bottles and mugs, chatting and laughing, obviously made of much sterner stuff than me. My feet were sore, my shoulders hurt after carrying the small day pack, and I was wet through. I yearned for a hot bath, a glass of something restorative and a soft mattress with clean sheets. I suspected there would be none of those.

However, I kept my grumpiness to myself and smiled bravely at my companions before following them inside. There was a large open area filled with tables and bench seats, a communal kitchen and bunkrooms off to each side.

It was first come, best bed, I was told and, yes, it was every man and woman for themselves — in other words, the bunk-rooms weren't segregated.

Our packs were waiting inside the door, miraculously dry after a watery boat trip. We left wet shoes and jackets at the door and, at Liz's urging, quickly bagsed our beds by depositing our sleeping bags on them. She'd been worried we would miss out, but we were just in time to get the last few beds in the hut. It meant three of us having to climb up to top bunks, but at that stage I didn't care. I was so wet and tired and hungry I could have slept on the floor.

We changed into dry clothes and sandals then Liz and Helen sorted through the various Tupperware containers of food to see what was for dinner.

I looked around the communal kitchen. No microwave.

'Hey, guys, what are we going to do? There's no electricity!'

'Penny, don't you ever listen! Of course there's no electricity. We're on a tramping trip, you noodle, not a luxury lodge tour. We have to cook it ourselves.' Liz looked disbelieving.

'Yes, but how?'

'With this, silly.' Liz held out a funny little contraption that looked like a miniature Sputnik. She laughed at my wide-eyed disbelief. 'It's a little gas cooker. See, this is the gas bottle and this is the stand for putting the pot on. You light it here.' She pointed at the shiny metal core. 'Look, I'll show you.' She miraculously found a spare space among all the others at the kitchen bench, shook the glutinous contents of a plastic container into a small billy and lit a flame under it. It hissed and spat and slowly the food started to sizzle. She turned it down and stirred it with a fork.

'I swear you're in another world sometimes, Penny. They were telling us all about this stuff this morning.'

'Oh.' I felt foolish. 'I can't have been listening.'

'This is fun!' Helen came up behind us with a bag of salad greens and a tiny pottle of dressing. 'I'm so glad we got those people to do all the preparation for us. I'd never have had time to do this. And certainly not as well.'

'And it smells divine,' Di said. 'These guys have put a lot of thought into it: chicken cacciatore, potato salad and cos.'

I couldn't believe how early we were eating — the kids would have called it rest-home hours — but, like the others, I was famished.

We dined off plastic plates; to my intense surprise it was very nice.

'You and Fran can do the dishes.'

'Sure,' I said. 'No problem.' I looked around. I wasn't stupid enough to think there would be a dishwasher, but it came as something of a shock to see there wasn't even a sink.

Liz laughed at my wild-eyed look. 'You're right. No hot water, Penny. And no basin. You wash everything outside in the billy under the cold tap.' She scrabbled around in the bag of goodies the tour company had left with our packs. 'Here.' She produced a tiny scrubber and a sachet of dishwashing liquid. 'I wouldn't let on we've got all this stuff. Most people haven't.'

I looked around. Indeed they hadn't. Some of them were even smirking at our comparative abundance.

'Tell you what. You go outside and clean up then I'll boil up some water and make coffee.'

I dutifully went out to the tap to wash up. It had stopped raining, thankfully, but the resulting swarm of sandflies was not pleasant. I got bitten while removing the gelatinous cacciatore from the pot and plates and had several red welts around my ankles and elbows by the time I returned to the kitchen.

'Bloody sandflies,' I complained to Helen.

'You should have put the stuff on.'

'I forgot.'

I left her with the clean pot of water to heat, went off to find the repellent and smothered all exposed skin — somewhat belatedly, I realised, scratching the itchy bites.

'Where's the loo?' I asked Di, who was in the bunkroom fiercely brushing her hair. Her normally ironed-flat hair had frizzed up in the rain so that it was sticking out almost horizontally. I figured it best to ignore it — Di was such a fusspot about appearances.

'Outside. Round the back.'

I looked quizzical. 'Outside?'

'Yes, Penny. We're in a national park. They don't have flush toilets indoors.'

'Oh.'

Damn! Another learning curve.

A tall bearded man with a foreign accent excused himself as he brushed past me.

'They're not segregated either, the toilets,' she added. 'And neither are the showers. You'll be able to see all the dangly bits while you shave under your arms.'

'What?'

She grinned at me.

'I won't be having a shower at all then!'

Di burst out laughing. 'Only joking,' she said.

I'd feared the ablutions. I'd already experienced the chemical toilets in the bush — with their ever-attendant sand-flies and wasps and evil smell. I'd quickly learned how to speed-pee.

I found the toilet block, screwed up my courage and my nose and entered. But to my surprise, there were flush toilets and no smell.

On my return two men about my age from our tour group were sitting near the entrance to the hut.

'Hi,' I said in response to their greetings.

'Your meal looked pretty good,' one of them said. He had a short beard, very short-cropped hair and nice, smiley eyes. I recognised them both from our bus earlier on.

'Yeah, we haven't even cooked ours yet,' said the other, tipping a plastic cup to his mouth. As I passed, I could smell rum.

'Not much to cook,' said the first.

'Plenty of time for that,' said the second. 'Cheers.' He

raised his glass, almost dismissively, and I continued inside.

'Who are they?' asked Fran, who was watching the Primus and its carefully balanced cargo.

'Dunno. I didn't ask.'

'They look quite nice.'

'Oh? I hadn't noticed.'

'Come on, Penny, I saw you smiling at that guy with the beard. Fancy him, do you?'

'Come off it, Fran! I just said "Hi". I don't know him from Adam.'

'Hmmm. We'll see.' I caught her grinning knowingly. 'Hey, you're blushing. Hey, guys. Penny's blushing!'

'Coffee's ready,' Liz called before the others had time to comment.

'Thanks Liz,' I said gratefully, selecting a steaming plastic mug and adding the little container of UHT milk.

'Come on, let's take it outside. The view is something else.'

They jostled me outside before I had time to protest about being set up and we sat on the grass overlooking the bay. It must have been incredibly early, but I'd deliberately left my watch behind — partly to save it from getting wet, but mostly to lose track of time.

When the others weren't looking, I glanced behind me to see if the man with the smiley eyes was still there. He and his friend had been joined by four teenagers — three boys and a girl — and seemed to be embroiled in some sort of negotiation about dinner.

'But we're starving,' one of the boys was saying loudly.

'We want dinner now,' added the tallest of the three.

'Please, Dad,' cried the girl.

Smiley Eyes got up and carried his cup inside. The kids

followed him. His friend stretched out, leant on his elbows and took another swig.

'Penny?'

I swung round. 'Yes?'

'You were miles away. Fran was asking if you wanted to go for a post-prandial stroll along the beach.'

'Sure,' I said.

'But you were busy staring at your fella,' Fran teased.

'He's not my fella!'

'Come on, let's stretch our legs — again.'

I clambered to my feet. Already my thighs were starting to protest.

We paddled through the cool, lapping water, picking up empty scallop shells and skimming them across the calm ocean, blue now under the newly emerged sun. We helped a couple push a dinghy back into the sea on the way back to their yacht. We stopped and listened to the distant laughter and voices from the many yachts anchored in the safe haven. And, after a dazzling sunset that turned the slowly disappearing clouds orange then pink, we watched a full moon rise up over the water, fooling us it was twice its normal size from the mirage caused by the nearby headland.

'Maybe this tramping lark isn't too bad, after all,' I conceded, mud-sliding hassles of the afternoon forgotten, as we sat on the damp sand and felt the warm evening breeze on our skin.

The tramping lark, however, turned pear-shaped overnight. Serenaded by a chorus of snores, farts and grunts from the surrounding bunks, I tossed and turned on a mattress that was made of just enough foam to keep me separated from the wooden slats until I wanted to turn over, whereupon my hipbone crunched into the hard wood. I was awoken

— though it felt like I'd not slept a wink — at what seemed like dawn, by Helen and Liz swinging their legs over and clambering down from the bunks on either side of me.

'Come on, guys, time to get up.' Helen patted my feet as she manoeuvred herself onto the ladder. 'We want to get across the estuary while the tide's still out or we'll have to wait until this afternoon.'

I closed my eyes again. This afternoon sounded much more civilised.

'Penny?' It was Helen again. 'Come on, wakey wakey. Time to rise and shine.'

I propped my head on my hands and raised myself up to eyeball her, causing me to bang my head on the side of the bunk.

'Ow!' My eyes felt like a piece of sandpaper had been wedged in each corner. And now my left temple hurt as well. 'Ow,' I added for emphasis.

'Mind your head!' Helen laughed. 'Come on.'

I gave in. I figured I'd be hopeless on my own if I waited until the afternoon so I'd better get over it and get up. I managed to hit my head on the side wall and ceiling no fewer than four more times while I twisted and turned to get onto the ladder, then another couple of times while I got down it, clutching my extra long T-shirt around my legs, aware that the woman and her boyfriend in the bunks below were getting the sort of eyeful that would undoubtedly put them off their breakfast, if not their whole day. The woman smiled sympathetically as my feet found terra firma.

'They do not make easy,' she said in an accent from somewhere in Europe.

I smiled back. 'No.' I pulled on my shorts, slipped into my sandals and made an urgent dash to the outside toilet. I would have thought the insect repellent would still have been working, but these damn sandflies proved immune, armed and dangerous.

Di persuaded us all into an early morning swim to start the blood pumping. She wasn't wrong. The water was so cold I thought my heart had actually stopped in the few seconds I plunged under the water. I was determined not to be the last in, but I worried for a moment if I would be able to get out, such was the shock. I wasn't alone — we all ran shrieking from the sea to the cold shower cubicle, doused ourselves in turn with fresh water (which now felt warm by comparison) and shampoo, and towelled ourselves dry in the small communal space outside.

'Well, that was quite a shower!' Di was glowing with pleasure. 'Don't you feel better?' She looked around at us, in various stages of dress and dampness, and laughed. 'Wasn't it great?'

'It feels good now,' I admitted, starting to warm up and tingle pleasantly. 'But it was flipping awful at the time.'

'No gain without pain, Penny.' She was still laughing, as were the others. I joined in.

Breakfast was a hasty affair of cereal with tinned peaches and milk, and tea. We left our packs as instructed, for the boatman to pick up, and set off in a light drizzle, which had unfortunately just come in from across the hills to the west.

By the time we'd slogged across the estuary, it was hosing down. But I was beyond worrying about being wet and muddy. Everyone looked the same: sodden, bare legs, boots and socks splashed with grime from the soggy track. As we passed people going the other way, they looked up, smiled and greeted us cheerily. Who was I to be the odd woman out? Grin and bear it, girl, I told myself, greeting them as cheerily as I could and plodding on.

We stopped for lunch at a high point overlooking the coast — Frenchman's Bay, Fran said after consulting the map — where you could just make out through the mist an offshore island. I tried to imagine the golden sands and blue sea under a brilliant sun, but it was not to be our luck. From there, it was a short slither downhill to Sandfly Bay, which didn't live up to its name because the sandflies were sheltering under a leaf or wherever sensible sandflies go to save themselves from drowning in the pouring rain.

At the back of the bay was the Falls River, which the guidebook had praised as being a highlight of the trip. As it transpired, it was a watershed in more ways than one.

Chapter 9

The swing bridge over the river had been on my mind all day. I'm not a cissy, not by any means, but I'm not all that fond of swinging in mid-air high above a rocky ravine. So I'd been steeling myself for some time to make the crossing without letting on that I was a teensy bit terrified. But as soon as she saw the thing, suspended high over a plunging waterfall and rocky riverbed, Fran confessed first to hating swing bridges, so the two of us were encouraged to cross mid-party, one by one.

Liz and Di went first, jumping up and down, shrieking and cavorting and enjoying every minute of it; as soon as the swaying stopped, Fran crossed, hesitant, terror-stricken, slowly edging forward, looking every which way but down. I put on much the same pathetic performance, my heart pounding, a sick feeling in the pit of my stomach, urged on by the others

— Fran the loudest of them — until I stood on the track once more and my world stopped swaying. Liz greeted me with a hug and they all cheered as Helen crossed last. Water bottles were extracted from the sides of packs and swigged on, but I had just one thing on my mind now: I needed to pee, urgently.

Somehow, the pent-up fear of the swing bridge had prevented me thinking of anything else except putting one foot in front of another until after I'd crossed. But now I realised I hadn't been to the loo since we'd left Anchorage. The relief of making the other side of the swaying monster swept through me, along with recognition of my bodily needs. I looked around: no loo in sight, of course. Not that I expected to find one here in the middle of nowhere, but at various points along the track, chemical toilets like little sentry boxes had popped out of the bushes. Falls Creek was not such a spot.

'You go on, guys, I'm going to duck in here for a comfort stop,' I said as everyone put their water bottles away and prepared to move on. 'I'll only be a sec. I'll be right behind you.'

Liz looked at me doubtfully. 'Are you sure?'

'Yeah, I'll be fine. I can handle anything now I'm over that bridge.'

I waved them on and, as soon as they'd disappeared from view, ducked off up an easy slope where I could see a cluster of bushes that should give me cover. It took a bit longer to find a hidden spot than I'd expected, as the thicket wasn't quite as thick as it looked, but desperation overcame me soon enough: I pulled down my shorts and knickers and, with only a small amount of prickling on my bare backside from the surrounding ferns and bushes, was soon mightily relieved.

With shorts and clothing rearranged and my day pack once again firmly on my shoulders, I headed back down to where I thought the track should have been. But I must have either trekked further up than I'd realised, or taken an unknown turning somewhere, because I couldn't find it. Suddenly, the ground became steeper and I had to pick my way with even greater care to avoid slipping. I stopped and looked around: this bit didn't look familiar at all. I listened for voices, but couldn't hear the girls anywhere. Bugger! I thought. I'm lost.

Fortunately, the voice of reason didn't abandon me; I stood still and took stock. I knew the track must be somewhere below me, and I could still hear the waterfall to my right. If I could just keep on edging downhill, I would surely find it before too long.

At that moment, I heard voices coming from down the hill to the right. It sounded like a couple of teenagers crossing the swing bridge, and from the wails it sounded like one of them, a girl, was protesting that the other was making the bridge sway while she was trying to cross it.

That spurred me on. Ignoring the voice of reason now, I hurried downhill to where I was sure the track must be. But I took it too quickly and tripped over a tree root. Suddenly I found myself sliding on my bottom down a muddy slope. I tried to grasp at saplings and fern trunks to stop the fall, but only succeeded in gathering speed until, whump! I came to a halt against a couple of boulders.

My ankle hurt like hell; I suspected it was broken. I tried to stand on it, but couldn't. My hands and arms were grazed and bleeding, my legs were covered in mud and leaves.

The voices below grew closer.

'You big baby,' the boy was saying.

'You big bully,' the girl rejoined.

'Stop it, you two,' the man said.

I realised I'd be stuck here forever if I didn't catch their attention.

'Help!' I wailed. 'Please, help!'

The arguing stopped.

'Hey, someone's up there,' the girl said.

'Help,' I cried again. 'Up here.'

Moments later, the man appeared from below the boulders — the same man I'd seen at the hut last night, Mr Smiley Eyes. His look was all concern.

'Are you okay?' He pulled himself up over the top of the boulder. 'Stupid question,' he added. 'Of course you're not. Here, let me help you up.'

'I can't stand. I think I've broken something.'

'Oh dear, that's not good.'

The teenagers had appeared by now — two tall and gangly kids who looked about the same age as mine.

'What's happened?' the boy said.

'Duh! She's hurt herself, stupid,' the girl said.

Their father — or at least I assumed he was their father — looked around as if help might appear out of the blue.

'Weren't you with some others?'

'Yes, my girlfriends. They're not far ahead. I told them to go on and not wait. I . . . er . . .' Even in my desperate situation, I wasn't going to admit that I'd fallen over after being caught short.

'Then it shouldn't be too hard to catch up with them.' He turned to the kids. 'Drew, Zak, go as fast as you can and let Miss . . . er, Mrs . . .' He looked at me shyly. 'I'm sorry, I haven't even asked your name.'

'Penny. I'm Penny Rushmore.'

'You can catch up with, er, Mrs Rushmore's friends and tell them to come back.'

A cloud passed across the girl's face, as if she might argue, but she must have thought better of it. 'Okay, Dad.'

'Come on, Drew, what are you standing there for?' The boy, Zak, had started already, slipping back down the boulder and thundering down the slope at speed. Drew followed just as quickly, their young limbs oblivious to the dangers of the slippery ground, and soon they were out of sight.

'Thank you for doing this.'

'No problem.' He smiled. 'Sorry, I should have said earlier, I'm Simon. Simon Wakefield.'

'Well, I'm extremely pleased to see you Simon. I could have been stuck here for hours.'

'Is there anything I can do to make you more comfortable?'

'I don't know. I don't want to move too much in case it is broken, but I wouldn't mind moving over here a bit so I don't feel as if I'm going to slide down further.'

I tried to wriggle sideways, but the pain made me wince.

'Here, I think I can help you with that so it doesn't hurt.'

He came up behind me, put a muscly forearm under each of my arms and hauled me up, back over the lip of the boulder so that I was perched more firmly on top. The movement made my ankle scream with pain but I don't think I could have stopped myself from falling further if I hadn't done it.

'There, is that better?'

The pain subsided as I remained still and I smiled wryly. The rain had eased off to a steady drizzle, but it was still enough to make the water drip off my nose and trickle uncomfortably down my bare and battered legs.

'What a mess I've got myself into. I'm sorry to hold you up.'

'It's nothing. Don't worry about it.' He paused. There was an awkward silence.

'I suppose it could be a while before they're back,' I said to fill the gap.

'Yes.' He looked around. Another awkward silence.

'I could . . .'

'Perhaps . . .' We both started to talk at once.

'Please go on.'

'I was just going to say, I always seem to get into scrapes like this.'

'You do?'

'Yes. I'm not an outdoorsy sort of person, really. I should have known better than to try this walk.'

'But you seemed to be doing so well, striding out with the others, coping with the sandflies and the rain.'

'It's all a sham.' I laughed, despite myself. 'The girls talked me into it. I've never been tramping in my life. I don't think I'm cut out for it.' I pointed at my ankle.

'My kids aren't all that keen on it either. I'm not sure I should have brought them. Their mother warned me it was a dumb idea.'

'You can never tell with teenagers, though. You'd swear they were having a dreadful time and then they get home and tell all their friends what a wicked holiday they had.'

He laughed. 'That's only too true. You must have teenagers too?'

'Yes. They look about the same age as yours.'

'Are they on the trip too then? I don't recall seeing them on the bus.'

'No, two of them are off with their father on the Gold

Coast. The oldest, Josh, is off in London doing his OE. I'm on my own.'

'Lucky you. No kids. A real holiday,' he said ruefully.

'In a way. Josh has been gone all year. But the other two are away on a guilt trip — their father has taken them to make up for the fact that he's also taken his new girlfriend.' I don't know what came over me to blurt all that out — I certainly hadn't meant to. I laughed, trying to pass it off as if I didn't care, but the laugh sounded hollow even to me.

'Oh. I see,' he said quietly, sucking in his breath slowly. 'And let me guess, she's half his age and he's having a midlife crisis.'

'It's a bit of a cliché, I know.'

'Well, welcome to the club!'

'What do you mean? How can you . . .'

'You'd be surprised what some women can do.' He looked around, as if checking that no one was listening. 'My wife left me three years ago for a man half her age and guess what? They split up after just a few months. But by then it was too late. Neither of us wanted to get back together. She'd changed. And so had I, I suppose.'

'Oh.' I didn't know what else to say. Three years seemed such a long time apart.

'It was prophetic really.' He laughed ironically. 'The pair of them were acting in a bedroom farce together for the local drama society. She was playing this older seductress character. It was *The Graduate* — you know, Mrs Robinson?' He started to sing the Simon and Garfunkel song.

'I remember that!'

'Well, Myra played the Mrs Robinson character that tempted the younger man to run away with her. And in the play, it didn't work out for them either. Except it was funnier in the play, with the bedroom doors slamming and these two characters running from room to room half undressed. I laughed and laughed. But the joke was on me . . .' He trailed off.

'I'm sorry.'

'Oh, don't be. It was for the best really. I know, that's what they all say when they're trying to be kind, but I can see now it would have happened sooner or later.' He looked apologetic. 'I don't know why I'm telling you all this out here in the bush, with the rain dripping down on you. I should be trying to shelter you or something.' He looked around but, apart from clumps of fern fronds and tree branches, there was nothing. 'I don't have an umbrella or anything to cover you with, not even a sleeping bag to wrap round you to keep you warm. I know.' He stood up. 'You can have my jacket. Here.'

'No, really, I'm fine. Really.' I waved him away. 'It's not cold. And I'm wet already. I can't get any wetter.'

'I wish I had a first aid kit with a thermal blanket. I'm getting worried about you. If you've broken it, you could be in shock.' He started rummaging through his pack. 'Here, have my towel. Drape it over your leg, at the very least.'

I let him wrap it round my nether regions, though I could tell it would only get damper by the minute. He looked genuinely stricken.

'I feel so helpless,' he said. 'I always told myself to take one of those first aid courses. They have them at work and you can go on them for nothing. Trouble is I never seemed to have the time.'

'Work must keep you busy then?'

'Oh, you know how it is. I lecture in Microbiology, so I'm not so busy I couldn't have done one of those courses if I'd really wanted to.'

'I always meant to go on one too, but there always seemed to be something more important. I've honestly no idea what I've done to my ankle. It could be broken, or just a sprain. I hope it's the latter. I couldn't bear having to be helicoptered out. It would be so embarrassing. Steve would never let me hear the end of it.'

'Steve's the one on the Gold Coast, I take it?'

'Yes. He's . . .'

The unmistakeable sound of Simon's teenagers bickering about exactly where to find me reached us both at once.

'They're back,' he cried.

'And by the sound of it, they've brought reinforcements.'

I could hear Liz's voice first, taking the lead and bossing the others as usual.

'Penny? Penny, where are you?'

'Are you up here, Penny?'

'Yes, up here.'

The teenagers' heads popped over the rocky outcrop first then the girls arrived one by one. Di was beside me in a flash.

'Here, let me have a look.' She eased my boot off and touched my ankle lightly, prodding gently with her fingers. I winced. 'Sorry, Penny,' she said. 'How did it happen?'

I described the fall, how I'd been wedged between two boulders, where it hurt most.

'Does it hurt here?'

'Not more than anywhere else.'

She prodded a bit more. 'Here?' She kept prodding gently, round the ankle bone, the foot, the calf. It all seemed much the same except round the outside part of the ankle.

'What sort of pain? Throbbing? A dull ache? A sharp stab?'

I pointed to the bit that hurt. 'Only here, really.'

'On a scale of one to ten, how bad is it, if ten is the worst?'

'Well, childbirth would have to be a ten. So I'd say about a five. Though it's not as bad now as at first. Maybe a four.'

She pushed down on my toenail.

'Well, your circulation's fine. And there's no pressure point, so I don't think it's broken.'

'Well, that's a relief.'

'There's a little bit of swelling, but it's not too bad. I think you'll be okay. Have you tried to walk on it?'

'Yes, but I couldn't stand. It hurt too much.'

Di opened a side pocket in her pack and pulled out a first aid kit from which she extracted an elastic bandage.

'I should be icing it. Or getting you to soak it in the cold river. But I think we'd do more damage getting you down there. So I'll just have to make do with a bandage. Here, hold still. I'll try to be gentle.' She bound my ankle with the bandage, sheltering it with her body as she worked, until it was neatly packaged. It felt firmer, more stable.

'Now, let's have another go.' She organised everyone to help me up so that I didn't have to move my right leg or put any weight on it until I was standing. It was quite an effort because I was stuck on top of a big boulder. But after much grunting and manoeuvring, I managed to stand on my left leg while Simon and Fran held me up and Di continued to deftly feel round my ankle bones. It still hurt each time she touched me, but not as much as before.

I tried putting my right foot on the ground and found it wasn't nearly as bad as I'd expected. I even managed to stand on it for a second or two; I could feel a dull ache rather than the searing stab of before.

'I think you'll be able to walk on it soon. You just need to rest it for a while.'

'I feel such a fool,' I said. 'I'm sorry about this, guys.'

Simon and Fran helped me hop slowly back down to the track while Helen carried my day pack and the others hovered anxiously around. The teenagers had long since returned to the track and were waiting impatiently.

'What do you think we should do?' Simon looked at Di, who seemed to have taken charge.

'I'm not sure.'

'But Di, you always know about these things.' Helen turned to Simon. 'She runs a big private hospital at home. She's the next best thing to a doctor.'

'Helen, you know that's not true. I don't know much at all. But I do keep my first aid up to date. I don't think it's broken.' She turned to me. 'But it's up to you. If you think you'll be able to walk on it, then we could help you get to the hut slowly. I think it's about half an hour off. If not, we can go ahead and get help.'

That spurred me on. I didn't want to hang about on this godforsaken rain-soaked track for much longer. While I rested my foot up on the ledge at the side of the track, the others ransacked the nearby bush until one of them found a sturdy walking stick. Di and Fran stayed with me while the others, including Simon and his kids, went ahead at my behest to see if they could get me a bottom bunk in Bark Bay Hut because I'd insisted on staying the night there. It was clear by now the ankle wasn't broken — I wouldn't have been able to walk at all if it was. Di had warned me it would swell and be even more painful if I didn't submit to being carried out, but I was damned if I was going through the humiliation of the stretcher treatment, so I struggled on, determined to make it, and hobbled for forty minutes all the way to Bark Bay.

Once there, it was kind of nice being made a fuss of. I didn't have to cope with any of the fearsome gadgets that heated the dinner or boiled the water. Instead, I limped across the dark sand, flopped into the briny and elevated my ankle in the cool salt water. Apart from a continual dull throb, it wasn't too bad. Later, a glass of wine at a bench table under the trees, with my leg elevated as per Di's instructions, and I was feeling a lot better.

'Good to see you back to normal,' Fran said, arriving with Helen and Di to join me. They swung their legs over the bench seats to sit down, Helen and Di opposite and Fran beside me.

'It's thanks to you lot,' I said, raising my glass to them. 'You came back to save me.'

'You would've done the same for us,' Di said, toasting me in return.

'Don't be too sure of that!' Helen said. 'I don't think Penny is cut out for the outdoors.'

'Not after today,' I laughed.

'Oh, that's a shame. I was hoping to see you on the Queen Charlotte next summer.' I looked around at the sound of that familiar voice. Simon must have overheard. Rum glass in hand, he introduced himself to everyone, apologising for not having done so earlier in the day.

'Think nothing of it,' Helen excused him. 'Quite understandable under the circumstances.'

'Come on everyone, let's go get dinner.' I looked up at Fran just in time to see her give a pronounced wink to the others.

'Yes, you're excused, Hopalong,' Di said to me, with a knowing smirk.

They vanished inside, leaving me and Simon alone, which of course had been their intention. There was no sign of his kids or his friend. I'd noticed all the kids earlier on the beach but hadn't seen them since.

I felt vaguely awkward. It was the first time in decades I'd been in this position — acutely aware of a man's presence and kind of liking it, but not knowing how to conduct myself. Was I supposed to flirt, to come on strong, to show him I felt some sort of attraction? Or was I supposed to pretend nothing had happened, that I didn't feel a thing? I honestly had no idea. It was such a long time ago that Steve and I courted, and even then I'd known him since university so it had never seemed like courting at all.

I picked up my plastic mug of wine and took a nervous swig. 'Have you . . .'

'How's your . . .' Again, we started to speak at the same time.

He laughed and continued. 'How's your foot?'

I held it up. 'Twice it's usual size now and a bit sore. But I'm so relieved I didn't have to be put on a stretcher or, worse, on a helicopter. I'd never have heard the end of it.'

'You're lucky it wasn't broken, that's for sure. I hope it hasn't put you off tramping for good, though.'

'I don't know about that. It wasn't a great start.'

'It'd be such a pity. There's nothing quite as satisfying for the body and soul as walking through bush like this — the outdoors, the people, the places you'd never see otherwise.'

'. . . the rain, the mud, the sandflies,' I continued, laughing. 'I've seen enough to know it can be absolutely brilliant. But I'd think seriously before doing it again.'

'I don't suppose you'll be walking anywhere tomorrow.'

'Probably not. Di said I should take the water taxi up to

Awaroa and meet you all at the lodge there.'

'Sounds very sensible. You wouldn't want to miss Awaroa.'

'So I've heard. I think I'll be able to cope with a boat trip and the short walk from the beach. But I don't think I could make the full day's walk.'

'Dad, when's dinner?' It was his daughter, Drew.

'Oz is getting it tonight, love, it was my turn to put the blowtorch under it last night. Ask Oz to get a move on.'

'Uh-hhh.' She pulled a face.

'Did you get your juice?'

'Yeah. I'd prefer a drink though.'

'Sorry, love, not tonight.' She grimaced again and flounced off.

He shrugged. 'They always want something more, no matter how much you give them.'

'Indeed.'

'Hopefully Oz will keep them occupied for a while. He's good at handling them at that age — he teaches high school Science. They take more notice of him than me.'

'He's got two of his own?'

'Yes, two boys. It's funny, Drew ignores them both, but I think she quite likes the older one, Tom. You'd never know it to listen to her though.'

'Ah, the teenage mind.'

'Bit of an oxymoron isn't it?' he laughed.

We talked about our kids and how they drove us crazy a lot of the time. We talked about going on holiday — with them and without them — and what it would be like in a few years when we could go without them. We talked about Awaroa and its fancy food and wine; we talked about favourite restaurants back home; about how much he liked to cook and how much I hated it; about my worst dinner party ever when I'd undercooked the coq au vin and served it rare and bloodied to a gathering of VIPs; about his worst dinner party when he'd set fire to the oven and then nearly set fire to the house; about coping on your own with teenagers; and about how little they seemed to mature by the time they got to university.

We even talked about tramping and my inauspicious introduction to it.

'The secret is having the right boots,' he said, holding out his long legs and wiggling his well-worn boots. 'These boots are made for tramping.'

'I'm surprised they make boots that big,' I said before I could stop myself.

He laughed. 'I know. I've got very big clodhoppers. My mother used to tell me I'd always have a very firm hold on New Zealand.' He wiggled them some more; they looked ludicrously large attached to such skinny legs. 'They helped me win a few swimming races though when I was at school. The kids used to call me Flipper.'

'I'll remember that,' I chuckled.

We talked until the sun — which had been making increasingly frequent appearances between the clouds — went down behind the hill and his kids arrived to say his dinner was getting cold. I looked at my watch.

'Good grief, it's nearly eight o'clock. Where did the time go?'

'I didn't notice it either.' He smiled lazily at me. If I knew more about it, I'd swear he was flirting. 'I'd better go or I'll be in trouble.' He stood up and brushed my bare shoulder with his hand. 'I hope to catch up with you at Awaroa.' And he was gone.

I should have followed him inside to see what the hell the

girls were doing, but I found I couldn't move. It wasn't my foot, which I'd managed to keep elevated like a good girl most of the time we were talking. It was just that, for some reason, I was rooted to the bench. I felt winded. My legs — even my good leg — felt like jelly.

'Hey, dreamer, what are you doing out here still?' It was Fran carrying a plate of the hot smoked salmon, rye bread and salad that was tonight's pre-ordered dinner. 'You must be hungry by now? We ate ages ago!'

'I lost track of the time. You should have come and got me.'

'Nah. You looked happy enough. We figured if you were hungry — for food that is — you'd come and tell us.'

'Stop it!' I protested half-heartedly. I was half enjoying the teasing, but I wasn't going to admit it. 'This is very kind of you, bringing it out here. And you must have gone to the trouble of reheating it.'

'Not a problem for the camping types among us,' she said. 'Liz did it in no time. She's almost got me persuaded those cooking gadgets are better than a microwave.'

'Yeah, right. I can just see you with one of those in your minimalist kitchen at home.'

'Mmm. Perhaps not. Anyway, you looked so blissful out here with your *friend*, we didn't like to disturb you.'

'Fran, you do jump to conclusions. He's not my *friend*.'

'You make the most of it, Penny, you deserve a nice man. And believe me they're not that easy to come by. When you get to our age, it's a bit like finding a carpark — all the good ones are taken and the rest are disabled.'

'Well, spare me from that fate worse than death,' Helen laughed, coming up behind us with a mug of coffee. 'Here, Liz sent this out for you.'

'Goodness, you guys are spoiling me. I'll be getting the wrong idea about tramping altogether.'

'Well, Simon doesn't want you to give it up, so we thought we'd better made it easy for you!' Helen chuckled.

• • •

The living was even easier the following night, which we spent at Awaroa Lodge. The sandflies were, as usual, a pain, but the pay-off was that the rain had stopped; it was a beautiful sunny day and the wind, thankfully, kept itself to a gentle breeze while I played Lady Muck by taking the water taxi along with our packs.

My foot was still swollen, but the overnight rest on the bottom bunk, followed by a day of very little walking, helped speed recovery. Apart from the boat trip and short hike from the beach to the lodge, my day involved nothing more than sitting outside under an umbrella reading a book while accepting an array of hot and cold drinks and the occasional morsel of food.

It was in this reclining position that the girls found me when they arrived hot and sweaty off the track.

'Look at you!' Helen cried, plonking down her day pack and getting out the camera.

'Give me ten minutes and I'll be out here with you,' Fran added.

I posed for the photo while the others hooted with laughter.

I showed them to our rooms. We were sharing, but it was a far cry from the communal bunkrooms of the past two nights. There were clean sheets, fluffy pillows, ensuite showers, designer accoutrements. If this was tramping, I could certainly get used to it.

Di headed straight for the bathroom '. . . to tame my bloody hair as best I can,' she said, while I pottered around the room in search of something to do. My toilet bag proved a mine of ideas to fill time: a mirror, nail clippers, nail file, tweezers. I attacked my typically out-of-control eyebrows then discovered to my horror a couple of stray black eyebrows had shifted south to under my chin — the sort of downward movement of body hair I'd noticed of late. Ginny said once it was making up for the gradual thinning of hair on top of your head or elsewhere — it all somehow migrated to your chin or, worse, onto your face in a really embarrassing place.

It was while I was rummaging round in the bottom of my pack looking for another top that I found my cellphone. I'd managed to forget about it for three whole days now and, happy to keep it that way, I quickly put it back. I had another day off tomorrow and then I could catch up with reality. Di, coming out of the shower and looking her usual calm and collected self — a far cry from the hot and bothered tramper of an hour ago — caught me and laughed.

'I've kept mine turned off too. I don't care what happens. I'm on holiday.'

'It's hard to believe, isn't it? Three days and we feel guilty for not phoning in.'

'I know. I told them there was no cellphone reception here anyway. They've got the phone number of this place and the tour company. If they really need to get hold of me, they will.'

'Same.' It was then I realised with a jolt that I had given work my contact details here, but not Steve or Dad. 'Oh, shit!'

'What?'

'I've just remembered something.' I dived back into my pack, pulled out the mobile again and turned it on. Nothing — just a 'No network coverage' message.

'What?'

'I forgot to give Steve and the kids this number. And this isn't working here.'

'They'll cope for a couple of days. Don't worry.'

We walked through flowering manuka to the restaurant where we ordered a bottle of Sam Neill's Two Paddocks Picnic Riesling and waited for the others to arrive.

'Paradise regained,' Di breathed, sipping the ambrosial aperitif, sitting back, closing her eyes and soaking up the last rays of the sun across the marshes.

I looked around the corner. Sweaty trampers were dotted about enjoying wine, beer and sodas, their packs and boots scattered round the perimeter of the open-air dining space. But there was also a smattering of corporate types looking like they'd just stepped off the superyacht anchored in the bay or off the big black Eurocopter I'd seen taking off and landing several times during the day. The accents of the dudes at the neighbouring table were pure New York; their chinos and loafers fresh from treading the luxury lodge route through New Zealand.

'Look, over there,' Di was indicating a nearby table with her thumb and forefinger. 'That's the chap who does what you do, PR. You know, Muldoon's nemesis. He used to work for the Queen, no less.'

'Simon Walker?' I turned around.

'Shhh, not so loud,' Di hissed. 'Yes, him. Apparently he brought one of the princes here one summer.'

'No!' I looked around as if royalty might appear at any minute.

Instead, Smiley Eyes Simon appeared, smelling of a crisp linen aftershave, clearly straight from the shower.

'Well, hello you two,' he said, approaching our table. 'Mind if I join you?' Di looked at me, grinned, and indicated a spare chair. He plumped down in it and picked up the wine list.

'This is a bit different from the last two nights, isn't it?' he said as he scanned the page. 'Not a bad selection. And I hear the food is top notch as well.'

'Seared tuna, scallops fresh out of the bay, manuka-smoked mussels, and wild fungi in hapuka . . . Sounds divine. If it was swimming yesterday, it's here today.'

'Goodness, Penny, you must have been swatting up on the menu.' Simon gave me that lazy smile again that made me go weak at the knees. Luckily I was sitting down.

'I've not had much else to do all day but think about what I'm going to eat next.'

'You missed a good day's tramping,' he said, smiling laconically. 'Even the kids liked it — sunny but not too hot, and plenty of time to stop at the bays for a swim.'

'I believe you. But I think I got a much better deal swanning about here.'

'I can see you're going to take some convincing to get those tramping boots on again.' He laughed at the face I pulled. 'How is your foot?'

'Can't feel a thing,' I replied, raising my glass.

Simon hailed a passing waiter — a young guy with a ponytail. 'Can I please order some wine?'

The waiter nodded. 'Certainly, sir. What can I get you?'

'I'd like a bottle of something white, please, since it looks like fish is the order of the day. How about this local wine, the pinot gris? Would you recommend it?'

The waiter nodded again. 'A very good choice.'

The waiter disappeared; we settled back in our chairs and drank in the view across the marshes, the sun still high over the distant ranges, a bellbird singing from the flowers of a nearby flax bush. High overhead, I thought I saw a falcon spiral skywards. I closed my eyes and breathed deeply, inhaling the slightly salty yet sweet smell of the wetlands.

'It doesn't get much better, does it?' Simon said quietly.

'No. This place is like heaven on earth.'

'I'll bet you'll find you want to come back here. It has a strong pull.'

'You've been here before?'

'Many times. Usually after a long hard tramp up the coast,' he grinned.

'I think I'll take the boat all the way next time.'

'You could always pay a few hundred and get yourself choppered in,' Di said.

'We'll turn Penny into a tramper yet,' Simon teased.

'I doubt it,' Di said.

'Well, I'll just have to make the most of it this time round.' I closed my eyes and breathed in the fresh sea air.

'Thank God for a few moments' peace,' Simon said at last.

'Where are your kids?' I asked. I feared the peace wouldn't last forever.

'Still down at the beach. There's a whole crowd of them. They seem to have made friends with some of the local bach owners' kids. The last I saw them they were kayaking down to the estuary. They could be gone for hours.' He looked extremely cheerful at the prospect. 'You should have seen them when we arrived off the track — straight into the shower then a beeline for the kitchen. They ordered up paninis as if they hadn't seen food in a month, and then disappeared off down to the beach. That's the life for me!' He raised his hand in a salute as the waiter reappeared with his pinot gris, which he unscrewed and poured. Simon waved him to keep pouring rather than formally tasting it, thanked the ponytailed dude and raised his glass to Di and me.

'Cheers,' he said. We raised ours and clinked them together. 'Cheers,' we both said.

'Cheers to you too,' chimed in Fran, arriving from the direction of the lodge. Behind her, Liz and Helen were approaching.

Simon offered his wine for them to drink, but Liz wanted a red and Fran her usual tonic and bitters. Then Oz arrived.

'Those kids are having a ball,' Oz said when introductions were over and the waiter had delivered more wine then gone off to fetch Oz a beer. 'They're right over the other side of the estuary in a whole pod of kayaks. I think they've found someone they know from school or the stables or somewhere. They told me they're going up to one of the houses over the back there afterwards for some sort of party.'

'Well, that's a relief,' Simon said. 'Drew was moaning all the way here about not being able to watch her favourite programme on TV and how boring it was at night with nothing to do. But I haven't heard a single complaint since we got here.'

'This menu's impossible,' Di said. 'Everything sounds absolutely divine. And it's even good for you. The restaurant has its own organic garden.'

'Don't give me organic food,' Fran protested. 'I need all the preservatives I can get.'

'Nonsense, darling, you don't look a day over fifty,' Liz said.

'Well thanks very much, Liz. I don't turn fifty until the end of the year!'

'I wouldn't worry about it. The older I get the more grateful I am,' Di laughed.

'Indeed. I'm not going to admit to being old until I'm sixty-five and ready to collect the pension,' I said.

'You wait,' Liz said. 'Sixty will be the new fifty.'

'I bet you won't even admit to being old, even then.'

'No, you'll still be running around trying to get everything done, complaining you've got too much on.'

'You can't slow down as you get older — you have to speed up because there's less time,' Helen said.

'I hope I can still manage to keep up at sixty-five,' I said. 'I don't want to retire and find I can't do all the things I've dreamed of doing.'

'You won't retire at sixty-five,' Di scoffed. 'You'll be spin doctoring 'til you die.'

'It's hard to break the habit of a lifetime,' I grinned.

• • •

After dinner, after we'd consumed coffee and a little nightcap, Simon walked me back to my room by what seemed a very circuitous route. At the point where we were looking over the marshes towards the distant hills, where the almost-full moon washed everything with a ghostly silver shimmer, he leant forward and kissed me full on the mouth and I responded with the enthusiasm that was his due. I could feel something arousing in the depths of my being that I hadn't felt for a very long time and it terrified me. But my instinct to flee was unrealisable. I couldn't move. I was glued to the gravel. I opened my eyes to the moon above, the flax and toi toi below, and

Simon's rapturous expression, eyes tight shut.

'Goodness,' I said at last. 'I wasn't expecting that.'

'Nor was I.'

We did it again. And again. I've no idea how long we stood by the rails overlooking the wetlands but eventually the call of a lonely morepork brought me back to reality.

'I'd better go,' I said with no motivation to move at all.

'Yes,' he said, kissing me again.

I was saved the dilemma of whether I should even consider going back to his room, or he to mine, since we were both sharing. Oz was already well ensconced, as was Di. By now she'd have completed her fanatical beauty routine and would be tucked up in her Trelise Cooper pyjamas in one of the two big beds in our room.

I slept fitfully, awaking several times, getting up to drink copious amounts of water and look out the window, staring at the moon and stars until, the last time I trod the bare boards, the moon had sunk below the hills, its memory but a distant shimmer. I opened the double door and went out onto the deck to breathe in the still night air, feeling uneasy yet excited at the same time, worried about what I might have started, yet thrilled and somehow curiously alive.

Chapter 10

There was no sign of Simon at breakfast, which was hardly surprising, since we all got up so late. I was just finishing a coffee outside with the rest of our team when he arrived, teenagers in tow, his feet covered in sand, his boardshorts still wet from the sea.

'Hey, you're all up,' he smiled that lazy smile and I felt a jolt strike me somewhere deep inside, below my breastbone.

'Come on, Dad, we need to get going,' his daughter said, tugging at his elbow.

'Yeah, the water taxi's leaving in half an hour,' the boy said. 'Come on, let's go.'

He headed towards the lodge, ignoring the rest of us. Drew followed, calling after her father, 'Hurry up, Dad,' in a voice I noticed carried more than a trace of a whine.

'Better go,' he said. 'I hope to see you again.' He directed this last remark specifically at me. But he made no attempt to get my phone number.

I went back to my room to pack. We were catching the midday boat back to Marahau and I threw my things into my pack in a desultory fashion, unable to concentrate, kicking myself for not saying anything more encouraging than a feeble, 'Yes, that would be nice.'

But when we went to check out, there was an envelope for me.

'Penny,' he had written. 'I enjoyed our brief time together and would like to see you back home. Please feel free to phone or email.' Then he wrote his contact details and signed it, 'Yours, Simon.'

I tucked the envelope and note inside a pocket in my pack and kept it a secret. Or at least I thought I did.

'I see lover boy wrote you a note,' Fran cried over the noise of the two hulking outboard motors at the back of the water taxi as we sped back to base. 'What did he say?'

'Fran! How did you know?'

'I saw him leaving it for you,' she said, pressing her forefinger to the side of her nose knowingly. 'Not much escapes us lot, you know.'

'He seems pretty keen on you,' Di said, twisting round in the seat in front to face me.

'He's nice,' Liz added, leaning across the narrow aisle.

'Good heavens, nothing is private around you lot!' I gasped.

'And you're surprised?' Di chuckled.

'Just be careful,' Fran confided. 'You know what they say about rebounds.'

'Fran, you're hardly one to talk,' Di said.

'Yes, Jack's belongings were not long retrieved from the

bottom of the driveway when you started dating that geek in R and D.'

'True, but he was the persistent type. He looked shy and retiring, but boy . . .'

'Please, spare us the gory details.'

At that moment, we hit a series of waves from the back of a passing ferry and conversation stopped abruptly. Once we'd passed the wake, Fran resumed her interrogation, but at least laid off the advice. Fortunately, the noise of the motor and the bumpy ride as the sturdy aluminium hull whacked down on wind-whipped waves interrupted her often enough to lose track. And when we passed the seals basking on the rocks at the back of one of the islands, she was distracted for good.

It set me wondering though, as we bounced up and down, whether I was indeed rebounding too quickly from Steve's sudden departure; whether I was so needy for male friendship that I had thrown myself, as my mother would have put it, at the first man that came my way.

• • •

We arrived in Nelson off the bus feeling flat.

It had been a great Philisophicals bonding expedition. However, the return to civilisation was accompanied by a number of complications. Di's hospital was still under threat of a strike and there were several urgent messages on her cellphone. And Fran's software firm was having security problems and needed to contact all its customers urgently. From the moment she picked up her messages, she was on the phone without a break.

Reluctantly, I turned on my mobile and dialled the

message service. The nice relaxed feeling of lethargy disappeared immediately when I heard Adam's unusually plaintive voice: 'Hi, Mum, it's me. I'm home early. I've been trying to get hold of you. When are you coming home?'

This threw me into a mild panic. Why had he come home early, I worried, and was he all right on his own? Sure, he was fifteen and old enough supposedly to cope with being home alone. But was he really up to it? Did he have enough money to pay for his food? And how many wet towels, dirty socks and undies had already piled up on the floor? Had he invited all his friends round for a party? And would there be anything left in the drinks cupboard? I returned the call immediately but he wasn't home so I texted his mobile. He responded a few moments later: 'At darrens b hm soon.'

I decided to wait. I didn't fancy a discussion with Darren in earshot so cooled my heels by following the girls around the Nelson shops while we waited the two hours to check-in to fly home. For a small town, the shopping wasn't bad and there were plenty of places to choose from for a late lunch.

I phoned Adam from a sidewalk café. We looked like a typical bunch of city slickers, each one of us either texting or talking into our cellphones, while the rest of the summer visitors relaxed in the sunshine.

'Hi, Mum,' he said when he finally picked up.

'Hi, darling. What are you doing home so soon? You're not supposed to be back until tomorrow.'

'I know. But Dad got me an early flight on Friday.'

'On Friday? That was days ago!'

'Yeah, I know. But I'm okay, really, you don't need to worry.'

'But why, Adam? Why couldn't you wait and come home with Charlotte tonight?'

'Oh, you know.' He paused. I waited. He said nothing further.

'No, I don't know. For Pete's sake, why?'

'Uh . . . I wanted to.' Another lengthy pause.

'Because?' It was like getting the proverbial blood out of a stone.

'It was gross, that's why. Dad was gross. She was gross. And Charlotte was the grossest of them all.'

'What sort of gross? Were they mean to you or something?'

'Nah, nothing like that. They were just gross, like, you know . . .'

'No, I don't know,' I said, exasperated. 'That's why I'm asking you. What was the problem? What was so bad you had to come home?'

There was a big sigh and another long pause. I was about to give up when he said, 'Charlotte was all over Jacinta like a rash and borrowing her clothes and getting her face made up all the time and going shopping like they were sisters and it was just gross.' He made a gagging sound. 'You should have seen them. You would have felt sick too, Mum. She bought Charlotte all these things that made her look like some random Barbie doll and they'd teeter off down in the lift giggling like they were sharing some big secret and all Dad would say was, "Isn't that nice, son, Jacks and your sister getting on so well. They're having such a great time." It was sick-making. And I had to listen to them giggling all night about boys. Charlotte would be telling her all about the random boys she knows and she'd talk about when she was at school like it was yesterday and going on about some boy there. Eee-argh.'

He sounded as if he really was being sick with that last one. I'd not heard such a long speech from Adam in ages. And

I didn't blame him for making an escape. I'd have wanted to get away from that sort of nauseating sucking-up too.

'I can understand your dilemma,' I said. 'Are you all right there? Have you got plenty to eat?'

'Yeah, course. I'm fine.'

'Well, I'll be home in a few hours now, hopefully before eight anyway.'

'Good. What'll we have for dinner?'

Adam's stomach was always on his mind.

'Why don't you get some mince out of the freezer and defrost it in the microwave? You could do spaghetti, couldn't you?'

'Okay.' He didn't sound overly excited about that, but at least it was something he could cook reasonably well. 'Oh, where's the dog?'

'At the kennels, of course. Where did you think?'

'Uh,' he grunted. He hadn't of course; he never stopped to think about anything that didn't directly affect him or his hunger pains.

'You can come with me and pick him up tomorrow after work. It'll take two of us to calm him down. The last time I got him from there he tried to eat my handbag.'

'Oh. Right. Well, see ya.'

'Yes, Adam, see you soon. It'll be nice to come home to a cooked meal. I'll look forward to it.' Nothing like a bit of positive reinforcement, I told myself, to kick-start him in the kitchen. It always took a bit of whip-cracking to get him going, but he wasn't half bad a cook once he put his mind to it.

I worried about him all the way home after that — worried he'd set the house on fire with the frypan, worried he'd demolished the contents of the liquor cabinet, worried he was scarred for life by his father's behaviour — or rather, his father's floozie's behaviour. Di, who sat next to me on the plane, regaled me with a horror story about her brother's son and his friends who had invited a few mates over for a beer one Friday night when his parents had gone away for the weekend and they were still all there when the parents came home on Sunday afternoon. Comatose bodies lay scattered across the living room and in all the bedrooms, with a boy and girl who would have only just made the legal age limit stretched out naked in the parents' double bed.

Thankfully, Adam had been up to none of that. When I arrived home, he hardly looked up from the television. He'd drawn the curtains against the sunny summer's evening and had made popcorn, which was now scattering itself all over the floor around the chair.

'Hi, Adam.' I went and stood between him and the TV so he'd have to acknowledge me.

He looked up, grunted, and went back to the screen. There was some loud action movie on with lots of shooting and screaming car wheels. I picked up the remote from the coffee table in front of him and turned it down. He grunted in mild protest, but didn't move.

'Hi there,' I tried again.

'Hi.' It could have been another grunt, but I accepted it as a greeting. He looked at me momentarily and went back to the screeching tyres and guns.

I gave up and carried my pack through to the washhouse, emptied the muddiest and mankiest clothes into the washing machine, tossed in heaps of powder and turned it on.

The kitchen was, needless to say, an appalling mess, with baked bean tins, sauce bottles, egg cartons, empty McDonald's wrappers and a vast array of detritus spread from one end of the bench to the other, and quite a bit of it spilled onto the floor. Because I'd been snowed under at work for the week before I'd left to go tramping, I'd not cleaned up either and I'd foolishly told my treasured cleaner not to come while I was away (not expecting teenage occupation in my absence), so the entire house looked like a tip. It needed industrial-strength elbow grease and a ride-on vacuum. But at least there was a bowl of spaghetti and meat sauce waiting on the bench for me to heat up.

'Thanks, honey,' I called, forking it up quickly without bothering to warm it up. I realised I was starving. There'd been nothing on the plane except the usual tea and water and dry biscuits. Adam's spaghetti was just what I needed.

While I polished it off, I picked up the phone and dialled up the message service. There were several saved messages, which meant that Adam must have listened to them already.

The first was from Steve, checking Adam was home all right and asking him to phone back. I didn't expect Adam would have bothered. Feeling contrary, I deleted it.

There were three messages from work, but I decided they could wait until the morning. There was nothing I could do right now anyway on a Sunday night and, besides, I was housebound with the car at the repair shop waiting to be picked up.

And in the middle of all the messages, there was a plea from Dad for me to ring. He wasn't feeling too good, he said.

That spurred me to action. Dad never admitted to feeling unwell, so it must have been pretty dire for him to mention it. I phoned his number. As luck would have it, Mum answered.

'Hello? Hello? Is that you, Susan?'

Oh dear, I thought, she's off again. Susan was a friend from her newlywed days in Te Kuiti when she'd been the champion marmalade maker four years in a row.

'Hi Mum it's me, your daughter, Penny.'

'Who? Penny?' There was a pause. 'Ron, who's this Penny? Is she a friend of yours?'

Dad came to the phone, thankfully.

'Hello there, lassie, it's good to hear your voice.'

'How are you, Dad? Your message said . . .'

'Oh, that was a bad day, Friday. I wasn't feeling at all good. But I seem to have come right since then. I think it was just a bad day, that's all. Your mother, she . . .'

He tailed off and I heard Mum giving him a hard time in the background. She had the radar of a fruit bat when it came to picking up any discussion about herself.

'Look, lassie, I'd better go now, she's not been good today. Perhaps I could see you tomorrow when you've finished your work.'

'Sure, Dad, I'll come round right after. Are you sure you'll be all right 'til then?'

'I'll be right, don't you worry now.'

'Okay, Dad. I'll see you tomorrow.'

I hung up, worried. I'd have to get round in my lunch break somehow, and before that I'd have to get a taxi to pick up the car, and then we'd have to get Tigger. Just a few hours back home and already the list was mounting.

• • •

After a week's holiday, there was so much to do at work that I didn't even have time to go to the toilet, let alone stop for lunch. My stomach behaved like my throat was cut, protesting all afternoon at the unaccustomed lack of food. If it weren't for Tracey delivering a cup of soup and endless tea, I'd have wasted away — I wish! Every time I put the phone down, it seemed someone else called, and on several occasions the mobile and desk phone were going at the same time.

Around noon, just when I thought I might escape with my mobile and see Dad, my funeral director client rang to say a TV news crew was outside his gate wanting to talk to him about the bottom falling out of the coffin at a funeral at the weekend.

'What?' I cried.

'This fella weighed over twenty stone so we had one of those double caskets we call The Boat. Some of the people we're burying are so heavy these days, you wonder how the pallbearers cope. Anyway, I don't know what happened, but the bottom started to creak and there was this gap starting to appear.'

'You're joking?' I prayed. There was silence. 'Is it true? Did the bottom really fall out?' A dire picture flashed in front of my eyes of a corpse thudding onto the chapel carpet watched by all the horrified mourners.

'Well, no. But it dropped enough to give Deralee a big fright.'

'That's not quite so bad then.'

'It's a total disaster. It could ruin our reputation.'

'I agree it's not good, Andy, but I think it's salvageable.'

I outlined a plan for dealing with the television news crew to get rid of the immediate threat and then talked through with Andy about resolving the situation with the family. Andy reckoned it was one particular relative who'd gone to the media — a woman, not in the immediate family, who had seemed a natural stirrer but who didn't seem to be particularly liked by other family members. She'd been the only one to react badly at the time.

'If you can get to the closest relatives before they start

to feel aggrieved, you might be all right,' I said. 'The idea is to apologise profusely, explain what went wrong, and offer to make amends somehow, like not bill them for the funeral . . .'

There was a sharp intake of breath at the other end.

'I know times are tough Andy, but imagine how tough it's going to get if the daughter starts weeping all over the six o'clock news. Nobody — but *nobody* — is going to ask you to do a funeral ever again.'

'But it wasn't our fault,' he protested. 'It's the casket maker who should be held accountable. It shouldn't matter if the body weighs over a tonne. It should always hold. It's his fault. He's the one who dropped us in it.'

'Well, almost dropped,' I added, finding it hard to keep a straight face. 'You've got one good thing going for you in this mess, and that's the fact that the body didn't actually drop. You've got to get some more positives out there, and the most obvious one is to somehow get as many members of the family as possible on your side.'

'Oh, all right,' Andy grumbled. There was a pause. 'You mean the whole funeral? I should waive the whole bill?' His voice was rising to a squeak of disbelief.

'Over to you. See how the family reacts to your approach. At the very least, you've got to give them the faulty casket for nothing. And from there on in, you've got to be prepared to give more if necessary.'

There was a pained silence.

'Okay,' he said at last. 'I see your point.'

'You don't want to have your firm look like the baddies in this, do you?'

'No, certainly not.'

'Well, you'd better get out to see them pronto and make them an offer.'

Andy rang off, meekly agreeing to do his best as soon as he'd put the TV people off for an hour or two. He was a personable sort of guy, Andy, and he was used to dealing with people in various stages of grief. He'd been in the business ever since he was old enough to earn pocket money for cleaning cars — except the cars in question were long, black hearses. As a result, he'd grown up with death and the bereaved in much the same way the rest of us grow up with dolls and Matchbox cars. He knew only too well that anger and blame are very high up in the stages of grief; he knew how to handle angry mourners who wanted to take some of their issues out on the funeral director — the fall guy in the dark suit. I just hoped he could manage to close the case of the collapsing coffin before it became national headlines.

Andy was on the phone to me on and off for the rest of the afternoon, reporting back, asking for further advice, discussing the contents of the written media statement I'd made for him and how to handle the television news crew. I picked up Rosie with her humming new big end or whatever it was that had cost so much money and drove to the funeral home, where I took Andy through the statement and ensured that he stuck to his key messages without straying off into dangerous territory.

He handled the TV interview quite well in the end, and encouraged the reporter to go and talk to the family spokesman, whom he'd managed to get the family to appoint (at my insistence, I might add). The TV reporter had, as we'd suspected, already interviewed the busybody aunt, so then I had to get the family spokesman to phone the TV newsroom and insist on being interviewed. Luckily, the busybody aunt was hated even more than the poorly nailed coffin, so getting someone to phone up and contest her claims didn't prove too difficult. But the whole afternoon was like being caught in a yo-yo — as soon as I thought we'd succeeded, we'd plummet down to the depths again from another sideswiping blow.

Exhaustion was creeping through me when I finally escaped from the funeral home and headed to Mum and Dad's. But I woke up pretty quickly when Mum answered the door and vaguely asked me to come in. She didn't recognise me — she hardly did these days — but she at least had the presence of mind to lead me along the hall to the bedroom. Dad was lying on the bed, deathly pale and not much more lifelike than the bodies I'd just seen backstage at the mortuary. I rushed over to him and checked his pulse — he was alive and breathing, but shallowly. I couldn't tell if he'd fainted or if it were something more serious.

Without hesitation, I phoned reception at St Joan's for help. The doctor, thankfully, was still on duty, carrying out his nightly visits, and was able to come immediately. I ushered him into the bedroom, where he quickly examined Dad, raised his head higher by plumping the pillows then asked for the phone.

'I'm calling the ambulance,' the doctor said tersely. 'He's been left far too long as it is. Have you any idea how long he's been lying here?'

Needless to say, I was guilt-stricken. 'Er, no, I don't.' I looked round at Mum but she still had the vagues. 'I spoke to him last night and he said he wasn't too good last Friday, but he was okay last night.' I realised it sounded like a pathetic excuse. But the doctor was no longer listening. He was on the phone to the office ordering oxygen. The minute that was done, he opened his bag and took out an array of gear, placed a substance under Dad's tongue then injected him with something.

An orderly arrived with the oxygen and the doctor started to administer it, smothering Dad with a big plastic mask. When the ambulance arrived, there was an even greater flurry of activity as the paramedics assisted the doctor then set about shifting Dad onto the wheeled stretcher. Even the retirement village manager arrived. She looked sternly at me, but she didn't say anything — yet. I could tell there'd be a St Joan's family discussion coming up soon. Dad had always kept them in the dark as much as possible about his health because he was terrified they'd try to separate him from Mum.

'If they thought for one minute,' he'd told me, 'that I'm not up to caring for Colleen, they'd pop her into the dementia ward quick as look at her.'

Now it seemed as if his dire predictions were about to come true.

Dad was wheeled out the door into the back of the ambulance, oxygen and a drip attached. I felt torn whether to go with him or stay with Mum. In the end, I didn't have a choice — the hospital manager took me aside and told me that Mum would have to go into the dreaded dementia ward until Dad was well enough to look after her again. Unless I wanted to have her at home. I was in no position to argue. I certainly couldn't care for her at home in her advanced addled state and there was no way she could stay in the villa on her own.

It was with a sinking heart and a sense of guilt shooting higher than the entire solar system that I helped the nurse and orderly gather up Mum's things and pack a bag for her. And all the while she was protesting, airing her oft-heard complaint that we were conspiring against her, that she wasn't going anywhere, that she was perfectly capable of looking after herself, thank you.

'But Mum, you're not allowed here on your own. It's not safe.'

'It's perfectly safe,' she argued. 'Look, I can lock all the doors and windows. Nobody can get in.'

It was pointless trying to argue. She refused to listen to any view other than her own, and she refused to budge from the house. In the end, she got so upset and belligerent that the doctor had to be recalled to give her a shot of something to calm her down. And that made me even more upset than watching Dad go off in the ambulance. I had to turn away when the needle came out; I couldn't watch them jab it into her. And the sound of her cries getting fainter was heart-wrenching.

I put my arms round her; I knew I ought to take her home with me. But even in her encroaching feeble state, she pushed me away.

The balmy summer evening hardly registered as I followed the staff outside and across the grounds to the dementia ward. The orderly carried her overnight bag while the nurse pushed Mum in a wheelchair. For the first time ever, my once stocky and bossy mother looked small and vulnerable. I hadn't noticed until now that she'd slowly been losing weight, that her sturdy limbs were sagging and frail, that her bearing — once confident, once the queen of her realm of three kids and a dog — had become stooped and anxious.

The sign 'Dementia Unit' was the barrier I knew I could not pass. I left them at the door, trying unsuccessfully to give Mum a kiss on the cheek before she disappeared inside. I'd been in there once — and that was enough. It wasn't that she wouldn't be cared for properly; the unit had one of the best reputations in town for its knowledge and care of people with Alzheimer's like Mum. It was the apparent madness of all the residents that got me down, knowing that Mum was going to be like them — was already like them most likely — and I didn't want to be confronted with the visible proof.

I walked briskly back to Mum and Dad's unit, got in the car and drove to the hospital.

There were several messages on my phone; I ignored them. I don't even recall the route I took or whether I obeyed any of the road rules. I felt as if I'd betrayed both of them.

The hospital sent me away, telling me I couldn't see Dad — he was under observation in intensive care and he wasn't allowed visitors until tomorrow at the earliest. I drove the rest of way home glumly, wishing that Stephanie was here.

By the time I got home I'd made up my mind: I was going to call my slippery sister and insist she come and help out.

'Please, Steph,' I begged. 'I know you're busy, but if we don't get her out of the dementia unit now, I have a feeling she'll be stuck in there forever. We should bring her home.'

'I just can't,' she said, brooking no argument as usual. 'My book comes out in a month and I'm tied up with all the publicity and interviews. I'll be on *Kim Hill* in a few days, live — I'm a bundle of nerves — and the *Sunday Star-Times* . . .'

'Stephanie, please, spare me the details. This isn't about you. It's Mum that needs you right now . . .'

'You've got to be kidding. I can't leave town. My publisher would kill me. They've set up all these interviews. No, I just can't do it. You'll have to hold the fort a bit longer.'

'So you could come later?'

There was an audible sigh of exasperation.

'Look, what part of the word "No" don't you understand? I'm tied up here for the next six weeks at the very least. Longer probably. There's the launch and the media and the book tour . . .'

'You're a great help,' I said sarcastically, feeling like hanging up on her. 'Thanks a bunch.'

After I put the phone down, I mooched off upstairs to find company. I was racked with guilt at my own inability to help Mum and livid with Stephanie for her intransigence.

Adam was still in his room, playing on the computer.

'Where's Tigger?' he greeted me.

'Oh no, I forgot! Poor creature, he's still at the dog home.'

'Mu-uum. How could you?'

I opened my mouth to tell him about his grandparents, but couldn't face it. His screen was filled with the flame-streaked boy-racer cars from *2 Fast 2 Furious*.

'I'll get him first thing and take him to work.' I left him to the street racing, grateful that the virtual version was enough to keep him occupied. He'd shown no signs, thankfully, of hankering after the real thing.

• • •

I got up an hour early to fit everything in, phoning the dog home to warn them I'd be out to get Tigger shortly, while eating breakfast, scanning the paper to see if there was anything in it about funeral homes (not a thing, fortunately), and listening to *Morning Report* for the same item (nothing there either).

Tigger just about knocked me over when he came bounding out of the kennel area, jumping all over me and covering me with sticky wet slobber. Knowing him well, I'd worn an old pair of jeans and my dog-walking polar fleece. My work clothes were stowed safely in the boot away from his dirty paws. Then he tore past me and leapt into the car, installing himself firmly in the back and refusing to budge.

But no sooner was I in and the door closed than he started to lick my ear and breathe his awful doggy breath all over me.

'Get in the back, you silly dog,' I laughed, fondling him. 'Come on, we're going into town and you've got to behave all day.' He'd been into the office before and knew the etiquette. As long as nobody left their lunch or anything edible in their handbag at Tigger level, he was okay.

It was quite a hike back into town and, before we got to the built-up area, I let him out in a grassy lay-by, where he repeatedly stamped his mark on the shrubbery. But as soon as I headed for the car, he streaked after me and beat me through the door, determined not to be left behind again.

By the time we got back into town he was happily asleep. I parked in the hospital carpark, opened the tops of both windows to give Tigger some air, and found Dad's ward. He was sitting up in bed looking pale and wan, with a tube coming out of the back of his hand and an oxygen mask across his face. He tried to take off his mask to speak but I put up my hand to stop him.

'Don't try to talk, Dad. The nurse has given me strict instructions not to tire you.' He looked as if he were about to protest. 'No, please, Dad. Let me talk for a minute.'

I held onto his hand and, for the first time in ages, told him how much I loved him, how much I'd been depending on him lately and how I could see now the toll it had taken on him. I told him that all was well at home — a slight exaggeration I admit — and I told him about the tramping trip and how good it had been to get away from things for a while, to see my life as if in a fishbowl, looking in from the outside and examining myself swimming round and round endlessly chasing my tail, pursuing a goal that seemed to change daily. I told him that Mum would be well looked after at the village

— I didn't mention the dementia unit; he'd probably guessed she was there anyway — and I finished off by telling him I'd met a man that I sort of fancied.

He waved his hand at that and gave me the thumbs up.

'I'm sorry, but I have to ask you to go now,' the nurse said, approaching the bed.

'That's okay,' I said, wishing I could stay a bit longer and hold Dad's hand. I said goodbye, kissed his forehead and squeezed his hand. He squeezed back and put his other hand on top of mine.

It was a wrench leaving him; he looked so vulnerable lying there surrounded by white sheets and pillows, tubes and clinical apparatus.

It was like that every day — I'd go in on the way to work and sometimes on the way home too. After a couple of days, his oxygen mask was off and he could talk, but he found it exhausting. Once I managed to get Adam to come with me, but wished I hadn't bothered. Normally cheerful and outgoing with his grandfather, happy to talk cars and engines ad infinitum, Adam was morose and hardly spoke the whole time we were there. Dad looked at me questioningly when Adam was standing by the window staring down into the carpark, but I couldn't explain. It was becoming evident that Adam had come home traumatised after his experience on the Gold Coast with his father — or rather with the Conniving Cow. Just how I should deal with it, I had no idea.

His mood had worsened when Charlotte came home from her father's guilt trip bubbling over with tales from the malls and the surf clubs. Jacinta, I quickly learned, was a *Baywatch*-type babe (why did that surprise me!) and had taken Charlotte to some surfing beach way south of where they'd been staying to visit an old surfie haunt she'd known in her youth (which, as I know only too well, was practically yesterday). Charlotte had been introduced to a horde of surfing hunks and had, of course, fallen in love with one of them.

Steve wasn't much help — neither with Adam nor me. When he dropped Charlotte off, he teased Adam about coming home early, causing him to slouch over to the corner of the room where he sat staring at the floor until Steve left.

With Adam out of the equation, Steve turned his attention to me.

'Charlotte told me your dad's in the hospital. Sorry to hear that.'

'Yes, they think he may have had a mild heart attack.'

'Huh. It's hardly surprising, you know — he runs around after that mother of yours all the time, it's a wonder he hasn't killed himself by now. You should have put your mother into some sort of proper care ages ago, Penny.'

'Yeah? Well, it's not as simple as that, he . . .'

'It's perfectly simple, you know. You should be more assertive with him. You've no problem being assertive with me.'

'Really?'

'Your mother's on a slippery slope, Penny, can't you see it? She needs to be in a hospital. It won't be long before she's in a vegetative state, dependent on some machine and fed on fluids from a bottle.'

'Sounds like you! Maybe you should unplug your TV and throw out all your beer,' I retorted. I was blowed if I was going to be lectured by Steve the smart-arse.

I don't think he quite got it. He sort of sniggered and looked sheepish. But at least he left pretty quickly, much to my relief.

Not long afterwards, the usual bickering between the two siblings turned into a full-scale conflagration, the flames fanned even further by Charlotte's new-found food fetish. Evidently brainwashed by the Conniving Cow's recent health kick, she suddenly refused to eat anything containing gluten or dairy products, hardly any carbohydrate, and had become obsessive about her weight, which provided Adam with plenty of fodder to tease, tempt and torment her.

Meals became a battleground, especially dinner time. She ate nothing for breakfast except spirulina, took a tuna or smoked chicken salad with a piece of fruit to work for lunch and covered the kitchen bench with kiwifruit skins, apple cores and orange peel from her early evening low-fat smoothies. Which was all very admirable, except that she didn't need to lose any weight to start with. She was enviably trim, thanks to sensible eating and nightly runs.

It galled me that she was trying to emulate an older woman and her picky eating habits when she needed more than diet food to sustain her standing about trying to sell wedding frocks all day, cycling miles at weekends to her rock-climbing site, staying up late on the phone, spending lunchtime in the gym and running most nights — sometimes with the Conniving Cow.

Over dinner one night I tried to reason with her. I'd compromised by grilling fish (and a burger pattie on a toasted bun for Adam, who hated fish), serving it with lots of salad and no rice or potato; I figured it wouldn't hurt me to cut down on the carbs too. For the first time that week, Charlotte thanked me for the meal instead of finding fault with it, and I silently congratulated myself as we sat down amicably for once together round the dining table. I'd even schooled Adam to shut up about Charlotte's eating habits and he tucked into his grilled burger without comment.

The peace lasted until we were nearly finished eating.

We'd been discussing Charlotte's day at the bridal salon and Adam's Science assignment that he was having trouble catching up with. It had been handed out while he was away and he was grumpy that he was behind already, since Biology was his best subject and one that he wanted to get good marks in so he could pursue his goal of being a marine biologist one day.

'Are you going to the supermarket tomorrow night, Mum?' Adam asked.

'Yes dear, why?'

'These burgers are yum. Can you buy more please?'

'I guess so. Anything else you need?'

'Nah.'

'Yes, I have,' Charlotte chimed in. 'I think we should be buying organic now, Mum. This mass-produced stuff is bad for us. You should see the list of fertiliser chemicals and pesticides they put on everything we eat.'

'But it costs four times as much, Charlie, I don't know we can afford it.'

'But it's worth it. What price can you put on your health?'

'Fine, you can pay for it out of all that money you earn with Bridezilla,' Adam chimed in. 'If there's anything left after you've spent it all on clothes.'

Charlotte ignored him.

'And we should be getting free-range eggs,' she continued. 'Those poor hens are subjected to the cruellest treatment, stuck together in battery cages with no room to move. They lose all their feathers, their bones are brittle, they . . .'

Adam started to mimic her, mouthing similar words and flapping his arms like a demented chicken.

'What would you know?' Charlotte turned on him. 'You'd

eat anything. Do you know how they make those burgers you're eating?'

Adam continued to imitate her, sticking his nose in the air like she had.

She ignored him again. 'Battery hens should be banned,' she said to me.

'You only started saying that when Jacinta did,' Adam taunted. 'You copy everything she does.'

'That's not true.'

''Tis so. Jacinta this. Jacinta that. Yes Jacinta. No Jacinta. Three bags full Jacinta.'

'Stop it, Adam,' I tried to intercede. 'You're just winding her up.'

'And anyway, how is Mum supposed to afford free-range eggs and organic everything. Have you seen how much it costs?'

'Then I'll help pay.'

'You? You couldn't pay for a mung bean. You spent all your holiday money in Australia out shopping with Jacinta.'

'I did not!'

'Did so. I saw all that stuff you brought home to show off every night. You just want to be like *her*.'

'That's so unfair.'

'Stop it, please!' I raised my voice much higher than usual; I hardly ever shouted at them and it had the desired effect.

'Adam, I'd like you to clear the table please and stack the dishwasher. I want to have a talk with Charlotte.'

He flashed his sister a look of triumph and stood to gather the plates. When he'd returned for the remainder and taken them away, I closed the door and sat down next to Charlotte.

'It's all right Mum, you don't need to lecture me. I know what I'm doing.'

'Do you? So tell me, what are you doing?'

'I'm being responsible for the first time about what I eat. I'm only eating food that is good for me and good for the earth.'

'Really? Well, I can understand you wanting to be responsible. That's very admirable.' I paused, trying to think of a way of saying it that wouldn't get her going again. 'But I'm worried that you'll get too thin. You're not . . .'

'Mu-uum,' she said in the tone you use when explaining something patiently to a child. 'I'm eating really healthily now. Lots of fruit and vegetables and salads and protein. I'm fine.'

'Yes, you're fine now. But it's not a balanced diet. And I'm worried that you're not getting enough to sustain the really active life you lead.'

'But I'm eating heaps. I'm fine.'

'It might be fine for a few days, Charlotte, but I'm worried how long you can keep it up. It's different for Jacinta. She's older than you. She doesn't need the sustenance you do . . .'

'But you don't understand. Jacinta knows so much about nutrition and she's onto this diet that really works. If you knew her, you'd see just how brilliant she really is.'

Charlotte broke off and had the decency to look sheepish. I think it had finally penetrated her warped teenage brain that she'd gone too far. 'Sorry, Mum. I forgot.'

I let it slide.

'Well, I'd like you to think about it and be careful, please. I don't want you wasting away.'

'Okay, Mum. Point taken.' She gave me a kiss and went out to the kitchen, where she and Adam were soon bickering again over who was going to unstack and who was going to stack the dishwasher.

Later that night, I picked up the phone and thought seriously about calling Simon — and not for the first time since I'd been home. In fact, every night I'd been tempted. But I put it down again quickly. I wasn't sure I could cope with another man in my life just yet. I had more than enough strife without attracting any more.

• • •

The next day I was late to work after having to see one of Adam's teachers over his lack of motivation at school. Shattered, I made it back to the car and phoned the office.

'Andy wants you to phone urgently,' Nicky said when she answered. 'Some women's magazine has picked up on the story apparently.'

I groaned. I thought we'd contained the collapsing coffin story to a short item on the TV news. It looked as though the busybody aunt was living up to her name.

Dealing with that took up most of the day, meaning I had to put almost everything else I was supposed to be doing on hold. By the time I got home, I was pooped.

'Hi, Mum. Here, this was in the letterbox.' Charlotte handed me the mail; I could see most of it was bills. One was from St Joan's.

'Hi, honey.' I smiled at Charlotte as she disappeared into the kitchen then opened the envelope. It was a bill for a very large sum. I'd been expecting an account with Dad in hospital and unable to write a cheque. 'What the . . .' It seemed we had to pay a whole lot extra for Mum to be in the dementia unit. Damn! I knew Dad had a little bit tucked away, but I could see it disappearing very quickly if this was going to be a monthly eventuality.

‘Oh, Mum,’ Charlotte looked up from the blender as I came in, ‘I meant to say, Dad says it’s all right with him if I come and live with him for a while. Is that all right with you?’

I collapsed in the nearest chair, winded. I should have seen this coming.

‘No, it’s not all right, really.’

‘But why? Dad says I can. Jacks says I can. Why can’t you?’

‘Because I don’t think it’s a good idea.’

‘But Mu-uum. I’m sick of having Adam around all the time, he’s so childish. You don’t understand.’

‘I think it’s you that doesn’t understand. It’s not appropriate for you to go and live with them both all the time. They’re home even less than me.’

‘But Mum, it’s not like that at all. Dad says . . .’

‘Your father can say what he likes, I’m not in favour of it. You’re in your first year at uni, starting next month. It’s really important you have some stability in your life.’

‘Yes I agree. That’s why I think I’ll stay with Dad for a bit. I’m old enough now to do what I like.’

Chapter 11

Her father won, of course, pulling the old sob story about access to his children and blaming me for being too clingy. However, I thought I detected something in Steve's voice that indicated he wasn't too sure about it himself. Sensing the experiment might prove more interesting than I'd first realised, I agreed. Charlotte went to stay on a trial basis to see how it worked out.

'You'll still need to have Adam to stay sometimes,' I bargained. 'It's not right to separate them completely.'

'Charlotte wouldn't agree with that,' Steve said wryly.

He was right. Splitting up Adam and Charlotte made for a much more peaceful time at home. There was no endless bickering, no fighting over the television or the stereo, no teasing each other about whatever particular weaknesses they might have at the time. Even Adam seemed to perk up a bit.

But when the weekend came, he refused to go to his father's — and his father seemed quite happy to keep it that way.

In the middle of all this, I was summoned into St Joan's for a meeting with the head honcho about Mum.

'Mr Rushmore is due home at the weekend and we are reluctant to let your mother go back to their villa again,' the big-bosomed woman boomed. 'We feel Mrs Rushmore has become too much for him to manage and it will only jeopardise his health again if he's left to look after her.'

I was inclined to agree but I knew Dad would steadfastly resist any attempt to separate them.

'Can we talk this through with my father when he comes back from hospital?' I asked plaintively. 'I know he'd like to be consulted.'

The head honcho agreed reluctantly, on the condition that Mum stayed in the dementia unit until she was convinced otherwise.

From: Penny Rushmore
To: Stephanie@StephanieScanlan.com
Subject: This time!

Hi Steph
I'm afraid the news about Mum is getting worse. The retirement village says she'll have to stay in the dementia unit even when Dad gets home from hospital. Dad will be so upset I don't know what to do.
The only solution is for you to come up here and look after her for a while. If you don't, I'll simply have to send her down to you. I know you've got *Kim Hill* on Saturday, so I'll give you until the middle of next week. If you're not here by then, she's on the next plane . . .

So there it is. You have a choice! This isn't like me to deliver an ultimatum to my big sister I know, but I can't see any other way out of it. Dad will be grief-stricken without Mum, and if Mum stays in that awful unit any longer, I don't think she'll ever get out again.
Penny

Not surprisingly, there was no immediate reply.

Adam, meanwhile, resisted even a suggestion of a day trip with his father and Jacinta — his father just didn't get it, as far as Adam was concerned, that anything involving Jacinta was out of bounds. If Steve had suggested a rally with his mates (in the now repainted Stag) or a boys' night out at some crappy action movie, Adam would have gone in a flash. But everything had to be with *her* tagging along, and probably Charlotte too. He refused to budge.

So rather than me waving both kids goodbye for a weekend with their father, it was Charlotte who packed her bag and somewhat reluctantly came to visit me and Adam.

It was late on Friday night, the day after I'd sent the ultimatum to Stephanie, and it was bucketing down outside. Charlotte arrived wet and grumpy, having run up the drive from Steve's car, announcing she had a party to get to in half an hour.

'That's a nice outfit,' I said to her disappearing back.

'Thanks.' She turned and smiled briefly. 'Jacks helped me buy it.' Then she continued on up.

Inwardly, I was seething. I'd seen the 'nice outfit' in the *Fashion Quarterly* magazine I'd been reading in the hairdresser's and it cost more than Charlotte would have netted in over a fortnight at the bridal salon.

'What's with Charlotte?' Adam said, coming downstairs.

'She's in a real stink.'

'Lord only knows. Friday-itis, maybe? Hopefully she'll get over it by the morning.' I shrugged, trying to pretend it was nothing.

'I wouldn't count on it. She's turned into a spoiled brat.'

'Adam, you shouldn't say that about your sister.'

'Well, it's true, you know it's true.'

Trouble was, it was close to the truth and I did know it. But I couldn't admit that to Adam.

'She's upset about the break up, I suppose. That sort of trauma can keep coming back to bite you for a long time afterwards.'

'Mum, you're so pathetic, just making excuses for her. The break up was more than nine months ago.'

Equally unsettling that weekend was the Saturday morning radio interview with Stephanie about her book. It shouldn't have upset me. I should have been proud of her and what she'd achieved. But even after reading some of her novel, I still felt as if she'd stolen something from me, something I couldn't quite put a name to, but something that made me feel as if the family's privacy had been violated.

Diary of a Suffragette wasn't in the bookstores yet, but according to Steph it was supposed to go on sale next week. Apart from the bits I'd read when she was down for Christmas, I didn't know much about it and was still not sure I wanted to.

Just the same, when the time came for the interview, I found myself sitting outside on the terrace with a coffee, the transistor tuned and waiting as the ten o'clock news and weather report came to an end.

The familiar voice of Kim Hill began the introduction: 'My guest this morning on *Playing Favourites* is Stephanie

Scanlan, author of eleven books for young adults that are, I'm told, even more popular overseas than they are here in New Zealand. *Tomorrow's Daughter* was translated into thirteen languages and is prescribed reading in schools from Dublin to Dubai.

'But her latest book, *Diary of a Suffragette*, is quite different from these fantasy creations for young people. It tells the story of her great-grandmother, a figure in New Zealand's suffragette movement in 1893 and a very inspiring woman.

'Stephanie, good morning.'

'Good morning, Kim.' My sister's voice was quavering with nerves, which was most unlike her.

'Your books for young adults have become popular around the world. What made you want to try for a new audience?'

'Well, I don't think it would have crossed my mind until I found out about my great-grandmother, Annie Jane Morrison,' Stephanie started hesitantly. She paused, as if she'd forgotten what she was going to say and, despite myself, I felt for her. 'She wrote . . . My mother gave me a bundle of her letters.' She paused again. I could imagine she was panicked by the enormity of the situation, sitting in a little studio opposite the great Kim Hill, choked up with sheer terror at the thousands upon thousands of people behind that microphone. I knew. I'd been there often enough in my days as a broadcast journalist to know just how a microphone could turn you into a dry-mouthed wreck.

'Ah . . . . to her sister. The letters were to Annie Jane's sister Jessie, one of the first editors of a ladies' page in a New Zealand newspaper,' She was gathering speed and confidence. 'I was so absorbed in her story I just knew it had to be told.'

I finished my coffee and listened as she laid bare our heritage without seeming to care that she had no one's permission to make us public property.

But she went further than that, she talked about our childhood: about her mother — my Mum! — who revered her grandmother's gumption to be counted among the brave women who stood up to the men in authority, about her little sister Penelope — me! — who didn't care about that sort of thing, and about her childhood — us three kids! — when life seemed an endless summer at the beach. And suddenly, the radio was playing the Beach Boys' 'Wouldn't It Be Nice' and I was taken back to 1967 when I was a gangly, pimply pre-teen whose togs hung loosely from my undeveloped chest while Steph was the oh-so-sophisticated high school surfer chick, her long hair blonded by the sun and her home-made pink-spotted bikini fitting over her long slim limbs like a Pirelli model.

And then I found myself singing along! Oh, how I'd longed to be older like my big sister Stephanie, who had no end of boyfriends on the phone and was always the most popular girl in her class.

In the middle of my reverie, Stephanie came back on air talking about her university days and the hippie movement. I thought, Oh no, she's going to play that clichéd song about going to San Francisco and wearing a flower in your hair, but she hardly drew breath before rollicking on to studying history and how women were just awakening then to the big blank that was 'her-story'.

Wait for it, I thought, we're in for Carly Simon or Carole King and that dreary old 45 Steph used to play about feeling like a natural woman. Or, worse, Joan Baez and 'We Shall Overcome' from the varsity sit-in. But I'd forgotten about that mother of all women's lib songs: Helen Reddy's 'I Am Woman'. And there I was again, transported to my old bedroom, listening to Steph's old gramophone in the next room, wondering what on earth it was all about, being kept down again. I could see her now, striding up and down our floral-wallpapered hallway, fist up in the air, singing that she could do anything because she was a woman, and an invincible one at that.

And Mum would come out of the kitchen in her apron, floured hands waving in the air. 'Turn off that awful racket, Stephanie,' she'd say. 'Whatever will the neighbours think?'

The phone was ringing inside. I ignored it.

When Helen Reddy finally shut up, the interview with Stephanie turned to her interest in history — or as Stephanie put it, *her*-story — and why she'd become so engrossed in her great-grandmother's story.

'The parallels with my own life were unbelievable,' Steph was saying. 'Here was this amazing woman on her own. Her husband had died and left her almost destitute with four daughters to raise so she had to go to work doing the only thing she knew how — teaching young girls. She never had a moment to herself. I can relate so much to that.'

I wanted to throw the radio into the garden; Stephanie had such an inflated opinion of herself and her 'busy-ness'. If the truth be known, she had it easy — a husband and daughter who never made a mess, a cleaning lady who had nothing much to clean, and a job in the room next to her lounge that she could start and finish any time she chose. She was forever jetting off round the world on book tours and holidays and never seemed short of money. And to cap it all, she'd started an affair with a league jock half her age. How on earth she thought she could compare her life to Annie Jane's required a giant stretch of the imagination. She was still waffling on: 'I identified so much with my great-grandmother . . .'

'I'm off to meet Jenna now, Mum. See ya.' Charlotte flew past on her way to the drive. 'She's picking me up in *her new car*.' She emphasised these last words as she always did when referring to Jenna's flash little RAV4. Her father had bought it for her seventeenth birthday and Charlotte was green with envy.

The sound of Jenna's peppy little SUV roaring off down the road brought me back to reality, as did the sudden disappearance of the sun, immediately followed by a few spots of rain. I flicked off the radio, picked it up with my mug and went inside looking for something vigorous and mind-numbing to do to take my mind off the lot of them.

It was while I was gouging out gunk from the depths of the oven, still of a mindset that they could all go to hell, that something in me started to rebel. Damn it! I thought. I'm going to do something *I* want to do for a change. And before I could change my mind, I whipped off the rubber gloves, flicked through the Yellow Pages and found the name of a woman Ginny always raves about for a facial. She had a cancellation later in the afternoon, she said, and booked me in.

Then, before I could talk myself out of it, I held onto the phone and dialled up Simon's mobile. He answered, sounding a bit short, but to my relief his voice softened when I said who was calling.

'Hi,' he said. 'Great to hear from you. I was getting worried you weren't going to call.'

'I can hardly hear you.' There were lots of voices in the background.

'Sorry. I'll go somewhere a bit quieter.' A whinnying sound interrupted him. 'Whoa girl.' There was a pause and a discussion I couldn't hear. 'That's Drew's horse, Skylark.

We're in the middle of nowhere at a weekend horse trial. I don't think the reception's very good here.'

'It's better now.' The background noise had stopped. 'Sorry I took a while to get back to you. I've been so busy . . .'

'That's okay. It's just nice to hear your voice again.'

I smiled, trying to quell the sudden pleasure that made me feel. I could picture his lazy smile and forgot what I was going to say.

'I . . . er . . .'

Get a grip, I told myself, you're a grown woman.

He talked about Drew and her horse and how she was doing well in some weekend event that involved jumping over what sounded like tall buildings and landing in water. I couldn't for the life of me understand why anyone would want to do such a scary, senseless thing, but didn't say so. Simon seemed quite caught up in it, praising Drew's ability, which so far had her placed third in the competition.

I talked about Charlotte and her recent reverence of her father's squeeze — although I didn't call her that — and he commented that the sensitivity of teenagers was on a par with Borat's.

He said he'd like to see me soon. How about next weekend?

I agreed, somewhat breathlessly, aware this was my first 'date' in well over quarter of a century. It felt weird. I promised to phone him during the week with a time and place to meet.

For some strange reason, when I put down the phone, I couldn't remember what I had been doing. After a while though, the pungent smell of oven cleaner reminded me.

'Bugger the oven,' I said to nobody at all, threw the cleaning gear in the laundry sink and left it there.

I day-dreamed all through the facial, imagining myself

turning into a new woman — youthful, beautiful, with a Penelope Cruz complexion — imagining all sorts of romantic scenarios while the aroma of ylang-ylang and orange blossom oil burned in the corner and the miracle woman massaged my face, hopefully wiping away all traces of these past few months. I declined to look in the mirror afterwards to maintain the pretence. Feeling much better, I wafted home, serene and uplifted, calm and confident. Not even the pungent aroma from the unfinished oven could get me down.

It was a different matter on Sunday, of course, the self-indulgence having worn off by then. Serenity had shifted to immunity. When the kids argued, I refused to intervene. When Charlotte complained about the contents of the fridge, I ignored her. When Adam stayed steadfastly in his room playing computer games, I didn't try to lure him out or suggest he try something less antisocial for a change. I gave up on ever being the Mother of the Year and left the kids to it. Instead, I went to see Mum and Dad.

Just like I predicted, Dad hated being at home without Mum and hated it even more having to visit her in the dementia unit. He'd come back to the village from hospital that morning and I arrived right after lunch, bearing flowers and his favourite car magazine. With still no word from Stephanie, I spent the rest of the day with him, trying to help him come to terms with the situation. But it wasn't looking too hopeful. He said just being there with Colleen in the unit for more than half an hour was enough to drive you crazy, and no wonder Mum had deteriorated since she'd been there.

I traversed the long path between their villa and the dementia unit twice with Dad, visiting the office in between to ask once more about Mum's options.

'She'll be fine here with me, lassie,' he kept saying. 'Why

won't they just let me have another chance with her at home? I'm right as rain now.'

But the big-bosomed boss lady wasn't having any of that. The fact that Mum seemed to be worse was proof enough, as far as she was concerned, that she was too much for Dad to handle. The only straw she held out for Dad to grab hold of was the promise of a case review the following week.

I was home just in time to take Charlotte back to Jacinta's apartment — a peculiar feeling as I was usually picking her up at that time after the weekend at her father's. I intended to leave her at the front entrance and make a quick getaway. But Steve, alerted by her texting, was waiting at the door. He came over to the car and made a fuss of getting Charlotte's things.

'How's the old girl, then?'

I gaped, thinking what an immense cheek he had, until it dawned on me he was referring to the car.

'She's going great now,' I replied.

'Yes, I heard about the big end.' I gaped again. Sometimes this town was no more than a village. 'You should have told me, you know, Penny. I could have done it myself.'

I bit back a retort about his own big end, and how he'd clearly been planning on walking out on me for some time.

'I was in a hurry, Steve, I couldn't have her out of action for too long.'

He looked rueful. 'Perfection takes time, you know. Like the Stag, *that's* perfection . . . or at least it was until *you* got hold of it.'

I ignored that.

'Come on, Dad, I've something to show you,' Charlotte interrupted from inside.

Fearful the Conniving Cow might appear behind her any minute, I made an excuse and took off home to cook

Adam a hasty Sunday dinner. After we'd eaten in front of the telly, he cleaned up the kitchen *and* stacked the dishwasher — unheard of when Charlotte was around. The phone rang. It was Stephanie and she sounded in a bit of a state.

'I'm sorry, Penny. You were right. I owe it to Mum and Dad. I'm coming up tomorrow.'

'Good God,' I said, stunned. 'I didn't think you'd . . .'

'No. I didn't think I would either. But I've had a change of heart.' There was a sound of something approaching a sniffle, followed by a sob. Surely my big sister wasn't crying? I started to feel guilty for making her feel so bad. 'I've booked the flight and everything. It gets in at 10.30am. Can you meet me?'

'Good God,' I said again. 'Yes, I suppose so.' I mentally ran through my diary for the morning and thought of the meetings I'd have to change and the work I'd have to postpone. But it would be worth it, I realised, if Stephanie could take some of the parental load off me.

'Good.' She gave me the flight details and rung off.

I sat there, truly amazed, and tried to gather my wits about me.

'What's the matter, Mum?' Adam was passing me on his way back upstairs after his cursory clean of the kitchen. A glance behind him at the detritus still on the bench soon brought me to my senses.

'Your aunt's coming up tomorrow to stay,' I said. 'And the house is in no state to pass her minute inspection. Come on, you can help.'

'But I've just cleaned up the kitchen . . .'

'I know. But it won't be sparkling enough for Stephanie. You can do the rubbish and tidy your room. I'll do the rest.'

I pulled out an array of cleaning stuff and set to, beginning with the oven, which was still lying in wait for me, then speed-cleaned the rest of the kitchen, lounge and spare room. Not even Tigger and his grungy basket escaped my attention. As usual, the more you clean, the more you find that still needs cleaning, so it was almost midnight when I fell into bed, worrying if blackmailing Steph to come was such a good idea.

• • •

It was a significantly subdued-looking Stephanie that arrived off the plane. This time she was lamb dressed as mutton. Beige was back; the sultry sexpot was no more.

It didn't take long to find out why. We'd just turned onto the motorway for the drive home when her phone rang. Uncharacteristically, she turned it off and threw it in her bag.

'You'll be pleased to know the affair with Tim Sayers is over,' she announced dramatically, holding the back of her hand to her forehead. She had all the pathos of a dying cow in a thunderstorm. 'He dropped me like a hot potato last Friday.'

'Oh, I'm sorry.' I wasn't really, of course, but I didn't know what else to say.

She gave a stifled sob. I looked sideways as I switched into the fast lane. There was a real tear in the corner of her eye.

'He left me for the team physio. His name is Barry.' This was accompanied by a louder sob.

'Oh, I'm sorry,' I repeated, still at a loss. Then I realised what she had said. 'Barry? He took up with a *guy*?'

'It's so embarrassing. He's bi. I never picked it.' She looked away out the window. After a while she added, 'I was a sort of a trophy, I suppose. He would tell all his mates how famous I was. I think he saw me as a bit of glamour, an old fag hag. That's what one of his gay friends called me when I ran into him and a bunch of his friends afterwards. Oh, it was hilariously funny at the time, we all laughed and laughed. But I was crying inside. I've never been so insulted.'

Staring sadly out the window, I saw a vulnerable side to my sister I don't recall ever seeing before. Stephanie was weak like the rest of us. And I suspected, also for the first time, she was floundering, out of her depth. Unusually for her, she'd lapped up the young gigolo's flattery and let herself be led into making some very foolish decisions. And now she was exposed to ridicule and a harsh loss of self-esteem.

'I don't think you should put yourself down like that. You're worth ten of him, you know that.'

She didn't answer, just kept staring out the window, dabbing at the tears then blowing her nose.

I figured going to see Mum right away would take her mind off it. But, as it turned out, it only made things worse.

Normally — if there is such a thing as normal with Mum — Steph is the golden-haired girl. Even when Mum moved in to become a fixture in la-la land, she always recognised her older daughter, always had time for her first-born. But not this time.

'Who are these people?' she demanded when Dad took us through to the unit. 'What have you brought them here for?'

'They're your daughters, Colleen,' Dad said patiently. 'Stephanie and Penelope. Stephanie's come all the way on the plane to see you.'

'Nonsense!' Mum declared. 'I don't have daughters. I'm much too young for daughters.'

'Hello, Mum,' Stephanie said, crossing the room to take Mum's hand.

But Mum pulled it away. 'Don't you manhandle me! I

know your tricks. You want to steal my purse. I'm not falling for that.'

She continued to deny all knowledge of us. Dad had at least gained some credence with her. She spoke to him as if to a suitor, flirting with him, harping on about their recent engagement and what a long time it would be before they could afford to get married.

Stephanie looked crushed.

'I guess there's not much point in staying with her when she's like this, lassies,' Dad said dejectedly. 'I'm sorry, after you've come all this way, Stephie. She's not been the best ever since I came home. The nursing staff say she's been like this since I went into hospital.'

'I'd like to stay and sit with her for a while,' Stephanie said bravely. 'I've come all this way . . .'

'Of course, of course.'

'You go, Penny. You've got work to do and a job to go to. I'll stay on. I can get a taxi to your place when I'm done.'

I gave her a spare house key, said my goodbyes and left my sister sitting silent and sad opposite an unknowing mother while Dad kept trying to explain to Mum who Stephanie was.

Steph texted me later to say she was home and Adam had made her a cup of tea. 'Must talk re mum,' the text concluded. 'And Adam,' a second text said moments later.

It was a typical Monday in PR — only crammed into half a day because I'd had to take the morning off to meet Stephanie. The Monday team meeting had been put off until Tuesday, but the various client demands couldn't be put off, so I rushed about putting out fires and typing furiously into my laptop until Nicky's cheery farewell made me realise how late it was. I drove home with Elgar's *Cello Concerto* up loud on the stereo to help me get my thoughts in a row.

The kitchen was pristine. There was no sign of Adam's dirty dishes or food scraps, Tigger was fed and, surprisingly, Charlotte was home.

'Hi, Mum,' she said cheerily. 'Aunt Stephanie texted me she was here so I thought I'd come home for dinner with you all. Hope you don't mind.'

'Mind? I'm delighted.'

'No need to worry what to cook for dinner,' Stephanie breezed into the kitchen. 'It's all in hand. Adam and I are doing a barbecue.' Adam appeared through the ranchslider, barbecue tools in hand.

'It's all cleaned now,' he said to his aunt. 'Ready to go.'

'Good. You go put your feet up, Penny. Adam and I can handle this. Eh, bro?' She gave him a high five as he passed and he grinned.

'You wouldn't like to move in?' I laughed. 'You seem to have the recipe for family harmony.'

'Yeah, well, I'm not doing so well with my family. I thought I'd have a go with yours,' Stephanie smiled wryly. 'Besides, I couldn't sit around here mooching for the rest of the day.'

'Well, I shall make the most of it.' I took myself off upstairs, kicked off my shoes, peeled off my work clothes, changed into something casual and took the morning's paper outside to the deck to catch up on the news — I hadn't had time to read it in the morning rush.

Dinner was a delight. There wasn't a single argument between the kids, Charlotte didn't mention the Conniving Cow once, Adam was almost animated talking to his aunt about school, and Stephanie had clearly buried her hurt beneath the brusque busyness of organising Adam and the dinner. She even managed to get Charlotte and Adam to stack the dishwasher and clean up the kitchen without a row.

Stephanie was out on the terrace beside the barbecue. I put two mugs of coffee on the outdoor table next to her.

'Behind every successful woman is a lot of coffee,' I quipped.

'More like a pile of dirty laundry,' she retorted.

She picked up the mug and blew on it. 'We need to talk about Mum and Dad,' she said, after thanking me. 'I had no idea how bad Mum was.'

'She is pretty bad.'

'It was a tremendous blow today when she didn't recognise me. She's always been fine with me. I couldn't believe it.'

'She's never been this bad before. I wouldn't take it too personally, Steph. I mean, she hasn't recognised me for a long time.'

Stephanie laughed despite herself. 'I know. It used to give me no end of pleasure. I always thought of myself as the special one and that used to sort of confirm it.'

'It used to drive me spare,' I confessed. 'I've always been jealous of you being the favourite. But now we're equals.'

'Yes, equals. That should cheer you up.'

'Not really. Despite being envious of you, it was always a bit of a relief to me when she recognised you. It meant she still had some hold on reality, however fragile. Now that's gone too.'

'Who would have thought I'd be the last sign of sanity, eh?' Stephanie sighed. 'It is sad, though, isn't it? I should have come up when you suggested it the first time. She might have still known me then.'

'It's hard to say if she's got worse because she's in the unit, where she's surrounded by people who are completely off their rocker, or if it would have happened anyway. But Dad is convinced it's because of the company she keeps there. He's convinced if she were back in the villa with him, she'd be just fine.'

'But he can't manage her any more. He's too frail. I can see that now.'

'I know. But there's no way he'll admit it.'

We agreed we needed to present a united front on it to him.

'It's too late tonight. He'll be tucked up in bed with car racing on Sky Sports.' She finished her tea then said, 'Now, tell me about Adam.'

'What's there to tell?'

'He was saying he'd been in trouble at school and that he'd had his cellphone confiscated.'

'Oh?' This was news to me.

'He was a bit coy about what had caused it all. Hopefully he's learned his lesson. He said he'd had to apologise to everyone. He hated it, but he had to do it, and he said things had been a lot better at school since.'

'Did he now,' I said, annoyed that I had to receive this piece of information from my sister instead of my son. 'Well, I'm glad to hear it. Maybe he'll settle down.'

'Here's hoping.'

We brought our empty cups inside and closed the door — the air had grown chilly.

I left Steph pottering around in the guest room and checked on Adam. He was engrossed in homework; I left him to it and decided not to mention the phone confiscation. Charlotte had brought an overnight bag and stayed on. She was still in bed when Steph and I left in the morning to see Dad.

'Let her sleep,' Stephanie said. 'She told me her lectures didn't start today until midday.'

'To tell the truth, it's nice to have her here. Especially with you around. She seems a lot calmer.'

'Must be you who winds her up then.' Stephanie prodded me in the ribs as we walked the path to the car.

I laughed hollowly. 'You're probably right. The more Charlotte talks about Jacinta, the more neurotic I become. Maybe I should take what she'd call a chill pill.'

Dad was fussing around with his breakfast dishes when we arrived. The sports pages were open on the dining table, next to a pile of accounts from St Joan's.

'Here, Penny and I will do the dishes, Dad. You sit down.'

'This is indeed a pleasure, having you both to myself like this,' Dad said, pulling out the dining chair he'd not long vacated. 'I'm a truly lucky man to have two such loving daughters.' He sat down, picked up the accounts and waved them around. 'These people know how to charge like wounded bulls. There's not a single item they give away. Look, they even charge for aspirin.' He stabbed his other forefinger at one of the bills.

'Well, look at it this way, Dad. Once you've spent all your money, the Government pays.'

'That's what is so fearful about this terrible business. I wanted to be able to leave you provided for.'

'There's no need to worry about us, Dad. We don't need any money. We're all doing fine.'

'Just the same, Penny, you never know what might happen. A wee nest egg for you both, that's what I hoped for.'

'We should have had one of those family trusts years ago,' Steph said. 'But we didn't. So we just have to accept it, Dad and pay up.'

'Well, at this rate, it won't take long for it all to go. The fees for that unit your poor mother is in are simply enormous. And it's not doing her a bit of good. She'd be much better . . .'

'I know, Dad,' Stephanie interrupted. 'But it's out of the question. You know it is. You're in no condition to look after her. The management here just won't let you.'

He looked downcast. 'They don't understand, lassie. I'm not myself without Colleen around.'

'But you're not yourself *with* her either, Dad,' I said. 'She's too much for you.'

'She's never too much for me. 'Til death do us part, I promised. And I don't like being parted unnecessarily.'

'Maybe I should have her at home, somehow. Have you both there,' I said.

'Don't be silly, Penny. You can't possibly. You've got enough on your plate with those two kids and that crazy dog. Where would Mum and Dad go?'

'But I feel I should. I can't bear seeing you suffer without her, Dad.'

'Nonsense, lassie. I wouldn't expect you to take us both on. Your mother's a sandwich short of a picnic these days, that's for sure.'

I can't say I was all that keen on the idea, but I felt I had to offer. But I still felt guilty I couldn't somehow wave a magic wand and make it all come right for him.

He was not to be moved: he wanted Mum back home with him and that was the end of it.

'What about both of you moving over to the main building where Mum can have nursing care?' Stephanie threw in after we'd realised we were getting nowhere.

'Could she? I didn't know about that.' Dad's eyes lit up.

'I don't think they'll let you,' I said, annoyed with Stephanie for throwing in such a useless red herring. 'They're quite insistent on Mum staying in the dementia unit. They say she's a safety issue now, that she has to be in a secure place where she can't wander off and get lost.'

'But I can keep an eye on her. I can make sure she doesn't wander off.'

'I know, Dad. But even with the best will in the world you can't watch her every minute of the day. She's already taken off a couple of times when you were looking the other way.' I was getting even more annoyed. I was the meanie destroying Dad's hopes while Steph was the good fairy trying to help him. Except she didn't have a clue what she was talking about.

'Then what about having a minder?' Dad said. 'There's enough money to pay for someone to help me out during the day. It would only have to be for as long as she's awake. I might as well use what money we've got left to pay for something that would make Colleen's life a bit better.'

I couldn't argue with that so the three of us traipsed over to the office to see the boss lady who was, as luck would have it, out. It meant having to come back at 3pm, which would nicely disrupt the entire afternoon's work, but it would be worth it to get the matter sorted.

Steph decided to take Dad shopping for some shirts and a pair of shoes as well as groceries, so Dad squeezed into the back seat and I dropped them off at the mall with a work taxi chit to get back to the villa and went on into the office.

After catching up on messages (seven people to phone), emails (thirty-three to answer, the rest could wait), spam (sixty-two to wipe out) and swapping weekend stories with the girls (two horror stories from Ginny beat my one), I immersed myself in the olive oilers, who were finally starting to get the sort of publicity they wanted — thanks to the hunky Panos, who charmed the young female foodie writers without any difficulty at all. I suspected he was shagging at least one of them.

But I was so worried about Dad that even the attractions of Panos couldn't hold my attention for too long. As usual when I needed comfort, I turned to food, and mooched off to the bakery down the road for some nice starchy rolls, savouries and — the ultimate — doughnuts. They were to share with the others, I told myself, but I knew I'd end up eating most of them — Ginny never ate before dark, Tracey usually brought a neat little lunchbox filled with a healthy sandwich, yoghurt and fruit, and Nicky was back on the South Beach Diet so she could wear her tight-fitting flame red bridesmaid's dress for her sister's Easter wedding.

I wedged myself into the low-slung seat of Crackling Rosie and took off for St Joan's again, my tummy full to bursting, resenting being squashed over by the bucket seat. Of course I'd immediately regretted the excessive intake of food but the mere thought of throwing up makes me queasy so I just had to bear it. Literally. I waddled across the courtyard of the retirement village and met Steph and Dad outside the boss lady's office.

Mrs Small (a particularly inapt name, I thought) treated Stephanie like royalty.

'Call me Paula, please,' she said obsequiously to my sister, who'd assumed a regal bearing in response to Paula Small's adoration — quite a change from the quietly unhappy person she'd been since she arrived. 'My daughter Bethany is one of your greatest fans. Oh, if only I'd known you were coming I'd have brought in some of her books for you to sign. Oh dear, she would have been just over the moon. Oh dear, if only I'd known.' The normally assertive, tubby-faced Mrs Small was all of a fluster. If I hadn't been just a wee bit envious I would have found it funny.

But she soon reasserted her fiefdom when Steph asked if Mum could move back in with Dad. It was out of the question, she said, repeating for Stephanie's benefit why Mum needed to be in secure care.

'But what if she had a minder with her the whole time she's awake? We'd be prepared to pay for someone to keep an eye on her and make sure she doesn't wander off.'

'Do you have any idea how much it would cost to have someone specially assigned? That would be two people on eight-hour shifts every day of the year.' She gave us a figure and even Steph blanched.

But she wasn't to be deterred. 'We could split that three ways,' she said, turning to me and Dad. 'We could afford it then.'

All very well for you, I thought, with your advances in the thousands and overseas sales earning you money while you sleep.

'No, you two mustn't be involved. I can take care of this myself.' Dad looked at both of us, alarmed.

'We can talk about this later,' I said, not wanting to get into a family row in front of the boss lady.

'But it's certainly worth thinking about, isn't it?' Steph said. 'See, I told you there was a way around this.'

I ignored her. 'Come on, Dad. We can discuss it over a cuppa.'

Back at his villa I fiddled about with cups and tea bags while Steph went over the accounts with Dad.

'Penny and I will help out, Dad. You just can't do this

on your own, much as you'd like to. Look, you've got all this tied up in fixed term accounts. You can't get that out without losing big-time. And after that, there's not much left. If you pay for it all yourself, you'll run out before too long. No, you have to let us help.'

I gritted my teeth. Without the joint income I'd been used to, the household accounts had started to look decidedly sick. How on earth was I supposed to find several hundred dollars more every week? Even divided into three, full-time care for Mum was still a sizeable sum. Yet I was riddled with guilt at the thought of saying no. How could I deny my father what he wanted most?

In the end, I had a quiet word with Steph on the way home, pointing out my impecuniousness. She gallantly offered to pay more than me since she could easily afford it, which made my contribution almost affordable, but only added further to my guilt.

It was too late to go back to work by then so I made a pretence at being a domestic goddess and cooked a fancy three-course meal for the four of us (Charlotte had come back again after lectures), which, as the kids commented, was almost unheard of.

'You should come more often, Aunt Stephanie,' Adam said with his mouth still half full of nectarine and peach clafoutis. 'Mum goes all-out to impress whenever you're here.'

'Thanks,' I said sarcastically. 'I was hoping Steph would think we always eat like this.'

'It's great having you here,' Charlotte added. 'You don't get in a titch like Mum does.'

'Your poor mother! You don't know how lucky you are, you two. I'd get in a great big titch if I were in her shoes, the way you treat her.'

And she proceeded to tell Adam off for being so taciturn and Charlotte for being so insensitive.

'How do you think she feels when you go off to your father and his new girlfriend's? Are you deliberately setting out to hurt her?'

Charlotte looked taken aback then flushed with what I hoped was embarrassment, if not shame.

'No, Aunt Stephanie,' she said quietly. 'I didn't mean to hurt her. I never thought . . .'

'No, that's the trouble with teenagers. You just don't think. But heavens Charlotte, you're nearly eighteen. You're old enough to know better.'

'Well, I suppose I could come home more often.'

'You could?' This was news to me.

'Yes.' She kept looking at Steph. 'I don't think Jacinta wants me around so much any more. She's started saying things, like how nice it would be to have just five minutes to herself, or like the treadmill is never free when she wants it, or why can't she watch what she wants on TV any more.'

'Oh,' Steph said, kicking me under the table. 'And has your father said anything?'

'No, he's never around when she says that stuff.'

'Well, I'm sure your mother would be delighted to have you back.' Steph shot me a questioning look; I nodded.

'Of course I would, honey. You know I never wanted you to go in the first place.'

'I know.' There was a big sigh. 'I was afraid you'd say "I told you so" or something.'

'Who, me?' No doubt it would have occurred to me, but not right now. I was far too ecstatic. I stood up from the dining table and she let me hug her. 'Would you like me to take you over in Rosie and pick up your things?'

'No, I'd better go back for the rest of the week. Jacinta's got stuff planned for me. I'll tell her later on. When she's in the right mood.'

'I'll clear up, Mum,' Adam offered. I nearly fell flat into my clafoutis crumbs. 'Charlotte can stack.'

She didn't even argue.

'Let's make the most of it and sit outside while it's still warm,' I said and led Steph out onto the terrace.

We sat companionably catching the last of the sun, talking through what would happen with Mum and Dad, when Steph's cellphone rang inside somewhere.

'Bother,' she said. 'I'd better get it.' She ran inside and after a few moments it stopped ringing. I heard her say hello to someone, then silence. She'd obviously taken it into the hall out of earshot. I eased back into the canvas chair and thought about Dad and how much happier he'd be when Steph and I told him we'd made all the arrangements for Mum to live with him again. I was still more than a little anxious about how I'd find the extra two hundred a week; I'd just have to work harder and get less distracted at work. Hopefully, with Dad happy and Mum under surveillance, I wouldn't have to spend so much time rushing backwards and forwards to the retirement village. And if the kids could stay as settled as they'd been lately, I might be able to concentrate more on catch-up work in the evenings.

'Oh dear. I think I'm in trouble.' Steph came back out on the terrace clutching her mobile, now firmly shut.

'Why, what's happened?'

'That was Marcus.' She plumped herself down in the chair opposite and put her head in her hands. 'He was upset about something but he wouldn't say what.' She looked up, elbows resting on her knees, chin cupped in her hands. 'He's insisting I come home right away. Says he wants to "taaaalk" to me. Like he's going to read me the riot act or something.'

'Oh. What do you think it's about?'

'I have a horrible feeling he's found out.'

'But how could he . . . ?'

'God only knows. I cleaned out my email before I came up, and I'm sure I haven't left anything around the house. I was so careful.'

'Then perhaps it's something else.'

'I sure hope so. It'd be just my luck that as soon as the affair is over, Marcus gets to hear of it. I mean, it's *over*.' She dropped her head in her hands again, a picture of despair.

I didn't know what to say. Ever since she'd told me she was bonking a fellow young enough to be her son, who also happened to be a heart-throb sports jock chased after by the media, I'd had a feeling there would be tears before bedtime, not to mention long after they'd vacated the extra-marital scratcher. But now I just felt sorry for her. She'd been duped by a young social climber, she'd lost her self-esteem and now it looked like she might lose her marriage and her reputation as well. I surprised myself: I'd always envied Steph her lot in life, always hoped her pride would lead to a fall. And now it had, I should have been joyously gloating. But I wasn't. All I felt was pity and just a teensy bit heartened that my hitherto perfect sister was human too.

She booked a flight home the next morning then we went back to St Joan's to see Dad and tell him she had to return home to help Seraya sort out a problem. I let her tell Dad that Mrs Small was finding two aides to work back-to-back shifts keeping an eye on Mum and as soon as they could start, Mum could come home. Dad still grumbled about wanting to pay for it, but he did finally admit that he wouldn't be able to sustain the payments for very long on his own. He was still showering us with thanks when we were back at the car.

'I suppose we've done the right thing,' Stephanie sighed when she got into the car next to me.

'It's a bit late to have doubts now. You've just told him it's all going to happen.'

'I know. It's just that he's so frail. I hope he can manage.'

'The minders will make sure he doesn't try to do too much. Besides, if Paula Small thinks it's okay, who are we to argue?'

'Yeah, I suppose. Mind you, Paula Small and her rest home are making a big pile of money out of the arrangement.' She pulled a wry face. 'I hope it works out. You must promise to let me know at once if there are any problems.'

I promised and we drove home.

Steph spent quite a bit of time with Adam and Charlotte before they went to bed then popped into my room to say goodnight.

'They're great kids, Penny. You've done really well with them since Steve left.'

'You think so? For a while there things were pretty dire.'

'Nothing you wouldn't expect after what he did to them.'

'Yes, but the fall-out seems to have been going on for so long.'

'I wouldn't worry too much, if I were you. Charlotte's quite chastened now. A bit like me.'

Chapter 12

I didn't hear from Steph for three days. In the meantime, Dad and I walked Mum out of the dementia unit and escorted her back to the villa, where a man wearing a navy and cream St Joan's polo shirt and crisply creased navy slacks was busying himself making tea.

'Ah, there you are,' he said pleasantly. 'I'm Nathan Woodhouse. I'm your minder until after lunch. Trudy will be here at 2pm to take over.' He went over to greet Mum and Dad. 'How are you again, Mrs Rushmore? Ron? Let me help you with those things.'

'Who's he?' Mum asked.

'Nathan. You know, he's looking after us now. You met him yesterday.'

'Nonsense. Never seen him before in my life.' She looked at Nathan disdainfully. 'If you're going to be looking after me, young man, you'd better learn how to make a decent cup of tea.'

I gave Nathan a sympathetic smile but he didn't seem at all perturbed about being given a lesson in heating the pot and turning it round three times before pouring it into her favourite china cups. Mrs Small had said the minders were fully trained in dementia care, so I figured he had the patience of a saint.

I stayed with them until the tea was finished and helped Mum put away her clothes — though she insisted on doing most of it herself, resulting in her nighties being left in a neat pile in the linen cupboard. I managed to extract her toiletries from the pantry and put them back in the bathroom when she wasn't looking and I left her and Dad happily watching ballet on television — although I suspected that Dad's blissful smile was due entirely to Mum being back with him and had nothing to do with the dancing, which he'd always detested.

That night after work I honoured one of my New Year's resolutions and cleaned out the study. I'd been meaning to give it a good going-over ever since Steve left. But every time I'd passed the study door, I'd managed to find an excuse not to do it. I hate throwing things away — to me junk is something you keep for years and inevitably chuck out two weeks before you need it. But this time I steeled myself to do it.

I filled five supermarket bags with rubbish from the drawers and shelves and gave the wooden desktop a thorough clean and polish before arranging everything back on it. Standing back to admire my handiwork, I noticed the digital camera sitting on top of the bookcase. I must have put it there when I got back from the tramping trip and forgotten all about it. I picked it up, sat down and pressed the 'on' button, intending to amuse myself with the photos stored in its memory. Typically, I hadn't saved anything off the camera onto my laptop photo file for a while.

The first pictures to come up on the camera's little display panel were from way back in December: Charlotte with her prize; Charlotte, Adam and me going to the ball; and Christmas Day pictures of Mum and Dad, Stephanie and the kids, with us all looking as if we didn't want to be there — except for Mum, of course, who didn't know where she was.

A few frames later and I was transported to the Abel Tasman, with me cavorting on the beach, me and the girls in our tramping gear in the rain, grinning like drowned Cheshire cats. Then, unexpectedly, there was Simon, smiling that lazy smile, in front of an azure sky and a beach of white-gold sand. I'd forgotten about that photo; in the rush and drama of coming back home it had completely slipped my mind. But there he was a world away in a long-departed paradise, looking extremely sexy.

It made me realise with a jolt just how much I liked him and reminded me it was time to phone and finalise the arrangements for Friday night. Not that I hadn't been thinking of him, but I'd been nervous about making the call and had put it off. I resolved then and there to phone. No reply. As soon as his answerphone clicked on, I left a message saying I'd call back the next day.

Unfortunately, things were so frantic at work all day I didn't have a moment to myself until after I'd popped in to see Mum and Dad.

Mum was her usual dotty self, convinced I was one of the nurses plotting to lock her up again until I calmed her down. Luckily she hadn't taken a dislike to Trudy, the minder, who was calmly sitting at the dining table watching over Mum ensconced on the sofa in front of the telly. Dad resumed his seat beside her and I went to talk to Trudy.

'How's Mum been?' I asked, knowing the sound of the TV would cover our conversation.

'Nothing untoward, really,' Trudy said. 'Nothing you wouldn't have seen or heard before.' She gave me a sympathetic smile. 'She's kept me on the hop though. It's been good to sit down for a bit.'

'What's that? Are you two talking about me? I know you are. I don't miss much, you know.'

'It's all right, Mum. We're just talking about getting some supper.'

'Tuh!' Mum expostulated. 'The food in this hotel is no good. They should all be given the sack.'

Dad ignored that with the practised art of the Alzheimer's caregiver and diverted her interest back to the television set. He'd sacrificed Sky Sports to watch an old musical with Mum on the TCM channel.

After a while, grateful I wasn't needed and that everything seemed to be working out, I said my farewells. I knew better than to try to kiss Mum goodbye any more — the last time I'd tried it you'd think I'd tried to sexually assault her. I'd come to accept over time that there was a barrier between us, a barrier it just wasn't worth trying to cross.

There was no sign of Adam when I got home, and no note. I made the most of the quiet house and dialled Simon's home number.

'Hi,' Drew answered.

She scared me, that girl. I nearly hung up, but steeled myself to keep going.

'Er, hi. This is Penny Rushmore. Is Simon there, please?'

'Yeah. Hang on.'

The sound of clumping feet was followed by, 'Dad, it's that woman who fell over on the track,' followed by a banging door.

'Hi, is that you, Penny?'

'Er, yes. Hi.' Unexpectedly, I felt a rush of shyness. 'I er, I . . . I'm sorry I didn't phone you earlier. I've been so busy I . . .'

'That's okay. I understand. Me too.'

There was a pause during which my stomach knotted and my mind went blank. Get a grip, I told myself firmly.

We arranged to meet at 7pm the next night at a bar not far from the waterfront, halfway between both our places. After I'd put the phone down, I couldn't think of anything else — how I'd get there (was it too far to walk, should I take a taxi?), what I'd tell Adam (nothing? Everything?) and most important of all, what I'd wear (something low-cut and sexy? Something demure and cute? Something straight from work?). And would I have time to get home after work, take a shower, change and make myself gorgeous in the space of three quarters of an hour? Knowing the major roadworks required to knock my face into shape these days, the required transformation wasn't looking too hopeful.

• • •

I rushed through Friday, compacting everything into half the time so I could be out the door early.

Charlotte was staying with Gemma for the weekend. You could tell Adam had been home though. He'd dropped his school gear in a trail from the door to the kitchen, eaten, dropped wrappers and juice cartons from the cupboard to the sink just short of the rubbish, gone upstairs, dropped his clothes on the floor of the bathroom, had a shower, dropped the towel on the floor of his room, and gone to work at McDonald's, where he was undoubtedly neat and tidy and never dropped anything anywhere.

Today, I didn't care about the mess. It could stay where it was until tomorrow. Today I was looking after number one: me, myself and I!

Despite having planned what I was going to wear and how simple it would be to accomplish a quick change, I ended up discarding the chosen outfit and seven others before I settled on something that didn't seem too loud, too frumpy, too sexy, too wimpy, too casual, overdressed, underdressed, or make my bum look big. Even then, I wasn't sure it was the right thing. It was black of course, which is supposed to hide a multitude of sins and chins and other unsightly features. The top had one of those square, set-back necklines and showed off still summer-brown skin without revealing the batwing underarms that become so embarrassing over the age of forty-something. The skirt was slightly flouncy and showed a bit of ankle. The shoes were slightly high, but not so high as to look tarty nor so strappy as to lay bare the entire foot.

The make-up was another problem altogether. My lips were rubbed sore from trying different colours, deciding the red made me look like a drag queen and the pink belonged on a girl half my age. I finally settled for a conservative rose, and was applying the final touches to my eye make-up (which was also showing drag-queen tendencies) when the cab I'd ordered tooted in the driveway. I looked at my watch. There was no time to clean up. For once, I left the discarded clothes and shoes scattered where they were, across the bed and around the bedroom floor.

As soon as the cab swept away around the corner, I wished I'd worn trousers and the little pink tweed jacket I'd picked up in the January sales. But it was too late to change — I was running late already for my first date in over twenty-five years and I was so nervous, I feared if I turned back now, I might chicken out and not go at all.

Simon was already at the bar when I arrived. He had commandeered an outside table with a view over the harbour — a couple had just left, he explained triumphantly as he greeted me warmly and complimented me on my appearance. I thanked him and we sat down together to discuss the wine list. On his recommendation, I opted for the pinot gris and he ordered two.

I don't know if it was the wine relaxing me or the company entrancing me, but the evening seemed enchanted. The time flew. He turned out to have a sense of humour that made everything suddenly seem incredibly funny. He didn't tell jokes as such, but his anecdotes, his wit and the way he told his stories had me in stitches. I haven't laughed so much in a long time. Not even when we were rolling with mirth at a Philosophical Society meeting, holding our sides they hurt so much, had the hilarity been so sustained or, more truthfully, tickled my fancy quite so much.

Not that it was all one-sided, I hasten to add. I did manage to make some contribution to the evening's entertainment, spurred on by anecdotes of teenage dramas and holiday disasters — I had plenty of those to recall.

'Ah, you've got to laugh, don't you?' he said after telling a bittersweet story about his daughter and her last horse: the mare had lingered and had to be put down, but the way he related Drew's dramatic overreaction and demands of a burial service requiring the services of an enormous digger/'dozer plus eight strong men to lower the poor animal into the grave had to be heard to be appreciated. 'If we weren't able to laugh at some of our predicaments, we'd drown ourselves in tears.'

I confided about my mother — a subject I rarely raised with anyone — and even managed to see the funny side of some of her antics, like the time I arrived to find her extracting Anzac biscuits off the baking tray with a fly swat instead of a spatula and the time she'd put cat food in the microwave to heat for lunch. His mother's closest friend had Alzheimer's, he said, and he knew how sad it had been for her to watch the slow deterioration into constant dementia, powerless to help or to stop it.

We seemed able to talk about anything, to share all sorts of intimate secrets about ourselves and our families. I completely lost track of time. The sun had long set and the harbour had become a series of twinkling lights; the waterfront a passing parade of revellers, not all of them completely upright. It was after midnight when he dropped me home in the taxi.

'Would you like to come in?' I asked, feeling like giggling at the cliché of those words and wondering if he felt as nervous as I did.

'Thank you, Penny, I would.' He grinned in that lazy way again, his eyes twinkling — whether with mirth, sexual excitement or embarrassment I didn't know. He paid the cab and we went in together. Adam, thankfully, had gone to a schoolfriend's after they both finished work at McDonald's. Charlotte had yet to fulfil her promise of returning home from Jacinta's. I couldn't have planned it better — or worse. I wasn't sure I could handle this! I remembered the terrible mess I'd left in the bedroom and hoped we didn't get that far. But at the same time, I hoped we did.

Tigger greeted Simon like a long-lost friend, even though

it was the first time he'd set eyes on him. I found him a biscuit then shut him firmly in the laundry with his basket beside the dog door. I didn't want Tigger getting in the way; it would be typical of him to try to hijack Simon's attention or jump all over us in the middle of a passionate moment — if there were actually going to be any such moments.

'Would you like a nightcap?' I asked. 'A glass of wine? I'm sorry, I don't have anything else. I don't even have beer any more . . .' I tailed off, realising how pathetic that sounded.

'Don't worry about it.' He smiled again.

'Oh, that is, I do have some brandy still,' I hedged. I wasn't sure if I was ready for this looking-in-the-eyes stuff yet. 'Would you like . . . ?'

'Hey, why not? Let's have one for luck.'

I smiled nervously back. Luck for what? I wondered. Would we need a lot of luck? I figured *I* would. I didn't recall feeling so nervous since Steve gave me a skydiving experience for my fortieth birthday. I'd wondered at the time, poised to jump out of the doorway at twenty-thousand feet, if he was trying to kill me off.

I fumbled my way through pouring the brandy, spilling some on the sideboard. And as I passed him his glass, my hands shook uncontrollably.

'Thanks,' he said, taking the glass and folding his hand over mine for a moment, steadying it.

He raised the glass and inhaled. 'Ah, a fine drop.' He savoured it slowly — a nice change from Steve's draining slurps — and smiled over the rim of his glass. 'I don't drink brandy very often, but I do appreciate a good drop like this when I do. Cheers.'

I refrained from telling him it was one of Steve's prized possessions that he had omitted to stash away in his suitcases the night he left. I also refrained from imbibing — I'd fulfilled my promise to myself to cut down on the drinking, and besides, it would not be a good look to pass out on the sofa on my first date.

My first date! How weird that felt. Even with a couple of glasses of wine on board and inhibitions lower than the hearth rug, I still couldn't come to grips with it. And I was even less able to cope with the situation I currently found myself in. Just thinking about it made me jumpy.

'I'd like to . . .' he started.

'I'll put a CD on,' I said at the same time, hurrying over to the stereo in the corner. 'What do you like? Something old? Something new?'

'Something borrowed or blue?' he finished, chuckling. Suddenly, he was right behind, bending over the CD stack with me, brushing against my neck and back, making me prickle with anticipation.

Goosebumps appeared on my bare arms and a funny feeling stirred deep within me — a feeling I'd parked somewhere many, many years ago.

'Here, let me help you with that.'

He reached out and walked his fingers up and down the rack for a moment then selected one — Bic Runga singing live with an orchestra. I slipped it into the player and turned it on, quickly turning down the volume when it came out at Adam's deafening decibel level.

'Don't you love it when they do that to you?' he said, smiling as he stood, never taking his eyes off mine. 'I reckon the next generation will be stone deaf before they're twenty.'

'I know.' I laughed. 'But I remember my mother saying just the same thing.'

'Yeah, mine too.' His eyes were still piercing into mine, drawing me in. I straightened up and stood next to him, not knowing whether to move back to the sofa or follow my instincts and lean into him.

He put one arm around me and pulled me towards him, then pressed his lips against mine, his soft beard tickling against my chin, a totally new sensation for me. But I didn't want to giggle; it was strangely sensual. I kissed him back, slowly, hesitantly, then more insistently as the stirring I'd felt before took control of me and urged me to go further, deeper, throw away caution, abandon reason.

'Hey,' he said softly. 'That was nice.'

'Yes,' I whispered. 'Let's do it again.'

He wrapped both arms around me and we slow-danced to the music, locked in a kiss that felt like forever.

It seemed but a movement from there to the bedroom. Thankfully he went to the bathroom on the way so I had a moment to scoop up my unworn clothes and shoes and deposit them in the bottom of the wardrobe, jamming the door shut before they could tumble out.

By the light from the hall, I started to undress but he was right behind me, unzipping my skirt, lifting my top over my head. Suddenly, I felt exposed. When he started fingering the clasp on my bra I stopped him.

'Let me,' I said, conscious of his hands against my skin and aware that any second my breasts would be in full view.

He let go while I took off my bra and came around to stand in front of me. I pulled back involuntarily, covering my breasts with my arms; I felt shy. Although the bedroom light wasn't on, I felt as if I were under a spotlight and I wanted to hide. I'd never felt terribly proud of my body, it had always been a bit of a disappointment to me — too chubby, too short, too freckled, too fair. And lately, the cellulite had started to make its crinkly appearance at the top of my legs and a roll had appeared around my middle. One morning I'd woken up and poof, I swear it came from nowhere. Ever since, I'd been trying to keep it hidden, buying forgiving stretch-fabric clothes.

He seemed to understand. Gently, he took my hands and pulled them towards his belt. Unsteadily, I fumbled with the buckle and undid it, then even more shakily started to pull down the zip. He put his hand over mine and helped, dropping his pants and his undies on the floor. Then, with a swift motion, he pulled off his open-neck shirt and was naked. Tentatively, hardly believing this was happening, I stroked the hairs on his chest in a gentle downward movement, down to his navel then, bravely, beyond. He shivered.

Without saying anything, he reached out and guided me towards the bed. I sat on the edge, scared to go further. He sat beside me and surrounded me with his arms, his body, his smell, his being. Together, we fell slowly back onto the duvet and lay there for a moment, taking each other in.

Again, instinctively, I tried to cover myself with my hands, using the corner of the duvet to help hide myself away. I wasn't used to such scrutiny. I shied away from it. I didn't like him seeing all my imperfections at once.

'Don't hide yourself away from me, Penny.' Languidly, he bent down and started to kiss me all over, down, down past my navel, down to my panties. He slipped them off while continuing to cover me with kisses. I felt my breath quicken. He kept on stroking, kissing, teasing until I was breathless.

He pulled away and reached over to the side of the bed where his trousers lay on the floor and pulled out a condom. It threw me for a moment, the sight of him extracting it from the packet and putting it on. I'd not seen one of those since Steve and I first started dating all those years ago. But as soon as he resumed his well-aimed ministrations on my body, I forgot all about it and I was transported into the realms of erotica; all concerns about how I looked, about my body, about my faults, had disappeared.

Afterwards, we said nothing. We just lay there smiling into each other's eyes, replete.

• • •

I awoke to a delicious tickling sensation on my inner thigh; I responded by stroking his leg and we made love again, slower this time, more surely. I must have fallen asleep again immediately afterwards because the next thing I knew the sun was shining behind the bedroom blinds and I was lying there semi-exposed amid the rumpled duvet with a bare white sheet covering the space where Simon should have been.

'Hey, sunshine, it's time for breakfast,' he called from the doorway. 'I've brought you something to replenish your energies after last night.'

He deposited a tray of coffee and croissants on his side of the bed and handed me the heavy weekend paper.

'Thank you. What a treat. Where did you . . . ?' As I looked across at him I caught sight of my semi-naked body. 'Oh my God.' I started to cover myself up, spilling the coffee onto the tray as I did so. 'Oh, sorry, oh no.' I hadn't felt so flustered in a long time. The thought of Simon seeing my cellulite and my excessively padded curves embarrassed me beyond belief.

'Hey, what are you doing? Don't cover up that beautiful body. It's been my inspiration since I awoke this morning.'

I gave up pulling on the sheets and duvet and covered my bare chest by turning on my side and folding one arm in front of it. 'Sorry about the coffee.'

'No problem.' He dashed out and returned with a roll of toilet paper. 'Not terribly romantic, is it? But I couldn't find the napkins.' He mopped up the coffee and crumpled the soggy paper in a ball in his hand.

'How did you find anything down there? It's such a mess. And the croissants . . . ?'

'I'm an early riser,' he said chirpily. 'I was up ages ago, so I took Tigger down to the shops for a paper and found the bakery.'

Morning people have advantages, I thought. Steve had been an early riser but had never in living memory used the extra time to whip out for croissants, or anything for that matter. For him, an early start to the day meant more time to tinker with engines or join his corporate mates for a round of over-par golf.

'I'm afraid I've never been great in the mornings. I'm more of a night owl myself.'

'You look just great to me,' he whispered, leaning across the tray carefully and giving me a lingering kiss. 'You *are* great.' Pulling back from the kiss, he gave me a knowing smile. 'And there's nothing I'd like more than to prove that again. But I mustn't let your breakfast get cold.'

I sat up cautiously, not daring to fiddle with the covers any more, trying to ignore my bareness, and buttered the warm croissant. I'd never been one for wearing lots to bed, but neither was I the sort that pranced round the bedroom showing off my body; my body was not the showing-off kind. So having Simon looking at me now made me feel totally self-conscious. Only when he looked away to deal to his pastry did I relax a little.

It wasn't until I finished my coffee that I could move safely to scoop the bedclothes up to my neck.

'You shouldn't be so scared of letting me see you,' he said, noticing immediately. 'You've a lovely soft, warm, curvy body.'

I didn't know what to say other than 'Thank you.' For me, a curvy body had meant never fitting into the clothes I wanted to buy and mid-life had seen the firmness in my breasts and other bits stretch and flop like perished knicker elastic.

'I can see you don't believe me. I'm going to have to prove it to you, I can see.' He lifted the tray onto the floor where I could hear Tigger making a swoop on the plates. 'Hey, you greedy little dog, that's enough.' Simon picked up the tray and deposited it high on the dresser, well out of Tigger's reach, then shooed him out of the bedroom, firmly closing the door. 'Now, where were we?' He looked at me mischievously. 'Ah, yes. Your nice, soft curves. Why is it, I wonder, that you don't appreciate them as much as I do?' He grinned as he flung himself onto the bed, reached under the covers I'd pulled protectively over me and started to fondle my breasts. 'That's better.'

He continued to look into my eyes, smiling his lazy, sexy smile, while stroking first my left breast, then my right, his motions becoming firmer, my resistance becoming weaker.

Suddenly he paused and his eyes switched from teasing to a look of concern. He started to say something then stopped, looking away.

'What's the matter?'

'There's . . . I don't know how to say this . . . It's not my . . . Look, did you know you have a lump on your right breast?'

I gasped. 'What? You're joking?'

'There's a lump. Just here.' He touched me under my right breast, not far from my armpit, the exact same spot I'd felt a lump a few months earlier.

'Oh, yes,' I said relieved. 'I felt it ages ago. But it was sort of squishy and moveable. It's bound to be a cyst.'

'Do you know that for sure?'

'Well, I didn't go to the doctor if that's what you mean. I'm sure it's a cyst.'

'Hmmm. Well, just the same, I think you should have it checked out. Better to be sure about something like that.'

'I suppose so.' I was annoyed he'd found it; it had completely spoiled the moment. I pulled the covers tightly around me again and sat up, my arms folded across my chest.

'Hey, don't be cross with me.'

'I'm not.'

'If that look you're giving me isn't cross, I'd hate to see what is!'

I looked away. 'I'm embarrassed, that's all. I can't believe that the first time we sleep together, something like this happens.'

'I can understand that. But I couldn't not say anything. It's not something you can ignore.'

I couldn't look at him. Instead, I picked up the paper and stared with little interest at the front-page headlines.

'Oh, look,' I said to change the subject, 'the man who abused that little girl has finally come forward and admitted it.'

'Penny, please don't push me away. At least promise me you'll go and see the doctor on Monday.'

'I'll think about it.' I continued to stare at the paper until Simon pulled the top of it down and tried to catch my eye. 'All right, I'll give her a call. I promise.'

'Good.' He leaned forward across the paper and gave me a gentle kiss then pushed himself off the bed, rearranged his clothes and went over to the window.

I turned back to the paper to distract myself — I just didn't want to think about it — and noticed an interview with Stephanie promo'd on the front of one of the sections. I flicked straight to it and read:

'Young-adult fiction writer Stephanie Scanlan has hit the jackpot with a tale for grown-ups this time. Rooted in New Zealand's history, *Diary of a Suffragette* swaps the realms of fantasy her young characters have inhabited all these years for the tough reality of the suffragette struggle to win the vote in 1893.'

'Crap!' I said out loud, without meaning to.

'What's crap?' Simon said, turning back from the window.

'This *Diary of a Suffragette* stuff. Pure crap!'

'Oh, that. It's been all over the papers and the radio lately, that book. Isn't it any good?'

'No, it's not that. It's fine. It's just . . . she's my sister.'

'Your sister? Crikey. Just as well I didn't say anything bad about it.' He came back over to the bed to sit beside me.

'Oh, it wouldn't matter if you did. Half of me hates this and half of me is proud of her for doing it.'

'Yeah?' He sounded like he didn't get it.

'It's our family history she's telling everybody and I'm not sure I like it.'

'Sometimes history has to be told so we can learn from it, learn not to make the same mistakes.'

'True. I hadn't thought of that. The thing is, I'm probably envious I didn't think of it first.'

I opened out the paper, gave it a shake to close the page

and folded it in half, placing it firmly on the bed. It had only just occurred to me that all the mumbo-jumbo I'd been coming out with, saying I resented having our family's story paraded in public, was a cover for envy. That was it: pure and simple. Children's authors never seemed to get much publicity, at least not in their own land. *Diary of a Suffragette* had been getting far too much attention for my liking. I was, as usual, jealous of my big sister's success, and even more jealous because I hadn't written the book. I'd had the opportunity to steal a march on her; I'd had Annie Jane Morrison's letters long before Stephanie and I hadn't even bothered to read them until Steph found out and asked to see them.

'Well, good luck to her,' I pronounced with a certain finality. With a lump in my breast and all the implications of that surging round my head, Stephanie's stupid book didn't seem so much of a big deal anymore. I found it hard to muster up anything other than apathy. I didn't care anymore about Annie Jane being public property. The green-eyed monster had been slain.

I picked up the classifieds section and looked at the job ads instead to see if any PR firms were advertising for staff; I liked to keep up with industry gossip. Simon glanced at the property section and sighed.

'You never know, I might be able to afford a place of my own one day,' he said, 'instead of having to rent while Myra sits tight in the big family home she shared with that gigolo.'

'At least he's gone now.'

'Yes, but it doesn't make it any easier. I still have to wait 'til the kids move out before we can sell.'

The morning disappeared quickly as we lay side by side on the bed and debated the lose-lose situation in the Middle East, the politics of staying in power back home in New Zealand,

and the joys of unplanned solo parenthood later in life.

Our politics were similar enough to erase the possibility of coming to blows or an acrimonious falling-out, while leaving enough difference to create debate. Simon sympathised more with the Arabs than I, but had a surprising antipathy for our Prime Minister, relegating her to the same basket as Sir Robert Muldoon; whereas I had no truck with the Arabs or the Jews and thought the PM was a pretty smart cookie if you ignored her ostrich-like attitude to the commercial realities of doing business amid all her government's red tape and high taxes.

But when it came to teenagers, we were of one mind: the sooner they grew up and left home the better.

As if he'd heard us, Adam arrived home at that point and, by the sounds coming from the kitchen below, commenced to raid the fridge and the cupboards. His friend George's mother, I knew, would have already fed them breakfast — she always did — but that seemed hardly to have touched the sides of his stomach.

'Oh dear, I'd forgotten all about Adam,' I said, looking at the bedside clock: 11.30. 'What'll we do?'

I was racked with guilt and something approaching terror. How was I going to get Simon past him unseen? I couldn't exactly spirit Simon out the top-floor window — he'd break a leg at the very least landing in the hydrangea bushes. And I doubted he'd agree to hide in the wardrobe for the rest of the day until Adam went out again.

'That's entirely up to you, Penny. What do you want to do?'

'I honestly don't know. I've never . . .'

'There's a first time for everything. I'll do whatever you think is right.'

'Oh, Lord.' Flummoxed, I started to get up then realised

my clothes were on the other side of the room. 'I need a shower. Would you like one too?'

'I'll have one at home.'

'Oh, okay.' I sat there trying to work it through. 'Tell you what, I'll go take a shower and you wait here for me. Then we can both go down and face Adam together.'

'Mu-uum, are you home?' Adam was shouting up from the bottom of the stairs.

'Yes,' I shouted back. He didn't hear.

'Mu-uuummm?'

Panicked that he would come upstairs and find us together, I abandoned shyness, leapt out of bed and called around the door, 'Yes, I'm up here. I'll be down in a minute.'

Moments later I heard him crashing around in the kitchen again then the radio went onto The Edge ultra loud.

'Shower time,' I said over my shoulder and disappeared into the bathroom.

In the shower, I thought momentarily of feeling below my right armpit, where Simon had found the lump, but couldn't bring myself to do it. What if it really was there? Then I'd have to do something about it. What if I couldn't feel a thing? I'd worry anyway. Instead, I deliberately avoided soaping myself anywhere near the spot in question.

When I came back out, shampooed and cleansed of all traces of illicit sex, Simon had made the bed, tidied up the scattered newspaper and breakfast things and was sitting on the edge of the bed looking nervous — the first sign of discomfort since our tryst began. I dressed hurriedly, pulling out a low-necked hot pink T-shirt people often said looked good on me, over jeans and sandals. I left my hair damp — the thought of blow-drying it while churning up inside about what I was going to say to Adam didn't appeal.

'Right, let's go.' I looked at Simon. He was smiling that stomach-knotting lazy smile again.

'Come over here,' he beckoned.

I did as he asked.

'You look even better with your hair wet from the shower.' He pulled me toward him and kissed me lightly. 'Relax. I'll bet your son won't mind one little bit.'

'I wouldn't be too sure.'

Frankly, I had no idea how Adam would take it. He'd given out hints of late that another man in my life might be a good idea eventually. But 'eventually' didn't necessarily mean right now.

I picked up the tray, Simon carried the paper and we headed downstairs to face the music.

'Hi, honey,' I said entering the kitchen, talking fast before Adam had a chance to comment. 'This is Simon Wakefield. Simon, this is my son Adam.'

'Hi, Adam.' Simon held his hand out. Looking nonplussed, Adam shook it hesitantly.

'Hi, er, Mr Wakefield.'

'Please, call me Simon.'

'Sure. Er . . .'

'Simon and I were out together last night. He stayed over.'

'Oh.' Adam's eyes widened. It looked like the penny was dropping — literally as well as figuratively.

'We met on the tramp in the Abel Tasman. Simon was the one who rescued me when I fell and hurt my ankle.'

'Oh. I see.'

'Well, Adam, I'll be seeing you around,' Simon said. 'I'd better be getting home. My kids will be wondering what's become of me.'

He started towards me but, while Adam was looking his way, I shook my head. It was enough for Adam to realise we might be an item without seeing us touching or, worse, kissing. I knew Adam well enough to know that would be a major turn-off.

'Bye, Simon.'

'Bye. *I'll* call *you* this time.'

And he was gone, just like that. The kitchen suddenly seemed empty.

'Mum, you've been keeping secrets.' Adam was smirking at me. I squirmed with embarrassment.

'Not really, Adam. I didn't know myself until last night that there was anything worth keeping secret.'

'What does he do?'

'He's a microbiology lecturer at the university.'

'Oh.' Adam looked even more interested. 'That's cool.'

It dawned on me then that, if Simon and I *were* to become an item, there could be some spin-offs for Adam with his passion for marine biology. I didn't know much about sciencey things, but surely different biology studies must be related in some way?

'And he's got two kids, Drew and Isaac — Zak. They're both about your age. Drew is a bit older. I think she's in her last year at school.'

'Oh.' Adam was being discouragingly non-committal. But I supposed that was better than coming out with something downright negative. He fidgeted with the toastie maker. 'Are you going to see him again?' he asked, without looking up.

'I hope so, honey. Is that okay with you?' I felt an idiot asking for his permission, but somehow I wanted his approval of Simon.

'Course.' Apparently unconcerned, he went back to his toastie and I figured the conversation was over.

I wasn't sure how I'd handle it with Charlotte — I could worry about that when she came home on Sunday night.

Adam came with me later to see Mum and Dad, which was quite something for him and a much-needed distraction for me. He and Charlotte had become increasingly reluctant to visit their grandparents since Mum had got bad and I didn't blame them; visiting was a stressful trial even on her good days. I let him drive me over, which I knew would be even more likely to take my mind off things. Adam was practising for his licence and without his father around to help him, I'd taken on the role of guinea pig.

He'd been having lessons since the beginning of the year with money saved from burger-turning and had become reliable enough for me to venture forth without a blindfold. But there were still moments when I wished we had one of those dual steering wheels and brakes you hear about. Every time we came to traffic lights or a roundabout I found my right foot trying to push itself through the floor in search of a brake pedal and remembering Liz's sage advice: never lend your car to someone you've given birth to.

I hung in there with him though, encouraging when needed and biting my tongue instead of criticising. I wanted him to pass his licence — I wanted him to have a bit more independence, to be able to drive to his friends' places sometimes, and to show his sister that he could do it. She was so scathing of his efforts behind the wheel that he refused to drive when she was in the car anymore.

The first time he'd sat the written test, he'd failed, which had caused Charlotte immense glee. She, of course, had passed first pop. He hadn't mentioned it when he went back for a re-sit in case he missed out. Even then, when he came home and announced he'd passed this time, she had to remind him she'd only had to do it once. She'd breezed through the practical test too; all she lacked now, as she often reminded me, was a car to drive. She'd been working really hard on her father to buy one and I didn't doubt that he'd succumb sooner or later.

Mum was much more of a trial than the car journey. She thought Adam was her younger brother Ned and kept telling him off all the time for taking pot shots at passing cars and neighbourhood dogs with his catapult. Trudy was there helping, keeping a completely straight face even when Mum came up with some of her howlers.

'What have you done with it, Ned?' Mum said to Adam. 'Where have you hidden it this time?'

Of course, Adam was completely baffled until I managed to sneak a moment when Mum was out of earshot to explain what was going on. Or at least I thought she was out of earshot.

'What's that you're saying, young lady? I'm not deaf, you know. My goodness, you two will be in for it when Father gets home.'

'I'm sorry, lassie,' Dad said when we were alone out in the kitchen for a moment. 'She's been back in her childhood most of the weekend. She's been there quite a lot since she came back from the unit. That manager woman, Mrs Small, came over here last week specially to tell me . . .'

But he didn't have time to finish telling me what the big-bosomed head honcho lady had to say because Mum's flapping ears brought her into the kitchen right on cue.

'What's that you're saying? I'm not going anywhere.'

'It's all right, Colleen. You can help make the tea, here.' Dad handed her the canister and she started to spoon the leaves into the cups he'd laid out neatly on the bench. He managed to stop her before she started to pour hot water into each one. 'Here, let me lift that jug for you, it's heavy. Could you please get the biscuits out of the cupboard, Colleen?'

Mum was easy to divert, as Dad well knew, and obligingly headed for the pantry. After a few moments, she returned with a jar of syrup of figs the doctor had recommended Dad take for his bowels.

'Lovely, thank you, dear.' Without skipping a beat, Dad took the jar, placed it on the windowsill and diverted Mum's attention to finding the sugar bowl while he put the syrup of figs back in its rightful place and returned with the shortbread — no longer home-baked by Mum, sadly. Hers used to be the butteriest, smoothest shortbread on the planet. Us kids used to fight over who got the last one on the plate when all the rellies left after Sunday afternoon tea and we scrapped for the leftovers.

Mum happily sipped her tea and allowed Adam to divert her with an old series on television while I quizzed Dad about what the St Joan's gerontologist had had to say.

'I don't know why they've got it in for her,' he said. 'She's not been so bad lately. Just the usual carry on. But this Dr . . . er, Dr Tomahawk or something, he wants Colleen back in the unit. He says she's a danger to herself and to me. I reckon one of those minders has been telling tales out of school.'

'Would they have anything to tell tales about, Dad?' I pried.

'Well, I wouldn't have thought so, lassie. Just the usual, you know . . .'

'Tell me.'

'Well, there was the time she swore like a trooper for daring to make her have a shower when she didn't want to. I don't know where she got some of that language from,' Dad started to chuckle, 'but I don't think Trudy had heard much of it before. She looked very shocked indeed when she came out of that bathroom.' He paused.

'Anything else, Dad?'

'She's been threatening to run away, of course. She's been on about that before, but this was the first time the minders heard of it. They got in a great tizz about it for a while there. But Colleen never went anywhere. It was all talk.'

'Not like the times when you were at home and she'd run away without any warning at all.'

'No. Mind you, there was one night when she went outside with a knife and a bowl full of potato peelings. That got poor Nathan ringing the alarm bell or whatever it is they do.' He chuckled again. 'But Colleen didn't mean anyone harm. She was going out to feed the chooks, she told them. All these people running round trying to restrain her and she was trying to feed the chooks!'

'But you never had chooks.'

'No, lassie, but your mother grew up on the outskirts of the city and her family had a big hen house in the back yard. She had to feed the chooks every day.'

'Potato peelings?'

'Who knows?' He chuckled again. 'Probably not. She probably thought it was the chook bucket though. She can't tell a potato from a carrot — or a handful of grain for that matter.'

'Was that all?' I was afraid to ask.

'I think so. You see, I told you she hasn't been too bad of late. She's been quite good, really. Mind you, she did accuse Trudy of stealing her diamond ring last week. That didn't go down too well with Dr Tomahawk.'

'Was her ring actually missing?'

'She thought so. But of course, she couldn't remember where she'd put it. I found it buried in the bottom of the laundry bag. I think she'd been trying to hide it so Trudy wouldn't steal it!'

'Oh dear.'

Dad started to laugh. 'You have to see the funny side of it, lassie, you do. Or you'd go mad.'

I recalled hearing that just last night from Simon.

'Are you looking after yourself, Dad?'

'I wouldn't have it any other way, lassie.' He paused. 'Look, I've got all the help I need here — the minders, even the meals laid on when I want them. They help me get Colleen up in the morning and make sure she's sound asleep in bed at night and not likely to get up and cause havoc. They shower her, dress her, feed her . . . I've never had it so good. You're the one to worry about, lassie. How've you been doing?'

I told him hesitantly about Simon.

'You need to get out and enjoy yourself,' he said when I finished. 'Is he a good man?'

Instead of answering him directly, I told him how much Simon had made me laugh, how much I'd enjoyed myself, how much we had in common living with teenagers and losing partners to younger lovers. I didn't tell him how Simon brought me breakfast in bed or how he seemed to be able to locate my G-spot with the precision of a military homing device. And I certainly didn't mention how he'd located a small lump with similar precision.

After we got home, without the diversion of Mum's eccentricities or Adam's erratic driving, my poor brain went into overdrive, totally preoccupied with the lump Simon had found. Finally, when I was about to go to bed and could stand it no longer, I raised my arm and felt round the side of my breast, palpating it slowly like the pamphlets say you should do.

Simon was right. There was something there. But it was still sort of squishy and it seemed to move sideways when I touched it. I didn't know much about breast cancer, but everything I'd read so far told me that malignant lumps are firm, hard even, and don't move around.

So there's nothing to worry about, I told myself, and slept much better than I expected.

Chapter 13

On Monday morning, filled with a lot more confidence, I allowed myself another underarm exploration in the shower. I'd read somewhere that letting warm water flow over you makes it easier to feel anything untoward. I knew exactly where to feel now — and, sure enough, it was still there, right where it had been on Saturday and, I knew only too well, where it had been for months. But this time it didn't feel quite so squishy or mobile. In fact, it was a lot firmer than it had been in front of the bedroom mirror.

Damn!

This is some sick joke being played on me, I thought, just as I'm embarking on a romantic attachment with someone who likes my soft curves. What will he think of me if one of the aforementioned soft curves is missing?

I didn't want to go any further along that train of thought, so hurriedly finished the shower and started towelling myself dry. I was halfway through when the phone rang.

Damn, damn!

I sped back to the bedroom, dripping the remains of the shower on the carpet while wrapping the towel around me.

'Hello?' I said, picking up the receiver.

'Penny?' It was Stephanie.

'Yes.'

'Thank God. I've been trying to get to the phone all weekend but Marcus was in my face all the time. He's just left for work.'

'Oh.'

'And Seraya went with him. So I'm alone at last.'

I could hear Steph sigh with relief. I, however, was not possessed of my sister's eagerness to spend half an hour on the phone talking about her ill-conceived affair.

'That's nice, look I've . . .'

'Oh God, Penny, you've no idea what a terrible time I've had since I left you. It's been absolute hell.'

'I'm sorry, but . . .'

'Marcus knew. It was so awful. He actually knew.'

I juggled the receiver and tried to towel the rest of myself dry, with the result that the phone dropped on the floor. Steph hadn't noticed.

'. . . his friend Philip told him he'd seen me and Tim kissing outside Tim's front door. So he confronted me, just like that, he said "You're having an affair with that oaf, aren't you?" I didn't know what to say. Just like that! What could I say?'

'It's a tricky one. Look, I've . . .'

But Steph wasn't really asking my opinion. She was in full flight. I gave up trying to stop her, carried the phone over to my undies drawer and started to get dressed. I listened to her tale of woe — how she'd tried to convince Marcus it was a passing fancy, that the kiss was as far as they'd gone, that she'd not seen him since etcetera etcetera — and managed to drop the phone twice more without her noticing. I was fully dressed and doing my make-up when she finally ran out of steam and said, 'So, how are you? The kids all right?'

'Yeah, fine. Charlotte's much more settled. She's promised to come home some time this week. Whatever you said to her seems to have worked.'

'Good.'

'So, thank you. Look, I've gotta go . . .'

'Sure, sure. Sorry to hold you up. I just had to talk to someone. This whole thing's a disaster. I should never have been so stupid.'

I couldn't possibly comment on that one. Not yet, anyway. In a month or two, I could expect Steph to see the funny side, to have a good laugh about it. But for now, even after only half listening to the saga, I could tell she was still very raw and quite low. I did my best to make comforting noises; they seemed to do the trick because ten minutes later, when I was in the kitchen spooning up cereal and a banana and throwing a few Meaty-Bites at Tigger, she rang off sounding much better.

I'd deliberately kept quiet about the lump. I was going to keep that to myself until after I'd seen the doctor — if I saw the doctor. I still wasn't convinced I needed to.

• • •

I changed my mind around lunchtime and made the call, prompted by a throwaway remark Tracey had made when going through the local paper, looking for a story I was expecting about a local property development.

'Those poor kids,' she said. 'Just like that, their mother is wiped out by a boy racer on the motorway and they're so young. It just shows we have to make the most of it, don't we? We could be run over by a bus tomorrow. Or more likely a street racer.'

I phoned the doctor, but couldn't get an appointment until the next morning.

From then on, I threw myself into my work and tried to forget about The Lump, but it kept nagging at me, the 'what ifs' going through my brain constantly. The day passed in a surreal blur. There was plenty to distract me, though not all of it was for the better. My colleagues didn't notice any untoward behaviour, fortunately, because the last thing I wanted to do was talk about it.

Tracey was busy with the accounts; Ginny was occupied with Panos, who'd turned his attentions from olives to oiling his way around her; Nicky was tied up with the local jockey club trying to raise their profile; and the day turned to complete custard somewhere around four when I got a phone call from Adam's senior teacher

Adam had, she said, been doing brilliantly at Biology (sigh of relief, perhaps the phone call wasn't going to be bad news) *but* (ah, here's the rub) he'd been completely ignoring his other subjects, especially English and Maths, and he was well on his way to failing Year 12 if he didn't pull his socks up right now (grovel and agree with her that I'd get on his case).

'There was the matter of misuse of his phone earlier on,' she continued. 'That seems to have stopped. But now there's something else that's worrying us,' she said. (Uh-oh; cut to the chase.) 'Adam used to be such a gregarious boy. He used to have lots of friends. But he's been quite withdrawn lately. Is there a problem at home?' (Where do I begin?)

'Ah, well, sort of.' I'd told his school last year that his father had flown the coop; I didn't feel like revisiting the subject and the long-lasting effect it was having. Besides, his grumpiness seemed to have abated somewhat since Steph had had a talk to him.

'Things have been a bit up and down. But I think you'll find he's a bit better now. Just this past week he's been a lot happier.'

'Oh, I see. Well, I'll keep an eye on him. And I'd like you to do the same.'

I promised I would watch him like a hawk, monitor his homework and study schedule, ban the internet in the short term, confiscate his mobile — again — and put a time limit on his phone calls.

Adam didn't seem to mind at all — in fact, I could have sworn he was grateful when I'd finished quizzing him and told him he had to pull his socks up.

His form teacher had said something to him several weeks ago, he said. 'But there's no problem now. Everything's sweet.'

'Well, you keep it that way,' I admonished him. 'I don't like getting these calls at work.'

Steph phoned again after dinner. Marcus had gone out to a meeting, she said, and she was desperate for someone to talk to about it.

'Steph, we talked just this morning.'

'I know, but I'm beside myself. I can't think of anything else. I'm at my wits' end. Marcus is so hurt. I feel so awful.'

'What did you expect, you nutcase? You knew when you went down that path what you were risking.'

'I know. I know. But I never thought he'd find out. I never meant to put our relationship at risk.'

'Good God. What did you think you were doing then?'

'I didn't really think. I just sort of got carried away and before I knew it, we were full on.'

Steph kept right on talking, going over and over what Marcus had said and what she'd said ad infinitum.

'Yes, you said,' I interjected when she started to repeat herself. I'd finished filing my nails and was getting bored.

'I know, I'm being selfish. How are things at your end?'

That caught me unawares. 'Oh, okay.'

'You sure? You sound a bit wobbly.'

'Do I?' I wasn't aware I'd given anything away. I checked no one was in earshot and took a deep breath. 'Well, I've found this lump on my right breast.'

There was a gasp at the other end. 'No! When did you find it?'

'On Saturday.' I wasn't going to tell her how; that was so humiliating.

'Oh, you poor thing. And there I was rabbiting on about myself all that time. You should have said. You didn't even tell me this morning.'

'Well, you were a bit distracted.'

'True. Oh, Penny, I'm so sorry.'

'Yes. Thank you.'

'Haven't you been to the doctor yet?'

'No. I phoned today. I'm seeing her tomorrow.'

'You should have said it was urgent. If you'd said why they might have squeezed you in between appointments.'

'I didn't like to make a fuss. It might be nothing.'

'But you need to know right away. God, if it was me, I'd be barging into the surgery and not going home until the doctor had seen me and let me know, one way or the other.'

'Well, I'll find out tomorrow.'

'Promise you'll phone me right away.'

'Yeah, okay.'

'If you don't, I'll phone you.'

Call-waiting blips came on the line. 'I've got to go Steph, there's someone trying to get through. Talk tomorrow.'

The caller waiting was Simon. Like Stephanie, he asked me if I'd seen the doctor yet.

'No, the appointment's tomorrow morning.'

Like Stephanie, he told me off for not insisting on seeing her today.

'I didn't like to put them out. It might be nothing.'

Like Stephanie, he thought that was a feeble excuse.

'You sound just like my sister.'

'Well, she knows what she's talking about.'

I didn't sleep nearly as well that night. Scenarios kept whirling round in my mind about what might happen. I'd known of others who'd been in my situation, though nobody close enough to call. I kept thinking of the kids, of Simon, of my business, and hoped like hell it was nothing.

• • •

What does a girl wear to the biggest examination of her life? Killer heels? A plunging neckline?

'Mutton dressed as lamb,' my mother would say.

Maybe something sensible to give the impression you're a clean-living girl at heart. One hundred per cent pure, perhaps, like linen?

'Crumpled like an unmade bed,' I could hear my sister's put-down.

I stood in front of the bedroom mirror, a freeze-frame of indecision.

'Make sure you've got clean underwear.' My mother's voice again. 'You never know when you might be run over by a bus.'

Right now, being run over by a bus seemed like an easier option than facing the news no woman wants to hear.

I fished the long-forgotten La Perla bra out of the bottom of my undies drawer. A little tight — unseen by mankind since Steve's departure — it was cobalt blue, lacy, just the thing to make a girl feel like a woman. Perfect. I slipped it on. Just because I was feeling like shit didn't mean I had to look like it.

But I dithered so long over the rest of the outfit, I ended up wearing much the same as any other day, although I made sure I had a stretchy top instead of a shirt — there's nothing worse than having to fiddle with tiny buttons when you're shaking with nerves.

Suzanne Piper, my GP, left me to undress after I told her why I was there and returned after a few moments to examine me. She started making sweeping, circular movements with her hands around my right breast, working her way into the centre then back out again, going over and over the place where I thought the lump was.

Then she repeated the motions on the other side.

Finally she checked under my armpits and at either side of my neck.

'Is there anything there?'

'I think so. yes. Here, you feel it.'

She placed my hand on the side of my right breast, deep underneath the nipple, so deep in fact it felt like my ribcage. With a sinking feeling, I felt something, not much bigger than a grape. I could understand why I'd never felt it before — it was so embedded, so far down, I'd not been able to distinguish it from my ribs.

'You can pop your clothes back on now,' she said at last.

I did up my bra and slipped my top back on.

She waited until I sat down and said, 'There's a small cyst at the side of your right breast, where you thought something might be.' She plucked a diagram of two perfectly formed semicircles out of a pile of papers and put a small 'X' on the spot. 'It's nothing to worry about. I think you'll find it will go when you have your next period or soon after.' I was just about to breathe a very big sigh of relief when she continued, 'But I'm afraid there's the lump you felt further in towards the centre of your right breast and it does concern me.' She drew a bigger 'X' on another spot on the diagram closer to the nipple. 'It's not a cyst. I'd like to have it checked out thoroughly with a mammogram. Are you free for the rest of the morning?'

'What? Uh . . . yes.' It was as if the world had stopped spinning and the air had lost all its oxygen. It was as if I was in a foreign country and words lost all meaning. It was as if someone had kicked me in the knees and the stomach at the same time.

I think poor Dr Piper said several other things but I've no idea what they were. I vaguely recall paying the bill and waiting while the nurse called a private breast clinic and made an appointment for a mammogram. I found myself standing in the carpark clutching the evil diagram and a referral note for the clinic. I had three quarters of an hour to fill before the appointment. The drive in the post-nine o'clock traffic would take about thirty minutes, so I stopped at a nearby coffee bar for a slug of caffeine. And then another. Which of course made me want to go to the loo. So then I had to make a speedy dash the rest of the way to the clinic, arriving just two minutes after 10am.

I probably shouldn't have driven. I wasn't really with it, but I didn't stop to think about it and besides I wouldn't have known who to call to take me. There was only a very short wait and I was ushered into a cubicle to take my bra and top off (with nobody to notice Madame Perla) and put on a complicated beige gown with three armholes.

'There's a picture on the wall that shows you how to do it,' the young woman said and left me to it.

If it was an intelligence test, I failed it miserably. I don't know how many times I tried to get the damn thing on the way it was in the picture, but each time I ended up with an armhole to spare. Once I got stuck and thought I'd have to call the young woman back to extract me, but managed to get myself free by twisting and turning like a contortionist — not easy in a cubicle the size of a test tube.

'Mrs Rushmore?' Another woman's voice this time from behind the curtain.

'Yes.'

'If you're ready, can you please come this way?'

'Er, I can't get this thing on. I'm afraid I need a hand.'

An older woman poked her head round the curtain. I just caught the start of a smirk before she managed to control herself and put on the Sympathy Face.

'Oh dear. Let me help you.' She picked up the shapeless item and held it out, indicating where I should put my arms, and in no time it was wrapped around me with the final bit covering my front. Simple! Why hadn't I thought of it? If I hadn't felt so emotionally numb, I would have been embarrassed at my ineptitude, but I had weightier matters on my mind.

I followed her into a small room dominated by an enormous machine. She guided me over to one side of it and that's when I saw it: The Clamp. My friends had often regaled me with their experiences of The Clamp.

'Like having your boobs held down while being run over by a bus,' one had said.

'Codename: Jaws,' said another.

Only a month ago I'd laughed out loud at one of those spam emails that told me a mammogram meant you had to put your breast in an envelope and mail it to the clinic. It didn't seem so funny now.

I'd managed to avoid the vice-like grip of The Clamp all my life. I probably should have been brave and visited it earlier, but I'd only just reached fifty; I hadn't yet been offered an appointment and I'd certainly never thought of having one voluntarily. This was the sort of thing that happened to other women; never to me.

'Just sit down here, dear,' the kindly woman said, 'and I'll check your details. She went through everything on the page, showing me the diagram of my boob as if I wanted to see it again, and explained what she was about to do. 'Now, if you'll just come up here,' she guided me over to The Clamp, 'and lean forward,' she helped me position myself, 'and place your breast here.'

I looked at my right boob spreadeagled in its lonely whiteness on top of a plastic plate waiting to have its picture taken. It wasn't smiling.

After several readjustments, the woman was satisfied and then it happened: The Clamp chomped down onto my flesh and gripped it in a vice. The analogy of being run over by a bus or trapped in a closing refrigerator door was close to the mark. I winced but didn't make a sound.

Then it was the turn of my other boob to undergo the indignity. It hurt too.

'Thank you, dear. Now, if you wouldn't mind waiting in your cubicle until I come by, I'll just check that the pictures have come out okay.'

Meekly, I shuffled off to the cubicle and sat in the ridiculous three-armed gown reading about Posh and Becks — as if I was interested — and waited. The magazines barely held my attention. My mind was in turmoil.

'Thank you, dear. The x-ray pictures are fine. The radiographer is checking them now. If you wouldn't mind waiting a bit longer?' The woman smiled sympathetically and was gone.

I wasn't sure if she meant the pictures were in focus, or if she meant there was nothing to worry about, but I didn't like to ask — I wasn't sure if I wanted to know.

So I read about Angelina and Brad, and Catherine and Michael, and Kate and William, without taking in a single thing. Deliberately ignoring the pamphlets about breast cancer, I picked up another magazine.

'Ah, Mrs Rushmore?'

'Yes.'

'The radiographer would like you to have further tests, please. He'd like you to have an ultrasound.'

I didn't know much about this sort of stuff, but I knew that needing 'further tests' was not a good sign.

'Oh, sure.'

What else could I say? No? I certainly felt like it. But the sensible part of my brain made me go through with it; made me stand up, gather my bag and clothes, and marched me along the corridor, with another line of discretely curtained cubicles. Posh and Becks, Paris and Brangelina were all waiting there for me. But this time I couldn't focus. I fiddled and fidgeted, checked my cellphone was still off (there were signs banning them everywhere), pulled out my diary (but couldn't muster any interest in the cancelled work appointments and missed deadlines), and ended up gazing at an old photo of the kids (taken in one of their rare non-combative moments), smiling innocently beside a sandcastle they'd made. Seconds later, from memory, the dog had dug a hole under the carefully decorated structure, Charlie had started wailing (not all that attractive for a 14-year-old) and Adam had begun taunting her for being a wuss.

'Mrs Rushmore?'

The nurse was back. She indicated I should follow, led me through a door at the end of the corridor and introduced me to a man whose name I promptly forgot.

He sat me down and explained that the lump showing in the mammogram had been drawn to his attention and he was going to carry out an ultrasound examination of it.

By now, my mind was so numb, the word 'ultrasound' didn't really register anything further than another brick in the wall. It was all becoming so horrific, I kind of expected it to keep on getting worse.

He asked me to lie down on a narrow bed and remove my designer hospital number. A nurse wiped some thick, clear goop across the offending part of my breast and he ran a flat nozzle thing over it again and again. The last time I'd had one of these I was pregnant, filled with new joyous life. This time was very different. This time, whatever was growing inside me, it wasn't going to bring any joy.

'There,' he said, and pointed to a fuzzy blue and white screen with strange lines and shadows on it.

'What?' I looked blank. I couldn't see anything other

than a very bad test pattern.

'There.' He pointed again and I could just make out a black blob the size of a ten cent coin in the middle of a whole lot of moving squiggles and blobs. He pushed buttons and things and a few moments later the nurse was wiping off the goop and offering me back the front part of my beige gown. At this rate, it was becoming an indispensible part of my wardrobe.

But just when I thought I was going to escape from the nightmare, he told me they'd like to do a biopsy.

So the gown and I went into another cubicle to read more stories about celebrities until another young woman came to get me and ushered me into another dark room where yet another man was waiting to deal unto me.

This time, he explained, he was going to jab a very long needle into me to get right inside the lump and extract some of the fluid from it so they could see what it was made of. Was this okay?

Of course it's not okay, I felt like saying. Would you like a very long needle shoved several inches down into your right boob? But instead I said, 'Oh, sure.' I was shifting into auto-response.

Someone gave me a local anaesthetic and The Needle made its debut appearance. It was so long it could have had a starring role in a horror movie. It stung a bit at first, going in, then, as he wiggled it about, it started to hurt. It also felt nauseating and very weird. I could tell it was in there, probing around, but I couldn't tell exactly where, and there was no way I was looking at the ultrasound screen this time to see it insinuating its way through the squiggles and dots. He was in there for an eternity, jiggling around, muttering about how small it was and therefore hard to pinpoint; he kept checking his progress on the nearby screen when finally he said, 'Ah, that's it.' A few moments later, it was all over.

The nurse told me I could get dressed; the doctor would see me shortly.

'The doctor? I didn't know all this was going to happen here. What does this all mean?'

'The doctor will be able to talk to you about it shortly. If you wouldn't mind getting dressed and waiting . . .'

'Oh, sure.'

So I said goodbye to the designer gown and returned to the main waiting room where I studied my fellow waiters with trepidation. Were they like me, waiting for News? Were they embarking on the same sort of unknown nightmare journey that I was? Or were they already well down the track, old hands at this terror waiting game? They gave nothing away of course and neither did I.

Surreptitiously, when I was sure everyone was buried in their magazines, I felt my prodded and probed breast. It still hurt. In fact, the whole experience had hurt more than anything I'd experienced so far. I patted it consolingly. It didn't do much good: within a couple of days, the poor thing would turn black and blue.

There were no Posh and Becks magazines left on the coffee table so I rummaged around in my bag for something to do. Not much inspiration there, though I did find my phone still switched off. I turned it back on to check for messages. There were none from Simon but, predictably, several from the office. I didn't reply — they could wait until this awfulness was over. I shoved it back in my bag, picked up the morning paper and tried the crossword without coming up with a single answer. I was onto my third reading of the weather page when my phone rang.

'Penny, it's Tracey. Where on earth have you got to? I've rung you twice already. I've been keeping all sorts of people at bay.'

'I'm sorry, Tracey. I had to go to the doctor's. I'm still there.'

'God, are you all right? You've been ages.'

'Yeah fine,' was my automatic response, even though I clearly wasn't. 'I had to wait. Shouldn't be too long now.'

'Oh well, I guess everyone can hang on until you're back. How long do you think you'll be?'

I looked at my watch. 11.30am! I'd been here for an hour and a half. 'Oh, maybe half an hour, then there's the traffic.'

'Ohhh. I see-eee.' The usually unflappable Tracey paused as if she was about to say something then obviously thought better of it. 'It'll just have to wait 'til you're back then.'

I didn't ask what the problem was. I didn't want to know. And I doubted I'd be able to handle it anyway. I ended the call and turned my phone off again.

'Mrs Rushmore?' Yet another man appeared from one of the doors leading off the waiting room and indicated I should follow him. This one was wearing one of those clubby striped shirts with a white collar and a tie that clashed badly — it must have been pretty dire for me to actually notice it, given the zombie-like state I'd reached. He sat me down opposite him at his desk and looked at me over his reading glasses.

'I'm afraid I don't have very good news for you,' he started. 'You have all the indications of early breast cancer . . .'

His words became a bit of a muddle after that. I'd already guessed, of course, but hearing it said like that was a huge shock. My mind went numb. It's not that I didn't want to know — I was only too well aware I needed to know what was going to happen next and why. But somehow my mind went into overdrive, thinking of the kids and Mum and Dad and what would happen to them if . . . and what would I do about work and all my clients and how would I be able to earn money if I was off work for months and . . .

'. . . did you hear me?'

'Er, sorry?' He'd stopped talking and there was a fearful silence.

'I was saying, this is a lot for you to take in under the circumstances. It would be a lot better if you had brought someone with you.'

'Er, yes, it would. But this all happened so quickly. There wasn't time really . . .' I was vaguely aware that one of the nurses had suggested over an hour ago that I might like to get my husband or a close friend along, but the mere mention of 'husband' had sent me into further denial.

'Well, when you go I'd like you to make another appointment for tomorrow and bring someone close to you so we can go through the arrangements. In the meantime, I'd like to see if my nurse can book you in for an operation. In your situation, I think a full mastectomy would be advisable but you might like to think about that overnight and talk to your husband about the options. A lumpectomy, as I explained a few moments ago, would be possible. I'll get my nurse to give you the information that tells you all about the options so you can have a think about it. If you choose to have a full mastectomy, as I was saying, there is the option of a replacement, either at the same time as the operation or several months later.'

'I'll go for the full mastectomy and immediate replacement,' I blurted. I just wanted to get it all over and done with as soon as possible, and a replacement was absolutely essential. The thought of having a half-flat chest and trying to live with a prosthesis falling out all the time filled me with total horror.

Besides, I absolutely had to have some sort of flesh there if I was going to have any sort of relationship with Simon.

Because as soon as he'd said the word 'mastectomy' it dawned on me that this was not an ideal time to be embarking on a romantic relationship. There was a very real possibility that Simon would run a mile from a titless wonder at such an early stage. Heavens, he hardly knew me with two boobs, let alone one.

'Are you sure, Mrs Rushmore? It's a major decision you're making and I think it best if you think about it overnight, just the same. I wouldn't want you to commit yourself in haste.'

'No, I want a mastectomy. I don't want to risk you finding something later and having to go through this all over again. I've read about all that and it seems to happen quite a lot. If I'm going to go through with this, I only want it to be once. And then I want a replacement right away.'

He explained about the cost and checked again that I had medical insurance. He suggested I give my insurer a call and find out what was possible under my scheme, then come back with my husband or another support person and see him in the morning.

That was the second time he'd mentioned the word 'husband' and I knew I should pull him up, but I couldn't cope with dredging all that up as well. Things were bad enough.

But I was starting to get the message — he wanted me to come back in the morning with someone who would a) listen properly, b) talk some sense into me, and c) take notes so they could explain to me later in words of one syllable. Good idea!

'Sure.' I thanked him, though for what I'm not sure, returned to reception to make another appointment and pick up screeds of information, then departed for the office.

There was nowhere else to go, really. I didn't want to go

home to an empty, messy house. I couldn't barge in on any of the Philly girls at work. And I didn't want to be on my own — that would mean stopping to think about what was happening and I didn't want to. I was in a river being rushed along by the current and I didn't want to swim for the bank. The bank was where you looked clearly and calmly at your situation and made rational decisions about how to extract yourself from the mess you were in. I preferred the river, where the current decided for you whether you were going to live or die.

Tracey was at reception with Nicky when I arrived, poring over a database. Ginny was in her office.

'Hi,' I said as breezily as I could. 'Sorry I'm so late.'

'Thank heavens you're here,' Tracey said. 'Everyone's been asking for you. There was Panos and . . .' She paused. 'Oh God, I forgot. Sorry! You've been to the doctor's. How are you? Everything all right?'

That was all it took. I burst into tears. 'Actually, no.'

Nicky came over and put her arm around me. 'Hey, what's happened? You're never sick. Well, hardly ever,' she added. 'You had the flu a lot last winter. Is that what the problem is?'

'No . . . Well, yes. I expect my poor old immune system couldn't cope.' I started blubbing big time now.

'Your immune system? Why, you haven't got ME, have you?'

'No!' I wailed. 'I've got breast cancer!' There, I'd said it for the first time. It didn't feel at all good.

'Fuck!' Ginny said, coming out of her office and throwing her arms round me too, making it a sort of group grope. 'Did you just say the C word?'

'You can't have,' Nicky said. 'You're too young!'

'I wish. If only I'd thought of it earlier. I'm in the target age group now. I'm fifty, remember.'

There was a stunned silence then they all sprang into action. Tracey brought tissues, Nicky kept hugging me and Ginny disappeared for a moment and came back with a bottle of her best Moët.

'Time to drown some sorrows,' she pronounced and popped the cork. 'Behind every woman just diagnosed with breast cancer is a large bottle of bubbly.'

I didn't even question how early it was in the day to be drinking; I simply accepted it and, I'm ashamed to say, glugged it down like a milkshake. And while we stared at our glasses and swirled the yeasty yellow liquid round and round, I recounted my morning's experience — or as much of it as I could remember. When I got to the bit about the mammogram, Ginny winced.

'You can tell those machines were invented by men,' she said. 'I'd like to see them put their balls in there and flatten them like we have to with our hooters.'

We all laughed uproariously, even me, and some of the tension was relieved; my tale became less one of woe.

When I was describing the biopsy, Ginny said, 'Don't tell me, when the doctor was getting ready to stick the needle into you, he said "I feel a right tit!"'

'He tried to hide it from me so I couldn't see it,' I laughed. 'But it was ginormous. You couldn't miss it, even in the half dark.'

Nobody mentioned the C word again, least of all me.

'Would you like me to come with you in the morning?' Nicky said. 'I'd be happy to. I could take notes or take my little tape recorder from my journalism days.'

'Would you? I'd love you to. I hadn't thought about who I'd ask but really, there's no one. Steve's out of the question,

Mum wouldn't be much use, Steph's just gone back home, and it would be too much to load onto Charlotte.'

It was agreed then that Nicky would pick me up at home, take me to the clinic and take notes when I was with the doctor, ask questions if she didn't think I was asking the right ones, and bring me back to the office afterwards. I didn't want to go home by myself — the office was much more collegial, even if I couldn't focus. In the meantime, I said I'd prefer to stick around — at least until I thought Adam and Charlotte would both be home around five.

'Okay, tell us how we can help you this afternoon,' Nicky said. 'You're going to find it impossible to concentrate. Maybe Ginny and I could take over some of your work.'

'Oh God, I hadn't thought. It won't just be this afternoon. It'll be for the next few weeks. I don't know when the operation's going to be. I doubt they'll fit me in this week, though.'

'Lucky you've got health insurance,' Tracey said. 'Imagine having to wait for the public system to take you.'

'Damn lucky,' I agreed. 'I've often wondered if those big premiums I've been forking out are worth it, but now it's payback time.'

'So what've you got on now?'

I briefed Nicky on a couple of jobs that were comparatively easy to hand over in the interim, with clients she'd worked with in the past. The rest weren't so easy.

'I'll have to think about what I'm going to do when I have the operation, whenever that is. I guess I'm going to be off work for a while. I don't remember how long the doctor said.'

'I'll do as much as I can, Penny. But I won't be able to take on all of your work. There's just too much of it. Ginny could help with some of it.'

'Some of it, sure. But a lot of the stuff I do is way out of her league. You want an event organised, you want glamour and schmoozing, Ginny's your gal. You want the serious stuff done though, you go elsewhere.'

'I know. But maybe we'll be able to divvy it up — Ginny can handle the media stuff pretty well and I can do the rest. I can just see her with those puppies.'

'Yeah right, like a Tui billboard! One drop of puppy pee on her Chanel suit and she'd drop the poor thing and run.'

I cleared my messages — including two from Steph wanting to know what had happened at the doctor's — then Tracey took notes while we all discussed what we could do. Going through the messages first made us realise we'd have to work out what we should say to all the clients about my absence. Then we went through my clients, one by one, looking at what needed to be done over the next day or two, then how to handle the weeks when I'd be off work completely.

'I bags Panos,' Ginny volunteered straight up.

'I thought you'd bagsed him already,' Nicky said grinning. 'After hours, anyway.'

Ginny opened her eyes wide, feigning innocence. 'Who, me?' she said, smirking.

'All that publicity stuff should be right up your alley,' I said. 'Along with the magnetic Panos.'

Much to my surprise, Nicky offered to take on the funeral homes.

'I've always had a morbid fascination with that sort of thing,' she said. 'Ever since I started watching *Six Feet Under* I've wanted to visit a morgue.'

'You should have told me, Morticia. You could have come and helped out at the open days.'

'Just as long as they don't have any more collapsing coffins.'

'They buried them,' Ginny quipped. 'It was a very grave situation.'

Tracey and Nicky started to laugh — cemetery jokes were as common as menopause gags in our office. But then they caught my eye and stopped — they could see I was struggling with the mortality issue for probably the first time since I'd taken on the client eight years ago.

We parcelled out the rest of the work, though nobody was too keen on taking on the irascible Jim Stephens.

'Come on, Ginny, you'd be so good at puppy puffery. A natural.'

'It's not the puppies . . .'

'I know, it's Jim.'

'He can't be that bad, Penny fancied him rotten a while ago.'

'Hey, that's going a bit far. . .'

'And he has women falling over him in all those society photos. He must be worth squillions.'

'Well, maybe I could consider it . . .'

We all laughed, despite ourselves.

'I think we can handle it,' Nicky said when we came to the end of the list. 'As long as none of them decides to have a crisis in the immediate future.'

Back in my room, I Googled 'breast cancer'. There were over 60 million links. I clicked on the first one and started to read, then the next one, and another. The options the poor doctor had been trying to explain were clearly outlined: I could choose between a lumpectomy, which would remove the tumour and possibly also the nipple but leave the remaining breast tissue untouched, followed by radiotherapy and chemotherapy (prognosis: might not get it all); or I could have a mastectomy, completely removing the whole breast and lymph nodes, followed by chemotherapy (prognosis: much more likely to get it all). The lumpectomy was more popular; the mastectomy was more radical.

After a few minutes, the barrage of information became way too much and way too daunting. I left the office early, refusing an offered ride home from Ginny ('You can leave the car here if you don't feel like driving') because I intended to stop by St Joan's on the way. But when I saw Dad so happy with Mum sitting beside him on the sofa — despite her cranky outbursts and dotty behaviour — I couldn't bring myself to tell him. It seemed more logical to wait until I was out of hospital before I said anything, otherwise he'd just worry. When I knew the operation date, I could tell him I was going on holiday for a fortnight or something — he'd never know.

There was a note on the kitchen bench when I got home — Adam had gone to see his friend George. Charlotte wasn't back from uni, so apart from the pitter patter of Tigger's feet, the house was quiet.

I fed him and, before I talked myself out of it, phoned Steph to break the news.

For once, she didn't talk about herself or her problems. She cut straight to the chase: 'So what did he say? Are you okay?'

'No. I'm not.' I bit my lip and steeled myself. 'I've got to have a mastectomy.'

'Oh, shit! Oh no. You poor thing. So there was a lump?'

'Yup. And it's malignant.' I felt my lip quiver but I managed not to cry.

I gave her a précis of the morning's events and explained I'd be going back in the morning with Nicky for the definitive version: what options I'd chosen, where I'd go for the op, who would do it etcetera.

Steph tried to talk me out of a full mastectomy. Lumpectomies, she said, were much less painful, much less destructive, and didn't require a replacement. And replacements, she said, were supposed to be the most painful of all.

'What are you trying to do to me here? Now I'm thoroughly confused.'

'Believe me, you don't want to have to go through all that replacement stuff. Do you know, they take it from your tummy?'

'No! In that case I'm all for it. My tummy's way too big.' I looked down at my midriff — it could certainly do with a slice or two off the front. I'd happily consign it up north and to the right a little.

'Well, that would certainly get rid of it in no time. And on health insurance, too.'

'At least there'll be a pay-off for all that drama, eh?' I said wryly.

Chapter 14

Charlotte arrived at that moment, all bounce and youthful verve, tossing her bag on the breakfast bar and starting to rummage in the fridge.

'I've gotta go, Steph. Charlotte's home.'

I promised to call her after the doctor's appointment and finished the call.

'Hi, Mum.' Charlotte passed me on the way to the lounge with a banana in one hand and her mail in the other.

'Hi, honey. Are you coming back home now?'

'Yes.' She paused while she opened an envelope and started to read. 'It's weird.'

'What's weird?'

'Jacinta's asked me to go to some channelling group with her.'

'Channelling?'

'Yes, some psychic medium who's in town. I'm not sure it's me.'

'Well, you don't have to . . .' I can't say I was overjoyed at Charlotte getting embroiled in all that hocus-pocus mumbo jumbo, but I wasn't at all surprised that the Conniving Cow was into it.

'That's why I thought I'd come home for a day or two. She's been talking real weird lately.' She sighed. 'I suppose I'd better go. Dad made her ask me; I overheard them. He was telling her off for being rude to me and driving me away and he was trying to make her do stuff with me.' To emphasise the point, Charlotte bit on her banana.

'Oh, I see.'

'You've no idea, Mum. She's such a cow sometimes.'

You took the words right out of my mouth, I felt like saying. But all I said was, 'Really?'

'She's so totally shallow, you know? She can't see past her Manolos and Armani. She thinks she's so cool, she's such a try-hard.'

'Oh, I see.' Who was I to disagree?

I left her to organise her social life, fed Tigger to stop him shadowing me, and opened the freezer to get dinner, but couldn't see anything I fancied. In fact, I couldn't see anything at all. My ability to focus on anything other than the sword hanging over my head had gone.

I took a soda through to the now empty lounge and switched on the TV. The news was on but I've no idea what it was about; I watched the pictures without seeing.

'Hi, Mum.' It was Adam. He surged into the room, dropping bags, books, clothes, shoes, a tie, a jacket and his bike helmet in his wake.

'Hi, honey. Had a good day?'

'Yeah, good.' He reached the kitchen and started to forage. 'What's for dinner?'

'I don't know, to be honest.'

'Can we have takeaways then?' He never let an opportunity pass him by for something with fries.

'Oh, sure. Soon. I want to have a talk with you both first.'

'Uh-oh. A "family conference". Has Charlotte done something wrong?'

'No such luck. And neither have you.'

'Oh. What is it then?'

'You'll have to wait for Charlotte. How'd you like to go get her? She must have gone upstairs.'

Adam went to the bottom of the stairs and roared, 'Charlotte. Mum wants you,' at the top of his lungs. I winced.

'I meant go *get* her, not go shout at her.'

'Yeah. Sorry.' He came and sat on the chair opposite me and turned the sound up on the TV.

Charlotte arrived after a few minutes, looking grumpy. 'I was just finding what I needed on Google. What is it?'

'Mum wants a "family conference",' Adam said.

'Oh. What's Adam done now?'

'Nothing,' I said. 'It's me.' I turned the sound down again.

'I know. You got caught by a speed camera again,' Adam crowed.

'No, it's not that. It's . . .'

'You're going on another diet? That was so major last time.'

'For God's sake, Adam, let Mum get a word in.'

There was silence at last; they were looking at me expectantly.

'I've got breast cancer,' I said quietly. 'I've got to go into hospital to have a cancerous lump removed.'

'Cancer? Oh no!' Charlotte looked shocked. Adam looked blank.

'Yes, I'm afraid so. I just found out today. I had no idea. But I don't want you to worry about me. These days, it's easy to cure.' I thought if I said that often enough, I might come to believe it eventually; inside, I didn't feel as confident as I sounded. 'They cut it out of you and give you special treatment and then it's all gone. Kaput.'

There wasn't much else I could say, really, without going into the gory details of the operation — and I didn't want to go there and neither would they. Charlotte asked a few questions, which I answered as best as I could, but of course I had no idea yet when the operation would be or how long I'd be in hospital.

'You can expect to be seeing a lot more of me around the house, though, afterwards,' I said, trying to sound breezy, despite the slight catch in my voice. 'And I'll be looking forward to you two waiting on me hand and foot.'

'Yeah, sure.' Adam's face was expressionless, although that didn't necessarily mean anything. He was often hard to read and sometimes, when he looked like he was deep in thought, he wasn't actually thinking anything at all. I hoped this was one of those times.

'One of the girls in our class last year had to stay home from school to look after her mum when she had cancer, and look after all her brothers and sisters.'

'Hey, can I do that?' Adam was always looking for an excuse to bunk school.

'No, you certainly can't. Besides, it would be more stressful having you around.'

'She was off school for three months. She said her mother was really sick and lost all her hair.'

'Well, I don't know if I'll lose mine or not. It depends on whether I have to have chemotherapy. Hopefully I won't need it.'

'How will you know?'

'They tell you after the operation. It depends on what type of cancer you have. But they don't know until they get inside you.'

Adam looked distinctly uncomfortable. He shifted from foot to foot then said, 'So can we go and get McDonald's now?'

'Oh, Adam . . .' Charlotte wailed. 'You're so insensitive.'

'He's all right,' I smiled, relieved that the tension had been broken.

'You don't get it, do you? Mum's got to go into hospital and have an operation for cancer. Like, *cancer*!'

'Charlotte, it's okay, Adam's fine.'

'Yeah, of course I get it. But there's no need to go on about it,' Adam said. 'You have to make such a drama out of everything.'

'I do not.'

'Please, both of you. Don't fight right now, okay?'

'Yeah, okay,' they mumbled ashamedly.

• • •

We'd just finished eating takeaways when my mobile rang. Simon's number showed on the display panel.

'Hi, Penny, how are you?'

'Not bad, all things considered,' I said, attempting to sound cheerful.

'So how did it go? What did the doctor say? I've been hoping you'd phone, but I couldn't wait any longer.'

'It's cancer.' I could feel my lip quivering again. I would've thought it'd be easier each time I had to tell someone, but it wasn't. Not yet, anyway.

'Oh, Penny, I'm so sorry. Would you like me to come round?'

'No, I'll be okay, thanks.'

'Come on, are you sure?'

I thought about it for a moment. I longed to throw myself into his arms, to feel comforted by him. But I wasn't sure how the kids would react to him being here at such a time. I hadn't even told Charlotte about him, though knowing Adam, he'd probably told her the minute she walked in the door on Monday night — the first time he would have seen her since she'd been at Gemma's for the weekend. Then I remembered Adam's deadpan response to the news and thought, damn it, why not.

'Yes, well, that would be nice.' It came out almost in a whisper; my voice seemed to have abandoned me.

'I'll be right over.'

It took him three quarters of an hour to cross town and I was a bit of a wreck by then. I'd resolutely stared at the television, but whatever was on failed to absorb me. My mind kept going over and over the possibilities, and no matter how often I banished them, worst-case scenarios kept worming their way back.

The doorbell rang.

'I'll get it,' Charlotte yelled from upstairs.

'No, I'm right here,' I yelled back and made a dash for it. I beat her — just. Tigger beat us all.

Simon was met consequently by a barking, bumptious

dog, a breathless nosy teenager and a woman several sandwiches short of a picnic.

'You must be Charlotte,' he said, shaking Tigger off. 'I'm Simon.'

'Ah yes, Simon. Simon Wakefield, this is my daughter Charlotte.' I said, flustered. I should have given some thought to how I would handle this but in my current state, it hadn't even crossed my mind. 'Simon's a . . .'

'. . . a microbiology lecturer at the university,' Adam said from behind me in a know-it-all voice. 'He's Mum's boyfriend.'

'Adam, that's not quite . . .'

'Yeah?' Charlotte was all agog. She turned to me. 'You never told me you had a boyfriend, Mum.' She sounded a bit miffed.

'No, well, it's all been a bit sudden. Adam met him at the weekend.'

'He was here at the weekend?'

'Well, er . . . Yes. Please, come inside, Simon. Please let the poor man in before the twenty questions.' I took him through into the lounge then gave the kids a meaningful look: 'Why don't you two pop back upstairs for a bit? I'd like to have a bit of privacy, if that's okay?'

Both kids looked disappointed but conceded; I could hear Charlotte interrogating Adam as they went up the stairs.

I offered Simon a cup of tea but he declined so we sat in the lounge while I related the day's sequence of events. When it came to the bit about the doctor sitting me down in his room and imparting the news, I got a bit shaky on it and had to sniff back the tears.

'That must have been devastating,' he said, shifting closer to me and putting his arms around me.

That did it; I burst into noisy, choking sobs. Pressed up against the comforting warmth of his Untouched World jersey, breathing in the smell of him, it felt safe at last to grieve. He held me firm, not moving, not flinching, until I stopped bawling.

'I'm sorry, I shouldn't have done this to you.'

'Don't be sorry, Penny. That's what friends are for. If I can't comfort you at a time like this . . .'

I snuggled into his chest, resting my head under his chin. 'Thank you.'

After a bit, I became aware of my dripping nose — I'd probably managed to cover the entire front of his merino top in snot and dribble — and retrieved the box of tissues from the other side of the coffee table. 'Sorry,' I said again, blowing my nose. But he didn't seem to care about his jersey. He enveloped me in another bear hug and waited for me to calm down.

'That's better,' he said at last, giving me one of his signature smiles.

We talked about tomorrow's visit and what might happen after that; I promised I'd call him when I knew.

I went to the door when the time came for him to go and called Charlotte down to say goodbye. He talked to her for a bit about his kids and about what she was doing at uni, gave me another hug, farewelled us both and was gone.

'You might have told me,' she said the second the door closed.

'I know, I'm sorry. I've been a bit preoccupied.'

'Yeah, I guess.' She looked at me. 'So when did you first feel the lump?'

'Not long ago. It's taken me a while to admit it to myself,' I said; I didn't mention I'd failed to take it seriously until Simon had found it. 'I phoned the doctor when I was at work on Monday, saw her first thing this morning then went over to the breast clinic and spent the rest of the morning having all these tests. It's all been a bit of a rush.'

'Poor Mum, you must be feeling a bit dazed.' She put her arm around me as we stood there in the hall but this time, thankfully, I didn't feel like crying.

'Yes, I am a bit. Thanks for being so understanding.'

'We'd better tell Josh, I suppose,' she said, looking at me questioningly.

I'd been putting it off, not knowing for once what to say.

'Ah, yes, I suppose so.'

Charlotte put her arm around me.

'Would you like me to do it?'

'Actually, yes, if you wouldn't mind?'

I followed her into the living room and sat down while she punched his UK mobile number into the phone. I picked up a family photo in a frame on the side table and stared longingly at the four of us, hoping what had been reduced to three of us wasn't about to become two.

'Mum, he says he wants to come home,' Charlotte said loudly.

'Oh, sorry, I wasn't listening.'

'You better talk to him now. He wants to jump on the next plane.' She handed me the receiver.

'Hi, honey. Sorry to have to do this to you,' I said. He sounded pretty choked up. 'Look, Josh, I don't want you to worry about me. I'm going to be fine.'

'But Mum, I ought to be there. I can get on a plane tomorrow . . .'

'No, Josh, really, there's no need. You're tied up with your new job. You've been after it for so long, you can't throw it in now.'

'The job doesn't matter . . .'

'Of course it matters. Besides, I'm not going to die, you know. I'm just going to have an operation and then I'll be fine.' I hoped I sounded more confident than I felt.

He protested for a while but eventually gave in to me after extracting numerous promises from both me and Charlotte that we'd phone and email often.

• • •

Early the next morning, before returning to the clinic, I phoned Di. I figured with her quasi-medical background she'd be used to both receiving and breaking this sort of news and would therefore be the best Philly member to tell first. She promised to call an emergency meeting of the Ladies' Philosophical Society forthwith. And she managed to impart more information about breast cancer and mastectomies than I'd picked up the previous day. Mind you, I'd been in such a state of shock as soon as I heard the 'further tests' pronouncement that I'd have been lucky to remember my name.

When I arrived at the clinic with Nicky, I realised I had no idea of the name of the doctor — or surgeon as it turned out — I'd seen the day before. I had to ask the receptionist.

'Dr Foster. Dr Mike Foster,' she said. I managed to refrain from a semi-hysterical rendition of 'Dr Foster went to Gloucester . . .' and took a seat in the now-familiar waiting room with Nicky.

'I think I must have read all these yesterday. I can tell you all you need to know about Posh and Becks, Kate and Wills . . .'

'Thanks. I'll pass,' Nicky said, taking the chair next to mine. Instead, we talked about work.

'Mrs Rushmore?' the receptionist called. 'Dr Foster will see you now.'

I don't know whether it was because Nicky was beside me writing pretty much everything down, or because I was in denial, but I still don't remember much of what he said. The gist of it was that I was booked into a private hospital next week for a full mastectomy and a reconstruction at the same time.

'Are you sure that's what you still want?' the surgeon asked.

I looked at Nicky.

'It's up to you,' she whispered.

I thought for a minute. I definitely wanted a replacement. And I didn't want it in six to nine months' time, or more. I'd managed to take that much in: if you had the new boob slapped on later, you had to wait until you were through all the treatment and that could take months, even a year. No way did I want to wait that long with only one boob. I definitely wasn't a prosthesis kind of girl.

And I definitely wanted the whole lot off. I'd heard enough horror stories of women having to go back a second and even a third time after just having the lump removed, when subsequent tests showed there were still cancer cells remaining. However, I didn't want to go to the extreme I'd heard some women did of having both breasts off at once to stop the other one developing a tumour. No thank you. I might be developing mild irrationality but I wasn't completely insane.

I confirmed it: mastectomy (just saying the word made me shudder) and reconstruction (which sounded like a motorway project), together, at the same time, concurrent, with no time for regrets. Next week.

'That will be Tuesday, March the thirteenth. It can be quite difficult to get two surgeons available at the same time, but we've managed to fit you in next Tuesday. Is that all right with you, Mrs Rushmore?'

'Yeah, sure. I think so.' I flipped open my diary; the page was almost a blank — just one appointment that could easily be changed. Then I realised I was being an idiot. It wouldn't matter if there were a hundred appointments on that day, of course I'd be available. This was the most significant appointment of my life — I had to be there or my next appointment would be with the angel of death.

I scrawled a dramatic line across the page, and the next page, and the one after that until Nicky's insistent tapping on my elbow brought me back to the present.

'. . . the appointment with the reconstructive surgeon and we'll expect you at the hospital at ten to eight then,' Dr Foster was saying.

'Er, yes, I'll be there.' As if I had a choice.

In a daze, I was guided out of the room by Nicky.

'We need a coffee, fast,' she said, steering me along the hall, out the clinic doors and across the carpark to her car.

We sat outside at a corner café and sipped flat whites while Nicky did her best to fill me in on the detail — the agenda for next Tuesday (a flurry of tests and checks followed by a long period of waiting), the names of the replacement surgeon (a woman I recalled reading about in a magazine somewhere), anaesthetist (unpronounceable), what would happen to me on the operating slab (unforgettable and therefore quickly erased from my mind), how they would carry out tests immediately on the tumour cells to find out if they had spread to the lymph nodes under my arm, and how these would be removed if affected.

'Would you like me to come with you when you check

in?' Nicky asked when she'd checked off her long list of things to tell me.

'I suppose I would, if you don't mind.' I looked at her and realised that after working with Nicky ever since we'd started Project PR years ago I'd taken her very much for granted. And apart from the intimate revelations she threw into our pot pourri of hilarious stories at after-work drinks, I didn't know all that much about her. Sure, I knew she had sole charge of the highly charged six-year-old Dylan after her ratbag husband departed soon after his birth; I knew she was even more capable than me of juggling with the usual jelly on the home front; and I knew she was bloody good at the business of communication management. But Nicky had kept a lot of her private life private.

'You're being a real brick, Nick. You must have been through something like this yourself to be so understanding.'

'No, not really.'

'Not really?'

'Well, there was the time I . . . Oh, it doesn't matter.' She became absorbed in her coffee, stirring it repeatedly even though she didn't take sugar.

'Nicky, don't leave me hanging like that. You don't have to worry — I won't tell a soul.'

'Well . . .' She paused and continued to stare at the patterned milk froth. 'I had to have a hysterectomy after Dylan was born. The birth was a real disaster and they had to do tests and everything. That's how they found out I had some bad cells in my cervix.'

'Was that why Donald left?'

'Yes, he couldn't face not having any more children. I think he wanted me to be barefoot and pregnant for the rest of my life. We'd always talked about having five or six.'

'Oh, I didn't realise. I never knew.'

'He's still a ratbag,' she chuckled. 'I know you've always said he was one, and you're right. I think it was just an excuse to leave, really. But he's missed so much not seeing Dylan growing up.'

It helped give me a sliver of perspective: Nicky was younger than me and in the prime of her life, but her loss meant she couldn't have children. What was my loss by comparison? Merely cosmetic.

• • •

I tried to hold that thought over the next few days as my anxiety increased along with my self-pity.

Nicky had written down the appointment time with the reconstructive surgeon and gallantly accompanied me. It was reassuring having a woman doing the replacement. For some reason I felt she'd be more sensitive; she was certainly compassionate. She made me undress and lie down (how many times had I had to do that already this week?) and inspected me deftly, asked me my bra size, and made copious notes. I found myself studying the women in her waiting room on the way out, wondering if they were in for a boob job too.

'Did you see that poor woman with the enormous knockers?' Nicky giggled when we were outside. 'I bet she's in for a breast reduction.'

'Perhaps I should have one while I'm about it.'

'Or you could go for one of those Hollywood jobs and end up looking like Pamela Anderson.'

'No thanks. I'll be quite happy just to have two, whatever the size.'

Simon responded to my wobbly call after seeing the surgeon by dropping everything and rushing over to see me. He arrived bearing flowers — my office was starting to look like a florists' shop — and two flat white takeaways that were still hot.

The Philly girls did their best to cheer me up that night too. We met at the usual bar after work on Thursday and they deluged me with flowers and gifts of champagne, which prompted me to tell them Ginny's line about its restorative powers during a crisis — any crisis.

'A woman can never be too thin, too rich, or have too much champagne,' Helen said, raising her glass.

I answered all their questions, this time finding it a bit easier, repeating things I'd said before, a bit like the standard answers I give some of my clients when being hounded by the media. The Lindauer flowed as usual, but instead of slugging back the bubbly, I couldn't bring myself to take more than a few sips.

'That's not like you, Penny,' Fran observed, chugging her ginger beer.

'I know. Somebody told me drinking too much wine can give you cancer. It's kind of put me off it.'

'God, people can be so stupid,' Di said. 'I see it all the time. They think they're being helpful, but they just make you feel worse coming up with all these crackpot theories.'

'Tell me about it. Someone else said it was using deodorant that causes it.'

'Deodorant? That's absurd . . . isn't it?' Helen said.

'Of course it is,' Di said. 'Next they'll be telling you it's from the ions in the air. Or outer space.'

I told them about the Conniving Cow's new fondness for 'channelling' visitors from beyond the grave.

'Pity she's not beyond the grave herself,' Helen said. 'I could happily help channel her there.'

I found that so funny I couldn't stop laughing but when I sounded close to choking, Liz had to start thumping me on the back.

'Sorry, guys. I've been a bit manic this week — one minute I'm in the throes of depression, the next I'm hysterical with laughter.'

'Perfectly understandable,' Liz said. 'You're holding up like a trooper, Penny. If it was me, I'd be hysterical all the time.'

'What really pisses me off,' I said, 'is how unfair it all is. I breastfed the kids, I don't have any rellies who've had it. And, I mean, all the stuff you read says how a healthy diet — you know, low-fat this and non-fat that, lots of fibre, fruit and vegetables — how it's supposed to help prevent cancer. Well, I ate enough broccoli to make me turn green, I always ordered the salad and even ate the beastly stalks, and I always chose the bran muffins though they're usually as hard as bullets. From now on I'm going to live on a diet of doughnuts and cream.'

'You go girl. If you ask me, it doesn't make a damn difference.'

'I reckon there must be something in that wheatgrass juice they sell,' Liz said.

'Go on, you're not the type to fall for all that faddish mumbo jumbo,' Di said.

'Well, wheatgrass can't be all bad for you,' I said. 'Whoever heard of a horse with breast cancer?'

'You'd have to be desperate to drink the stuff,' Helen said. 'It smells like horse shit and tastes like it too — or at least how I imagine it tastes.'

'Well, that's where grass goes after the horse has finished

with it,' Liz said. 'What can you expect?'

'Typical,' Helen said. 'We've been here less than half an hour and already the conversation has turned to crap.' She swigged back her bubbles and reached for the bottle. 'Hey, it's finished. Better order another. And maybe some food.'

'As long as it's not low-fat or high-fibre,' I said. 'And make sure there's plenty of it. I'm eating for two now — me and my tumour. It's got five days to live it up before it gets the chop.' It occurred to me as I said it that I had five days to live it up too before I got the chop. That was the irony of it — apart from what was roiling around in my head, I felt fine. After Tuesday, I'd feel like shit.

Helen called the waiter and ordered up a platter and another bottle. 'And I'd like fries with that,' I added.

I felt a lot better after seeing the girls — and not just because I ate most of the fries and all of the sour cream. Laughter had definitely been the best medicine, just like Simon had said on our first date. I arrived home feeling markedly better.

That night, Steve phoned.

'I'm sorry to hear the news,' he said. 'Charlotte's just told me.'

Once again, I found myself taking on the role of comforter as I went through the story one more time. I hadn't expected him to be so affected — after all, he'd traded me in just on a year ago for a younger model — but he seemed devastated and kept seeking reassurance that I was okay.

'Would you like me to come round?'

'No, thank you,' I said without a moment's hesitation. 'It's kind of you to offer.'

There followed an awkward silence which I eventually filled with the first bit of small talk that sprang into my head: 'So, how's Jacinta?'

'Oh, she's fine . . . I think. Uh, she's not here right now.'

'Oh.' I was beginning to suspect, from the way he was talking, he'd had a few whiskies.

'Yes. She phoned earlier. She's out with her girlfriends. They're planning a weekend away.'

'Ohhh.'

'I was wondering, Penny, about our separation . . .'

'Yes.'

'Well, maybe we don't need to go through all that.'

'No?' I was aware my voice had risen to a squeak. I was finding this hard to believe.

'No. I was thinking maybe we should wait a bit. You know, see how things go.'

'Really?'

'Yes. I mean, we don't want to rush things, do we?'

'It's a bit late for that now. We've signed everything now that all the property stuff is settled.'

'Yes, I know. But I meant about going through with the rest of it. We don't need to do the whole divorce thing, do we?'

'Look, Steve, I think you'd better let our lawyers talk about this. If you're changing your mind . . .'

'I . . . I don't know, to be honest. I just don't want it to be so final.'

'You sound like you want to have a dollar each way, Steve,' I laughed. 'You can't be a bigamist, you know. It's illegal.'

I put the phone down puzzled but also with a new confidence. It seemed as though I wasn't as unattractive to Steve after all.

To further cheer me up, Simon phoned a few minutes later.

He offered to pick me up on Saturday afternoon and take

me to watch Drew ride. He explained how he'd be running after his kids most of the day but the evening was ours.

'I hope you don't mind all that to-ing and fro-ing,' he said on the phone. 'I'd really like you to spend some of the weekend with me, but all my days off now are taken up with kids and horses and chauffeuring them back and forth. Myra has seen to that. I've got to come back into town to pick Zak up from touch at noon, take him home, hose him down, feed him and drop him round at a friend's for the afternoon. His friend's place is just round the corner from yours so then I could pick you up.'

'It all sounds very busy,' I'd said gratefully. 'And I'd love to come. A day in the country will be a terrific diversion.'

On Saturday, I would have three sleeps until the big day, three sleeps that would probably be spent in a state of perpetual panic. Monday would probably be okay, with clients to keep me on the run and work to finish off, ready to hand over. But the weekend and evenings worried me.

'Would you like to bring Adam along?'

'I'll ask. I don't expect he'll be keen. But thanks for the offer.'

To my surprise, however, Adam agreed to come. He liked horses, he said, had seen these big eventing competitions on the television and had always wanted to see them for real. That came as a surprise too — I'd never had any inkling that horses appealed. But he'd always kept himself to himself; even before this withdrawn phase his teacher alluded to he'd kept pretty quiet about his feelings and desires. So I accepted his company with a mixture of pleasure at having him with me in a rare mother-son outing and fear at how he would get along with Simon's kids.

It transpired that this weekend, the Conniving Cow had

planned a trip out of town with a couple of girlfriends to see some big motor-racing event they'd always hung out at. I could just picture her draped over the bonnet of a red Ferrari or something equally tacky, a siren on wheels, chatting up the hunky European drivers in the pits, batting her eyelashes over the air cooler, flashing her cleavage over the carburettor. The pits were appropriate for her, I figured.

I told Charlotte I'd be out for the day with Simon and that Adam was coming along for the ride.

'Cool, can I come too?'

'Okay,' I said after a mental tussle to say no — that would mean not one but two offspring to worry about getting offside with his kids. 'He has a daughter a year or so younger than you called Drew. We're going to watch her ride her horse over these enormous rails and water races at a competitive event. It would be really, really nice if you can get on with her.'

Charlotte reminded me she'd be working late on Friday and that I'd promised to come in and get her at closing time. I'd forgotten of course. I didn't seem to be able to retain much at the moment.

It took me ages to get through the Friday night traffic to the bridal shop so by the time I arrived she was waiting on the pavement in front of the illuminated display window. She was laden down with two bags and a big flat parcel wrapped in brown paper that looked like one of her design portfolios. She opened Rosie's permanently unlocked boot, tossed her things in, and came round to the passenger door. Tigger, who'd come along for the ride, pawed eagerly at the window and barked excitedly.

'Hi, Mum,' she said, opening the door and throwing herself lithely onto the low-slung leather seat. 'Get off, you stupid dog.' She pushed Tigger's face away from hers. He retreated to the tiny back seat and panted happily. 'You took a long time to get here,' she added, turning to me.

'Yes, sorry, traffic was appalling,' I said and slipped Rosie into drive.

It took just as long to get home, with a sudden downpour holding traffic up even more.

'Let me help you with that,' I said as Charlotte struggled with her gear from the boot.

'It's okay, Mum, I can manage. You go on in.'

'I'm not a cot case you know, just because I've . . .'

'It's not that, I can manage. Go on, I'm just coming.'

I left her to it and headed for the kitchen to make a hot chocolate for us both. Adam was doing his late-night shift.

I heard her come in and drop her bags on the floor.

'I'm making a hot choccie for you,' I called.

'Be there in a minute.' She hurried through the lounge to the dining room, carrying her portfolio. I heard the paper ripping and some clunking sounds. She came back in looking flushed.

'I've got something to show you,' she said.

'The jug hasn't boiled yet. Can it wait?'

'No, I want to show you now. But you have to have a blindfold. Here.' She whipped a clean tea towel out of the dresser drawer. 'This'll do. Now, put it on.' She folded it on the diagonal, wrapped it over my eyes and tied it.

'You'll have to guide me through the lounge. I don't want to trip over the coffee table or the dog.'

'Don't worry. Here.' She took my arm and steered me deftly through the furniture.

'What is it? Have you got your design project back?'

'No, it's not that. Wait and see.' A few moments later she said, 'Right, you can take it off now.'

She helped me slip the tea towel down and I gasped in surprise. Right in front of my eyes was none other than the Grahame Sydney painting, back in its rightful place.

'Charlotte, that's so . . . Oh, thank you.' Then it occurred to me she'd stolen it from her father. 'How did you . . . ?'

'It's all right, Mum, you don't have to worry, Dad knows,' she laughed. 'It was a bit of a struggle to get him to agree, but he came round in the end.'

I was gobsmacked. Steve had been totally irrational over keeping the Sydney as part of the settlement, to the extent that he'd conceded a lot of other things in its place. For him to let it go now was a major change of heart.

'Oh God.'

'What?'

'He didn't say he was planning to come back with it?'

'No.' Charlotte's eyes widened. 'Would he?'

'No way. He's still attached to Jacinta. I just can't believe he let you have it.'

'Well . . .'

'Charlotte, you haven't stolen it?'

'No, not really. He knows I've taken it. He thinks it's just a loan. But I remembered what you said ages ago, after he left, about possession being nine-tenths of the law, so I figured you'd end up keeping it. I can't see him marching round here to claim it back anytime soon.'

'No.' I pulled a wry face. 'I'll just have to pull the sympathy card with him a bit longer.' I couldn't take my eyes off the painting and felt a lump in my throat. It was a crazy thing to think, but the awfulness of the breast cancer diagnosis seemed to have coincided with — or possibly even caused — some really positive things to occur. 'Thank you, honey. It's good to have it back.'

'Oh, and by the way, I'm moving home now for good.'

'That's great, Charlie. I'm so pleased.' I gave her a hug; she tolerated it for longer than usual then escaped my grasp.

'Look, Tigger,' she said, bending down to take the dog's head between her hands and pointing him in the direction of the Sydney. 'You have to guard that with your life. You have to be a proper watchdog and earn your Meaty-Bites.'

At the mention of his favourite food, Tigger started jumping around, barking.

'You daft dog,' I said. 'You wouldn't have a clue how to guard anything but your food bowl.'

• • •

I locked up very carefully the next afternoon when Charlotte, Adam and I left Tigger in charge of the Sydney and the house and piled into Simon's elderly black Range Rover.

'Sorry, that's Zak's sports bag. Just chuck it over into the back to make more room,' Simon said. 'I thought he'd taken it with him.'

Simon drove us through the stop-start motorway traffic south to the farm where the two-day event was being held.

There were horsetrucks and trailers everywhere, people young and not so young in riding gear — some like a Thurber cartoon in full hat, cravat, jacket, gleaming white breeches and shiny black riding boots, their faces tense with nerves; others, who'd obviously ridden, were dishevelled, half undressed, breeches and faces covered in mud, pink-cheeked and pooped.

Simon seemed to know his way through the throng and parked in an adjacent paddock where there were more horsetrucks with horses attached, riders grooming them and fussing around. We opened the door to a strong smell of liniment, horse dung, sweat and hay mixed together and the sound of horses whinnying, loudspeakers announcing results, people hollering and engines stopping and starting.

'Come on, over here,' Simon called, leading the way between the parked cars and trailers to a series of tents and roped-off areas where more horses and riders were gathered, Simon explained, for the dressage.

'Drew did her dressage this morning,' he said as we passed the ring. 'Skylark was jumpy though and didn't do her best. Drew was a bit upset.'

Uh-oh, I thought. This didn't presage too well. Drew could be cantankerous at the best of times, if her behaviour on the track was anything to go by.

'But she should have better luck this afternoon in the show-jumping.' I crossed my fingers for that one. I so wanted the encounter between the kids to go well.

'Show-jumping is Skylark's specialty,' Simon added as we took a seat on the slightly raised grassy area beside the ring. 'We should know how she's doing soon if they're running on time.'

They weren't, so we didn't get to find out for another hour if Drew was likely to be in a better mood. But luck — or Drew's good management — was on my side because we cheered her on to a clear round in 'not a bad time', according to Simon. 'Let's go and congratulate her.'

'I'd like to wait here for a bit, if that's okay,' Adam said. 'I want to watch the rest of the jumping.'

Simon looked at me.

'Okay,' I said. 'I'll come and pick you up later.'

Drew was sweetness and light when Simon introduced us.

'Remember Penny Rushmore from the Abel Tasman? And this is her daughter, Charlotte.'

'Oh hi, Mrs Rushmore. Good to see you again.' She smiled at me then at Charlotte. 'Hi,' she said.

'Congratulations, Drew. We saw you jump,' Charlotte said.

'You did really well,' I added.

'Yeah, it wasn't bad, thanks. Just as well you didn't see us this morning. Skylark was awful. I couldn't do anything with her.'

'Do you know your aggregate results?' Simon asked.

'No, they're not up on the board yet.'

Simon went off with her and Skylark to the trailer to give the sturdy big roan a rub-down, feed and water. He arranged to meet up in half an hour by the gate with the horsebox hitched to the Range Rover, ready to go.

Drew was wriggling gleefully about in the front seat, having come second overall from this first day and was counting off the competition for the big course to cover on Sunday.

'Hop in the back for Mrs Rushmore, please,' her father said.

Her face clouded momentarily, but she obediently opened the door and started to climb down.

'It's okay, really, I'm fine,' I said, opening the back door. 'I'll sit in the back with Adam and Charlotte.'

'No, please, sit here.' Drew was already out and offering me her seat. I took it with a smile, though inwardly unsure of how the three teenagers would cope together for the first time.

There was silence for a long time as we followed the procession of horse floats and SUVs along country roads towards the highway. Simon turned up the stereo to fill the gap. 'Da-aad,' Drew cried. 'Not that old people's stuff.'

I heard Adam and Charlotte chuckle in sympathy.

'I suppose you want The Edge?'

'Thanks.'

Simon pushed one of the pre-set buttons and a rap song with some execrable language came on. Simon gave me a conspiratorial glance.

'Nice tune, huh?'

'Yeah, let's hum along,' I said wryly.

However, the music seemed to cut the ice with the kids who started chatting congenially over the din. They talked about horses first, with Adam quizzing Drew intently, then moved onto talking about school, teachers, friends and their various sporting interests.

Once, when they all laughed at something together, Simon looked at me and smiled.

'Good they're getting along, eh?'

'A huge relief. I was a bit worried how they'd make out.'

'Yeah, same.' He paused then said, 'So how are you getting along?'

'Oh, okay, I suppose. It's like being in limbo. I've got this terrible thing hanging over me and I know something's going to be done to get rid of it, but waiting is awful.'

'Couldn't you get it any earlier?'

'Only if I'd . . . er,' I was coy about going into the details. It didn't seem right, somehow, discussing my intimate anatomy with him. 'I had to wait for the other surgeon to come free.'

Thankfully he knew what I was talking about. 'Oh, I see.'

'So I'm afraid I'm stuck with it. I don't seem to be able to go for long without thinking about it.'

'Well, I'll just have to help take your mind off it, won't

I?' He flashed me a sexy grin. Despite my preoccupation with you-know-what, I began to feel weak at the knees.

Chapter 15

When we dropped Drew off at the stables, my two asked if they could go with her and help.

'Sure,' Drew agreed.

So we left the three of them behind and drove further into the country to find a café Simon recommended. After a while, in the middle of nowhere, surrounded by fields of dairy cows and sheep, he stopped the car, leant over and kissed me.

'I've been wanting to do that all afternoon,' he said quietly.

'Oh. I'm not so . . . are you sure?'

'Why wouldn't I be?' He looked at me closely. 'You're not any different, you know. You're just the same beautiful woman I made love to for the first time last weekend and I want you to make love to me again this weekend. Now in fact.'

'What, now? Here?'

'Why not?'

I looked around. I wasn't sure I was ready for this. 'Someone might come by and see us.'

'They might.' He smiled that lazy smile and his eyes twinkled. He was teasing me.

'But that would be terrible.'

'Would it?' He reached over and wrapped his arms around me. 'Did you know these cars have a very, very big back seat?'

'No, can't say I did. How do you know?'

'I had to sleep in it after Myra tossed me out of the house.'

'She didn't!'

'She did. After lover boy moved in with her, I became homeless overnight. I had no idea until it happened. No warning. And so I slept in the car. Where else was I to go?'

'I'll take your word for it.'

'I think you should investigate it thoroughly, make sure I'm not fibbing,' he teased, pulling me closer across the gear stick.

'Really? I don't know . . .' He kissed my mouth every time I opened it to talk. Any minute now he would drop his hand towards my breast and then what?

'Don't be frightened, Penny,' he said, as if reading my mind. 'It's not going to be any different than last time. Your body is exactly the same. It's only your mind that's in a different state. All you need to do is stop thinking for a minute and let your feelings take over.'

'That's easier said than done.'

'I take that as a personal challenge, Ms Rushmore.' He started not from my top but my nether regions, stroking me just where he knew I would respond until my mind started to give way to my senses. Suddenly, as he found just the right spot, the thought of making mad, passionate love on a side road in the countryside seemed a very good, life-affirming idea and the thought of discovery was lending it an edge that was even more appealing. Without saying anything, I got out of the car and hopped in the back, patting the seat beside me. 'Care to join me then? Or are you too chicken?'

He was beside me in a flash, covering me with kisses and wrapping his long, wiry arms around me tightly.

But despite all his entreaties, I kept my top on. Now that I knew there was something 'in there', I felt tainted somehow. I didn't want him touching my breast. But that didn't stop me from encouraging other erotic investigations.

Taking our clothes off, however, was a slapstick and tickle experience.

'You might have a big back seat, buster, but it's not big enough for both of us to undress at once,' I said as I struggled with my jeans. They simply refused to come right off.

'Here, let me', he said and gallantly tried to remove them. It would have been an ungainly and somewhat hilarious sight had anyone stopped to have a look through the steaming-up windows. At least two cars passed but fortunately kept going. I felt my heart quicken each time I heard an engine approach; it seemed to put even more passion into our amorous activities.

Afterwards, we lay back panting, our clothes in a tangle.

'We'll still have time for that coffee if we get a move on,' he said, gathering up my jeans from under the front seat and presenting them to me.

I felt a bit like a thief in the night, sitting in the little country restaurant sipping a flat white and holding hands across the table top. I felt like I'd been very naughty, but I also felt surprisingly comforted. I'd overcome a small hurdle: I'd been terrified Simon and I would never make love again — either he wouldn't want to or I wouldn't be able to.

'You're amazing, Penny, you know that?'

'Me? Amazing?'

'Yes, you are. I've never known anyone as spunky as you.'

'Spunky?'

'There's no need to repeat everything,' he laughed. 'I can see you don't believe me. But you are, you know. You're a spunky, funny, warm, delicious woman and I can't get enough of you.'

'Oh.' I was taken aback. I'd never thought of myself as anything other than a wife, a mum, a friend or a workmate — always in association with somebody else. 'Thank you. I'll hold that thought when I go under the knife.'

The kids were all still getting along just fine when we went to pick them up at the stables. Drew was bubbling about her results in the ring, Adam was clamouring to learn to ride and Charlotte had picked up the equine enthusiasm too.

'Drew says she'll bring me out one weekend when she's not competing and let me have a go,' Charlotte said.

'And me too,' Adam chimed in.

'Yes, you too,' Drew laughed. 'I said you could come.'

She seemed to be enjoying being the centre of my kids' envy and attention; she was quite a different child from the surly teenager I'd witnessed on the walking track.

When we got into town, Simon picked Zak up from his friend's. He was buzzing with a tale of woe about losing the touch game to a rival school that was much despised. Fortunately, it wasn't Adam's school.

'Hey, that's the school we thrashed in February,' Adam

cried, and went on to describe in vivid detail what a pack of stuck-up wankers they were and how they played dirty. He and Zak then swapped anti-private-school stories and touch stories and found they had several friends who knew each other.

'That's good. Long may it last,' I said very quietly to Simon. What with the incessant rap music, the boys' eager sports talk and the girls giggling about a group of boys they both knew, I figured they wouldn't overhear.

'Maybe we could do something at Easter — your kids and mine?' he said. 'Have you anything planned?'

'Not really. I haven't thought much past Tuesday to be honest. Maybe it would be a good idea. The doctor said I'd need to rest and not do anything strenuous.'

'Maybe we could go some place together, some place quiet, stay a couple of nights even, and you can put your feet up?'

'Maybe. We'd be lucky to find any accommodation at this late stage.'

Simon thought his friend Oz knew someone who had a house to rent in a popular resort town a couple of hours' drive away.

'Oz was saying last week that his friend had a late cancellation and was really hosed off at losing the money.'

'Do you think it would be wise to put us all in a house together so soon?'

'Good point. But I think this house is really big. Oz told me about a boys' weekend there once when there were around ten of them spread out in several rooms. I'll ask. Wouldn't it be great to get away together?'

'The two of us, yes. But I'm not sure about en masse!'

'I'll find out if it's available. Then we can talk numbers.'

Simon dropped us off at home, promising to pick me up

at seven for dinner. Charlotte had arranged, in a frenzy of texting, to go to her friend Jenna's for the night and Adam had his usual shift at McDonald's, so fortunately neither of them were home to witness the terrible dither I got myself into yet again over what to wear.

It was a superbly diverting candle-lit dinner in a small suburban restaurant. I felt relaxed enough by now to have a little wine and, thanks to Simon's efforts, managed to laugh quite a lot at his tales from the lecture room. Later, he drove me home and once again I invited him inside. We sat on the sofa listening to Amici. I had just snuggled into Simon's embrace and responded to a gentle kiss when Adam put his head around the door and wrinkled up his nose — whether from the fogey music, as he called it, or the sight of his mother pashing I didn't dare ask — and exited quickly upstairs. The moment I saw him, I tried to pretend I was calm and composed, but I was immediately un-composed again by Simon, who resumed his amorous attentions as soon as he'd gone.

'We're the ones behaving like teenagers this time,' I chuckled. 'It's a nice reversal of roles when my teenage son comes home and finds his mother misbehaving on the couch.'

'You ain't misbehaving,' Simon chuckled. 'You're behaving brilliantly as far as I'm concerned.'

It was a natural progression — after giving Adam plenty of time to text his friends before finally falling asleep — from the sofa to the bed.

I was still shy of letting him touch my breasts, but after the comfort of the afternoon, something made me want to make love as if there were no tomorrow. I don't think I've ever been so abandoned.

Afterwards, he said he should go. It was enough for Adam to see us together last weekend, he said, without us hitting him with it twice in a row.

'But you could sneak out long before Adam's awake,' I said.

'I don't want to have to do any sneaking,' he replied. 'I want to be open with the kids — with all the kids — about what's going on.'

'But they'd rather not know, I bet you. They hate to think about that sort of thing, even when you're married.'

'That may be true, but I still don't want to sneak around like I'm ashamed. We've nothing to hide.'

'It's not really sneaking around if we have breakfast together and you just happen to leave before Adam gets up. I mean, he's hardly ever up before noon on a Sunday.'

But Simon didn't agree and I conceded. He got up, dressed and kissed me goodnight, saying he'd let himself out before leaving me lying there, feeling very much alone.

I felt like calling out to him to come back, that I was afraid of being alone, afraid of the dark and the dark thoughts it engendered. But it was too late. He'd gone.

It was not a good night.

• • •

The next day, Charlotte came home from Jenna's unusually quiet. It didn't take me long to find out why: Jenna's grandmother had just died from cancer — though not breast cancer — and Charlotte had extrapolated her fate to mine.

'Try not to think like that, honey,' I said. 'Cancer isn't a death sentence these days. There's a huge survival rate for breast cancer, especially if you catch it early, like mine has been.'

She didn't look too convinced so I showed her what I'd found on Google — the increasingly high survival rates, the good news stories. I knew by now how to avoid the bad stories.

Just before dinner, Steve turned up unannounced, carrying a bunch of flowers. I took them graciously, thanked him, invited him in for a drink — although I could tell he'd had a couple already — and found a place for his flowers on the coffee table. There was already a bunch from Stephanie and the huge bouquet from Simon that I'd brought home from the office.

'So, how are you? I've been thinking of you.'

'Oh, I'm as good as can be expected with the sword of Damocles hanging over my head.'

He smiled sympathetically. 'I suppose that's what it must feel like. If there's anything I can do . . .'

'No, I'm fine thanks, Steve. The kids have been great. Adam even cooked dinner tonight and Charlotte cleaned up without a murmur of protest.'

'I wish there was something . . . I feel terrible.'

'Really, I'm fine.'

'You like having the Sydney back in its old place?'

'Yes, I do, thank you very much.'

'It's only a loan, mind you.'

'Yes, Charlotte told me.'

There was a pause. We both sipped at the pinot gris while Tigger made a renewed attempt at getting Steve to tickle him under his ears, like he used to in the old days. Adam trotted through on his way upstairs carrying a peanut butter sandwich and giving his father a disapproving glare. I heard his door bang upstairs.

'I heard you've met someone,' Steve said eventually.

'Yes. I suppose Charlotte told you?'

'Yes.'

'What did she tell you?'

'Oh, just that . . .' He looked nonplussed. 'Uh, that he was a science lecturer of some sort and he seemed okay.'

'Anything else?'

Steve pulled a face. 'Just that he had a beard and needed a decent haircut.'

I grimaced. 'She would.'

'And he's got kids of his own?'

'Yes. Two.'

'It's not too late, you know,' he said.

'What?'

'You know. It's not too late for us.'

'For us?' I heard myself squeak. I couldn't believe the cheek of the man.

'Yes. I've been thinking we could give it another try.'

'What? Just like that? You're crazy.'

'No, seriously Penny, I'd like to give it a try.'

'What about Jacinta?'

'Well, I don't think she . . . that is, she's not really . . .' He trailed off.

'What, Steve? She's not really what?'

'She's hasn't come home yet after the weekend. She's staying on a bit longer.'

'Oh.'

Adam came banging down the stairs in search of further sustenance. He gave his father another filthy look as he passed.

'Well, I suppose I'd better go,' Steve said, getting the filial message. 'Bye, son.' He stood up and waved at Adam. Adam barely nodded, grunting an acknowledgement.

'Maybe we could talk about it tomorrow,' he said sotto voce to me as he departed.

'I don't think there's anything to talk about,' I said, finally coming to my senses. 'It's too late to go back. Besides, this is really not a good time for me.'

'Of course, I'm sorry. I shouldn't have brought it up.'

'Probably not.'

He departed, looking hopefully back at me.

Well, I might be green but I'm not a bloomin' broccoli, as my mother used to say before she went dotty. I could see right through his little game: Jacinta had been out of town a few days and he'd been on his own for once. With no one else to keep him entertained, he'd actually started to think for the first time in a whole year about the situation he was in and I suspect he didn't like it as much as he thought he would. If the Conniving Cow was true to her name and had been up to her old tricks, playing up to the grease monkeys and spannermen at the race track, well ha bloody ha, I thought. Serve him right.

I smiled to myself. I was feeling a lot better suddenly, and I hadn't given breast cancer a single thought for the whole twenty minutes that Steve was being so utterly ridiculous.

• • •

Monday dragged on interminably. We'd agreed the previous week what to say to the clients but had held off until just before the operation to tell them. Tracey was responsible for pushing the button on the blind-copied email to them all, announcing that I'd be off work for three weeks for a routine operation. She sent it at 12.04pm and within minutes the phone started ringing with kindly inquiries as to how I was and the nature of the op. Tracey fielded them all. I swear she didn't tell any of them the real reason for my absence but, whether they knew or whether they were responding to the 'routine' message, the first flower delivery arrived at 3.30. It was from Jim.

'Sorry to hear the news,' he scrawled in his oversized angular script. 'The puppies will miss you. Get well soon.' His secretary (it sure as hell wouldn't have been Jim) had drawn cute puppy pawprints at the bottom in pink felt-tip.

More flowers arrived over the next two hours, adding to the brilliant array already covering my desk and reception. The cards nearly had me in tears.

'I had no idea I was so popular,' I said when another floral delivery arrived.

'Go on, everybody loves you,' Ginny said. 'Grade one schmoozing like yours always pays off in the end. Pity they didn't think to send champagne instead of flowers — it'll be much more useful after Tuesday.'

'I don't think I'll be swilling champagne in the hospital,' I said.

'Just you wait. You'll be crying out for it after a day or two. I know you. It's in your system. You'll get withdrawal symptoms.'

'Who me? That sounds more like you.'

'You should ask them to mainline it, instead of that awful stuff they feed into you through the drip.'

'Now that's not a bad idea.'

As she spoke, a huge bouquet arrived from Andy and the funeral boys.

'I hope they didn't nick 'em from one of their clients,' Ginny added when I read out the card.

'God, Ginny, you've got absolutely no couth,' Nicky said, overhearing.

'Well, they're not white lilies, so it's unlikely,' I said, refusing to be offended.

That night, Simon took me to the movies and then to dinner, which helped take my mind off the following morning. He brought me home and I asked him to come in with me because the house was so empty without the kids. They'd gone to their father's for as long as I was out of action and I couldn't face being alone. But it was an unspoken agreement that he wouldn't stay — we both knew intimacy was out of the question.

After a near sleepless night — despite downing two of the sleeping pills Ginny had given me — I arrived at the hospital at precisely ten to eight. Such punctuality was due entirely to Nicky picking me up in plenty of time; if I'd been left to my own devices, I don't think I'd ever have left home. It's not that I wasn't ready — I'd been ready and waiting for nearly an hour.

Mind you, getting dressed took some time in itself because I couldn't decide what was right. I mean, do you turn up to have your boob removed in your best designer outfit to cut a deliberate dash? Or should you dress down in your frumpiest trousers and grungy top, to look how you feel? Are stilettos de rigueur for a private hospital? Or would they make the sensibly shod nurses hate you? In the end I aimed for a show of style at the lower end of the wardrobe — no little designer numbers, no high heels, but something stylish (for confidence) in vibrant colours (to cheer me up).

Packing my bag had been easier. Since I only possessed one nightie and a pair of PJs, there wasn't much choice. I'd burrowed my long-abandoned bathrobe out of the dressing-up chest, where it had lain since I was last in hospital, giving birth to Adam, borrowed Charlotte's Chinese-patterned pumps to use as slippers, and filled my toilet bag with a bucket-load of treasures I'd been saving for a rainy day. If this wasn't a rainy day, I reasoned, then what use were they?

Passing the time until Nicky came to pick me up, I watched breakfast TV and read the paper (which reminded me it was the thirteenth of the month; I hoped it wasn't unlucky), but found it hard to focus, especially without my usual cup of tea. I'd been told not to have anything after midnight so I'd be ready for the operation some twelve hours later. But knowing I couldn't have a cuppa made me want one even more. I was gasping by the time Nicky arrived in her teensy wee Smart car. As she commented when we arrived at the hospital and had no trouble parking, they're great for squeezing into tiny spaces.

The receptionist gave me some forms to fill out and a nurse showed me and Nicky to my room. It was filled with flowers.

'You must be popular,' the nurse said, smiling. 'They've been arriving for you since last night.'

'But how did so many people know I was going to be here?' I looked at Nicky; she grinned.

'Some of those clients of yours are really insistent,' she said.

'I'll leave you to it,' the nurse said. 'The cupboard with the flower vases is down the corridor on the right. I'll give you plenty of warning when you need to get changed for the operation. The anaesthetist will pop in shortly.'

I went over to the bedside table and buried my nose in a bunch of pink and white roses and freesias.

'They're lovely.' I looked at the card: Ginny. I went round and read all the cards. Simon had sent an enormous bouquet of red roses mixed with other flowers. There was nothing from Steph, which was a disappointment. I hadn't heard from her since the weekend.

'You've got a lot of friends out there.' Nicky was smiling. She came and put an arm around me. 'There's a lot of love for you, you know.'

I sat down, feeling shaky.

'Come on. Let's get these into some water.' Nicky gathered up three of the bunches and headed towards the door, indicating I should bring some with me. Finding vases to fit the size of each arrangement and traipsing back and forward to my room was diverting enough. Then Nicky encouraged me to unpack and put some of my things around to make the room look more homely.

'Oh, I brought you these,' she said, extracting a *Harper's* and a *Vogue* from her bag. 'Every girl's favourite reading when she has the time.'

'And boy, have I got a lot of time now. I can't believe it. Three weeks stretching ahead of me with no appointments. Except for a certain appointment in a couple of hours' time.'

I stretched out the unpacking as long as I could and was beginning to wonder what I could do next when the anaesthetist arrived. Nicky said she'd wait in the TV room.

'You don't have to stay, Nicky. I'll be fine now I'm here.'

'Are you sure? I don't mind. I've got the whole morning free to be with you.'

'I'll be a bit drowsy soon. He's going to give me a pre-op which is supposed to make me relax so I don't scream all the way to the theatre.'

'Well, if you're sure . . .'

I glanced at the anaesthetist and his bag of tricks, turned back to Nicky and nodded.

'I'll be fine. With a bit of luck, I'll doze off into la-la land

and wake up tonight when it's all over.'

Nicky gave me a hug and a peck on the cheek and departed.

The pre-op didn't make me nearly as drowsy as I'd hoped, but I couldn't focus on the magazine properly, or the TV hanging down from a swing-arm arrangement above the bed. I switched on the radio and listened to Katherine Ryan interrogating some hapless politician. She was just winding up her show when the nurse returned and said it was time to get into my theatre gown.

If I thought the little beige number at the breast clinic was downmarket, this was even worse. It went on like a strait-jacket, front first, and had to be tied at the back, leaving my bottom mercilessly exposed. I sat down on the big armchair to hide it.

I was starting to feel horrendously hungry so it was almost a relief when the nurse returned a while later with a trolley bed to tell me I was on my way. She helped me up onto the trolley and I was wheeled off on the journey of a lifetime. For the first time, I felt horrendously sorry for myself. As the bright energy-saving lights flashed past one by one, I became aware that this was it — this was the last time I would have my own two breasts, the last time I'd be whole and possibly the last time I'd feel well. Why me? This wasn't supposed to happen to me. I could feel my eyes prickling and a tear tickled its way down the side of my left temple, through my hair, across the bottom of my ear and came to rest in the fold of my neck. Nobody noticed.

The anaesthetist was waiting for me along with several others as soon as we arrived at a brightly lit room. From my prone position, that was pretty much all I could see — their faces poring over me and the bright lights shining down.

I felt another tear trickle down while he chatted away, telling me once again what he was about to do, and before I knew it I felt a small jab and a sting on the back of my hand. He asked me to count to ten.

'One, two, three, four . . .' That was the last thing I remembered. Everything went black.

• • •

I came to, disoriented and groggy, in another well-illuminated room. I couldn't feel a thing — no pain, nothing. And I couldn't talk. I opened my mouth, but couldn't make a sound.

A nurse scurried up and greeted me. I couldn't respond. He explained I'd have a sore throat for a while from the tube, but that I was on metered doses of morphine so it shouldn't hurt too much. I drifted in and out of consciousness, aware only of a terrible thirst that was only marginally slaked by sucking the ice cubes they brought me, until I found myself back in my room, surrounded by flowers. Seemingly in no time, Steve was standing beside me. Even in my befuddled state, I was surprised.

'Hello, Penny. How are you?'

'Awful. I'm feeling awful.'

'They said I could come in. They're only letting family in. The kids want to see you.'

'I don't think they should see me yet. It'll be too much of a shock.'

'Well, okay, if you're sure.'

He sat down on the chair beside me.

'Steve, I don't think I'm up to visitors yet.'

He looked blank.

'I mean you, too.'

'Oh. Oh, I see. Well, I'd better go then. Shall I bring them tomorrow?'

'Yes, I should be more up to it by then. Thanks Steve.' I turned away and closed my eyes.

I drifted in and out of consciousness for the rest of the day and the next. There wasn't much I was capable of doing, but I did manage to avoid looking under the covers. I didn't want to know what I looked like. When the nurses came to check my wound, I turned the other way and closed my eyes.

The kids arrived without Steve later the next afternoon. Adam gave me a kiss on the cheek and handed me a framed photo of Tigger. Charlotte fainted, collapsing in a limp little heap on the floor. I pressed my call button while Adam flapped around helplessly then dived out into the corridor to find help. A nurse arrived in no time with Adam in tow and took over, quickly bringing Charlotte round again then giving her sips of water. When she seemed fully recovered, the nurse said, 'I think it must have been too much for her, seeing you so soon. Would you like me to arrange for her to go home?'

'No, I'm fine now,' Charlotte said quickly. 'I don't know what came over me. But I'll be fine.'

The nurse looked at me and I shrugged. 'I expect she'll be all right.' She turned to Charlotte. 'You should stay in the chair for a while longer, just to be sure. Call me if you need to, Penny,' she said and bustled out.

'I'm fine, Mum, really. Stop looking at me like that.'

'Tigger misses you, Mum,' Adam said, having a second go at giving me the photo. 'He doesn't like it at Dad's new apartment. He's only allowed in the kitchen and back porch and he's got this pathetic box to do his business . . .'

'Adam, don't be gross.' Charlotte pulled a face.

'I'm surprised he's still there,' I said, smiling weakly. 'He's such a badly behaved dog most of the time.'

'Dad insisted,' Adam said. 'Jacinta didn't have any choice.'

'He's had lots of walks,' Charlotte added. 'Dad goes running every morning with Jacks and they take Tigger too.'

'Except this morning he tripped her up. She was real mad.'

I found myself laughing; it hurt but I didn't care. It felt good inside, the very first laugh since the op. In the days leading up to it, I felt I'd never laugh again.

'Hey, Penny, you sound pretty cheerful. Sounds like I needn't have bothered coming up after all.' My eyes nearly popped out: it was Steph!

'Good God, how did *you* get here?'

'Now what sort of welcome is that? Nice to see you too!'

'Oh, Steph, it's *so* good to see you.' I could feel tears starting to trickle. I brushed at them with the side of my capacious gown. 'I thought you'd forgotten about me.'

'Forgotten you? How could I forget you? You were a major thorn in my side for nineteen years. I'll never forget you, you big ninny.'

'So how did you get here?'

'I flew up this morning. I've been to see Mum and Dad, and I've told Dad what's going on . . .'

'You didn't! I wasn't going to . . .'

'I know, I know. But he'd never have forgiven me if I'd kept it a secret. I've promised him he can come and see you tomorrow or the next day. I thought I'd better see you first, see what sort of state you're in. I don't want you giving the poor old boy a fright.'

'Thanks! You're right though, I just gave poor Charlotte

the heebie-jeebies. She fainted.'

Steph turned to Charlotte and grinned. 'Don't blame you. She does look scary, doesn't she?' She turned back to me. 'I can see we're going to have to take you in hand. Just because you're hurting all over doesn't mean you have to look like you don't care.'

'But I don't,' I protested.

'Well, I don't believe you. You've always cared about how you look. Now, let's see . . .' She started to rummage in my drawers.

'Hey, that's my stuff in there, you can't . . .'

'Look, the fancy nightie I gave you two Christmases ago. And hardly worn. You need to get it on, Penny. You can't get around in that hospital gown any longer. It's no good for your self-esteem.'

'Give me a break! You're worse than the nurses. They had me up the first night after the operation. It was simply dreadful. And now you want me leaping out of bed just to put a nightie on.'

'I didn't mean right now, necessarily. But . . .'

'I promise I'll put it on after I have a shower in the morning. I'm not looking forward to that either.'

'So how's your tummy?' Steph started to pull back the covers to have a look. 'Nice and thin?'

I pulled the sheets back on top of me. There was no way I was having a show and tell, especially in front of the kids. 'It's not bad actually. There's nothing left.'

'There's got to be some compensation,' Steph said. 'I wish I had a flat tummy. Mind you, I wouldn't want to go through what you've had to, to get it.'

Charlotte was looking aghast.

'Careful, Steph, you're frightening the children. I don't

want Charlotte fainting on me again.'

'Stop going on about it, Mum. I'm fine.'

'Did your mother tell you she'd get a nice flat tummy after the op?'

'Yes, I did. But I think she's of an age where she'd rather not hear about it,' I said. 'And I know Adam is.'

Adam was studiously looking at the TV set, which he'd surreptitiously switched on to Sky motor racing, with the sound off.

'Just like his father,' Steph sighed.

'Just as well,' I said, 'or he'd be making sick noises by now.'

'So am I allowed to ask how the new boob looks?' Steph said.

I glanced at Charlotte. 'Probably not the right time.'

'Mu-uum, stop treating me like a baby. I know you've got a new boob to replace the one they had to remove. I read all about it on the internet. It's cool what they can do. That girl at school whose mother lost her breast, she's at uni now. She said her mother never had a replacement and wished she had. I told her you were having one. She thought that was cool.'

'You're right, Charlie, I've been overprotective of you. I forget you're not a kid anymore.'

'I'm so pissed off with myself for fainting like that. It was so embarrassing.'

'She always was a drama queen,' Adam interrupted.

'I am not.'

'Adam, I thought you were watching the motor racing.'

'Yeah. Sort of. What's for tea?'

I laughed again. It still hurt. 'Oh, Adam, you never change, do you? I expect your father will be getting you dinner again tonight.'

'It was takeaways last night,' Charlotte interjected. 'Jacks was out.'

'Tigger will want his dinner soon,' Adam said, looking at his watch.

'Why, what time is it?' I still hadn't put my watch back on. Meals and visitors all arrived at the appointed hour; what did I need to know the time for?

'Just after five. Aunt Stephanie, can you come and stay with us back home? Then Tigger will be happy.'

'Well, I suppose so. I was going to stay at the motel near your grandparents. What do you think, Penny?'

'Of course. Great idea. We can't have Tigger tinkling all over Jacks's plush-pile carpet or whatever.'

'He ate the fillet steak off the bench on Monday night,' Adam said proudly. 'The Conniv . . . Jacinta was furious. Big deal! She made such a fuss Dad went out to buy sausages. That made her even madder.'

I found myself laughing again. And I felt incredibly tired.

They didn't stay long after that. Steph made me promise to dress properly in the morning — 'I'll be coming by after lunch to check on you' — and the three of them gave me a careful hug (Adam somewhat hesitantly) and a peck on the cheek before departing.

Cheered by their visit, I found the night passed more quickly. I even managed to thumb through Nicky's *Vogue* and watch bits of the news on TV. I wasn't allowed proper food yet — you have to pass the digestion test before they let you at the solids again — but the soup-and-jelly gummies' food was better than nothing.

• • •

But the next morning, something was very wrong.

I'd deliberately been weaning myself off the morphine, and this morning the pain was palpable.

I looked down at my chest and lifted the side of the bandage. It wasn't a pretty sight. I touched the bandages and a feeling of insurmountable sadness swept over me. The bandages were the representation of everything that was wrong and I suddenly felt incredibly powerless and terribly alone. A trickle of tears soon became a torrent and without realising what was happening, I was bawling my eyes out.

A nurse came running and, seeing the state I was in, offered me tissues and rested her hand consolingly on my shoulder.

'What's the matter? Can I help?'

'I don't know,' I wailed. 'I just feel terrible.'

'Would you like me to call someone? Your husband?' That set me off again.

'I don't have a husband any more,' I finally stuttered. 'My sister . . .'

'She came in yesterday, didn't she? She left her cellphone number with us. Would you like me to call her?'

'Yes, please.' I blew my nose loudly. I couldn't stop the tears, but I'd at least managed to quit sobbing so loudly. I could imagine everyone along the corridor would have heard.

Steph arrived after what seemed an eternity, having battled the early morning rush-hour traffic. She was carrying an oversized shoulder bag which she deposited on the floor by the bed. It started to wriggle.

'Shh!' she whispered and shot over to close the door. 'It sounded like you needed a dose of you-know-who.'

Within seconds, Tigger broke free of the confines of the bag and tried to jump up on the bed.

'Hey, you silly dog, calm down.' She bent down to pick him up and only just managed to keep hold of his wriggling, jiggling body as she presented him to me.

He slobbered all over my face and arms — still encased in the dreaded gown — and made the excited squeaking noises he usually makes when he's about to get fed. I couldn't help but laugh. I had to clutch onto my bandages to stop my tummy hurting, but I couldn't stop myself. Tears of sorrow quickly turned into tears of mirth.

'Steph, you'll get into terrible trouble if they see him,' I said when I could catch my breath.

'Who cares? It did the trick,' she said unrepentantly, lifting Tigger down onto the floor. He tried to jump up on the bed again. Fortunately it was too high or he would probably have ripped my stitches out. 'God, you're a crazy dog. What am I going to do with you? Here.' She lifted him up again but held him firmly at a distance. 'You can have one last look and then I'm taking you back to the car.'

'Heavens, I forgot. I should have given you the keys to Crackling Rosie.'

'Are you mad? I wouldn't drive that thing if you paid me. No, I picked up a rental at the airport. Much more reliable. And it uses about a quarter of the gas. I don't know how you keep it on the road.'

'No, nor do I. Sheer bloody-mindedness probably. And proving to Steve I can do perfectly well without him to keep things going.'

Steph shoved a protesting Tigger back in the bag, buttoned the top and disappeared out the door, the bag jumping and twisting under her shoulder.

'I'll be back shortly,' she said. 'As soon as he's done his you-know-what.'

'Your sister seems to have cheered you up a bit,' the nurse said when she came in a few moments later.

'I don't know what came over me.'

'Probably the five-day blues,' she said. 'Except you've had yours early. It's very common after a big operation like this.'

'Oh, I see. I had no idea . . .'

'No, well, it doesn't always happen. I think the best thing now is to get you up and give you a shower, nice and early, before breakfast.'

'Why, what time is it?'

'Nearly eight o'clock. Just time for a shower and this morning we could wash your hair. What do you think?'

'Good idea.'

It didn't seem such a good idea after all when I was standing under the warm jets. It had taken every ounce of control not to cry out with the pain of getting undressed and unbandaged before stepping into the shower cubicle.

And then there was the added dismay from seeing my poor exposed right boob with a raw red slash across the top where the bad bits had come out and the good bits had gone in. Magic transparent film had been sprayed across it and now there wasn't even a piece of sticky tape in sight.

But at least it was still a boob. Nice and round and just the shape a boob should be. The nipple was missing but, hey, a girl can't have everything. I'd been told if I wanted one, they could make it by whipping a piece of skin off somewhere it wasn't needed, twisting it round, and slapping it where a nipple should be. I was in no hurry for that. It sounded gross, as Charlotte would say. Besides, I'd had quite enough slashing and stitching for one year, thank you.

I was lying back in bed exhausted from such a pathetic amount of activity when Steph breezed back in.

'That's better. Your nightie's much more becoming than hospital blue.' She came over to the bed and gave me a hug. 'Now I can get near you without that appalling dog getting in the way.' She stood back and inspected me. 'Much too pale. You need a bit of colour in those cheeks.' She rummaged around in her handbag — not nearly as big as the large bag that had accommodated Tigger — and found her make-up. 'A little bronzer should fix that.'

'Don't you dare make me look a fright. It's far too early to be wearing make-up at this hour of the morning.'

'Don't think of it as make-up. It's bringing colour to your cheeks. They've taken on a sort of greyish-off-white hue. Very unbecoming.'

I let her have her way but insisted on a mirror to inspect her handiwork.

'Looks the same to me.'

'Good. That means it's not over the top. Believe me, you're not grey any more.'

'Well, I feel it. I've never felt so knackered after doing so little.'

'I'll leave you to rest then,' she said as an approaching breakfast trolley clattered in the corridor. 'Sounds like you're about to be fed.'

'At last. I'm allowed my first proper solids this morning. I've been looking forward to this moment for two days.'

'A small milestone on your road to recovery.' She kissed me on the cheek. 'I'd better get that dreadful dog home before he eats the contents of the car. I'll come back this afternoon with Dad.' And she was gone before I could protest about Dad.

The day streamed by with constant interruptions — someone to bring my breakfast and take it away again, a nurse to take my temperature and blood pressure and record it on a chart, a cleaner, one of my surgeons, another nurse to unhitch and take away the morphine pump as prescribed by the doctor, someone to bring morning tea, someone to take it away, the other surgeon, another nurse with new medication, someone to bring lunch, someone to take it away, another nurse to check my signs of life, and finally some peace. I lay back on the pillow and closed my eyes. But seemingly moments later, Nicky arrived, followed soon after by Simon. Then Nicky left and Charlotte arrived, proud of herself for biking all the way from uni. Simon left as soon as the afternoon tea lady arrived, then Steph came in with Dad. Until then, for the life of me, I had no idea what any of them had said.

'Eh, lassie, this is a bit of a surprise, you being here like this.' Dad came over to the bed and held my hand. 'You're a bit of a dark horse.'

'I was going to tell you, Dad, but not until I was out of hospital.'

'Och, I know I'm too old to be of much use now.'

'No, Dad, it's not that. I just didn't want to worry you. You've got enough with Mum.'

'That's true, lassie. She's not taken too kindly to me leaving her there with Nathan. But I wanted to come and see you.'

'Well, it's good to have you here,' I said, letting his hand go. I tried to give him an encouraging smile but I was feeling so pooped it was fleeting.

He chatted away about Mum and a bowls tournament he was taking part in, despite Mum's protests about him leaving the villa, then Steph and Charlotte joined in and I have a feeling I nodded off.

'I can see I don't have to worry about wearing you out, you are already,' Ginny cried. I came to from semi-sleep to see her approaching with a large stuffed Pooh bear clutching a bottle of Moët. The bear looked a bit tipsy, probably after surviving the rough and tumble of Ginny's car. She deposited both bear and bottle on the narrow table over the bed, gave me an air kiss and perched on the side of the bed to show me a foodie magazine with a huge picture of Panos up close and personal with an olive tree.

'Look, they've got four pages,' Ginny said pointing at the spread. 'You did that.'

It was like a blast from the real world hurtling through the door.

'That's great,' I said feebly.

'Oh, you poor dear,' Ginny said, leaping up, all concern. 'You look shattered. Would you like some champagne?'

'No, thank you.' I smiled despite myself. 'Ginny, you're incorrigible. You think that champagne can cure anything.'

'Well, can't it?'

'I know this is hard to believe, but right now I couldn't face anything stronger than tea.'

A nurse came bustling in and summed up the situation.

'I think Penny's had more than enough excitement for now,' she said. 'She should really only have two visitors at a time at this stage. She's not up to too many of you at once.'

'Okay, I get the message,' Ginny said. 'We should go.'

'Yes, we all should,' Steph concurred. 'I'm sorry, Penny, I didn't realise.'

For once, I didn't argue. I was fighting to keep my eyes open and, though I found it hard to believe, the cacophony of visitors was too much for me.

'I'm sorry, I'm not much company,' I said to Ginny as she said goodbye.

'Don't worry about it, sweetie. Everything's fine at work.

I'll come and see you in a few days.'

The others departed soon after.

'It's hard at first,' the nurse said when she came to settle me back on the pillows. 'Everyone wants to see you're all right and they always seem to come at once. But look at it this way,' she added, sweeping her hands round the room, taking in all the flowers and cards and gifts, 'to have such an overwhelming response, you must be much loved.' She gave me an encouraging smile and disappeared to take her ray of sunshine to some other hapless wretch along the corridor.

I lay back and thought about what she'd said. I'd never realised I had so many friends or that they held me in such high regard, yet the messages on the cards were so uplifting I should have been levitating. What a bugger, I thought, that in order to receive so much affection I had to go through so much misery.

Chapter 16

The cancer doctor (as opposed to the boob-rebuilding doctor) came to visit early the next morning on his rounds.

'Good news at last,' he said as he bustled in, all club shirt and bespoke tailoring. 'Yours is a low-grade tumour. That's much better than a higher grade.'

'Really? I always was a low-grade girl. Especially at school. But this is the first time I've been told it's a good thing.'

He smiled distractedly. I was clearly putting him off making his point.

'You won't need to have any further treatment,' he continued, his smile firmer now. 'No chemotherapy. No radiotherapy. You'll be able to recuperate in peace.'

'That's good,' I said, relieved. I'd been told chemo was a possibility, depending on the test results, and I'd been dreading it.

‘Two of the lymph nodes were affected and they have been removed. All the other tests confirm that further treatment won’t be required.’

‘That is a huge relief. I was terrified I’d have to have chemotherapy.’

‘No, that won’t be necessary.’

With that bugbear out of the way, I asked him the next most important question: ‘Will I be able to go home soon?’ Over the past twenty-four hours it had become very important to be on familiar ground.

‘Tomorrow, I think. I’ll ask your reconstructive surgeon what she thinks. If she’s happy, you can go home tomorrow morning.’

‘That would be great.’

At ten on the dot the next day, Steph came to get me. She took over, spiriting off the armfuls of flowers, cards and presents that had accumulated over my stay.

‘Just as well I left Tigger at home. There wouldn’t be any room for him,’ she said, surveying the back seat flower market threatening to burst out of its confined space.

Steph explained the miniscule car was a result of her Scottish heritage. ‘I like to think I’m doing my bit for the planet, saving fossil fuels,’ she said, ‘but really it’s because I’m too mean to pay for anything bigger.’

I clambered in, carefully lowering myself into the narrow front seat, arranging my drains on the floor. The deal with coming home so soon was that I had to cope with two big ugly containers draining my wound for the next two days, when my breast surgeon had promised to take them out. After that, I’d have to visit her every second day for her to drain them with a needle. The thought was not pleasant.

The judder bars coming out of the carpark were hell.

'Owww!' I cried as the little rental bounced over the hump. 'My stitches.'

'Sorry. I'll take it slowly.'

'Just watch the bumps.'

She did slow down — for Steph. But every time we crossed a pothole, I groaned.

'I can't help it,' I protested after about the tenth moan. 'It hurts.'

When we got home, the kids were waiting at the front door under a big felt-pen sign saying 'Welcome Home'. Needless to say, in my enfeebled state, it made me cry.

'Hi, Mum,' they chorused.

'Why . . . ? How come?'

'Aunt Stephanie arranged for me to have the day off school,' Adam said elatedly.

'We wanted to give you a good welcome,' Charlotte said. 'I'm only missing a Film Studies tute. Nothing I can't pick up from Jenna.'

'Well, it's a tonic to see you both here. I never expected . . .'

I pulled a tissue out of my bag and dabbed at my eyes before hugging them both.

'Come on you two, make yourselves useful. There's a virtual garden in the car to bring in.'

Charlotte laughed. 'You wait until you see what's in the lounge.'

'Not more . . . ?'

'Yup. Not just flowers, though. Come and see.' She led me through into the living room. The heady perfume hit me even before I could see them — a blaze of colour and joy. 'And look.' She took my arm and pulled me over to the kitchen counter, which was covered with an array of home baking and casseroles. 'I've been answering the door all morning.'

'Ah, there you are, dear.' Davina bustled in through the open front door. 'I've brought you a bacon and egg pie for lunch. You and Adam always were fans of my pie. And a batch of scones for morning tea.' She carried them through to the kitchen and put the jug on. 'I'll take care of this, Stephanie dear. You look after Penny.'

Steph sent the kids out to empty the car then sat me down on the sofa, recoiling at the sight of one of my drains. She quickly tucked a rug over it. 'You put your feet up, now. All that effort of getting here will have worn you out.' For once there wasn't a trace of irony in her voice.

I was suddenly aware of an unusual quiet. Then I realised why. 'Where's Tigger?' I looked around. No sign of him.

'He's out the back with a bone,' Adam said. 'Aunt Stephanie said to give it to him at ten-thirty so he'd still be out there when you got home.'

'You guys have thought of everything. I'm really spoiled,' I said smiling. 'It sure is great to be home.'

At that moment the dog door burst open and Tigger hurled himself through, heading straight for me.

'No you don't, you stupid dog,' Steph said, catching him by the collar. 'Just have some manners for a change.' Despite her firm hand, he inched his way forward, whimpering with excitement, pawing at me for attention. I reached down gingerly and patted him. He slobbered all over my hand and tried to jump up. 'Whoa,' Steph said pulling him back. He nuzzled at my knees then finally got the message and settled on top of my feet, effectively nailing them to the floor.

'Well, I guess that's going to keep me here for a while,' I said happily.

Davina brought the tea tray, with proper tea in the teapot,

her date scones swimming with butter on one of my fancy plates.

'You certainly know your way around the house,' I said. 'I couldn't have found that teapot if you asked me.'

'It may surprise you to know that Charlotte knew just where it was. Now, dear, tea?'

I allowed myself to be pampered and run after for the rest of the day. I even let Steph vet the number of visitors I was allowed. I heard her on the phone putting them all off, and organising them so they came on different days and not all at once.

'I'm not letting anyone come today. You need to settle in first.' I was enjoying a side of Steph I couldn't recall ever seeing before. Right up until the time she left home, when I was in my teens and still at school, she was the bossy-boots, the superior being who looked down on me as an irritating blowfly, buzzing around, in need of swatting away or, whenever possible, squashing.

To my astonishment, she seemed to enjoy playing the part of nursemaid, protector, chief cook and PA.

While dinner was cooking, wafting wonderful aromas through the house, she brought us both a lime and soda, sat down next to me and asked me all about it, 'from whoa to go,' she said. 'I want to know. There wasn't much of a chance in the hospital. There always seemed to be someone else around. God, it was worse than rush hour in the Koru Lounge.'

So I told her. 'Thanks for letting me do that,' I concluded. 'It sure felt good to get it off my chest.'

Steph roared with laughter. 'You've been getting a helluva lot off your chest these past few days.'

'And on again,' I added, joining in the laughter, which necessitated holding my stitches at the same time.

'You look like you think they're going to burst,' Steph said, pointing at me clutching my sides. 'I'm sure they're firmly sewn together.'

'They'd better be. No, it's not that. It just hurts to laugh. But don't make me stop. It's great to be able to. I thought for a while there I'd never laugh again.'

'You have been through the mill — you must have felt like crap. That's why I wanted to come up and help out a bit. I've been pretty mean to you these past few years, leaving you to cope with Mum. I've been feeling bad about that lately, since you . . .'

'Stephanie, that's not like you, helping the weak and the maimed.'

'I haven't exactly been the good Samaritan, have I? But you getting sick has made me realise I shouldn't have piled so much onto you. I should have taken some of the responsibility for Mum too.'

'I didn't get sick because of looking after Mum. You don't get cancer from running round after your parents.'

'Maybe not. But there is supposed to be an element of stress involved. I shouldn't have let you take it all on yourself. From now on, I'm going to be of some use. Any time you need me, just call. I'll be right up.'

'You can't do that. You're away overseas two months of the year promoting your books.'

'Not this year I'm not. I've told my publisher I'm not going out of the country for at least the next six months, maybe longer, depending on how Mum is.'

'But what about *Diary*?'

'Yes, I'll still do all that. That's not likely to sell overseas anyway, not like my children's books. I've got a New Zealand tour for *Diary* coming up soon. But I'll always be near an airport. If you need me, I can jump on a plane.'

'When's the book tour?'

'Just after Easter. I'll be on the road for about a month. They've got me going to towns so small I've never heard of them. But it's always great when people tell you they liked your book. That always makes a night in a cheap motel with a mustard-coloured candlewick bedspread and orange-patterned carpet worthwhile.'

'How's the book going?'

'Really well. The sales have shot away and the publisher's really pleased. The reviews have been pretty good, on the whole. There's always some smarty-pants who has to show how much they know about the subject or the genre, and I've had a few of those. But overall, yeah, good.'

'Is Marcus going with you?'

'No.' Her face clouded momentarily. 'He's staying home this time. Says he's got a big project on at work he has to finish.'

'You sound doubtful.'

'Hmmm. I suppose I am. But I daren't say anything. I don't want to provoke another row.'

'He's been a bit tetchy then?'

'He sure has. When he's at home, anyway — he's at work most of the time.'

'Well, it's a tough market these days — the advertising dollar is stretched to breaking point. He'll have to work twice as hard to pull in the commissions.'

'You sound just like him. Did he hire you as his PR person without me knowing?'

'Ha ha, very funny.'

'Well, whatever, it's driving me crazy. He's been like that for nearly a year — never home. I thought at first it was me.

You know, that he didn't like being with me any more. Like I was too old, or something.'

'Stephanie, you big baby. You're more attractive than you ever were. You're one of those lucky women who improves with age.'

'You really think so?' I could have sworn she started to preen herself, she looked so pleased. 'Well, it didn't feel like it.'

'So I suppose when Tiger Tim started to chat you up, you were ripe for the taking?'

'Don't call him that, Penny. It's . . .'

'Your boudoir nickname, I know.'

She looked shocked, but carried on: 'You're right. When he flattered me with his attentions, I fell for it, hook, line and sinker.'

'And you've really sunk to the bottom, haven't you?'

'Oh, I don't know about that.' She straightened her shoulders defensively. 'I'm only too ready to admit I was wrong, that I shouldn't have done it, but put yourself in my shoes, Penny . . .'

'No thanks. I couldn't afford them for a start.'

'Oh, I might have known you'd make a joke out of it.'

'Well, it was a bit of a joke, wasn't it, the way you ran after him?'

'Why don't you tell me what you *really* think? God, you can be so critical.'

'Stephanie, wakey wakey. You made a total ass of yourself.'

'Marcus certainly thinks so. It nearly spelled the end of the marriage.'

'No!'

'Yes. Things got pretty dire. In the end it was Seraya that saved us.'

'Seraya?'

'Yes, bless her. She heard us arguing one night when I thought she was out. She came in and said we should work it through, that we had too much going for us and that I'd realised what an idiot I'd made of myself and would never do it again.'

'She said that?'

'Yeah.'

'And *had* you admitted what an idiot you'd made of yourself?'

'Well, I had to then, didn't I? I had no choice.'

'And what did Marcus say?'

'He didn't say anything for a while. I thought he was going to tell her to naff off and mind her own business. But he just stood there, speechless. I didn't like to say anything. I'd have only made it worse. So I just waited. We all waited. Then he started laughing and laughing like he was going to burst and he said she was right. And that was it.'

'That was it?'

'Yes. He said I'd better have learned my lesson and that he would never refer to it again — and he hasn't.'

'Well, you're very lucky.'

'I know. I came very close to losing him. There's no doubt about that.'

'But you must have known at the time a toy boy wasn't a good idea.'

'Of course I knew. But I wasn't going to listen to that rational little voice in my head. I was totally bewitched by the flattering notion that someone younger than me thought I was still hot. How sad is that? I mean, he just wanted a trophy handbag — you know, like my old Hermés Kelly bag — to have attached to his arm when he wanted to show off to his gay friends.'

'You shouldn't put yourself down like that.'

'But it's true. I could see plain as day afterwards. If only I'd seen it at the time.'

'Hindsight, as they say . . .'

• • •

Steph left the next afternoon, happy that I was becoming much more mobile and commending me on my good spirits: 'You've got a great positive attitude, Penny, and they say that's worth a thousand doctors when it comes to kicking cancer. You keep that up, you'll be fine.' She gave me a big hug — which still hurt, but not as much as before — and tootled off in her tiny car.

Simon invited himself over that night and admitted that Stephanie frightened him.

'I didn't dare come round while she was here with you,' he said, settling beside me on the sofa with a cup of coffee he'd made for himself. 'She always looks like she's going to eat me. I don't think she likes me.'

'Nonsense. She's just jealous.'

'Jealous? Why, does she fancy me?' He suddenly looked very pleased with himself.

'No. Sorry. It's not you. It's me. She's jealous of me having someone like you around.'

'But she's got Marcus.'

Only by a sliver of fate, I thought.

'That doesn't matter to her. We've always been jealous of each other having something good.'

'Ah. So I'm good!'

'Yes, you most certainly are, you compliment seeker.'

We talked about the Easter holiday. Oz's friend had agreed to rent us his bach by the sea, and Simon insisted on doing all the shopping and arranging, as well as driving us all there and back.

'It'll be great to have a weekend away from the show-jumping ring,' he said. 'I love Drew and her horse dearly, but I do get heartily sick of it after a while.'

'It'll be a sea change,' I threw in.

'So it will,' he laughed. 'And it'll be a chance to get to know you a lot better.' He added some hefty innuendo to the last bit and smiled provocatively at me.

'Er, yes,' I said without conviction.

He put his coffee cup down and slipped his hand into mine. I held onto it, uncomfortable.

'You don't have to worry, Penny, I'll never push you into something you don't want to do,' he said, as if reading my mind.

'Thank you. I don't feel so sure of myself any more.'

He studied me closely.

'You are still a spunky, funny, warm, delicious woman and you're still very beautiful. In fact, you're no different to me than you were a couple of weeks ago.'

I squirmed.

'It's just that I . . . my body . . . I don't think I'll be able to . . .'

'I know, and I wouldn't want you to do anything you don't want to.'

'I'm sorry.'

'Hey, there's no need to be sorry.' He gave me a gentle, broad smile. 'How would you like to come out next Friday for a drink or a meal? We could go to the café up the road and have a quiet night out, get you used to the real world again!'

I agreed, not sure if I would be able to cope, but not wanting to hurt him.

However, by the time Friday rolled round, I was starting to suffer from cabin fever. My initial reluctance to have visitors very quickly wore off and by the end of the week I clung onto all the news people brought me from the outside world and welcomed visitors with the fervour of the housebound. I was still stiff and sore, but not nearly as much as earlier in the week. With my stitches due to be taken out on Monday, I was twitchy but much closer to normal.

I spent much longer than usual getting ready. And it's usually a bit of a mission anyway; all the little tricks with light and shade, all the pathetic attempts at turning back the clock, at rediscovering the fountain of youth. This time it required even more skill, even more light and a lot less shade. My complexion seemed to have taken on a sort of grey hue, tinged with yellow. The post-op look was definitely not a fashion statement and had to be plastered over as quickly as possible.

Simon drove me down to Bertolli's and found us a table for two away from the noisy crowd. He ordered two pinot noirs and launched into his plans for the long weekend.

'Probably too soon for you to bring your swimsuit,' he said grinning, 'but make sure the kids do. And Oz has offered the use of his runabout, so we might be able to do some fishing.'

'I expect you'll be able to give us chapter and verse about every fish we reel in,' I teased. 'Along with its parentage, its bone structure, and what it had for breakfast.'

'You bet. And I can even barbecue or smoke it for tea. There's no point in knowing all about fish and seafood unless you know how to cook it. I'll make sure I bring my arsenal of sauces, herbs and spices.'

'Mmmm. I can't wait.'

'Mind you, there's the small matter of catching it first. I hear the fishing up there has been a bit sparse lately.'

For the first time since the op I enjoyed a glass of pinot and had just finished a superb cannelloni when we were rudely interrupted by the sound of my mobile ringing.

'I'm sorry, I thought I'd turned it off. Just my luck something will have happened to Mum. I suppose I'd better answer it.' I rummaged around in my bag and found it, just catching the call before it switched to answerphone.

'Hi, Penny speaking.'

'Mum, it's me.' It was Adam and he sounded upset.

'Hi honey, what's the problem?'

'I'm at the police station.' My heart skipped a beat.

'What?'

'It's all right, don't panic. I'm okay. I'm in a bit of trouble though.'

'Why? What have you done?'

'I . . . er . . . I threw a bottle at a car and these guys stopped the car and had a go at me and the police came and so they brought us all in.'

'Oh my God. Are you all right?'

'Yes, Mum. I said I'm fine. I just need you to pick me up.'

'Now?'

'Yes. The cop said I could go if one of my parents came and got me.'

'Is that all? Have you been charged with anything? You're not being bailed, are you?'

'No. At least I don't think so. Look, I just need you to come down here.'

There was a break in his voice. I could just see him, scared, surrounded by crims and undesirables, frightened out of his wits, wishing he was home. My heart went out to him. I forgot about my present situation, about not being able to drive yet, about being supposed to take it easy.

'I'll be there as soon as I can. Which police station are you at?'

'The one up the road from George's place. I don't know what it's called.'

'I'm on my way.' I put the phone back in my bag and looked up at Simon.

'I guess you heard. Adam's in a spot of bother with the police.'

'Great timing,' he said. 'Doesn't he know you're just out of hospital?'

'I don't think teenagers think like that. The world revolves around them, not their mother's health.'

'Typical.' He shrugged. 'I'll come with you, if you like. You'll need a chauffeur anyway.'

'Would you? I'm sorry, you know I can't drive yet.'

'It'll be scary on your own. Besides, I know the ropes, I've been there before.'

'You have? What, with . . . ?'

'Yes. 'Fraid so,' Simon stood, went up to the counter and paid. He returned to the table and helped me on with my jacket. 'Zak got himself into a scrap one night down by the mall carpark with some mates,' he continued. 'They didn't charge him or anything, but it sure gave him a fright.'

'Well, it would be good to have some moral support, thank you. I'll accept your offer.' I smiled up at him and he gave me a quick hug as we reached the restaurant door.

'Come on, let's beat it.'

When we got to the police station, he took me by the arm and ushered me gently through the big double doors. I tried to steel myself; I was shaking with nerves. But I forgot about my own state quickly enough when I caught sight of Adam — his sandy hair matted with blood, freckles standing out on his white, bloodied face, his clothes torn and muddied.

'Oh my God, what have you been doing?'

He had the sense to look shame-faced.

'I told you, I got in this fight. These guys . . .'

'Oh, Adam, how could you? What'll your father say?'

'Don't tell him, please!'

'Well, I don't know about that. He should be told . . .'

'No, please!'

'I'll see.' I looked around. He was in a tiny cell with his friend George, who was sitting in a chair in the far corner, trying to pretend he wasn't there. 'George, you too?'

'Yes, Mrs Rushmore.'

'Are your parents coming?'

'Yes, Mrs Rushmore.' He hung his head. I noticed he wasn't covered in blood like Adam, but it wasn't the time to ask. The policeman was breathing down my neck.

'So, Mrs Rushmore, ma'am, if you wouldn't mind signing here, please . . .' He put a form under my nose. I signed. 'And here.' I signed again, barely taking in what I was signing.

He handed me Adam's cellphone. 'We had to take this off him. He was texting his mates to come and join in the stoush.'

I looked at him in disbelief; he shrugged.

'Your son is being let off with a stern warning this time. We figure it's one-all.' The policeman indicated at Adam. 'He threw a bottle at the windscreen of a passing car. Luckily it bounced off. But the lads in the car weren't too impressed. They stopped the car, jumped out and punched your son on the nose.' He noticed my look of alarm. 'It's been checked, and it's not broken.' He walked over to Adam. 'So, you're being let off this time, young man, but I don't expect to see you in here again, or it will be a different story. Understand?'

Adam hung his head and nodded silently.

'You can go now your mother's here.' He looked across at me and smiled sympathetically. 'It's all right, Mrs Rushmore. You can take him.'

We met up with Simon at the front entrance, where he was waiting patiently amidst an assortment of people from every imaginable walk of life, several of them totally legless.

'How ya doin'?' he said to Adam, tactfully omitting to comment on his condition.

'Hey,' Adam said in a very subdued voice. 'Thanks for bringing Mum to get me.'

'S'okay, happy to help.' He opened the door and ushered us out. 'Come on, let's get you home and cleaned up.'

'But your seats,' I protested. 'Have you got a towel? They'll get covered in blood.'

'Don't worry about it. They're fairly manky as it is, what with the stables and the stuff from work.'

I noticed some newspaper on the floor and shoved it under Adam's backside as he sat down. He sat silently, looking ashamed of himself. I figured it best to wait 'til we got home to hear his side of the story.

Simon, however, had other ideas.

'This really wasn't good timing, was it, Adam?' he said, turning briefly to look at him in the back seat. 'Your mother's not long out of hospital, she's not strong yet. What on earth were you thinking about, doing something silly like that?'

Adam grunted what sounded like an apology.

'Yes, well, I think you'll need to say a lot more than that to make it up to her. She shouldn't be running round late at night after you and worrying herself sick.'

Adam grunted again.

'What was that?'

'Sorry, Mum. And sorry you had to come out too, Mr Wakefield.'

'That's okay. Apology accepted.'

Simon turned to me and grinned. 'Welcome back to the real world, Penny. You can't be sick any more. Your son's just been released from questioning by the police!'

He dropped Adam and me off at the door, saying he'd leave me to it; he didn't want to be in the way.

'Sorry about all this,' I said.

'Don't mention it,' he said. 'I'll call you during the week about going away. You can tell me what you want for Easter dinner.' He smiled easily and was gone.

By the time I'd washed the blood out of Adam's hair and dabbed his face with antiseptic wash, I'd heard most of his tale of woe — much as the policeman had said, but with a few embellishments and expletives when he was describing the boys in the car. According to his excessively biased view, they'd asked for it by giving him and George the bird when they'd driven past before.

'And how many times did they actually go past you?'

'Dunno. Quite a few.'

'So why did you hang around? Couldn't you see you'd get into trouble?'

He grunted no.

'You kids you think you're bulletproof.'

He grunted again.

'Actually, you just don't think at all. Or you'd be able to see the consequences coming a mile off.'

Another grunt.

'Come on, then, I think you'd better go to bed.'

'Can I have my cellphone, Mum?' He looked across the room to my bag, sitting on the kitchen bench. He knew the phone was still in there.

'No, you can't. You can consider it confiscated for at least a week.'

'Mu-uum, you can't do that!'

'I can and I just have. There have to be some consequences for behaving so stupidly. And this is one of them.'

'You mean, there's more?'

'Probably, yes. I'll think about it overnight.'

'But I'll be a loser without the phone.'

'Well you should have thought of that earlier.'

'But Mu-uum.'

'No. And that's final. Now scoot off to bed before I think of another punishment.'

He ambled off, dejected, ashamed; his door banged shut moments later.

I sat down and tried to gather my thoughts. The bloodied bathroom could wait. I found myself wishing Simon were here with me. Not for anything amorous, mind you — I certainly wasn't ready for any hanky panky. In fact, I doubted I ever would be again, with a big scar where one of my erogenous zones should be. But it came as a surprise to realise that when I needed someone to turn to, someone sort of masculine and protective, it was Simon who sprang straight into my mind rather than Steve.

• • •

I found myself falling back on his seemingly endless patience and common sense two days later when another member of my family played up. It was Sunday afternoon and I'd just farewelled an ebullient Ginny and Nicky, who'd come bearing gossip and news from the client front.

'Is that Mrs Rushmore?' a stranger's voice said when I answered the phone.

'Yes, why?'

'It's Bernie Lawson here, Mrs Rushmore. I'm the manager on duty at St Joan's. I'm afraid there's been a bit of an accident. Your father, he . . .'

'Dad? What's happened to Dad?'

'He's being seen by the doctor. I thought I'd better let you know.'

'Is he all right?'

'I think so. A few bruises and a cut lip, by the look of him.'

'Whatever's happened?'

'Well, your mother, she seems to have had a bit of a turn. She took to him earlier. She can pack quite a punch, your mother.'

'Oh no!'

'Yes, I'm afraid we had to restrain her. She thought your father was part of a television programme about a robbery. She was still calling for the police when we arrived.'

'But what about the minders? Wasn't someone with her? Why didn't they . . . ?'

'Best you discuss it when you get here, Mrs Rushmore.'

'Is she . . . ?'

'She's been placed in the unit under sedation. And your father is sedated too. He was very upset. But he seemed more worried about what was going to happen to your mother than himself.'

'That's typical of Dad. I'll be right over.'

'Thank you, Mrs Rushmore.'

So much for taking it easy for a few weeks, I thought, as I eased Crackling Rosie out of the garage and down the drive. The three-point turn hurt like hell, but I figured there was no alternative. If I didn't drive, I wasn't going to get to St Joan's. If Adam had been at home, he could have taken me, erratic though he was behind the wheel, but as luck would have it he was on day shift — his black eye covered by dark glasses — and Charlotte, who could drive perfectly well, was at her father's.

Rosie was on her best behaviour for me. The power steering and automatic transmission made it almost easy. We slid into a park right outside Mum and Dad's villa. Hesitantly, afraid of what I'd find, I made my way up the path to knock on the door.

Nobody answered. I peered in the window. Nobody there.

I took myself off to the main entrance and found Bernie Lawson at reception.

'Ah, Mrs Rushmore. There you are. Thank you for coming in. Your father is under sedation so they've taken him over to the hospital. You can see him there if you like.'

'Sure. But can you just run through the sequence of what happened again, please? I'd like to find out how it happened, what with the minders there and all.'

So Bernie explained patiently how Mum had clocked Dad with the fruit bowl, temporarily knocking him out, thinking he had something to do with the burglary on the telly.

'It all happened so fast Trudy was unable to restrain her. By the time she got to your mother, the contents of the fruit bowl were on the floor and so was your dad.'

I said that this seemed a bit poor, given that we were

paying so much money to have Trudy et al there to stop this sort of thing occurring.

'I'm sorry it's happened, Mrs Rushmore — it is indeed most regrettable — but we did make it clear right from the outset that our minders cannot be policemen. If your mother became violent, we warned you that she would have to go back to the unit.'

I sighed heavily. I could see where this was going and I didn't like it. But if Mum was going to behave like she was in a Laurel and Hardy movie, I wouldn't have much chance of saving her from the dreaded dementia unit.

When I saw Dad lying back on his hospital bed, his once sturdy wiry frame reduced to frailty, I felt like crying. His head was bandaged, covering his right eye, and he had the start of a big shiny bruiser across his right cheek all the way up to his temple. His left eye was open but he didn't see me approach. I touched his arm and he looked groggily at me.

'I'm sorry, lassie,' he said feebly once he recognised who I was. 'I couldn't stop her . . .'

'It's okay, Dad. It's not your fault. She has the strength of an ironman when she's possessed like that. I've seen her.'

'I didn't want this to happen . . .' He flailed his hand to indicate the hospital room.

'I know. You've done everything you could.'

'No, lassie. Not enough. I should have stopped her.' He paused to get his breath, looking absolutely desolate. 'And now I suppose they've taken her away to that awful place again.'

'Yes, I'm afraid so.'

'Have you seen her yet?'

'No, I came straight to see how you were first.'

'Oh, I'm all right. It's her I worry about. Can you go to her for me and see she's okay?'

I could see he wasn't going to rest until I'd been to visit Mum and reported back to him so I left the hospital building and walked back past reception to the secure unit. Mum was in the day room where several men and women were seated around a blaring television, seemingly oblivious to it. One was flapping a magazine in the air trying to show the others, another was calling out every few seconds for help, and a third was playing with herself. Mum was just sitting there, staring at the telly. I went over and sat beside her.

'Hello, Mum,' I said, trying to take her hand. But she would have none of that.

'Who are you?' she demanded. 'I don't know you.'

We went through the old routine, me trying to establish some recognition, some rapport. But it was useless; she was completely away with the fairies. I gave up after a while. She was certainly none the worse for wear after her exertions with the fruit bowl and had absolutely no recollection of it; in fact, when I mentioned it, she became quite indignant and accused me of concocting a gross slander.

'I don't even know this Ron you are talking about,' she said. 'Who is he?'

'He's your husband. You've been married for nearly sixty years.'

'Tosh,' she said. 'I'm not married. I'm far too young to be married.'

She didn't even notice when I left.

Dad had turned on his side and was lying in a semi-foetal position, his back to the door, looking like he'd lost all hope.

'Dad,' I called softly to catch his attention. He didn't move. I tiptoed round the side of the bed so he was facing me. His eyes were closed. 'Dad,' I said, a bit louder this time. His eyes flickered then opened when he saw who it was.

'So how is she?' He didn't sound hopeful.

'She's the same as ever — in another world. She has no idea what she's done. She's back to complaining about the standard of service. She still thinks she's in a hotel.'

'Maybe if we didn't have the television on she'd be all right,' he said, propping himself up on his elbow and looking hopefully at me. 'Maybe if we got rid of everything that could get her excited . . .'

'I think she's lost to us, Dad. I don't know that they'll let her out of there now.'

'Poor Colleen. She hates it there.'

'She doesn't know where she is, though. She'd complain wherever she was.'

'But she never complained when she was here with me.'

'She did, Dad. You know she did. And then she went and hit you over the head with the fruit bowl.'

'But she didn't mean to . . . It was that awful programme on the television. I should have known it would set her off.'

'Dad,' I said, taking his hand, 'I think we have to accept that she's too much for us now. Even with the minder. She's just too much. If she has the chance to have another go at you, she might finish you off for good.'

'She wouldn't do that.'

'No? How do you know? She's a devil when she gets something like that into her head.'

'She always was as strong as an ox,' he said ruefully. 'She used to say it was all the housework that gave her such strength. She said I should try it sometimes.' He grimaced. 'Oh, I long for her to be like that again, the old Colleen we knew.' A tear formed in the corner of his eye and trickled slowly down his nose.

'I know, Dad. I know. She was a good mum. A bit scary sometimes. But we had some good times, eh?'

'I can't believe there's nothing we can do. What about Dr Tomahawk? Or that Mrs Small? Surely there's something they can do to help?'

'I think they've given up on her. I'll certainly ask though.'

'Anything's worth a try, lassie.'

'But I wouldn't get your hopes up. You've been so patient and understanding, but I think the time has come . . .'

'No, I don't want to hear it. Don't say it.' He removed his hand and resolutely turned himself over, facing the other way.

'Would you like me to get Stephanie up again? She might be able to do something.'

'What could she do that you haven't tried already?'

'I don't know. But she might.'

'Well, it's up to you.'

• • •

I phoned Steph soon after I got home to see if she could come. It was a test, in a way. Had she really meant it when she said she'd drop everything if I needed her?

Not a chance, I soon realised. She hummed and hah-ed and cleverly put the ball back in my court by insinuating I'd already done the deal.

'Look, Penny, you said yourself they're unlikely to let her out of there again. So what's the problem?'

'I just thought you might be able to help. Like if there were two of us arguing for her . . .'

But she wasn't to be persuaded. I suspect she was booked

up at the beauty spa for her usual manicure, pedicure, facial and body polish in preparation for her forthcoming book tour. She'd never dream of facing her adoring public without her roots obliterated, her foils furled, and anything else that showed given the full treatment first.

Disappointed, I called Simon for consolation.

'I feel so awful,' I blurted before he had time to talk about anything else. 'Dad's going to be beside himself without Mum. Even though it's not really Mum anymore, even though she behaves like a complete stranger, he still wants her there.'

'Of course he does. I mean, how long have they been married? Nearly sixty years. He's spent most of his life with her. He doesn't know how to live without her.'

'But he has to do everything. And she's so awful to him. She knocked him out, for heaven's sake. What does she have to do for him to get the message it's not safe with her any more?'

'I don't think he'll ever come to that conclusion. His heart is ruling his head.'

I had to agree.

We made plans for the weekend. Simon would collect me and the kids in his commodious old Range Rover on Thursday afternoon, hopefully in time to beat the queue of holiday commuters stalled on the motorway north.

He wouldn't let me bring anything except myself and the kids and our gear. He'd planned all the food and, he reminded me, we wouldn't have to worry about a greedy dog stealing it when we weren't looking — Tigger would have to go to the dreaded dog home.

The week dragged by. Having survived my first driving experience, I could at least get out and about, which helped, even though it still hurt to back out of the drive and to park. I even went to the supermarket and gleefully bought green bananas and a two-hundred-metre roll of dental floss — nothing like affirming you'll be around for the bananas to ripen or another thousand flosses.

But my first foray into the office was not received as enthusiastically as I'd expected.

'You're not supposed to be back at work until well after Easter,' Tracey admonished me as I walked into reception. 'You told us you were under doctor's orders to rest up.'

'Yes, I know, but that's when I was feeling sore and sorry for myself. Now I'm just bored and desperate for something to do.'

'Well, it's all under control here. Just,' Ginny said, coming through.

'Hi, Ginny. How's Panos?'

'Oh, he's fine. He's very excited about that story in the foodie magazine. I think it's gone to his head a bit. Did you see the headline they used, "The Good Oil"? Well, he's taken it to heart and tells everyone that's him. He thinks it's really funny.'

'That's not nearly as good as that awful newspaper headline you had at the dairy company, "Milk drinkers turning to powder".'

'It took me a long time to live that one down. The CEO kept teasing me that I'd written it myself. As if!'

'Jim still goes on about the toilet paper "Puppies on a roll" headline he got.'

'At least they never got flushed,' Ginny laughed. 'He wouldn't have been too keen about that.'

We sat down and had coffee together but soon afterwards Nicky, followed by Tracey, then even the usually social Ginny, made an excuse and departed, leaving me alone and unoccupied. I poked around in my office and checked emails but Tracey had already dealt with them all. It was a really weird feeling to have no work to do.

Superfluous at the office, I made an appointment to see the redoubtable Paula Small and headed for St Joan's.

It was as I feared. Her patience had run out. Mum had overstepped the boundary and put herself into the security-risk category. It was the dementia unit or nothing. If we didn't like it, Mum would have to go elsewhere.

'Mr Rushmore is welcome to stay in his villa as long as he likes but I'm afraid your mother can no longer stay there with him. It's just not safe.'

I was annoyed that Stephanie wasn't with me. I felt sure she'd be able to deal with the old harridan. She was much better at sweet-talking battleaxes. Besides, these days, I'd noticed, my tolerance of her failure to help had dropped dramatically. I was no longer Penny the patient, passive, submissive doormat.

Back in the car, I tried Steph's number on my mobile, but got switched to her message system.

'Hi, it's Penny,' I said crossly when the thing beeped at me to leave a message. 'I've just been talking to the people at St Joan's and they're determined to keep Mum in the unit. Dad's in a bad way. I don't know what to do. Call me.'

It wasn't until that night that she got back to me.

'When I was with Dad this afternoon, he'd slipped into the most terrible despair,' I said. 'I wish you were here.'

'I don't know what to do any more than you, Penny. There doesn't seem to be any way out of this other than what they're suggesting.'

'But there must be. If you and I went to see them together . . .'

'What difference is that going to make? Mum's not going to get any better. Now that she's started throwing fruit bowls around you can understand their concern.'

'Whose side are you on? I need you to go into bat for Dad, not for that awful woman.'

'Hey, that's not fair. I'm just pointing out they've got good reason to be concerned. Besides, I can't do anything you can't do. I'm not more likely to talk them round than you.'

'Yes you are. You're much better at persuading people to soften their stance.'

'Huh! That's funny coming from you. You're the hidden persuader in the family. You do it for a living.'

I could see I was getting nowhere.

'Look, Steph, you said you'd come up at the drop of a hat if I needed you. Well, I need you to help me out here. I'm not feeling that great. Dad's in a mess and Mum's gone completely ga-ga. Are you coming up or not?'

'I can't. I know I said I would, but I was fired up at the time. I've got to be on *Breakfast* tomorrow morning at 7.30am, then radio at 11am and at another station at 3am. Then there's a photographer coming round to do a shoot for the *Woman's Weekly*. I'm up to my eyeballs. And next week it's the book tour. I'm sorry, Penny . . .'

'I might have known,' I fumed. 'You had absolutely no intention of helping out. You're too busy looking after number one.'

'Hey, that's so not true. I did mean to come, honest. I just forgot I had so many commitments. Besides, I wasn't expecting this to happen so soon. I was only up there last week.'

'I should have asked Mum to hold off hitting Dad over the head for another couple of months, so it would fit in with your schedule,' I said sarcastically. I don't get really cross very often, but I could feel my cheeks flushing and I was burning up inside. It was taking all my self-control not to shout and use a lot of very bad words.

'Don't get like that. I'll be up your way in six weeks anyway.'

'Fat lot of use that'll be. Mum'll be under permanent lock and key well before then.'

But Steph wasn't to be persuaded. I was on my own again.

'Well, don't complain later if I have to make decisions you don't like. And don't blame me if Dad plunges into the depths of depression and stays there.'

'It's all decided for us,' she concluded. 'There's nothing you or I can do to turn this one around.'

I ended the call angrily; Steph was unrepentant. She just didn't seem to think there was a problem. All the vulnerability and humanity I'd seen when she'd been down over her gigolo had fast disappeared.

I went to see Dad the next morning, still totally out of sorts. The kids had done their best to cheer me up, chatting about the forthcoming Easter break up north. But they agreed with their aunt — there wasn't much of a choice.

By the time I got to St Joan's I was feeling almost as sorry for myself as for my father. I was supposed to be resting up after major surgery and instead I was running round after kids and parents in never-ending circles while my sister continued to swan around earning obscene amounts of money. My tummy was hurting where the stitches had been removed the day before; every time I turned round, I felt as if my wound was about to split open. I couldn't feel a thing around my boob — it was completely numb — but the muscles under my arms felt like they'd been cut in half and I couldn't get them to work properly.

That morning, I'd inspected myself closely in the shower

and had looked at my body with disgust and dismay. My body had let me down and now I was disfigured — there was a hideous slash across the top of my right boob covering a pile of extraneous fat that had been deposited inside. My tummy was, as a consequence, flat as a pancake. But instead of that I would rather have had my old, genuine boob back. I'd become as attached to it as I had to my rounded tummy.

I'd looked down and wept, the tears running down my face lost in the stream from the shower. I couldn't possibly let anyone see me like this.

Chapter 17

The six of us piled into the old Range Rover just after 3pm the day before Good Friday and headed up the coast to Oz's friend's holiday house. Tigger had been packed off the day before to the kennels, which was just as well because the car was filled to the gunwales with food and sports bags, sheets and towels, snorkels and wetsuits, soft drinks and enough wine to drown in, and only a tiny space in the back for one of the kids to sit in. And on the roof rack, a kayak and Zak's windsurfer. Adam's eyes had widened with excitement when he saw it approaching up the street.

'Do you think I can have a go on that?' he asked.

'We can ask him. Do you know how to do it?'

'No, but I've always wanted to give it a try.'

Simon helped us stash our stuff into every available nook and cranny and crammed the back door shut before it all fell out. The kids piled into the back, squashing up amicably enough, and I climbed into the front.

'Let's hit the road,' Simon said, smiling, and backed the truck out of the drive.

We arrived at the house four hours later, enduring bumper-to-bumper traffic most of the way. It was several sections back from the beach, on a slight hill, giving the deck and front room a lovely view up the coast and out to sea. Even though it was mostly cloudy, it was still warm enough for a flotilla of motor boats and small yachts to crowd the water and a few brave souls were swimming in the sea.

'What a great place,' I said.

'Cool,' said Adam. 'Can we go down to the beach?'

'Sure,' I laughed. 'As soon as everything's in out of the car and your stuff is in your room.' I held up the key Simon had given me for safekeeping.

'Bags the top bunk,' Zak said.

The boys started unpacking and the girls followed me in.

'This is our room,' Drew said, leading Charlotte to the back of the house.

A slightly musty smell hit me as I entered, but it was soon blown away by the sea breeze. The view from the lounge was stunning. It was a large room, taking in a dining area and kitchen with breakfast bar at the far end. I dropped my handbag on a nearby chair and went to check out the rest of the place: a bare-floored bathroom with a shower but no bath; a laundry with a washer but no dryer; a back porch leading to a sandy, barren garden; and back through the lounge to the bedrooms. Charlotte and Drew were already making the room with two single beds theirs. The boys were dumping wetsuits and plastic bags in their bunkroom, a tiny dark room at the back of the house. They didn't seem to care.

'Come on, let's get all the stuff out so we can get to the beach,' Zak called to Adam as they slipped past.

The double bedroom only had a miniscule space on either side of the bed, but its cramped confines were extended by a large window overlooking the sparse back lawn. I didn't dare linger. Simon and I had talked about the effect on the kids of us sharing a room and had decided it would look extremely odd if we didn't; the hope was they'd accept it without comment.

I caught sight of myself in the bedroom mirror as I retreated: anxious, jumpy and overdressed. My city clothes looked ridiculously out of place in this beach house, with its student-flat furniture draped with ancient throws and tatty fringed cushions.

'Come on, let's get this all inside,' I called to the boys to hurry them along; they'd stopped to explore the section. 'The sooner it's done, the sooner you can disappear.'

'Let me help you with that.' Simon took my bag in his free hand, and deposited it and the heavy chillybin inside. I started to help him pack its contents into the fridge.

'No, you take it easy,' he said. 'I can do this. It'll only take a minute. Besides, I'm in charge of the kitchen. It's my domain.'

'Except for Sunday night,' I reminded him. 'You said you'd let me do one meal. I've got to learn how to be a domestic goddess all over again. I'm in danger of forgetting with everyone looking after me so well.'

'Ee-eew, Mum,' Charlotte called from her bedroom. 'There's a dead mouse in here.'

'Where?' Adam cried with the homing instinct of a harrier hawk. 'Look, quite dead,' he said as he carried the small, stiff vermin out into the lounge and waved it in front of us all. 'I'll see if I can find you a live one.'

'Ee-eew, Adam,' Charlotte squealed, pulling a face. 'You're so gross. Take it out of here.'

Simon supervised the mouse burial in the bottom of the rubbish bin then emptied the supermarket bags onto the bench, while I returned to the bedroom to change into something more casual.

'Are you sleeping in here?' Charlotte said behind me. I looked up from pulling clothes out of the bag. She had a funny expression on her face.

'Yes.'

'Oh.'

'Is there a problem?' I made my voice light; I didn't want to make an issue of it.

'Oh, no. Not really.' She shrugged and went to her room.

After I'd changed into a loose dress and sandals, I checked the boys' room. Sure enough, everything was dumped in the middle of the floor and they were nowhere in sight. I restrained the urge to spread out their sleeping bags and pillowcases and headed instead into the kitchen, where Simon had finished unpacking and was searching through the cupboards.

'Must be some wineglasses somewhere here,' he said. 'Ah.' He turned to me holding up a small round glass on a stem; it looked like a refugee from the seventies. 'Sun's well and truly over the yardarm now. Fancy one?'

I looked at my watch: 7.30pm. 'Goodness, the time's flown. I'd love one, thanks.'

He opened a bottle and poured one for me then fished a beer out of the fridge. 'Not as cold as it could be, but it'll do just fine,' he said, pulling the top off the can. He took a swig. 'Ahh, that's better.'

'Here's to a peaceful weekend,' I said, raising my glass.

'Indeed. I think peaceful is something to wish for.'

We walked out onto the terrace together and took in the view. Way behind us, I heard the girls giggling in the bedroom. We leant on the railings and stared across the rooftops at the sea, where there were still a few boats puttering about.

'I'll get us a chair,' Simon said eventually, and extracted two white plastic outdoor chairs from a pile in the corner. 'Spare no expense,' he laughed as he set them where there was a good view.

We sat and I felt myself begin to breathe out comfortably, with only a tiny seed of anxiety remaining in the pit of my stomach. Inside, the sound of one of Charlotte's CDs could be heard on the mini-system in the lounge.

'Just as well there's no TV or that would be blaring by now,' I said.

'Mum, is there anything to eat?' Charlotte was standing by the ranchslider.

'Just help yourself to something. There's plenty of snack food and soft drinks,' Simon said.

'Can we have a glass of wine, Dad?' Drew had joined Charlotte in the doorway.

'No, Drew. Not tonight. Maybe Easter Sunday with dinner.'

'Aw-www.'

'Sunday,' he said firmly.

There was a big sigh from beside the ranchslider then the sound of the fridge door opening and packets being ripped open.

'She's usually fussy about chips and nuts and stuff like that. Says she doesn't want to get fat. But hopefully she'll relax her rules a bit while we're here.'

I turned around. 'Looks like we're okay for a bit longer. They're into the nuts and cheese.'

'Good. That'll keep them quiet for at least half an hour.'

The boys came back from the beach and ran inside to plunder the rest of the nuts before the girls finished them off.

'What's for tea, Dad?' Zak asked.

'Pizza,' Simon replied. 'In half an hour.'

'Yum,' he said and disappeared.

We sat companionably for a bit longer, enjoying the view and the intermittent chatter of the children. Occasionally it erupted into sarcastic banter as the boys teased the girls or vice versa, but never serious enough to warrant intercession by a parent.

The pizzas went down well, as Simon said they would, and the kids took off together down to the beach again.

'It'll be dark soon, don't be too long,' I said to their departing backs.

I left the mess in the kitchen and found one of the CDs I'd brought for just such a moment. We talked without noticing the time until I realised it was dark, and probably had been for some time.

'Heavens, it's nearly nine o'clock. We'd better go and find the kids.'

'They'll be fine,' Simon reassured. 'Oz says the kids all congregate together down by one of the waterfront houses and they're always fine. I wouldn't worry.'

He was right. They came back less than an hour later, the boys first, the girls soon after, and sprawled over the sofas and chairs, talking about their evening and the other kids they'd met.

Simon yawned. 'Must be the sea air. Time for bed, I think,' he said, standing and heading to the bathroom.

I followed him to the bedroom after a discreet interval. The kids never said a word; in fact they were so busy with their own discussions I don't think they even noticed.

Simon was reading a thriller; I got out my Philippa Gregory and snuggled in beside him, appreciating the smell and the warmth of a man beside me in the bed. He reached over and hugged me and we kissed — briefly and platonically. We knew only too well that four pairs of ears would detect even the slightest hint of sexual activity, which would have brought on howls of disgust.

• • •

When I awoke, it was dead quiet; the sound of four teenagers sleeping. Simon was lying on his back, his eyes open. My movement stirred him and he turned to look at me, smiling lazily into my eyes.

'Hey,' he said. 'Good morning.' He leant over and kissed me gently.

'Good morning.' I kissed him back, hesitantly. 'It looks like it's going to be a beautiful day.' The sun was already up and beating through the gap in the curtains.

'It does indeed.' He moved a little closer to me and cupped his hand under my chin. 'And you're the most beautiful part of it.'

Instinctively, I pulled back. I wasn't sure I could follow where he seemed to be heading, especially now it was so light.

'Don't be shy.'

'I'm not,' I lied.

'You're trying to hide yourself from me, I can tell. But there's no need. You're a beautiful woman, Penny.' He smiled again and I could feel something arouse inside me, overcoming some of my reticence.

'I'm not sure I can handle this.'

He used all his wiles to persuade me otherwise; he even closed the curtain tight so my scars wouldn't be so visible in the daylight, but finally he acknowledged my reluctance.

'We don't have to make love if you don't want to,' he said quietly.

Instead, he eased me beside him and, while smiling that lazy, sexy smile that made his eyes and his whole being sparkle, he stroked with a sensuality I'd never known those parts of me I'd been ashamed of him seeing. He made me feel so loved that I was overwhelmed. I felt a joy I'd not thought possible a month or two ago; I felt an inexpressible thrill to be alive.

'Do you know,' I said some time later, when I was lying beside him, my head tucked into the crook of his arm, 'ever since the operation, I've been dreading the moment when we would be lying together and you would see me. I didn't think we could ever be intimate again.'

He went to say something but I held up my hand. 'I didn't think I could ever let anyone see my body again. All I could think about was how awful I'd look, what you would think of me. But you've shown me it doesn't matter. What really matters is that I can still feel like I've just felt now.'

'I'm very glad to hear it,' he said, smiling.

'What does one silly old boob mean in the scheme of things, eh? It's nothing compared to being here with you, being alive.'

'A small sacrifice, really, in the scheme of things.'

'Indeed. Besides, I've got a new one to make up for it.'

'And you should be very proud of it. It looks just like the

other one. A perfect pair.' He cupped his hand around my new boob and chuckled.

'I suppose I should, in a way.'

'And besides, it's saved your life. You should be thanking it, not hating it. So promise me not to try and hide it away again.'

I promised. 'You're right,' I added. 'If it wasn't for this, I could have been dead in a year.' I paused for a moment as I realised what I'd said. It was the first time I'd admitted it to myself: this godawful experience I'd been through had undoubtedly saved me. And, just a few moments ago, I'd had all the proof I needed that I was still very much alive.

'You know,' I said, hugging him very tightly, 'I've just realised what makes life worth living is remembering the day you thought you were going to die.'

We lay there a while longer, talking, then got up, showered and breakfasted. It wasn't until late morning that the kids gradually emerged, sleepy-eyed, bed-haired, yawning, blinking at the sun pouring in the windows and asking what time it was. Simon and I had not long returned from a walk along the beach and were sitting on the deck having plunger coffee and muffins bought from the general store. I sprang up to get breakfast for everyone but Simon restrained me.

'Relax,' he said. 'They'll sort themselves out. There's plenty for them to eat.'

'What's for breakfast?' Adam was standing in the doorway less than five minutes later.

I grinned at Simon.

'Have a look. There's plenty of stuff you like.'

He grunted and joined Zak in a cupboard-rummaging frenzy that involved a lot of door and drawer banging, cutlery rattling and toaster popping. The girls could be heard talking in their room where they'd retreated after the boys filled the tiny kitchen.

I enjoyed the last of my muffin, slurped the rest of the coffee and leant back in the wooden deck chair which Simon had managed to find in the basement.

'By God, it's good to be alive,' I marvelled. 'Look at the view. Isn't it just perfect?'

'Mmmm,' Simon agreed, his mouth full of muffin.

I closed my eyes and felt the sun warm my body; my breast was sort of tingling under the sun's heat — the first time I'd actually felt anything there since the op. I smiled to myself: my whole body had undergone something like an awakening since this morning; this was further evidence.

My thoughts roamed over the past few weeks, over the unexpected benefits of trauma. I'd never known such an outpouring of affection and regard; the cards would be kept as a permanent reminder, in case there was ever a day when I didn't feel loved. But there was just one major problem that remained to be resolved: what to do about Dad. I was almost dozing off when I had a rare eureka moment.

'I've got it!' I cried, leaping up and rushing into the kitchen, surprising Charlotte and Drew eating scrambled eggs on toast. 'I've just had a brilliant idea.'

'What?' Charlotte mumbled, chewing her toast.

'Grandpa can come and live with us!'

'What?' she reiterated, with a bit more emphasis this time.

'He can come and live with us. There's a spare room. We can fix it up for him. He'd love it at home. And now that Mum is lost to the unit, she won't notice he's not there.'

'But Mum,' Charlotte said, 'you're never home during the week. He'd be lonely.'

'He'd have Tigger,' I countered. But the instant I said it,

I knew that wouldn't work; Tigger would be almost as much hard work as Mum.

'You're right, I suppose. He'd be on his own all day.'

'He could go to St Joan's during the day and be with Grandma,' Adam chipped in, coming in from his room.

'Well, that's a thought. It might just work.'

'And he'd be there when I got home from school. There's never been anyone. It'd be cool to have someone to come home to.'

'Good grief, you poor deprived child,' I said, grinning.

'Yeah, that's me. Though all my friends are the same.'

'Yeah, that's why you all get up to no good after school,' Charlotte interjected.

'I do not!'

'Hey, don't start,' I warned.

'Can I go windsurfing with Zak, Mum?'

I looked at Simon through the ranchslider. He nodded.

'Sure.'

'You can take the kayak down too if you like. You'll find Zak'll be out on his board for quite a while,' Simon added. 'I'll come with you and give you both a hand.'

It was quite a procession to the beach, backwards and forwards with all the gear, and back another time when Zak forgot his gloves.

Adam learned how to launch the kayak the hard way — by tipping over and getting wet every time one of the low waves washed over him — while I stood ineffectually by. Simon helped his son to get started on the windsurfer and we retreated to the dry sand to watch both boys take to the water. Adam, wearing one of Zak's lifejackets, soon became more proficient and was paddling confidently beyond the breakers, while Zak was skimming up and down, jumping the occasional wave like a pro.

'He's good, isn't he?'

Simon looked proudly out to sea at his son. 'He's not bad. He wants to go in competitions next summer. But he's got to learn how to jump the waves better first.'

'Looks pretty good to me.'

Eventually the girls came down to the beach, showing off their summer tans with bare midriffs and short shorts.

'Make the most of the sunshine,' Simon said. 'I don't think it'll be so good tomorrow.'

They went on into the sea, making a fuss about the cold water, shrieking when a wave washed over their knees.

I waded through the deepening water, enjoying the low waves splashing against my bare legs. Simon powered past and dived through a wave, emerging with a big grin on his face.

'Water's not too bad,' he said. 'I thought it would be colder at this time of year.'

He went out further and swam beyond the breaking waves while I stayed in the shallows, swirling the salty water around me, following the flow of the tide. I jumped the waves, revelling in the complete absence of pain or even discomfort. I felt free.

'This was such a good idea, coming here,' I said as we made our way back up the beach.

'It's a great spot. And great company.' He looked at me, then at the girls finally getting wet, then at the boys further out to sea. 'I'm glad we're all here together.' He took my arm and gave it a squeeze. 'See, you didn't need to worry.'

'So far,' I said laughing. 'There's three days to go yet. Let's not speak too soon.'

Back at the house, I helped make lunch. The kitchen

was a disaster area, but it didn't bother me. I'd noticed there were quite a few things that didn't bother me now. I seemed to be much more laid back.

'I wouldn't worry about making anything for the kids, not for my two anyway,' Simon said. 'They'll get their own.'

'Oh, okay. Just for us then. Would you like a ham salad sandwich?'

'Sounds great. I'll help.'

We'd just finished hard-boiling the eggs and washing the lettuce when the girls returned from the beach, sandy, damp and full of high spirits.

'Mmm, that looks good, Mum. Can I have some?'

Charlotte had thankfully gotten over her gluten-free organic-everything diet.

'Sure, honey.' I looked at Drew inquiringly, not wanting her to feel left out. 'You too?'

'No, thanks. I don't eat meat.'

'I can easily make one without ham.'

'It's okay, thanks. I'll get my own.'

I looked at Simon and grinned; he gave me an 'I told you so' smile.

The three of us sat down to salad sandwiches and juice while Drew rustled round in the kitchen. Just as we were finishing she joined us with a pile of lettuce, tomato, cucumber, tuna and sprouts and proceeded to pick at it. For some reason, this struck me as very funny and I had to hide my mirth.

Then the boys arrived and slathered peanut butter all over bread, followed by a layer of jam, eating it as they went. Adam came over to the table and poured a juice, downed it in one gulp, and poured another.

'Good time, honey?'

'Ah-huh,' he grunted in between mouthfuls.

'Did Zak let you have a go on his board?' Simon asked.

'Ah-huh.'

'He kept falling off though,' Zak laughed.

'Hnnn, huh,' Adam grunted with his mouth full.

'I'm going to give him a proper lesson this afternoon. He'll get the hang of it soon.'

After we'd eaten, I cleared the table and was about to ask the boys to clean up after them when they disappeared back off down the path to the beach again. I turned to Charlotte.

'Would you clean up the kitchen for me please?'

'Sure,' she said and did so, glancing at Drew several times to see if she was going to help. But Drew kept on chomping her way through the salad.

I came back from the loo to find her plate still on the table and no sign of her or Charlotte. The kitchen was passably clean.

'They've gone back to the beach too,' Simon said, coming in from outside. 'Don't know how long they'll be gone, though. There are some big black clouds on the horizon. I think we're in for a change.'

'Darn.' I went out on the deck to have a look. Sure enough, rain clouds were gathering on the southern coast.

'Better make the most of the sunshine then. Come on, let's sit outside.' Simon picked up his thriller from the coffee table and plonked himself on a deck chair.

'You're right, we're on holiday.' I fetched my book from the bedroom and joined him.

I stretched out on a neighbouring deckchair with my books, feeling nicely lazy, warmed by the late summer sun, and became embroiled in the machinations of King Henry VIII's court.

After a while I closed the book and shut my eyes, letting

the sun radiate through my eyelids. Crimson shapes danced around haphazardly as the warmth spread through my whole body. I stretched and yawned and dozed.

My reverie was interrupted by little pings of water on my face. Instinctively, I wiped the sides of my mouth in case I'd been dribbling in my sleep. I looked across at Simon to see if he'd noticed, hoping I hadn't been snoring either, but he was absorbed in his book.

'All good things must come to an end,' I sighed after a while.

'Sadly, yes.' Simon sighed too and together we picked up our books, stood and carried the chairs under the shelter of the eaves.

Suddenly, the sun was gone and the air went cold. I shivered.

'That was quick. I think I'll get something a bit warmer on.'

We'd both just finished adding clothes when the kids rocketed up the path, two to a kayak and surfboard.

'Come on, Adam, come and help me bring up the sail.'

Simon directed the girls in the rinsing and stashing away of the kayak and board, and then the house was full again with everyone wanting showers, towels, shampoo, something to eat, something to drink and, inevitably, something to do.

'You guys can clean up the kitchen for a start,' Simon said sternly to all four of them. The girls, who'd bagsed the shower first, had only just emerged from the bedroom after blow-drying hair, trying out each other's cosmetics and deciding several times over what to wear. The boys had gone straight from the shower to the kitchen, without stopping to even brush their hair, and came through to the lounge carrying a packet of chips and cans of soft drink.

'Can we have a beer, Dad?' Zak asked.

'We'll see. Maybe later. But you've got to clean up first. I want this place looking ship-shape.'

'Aww-www,' Zak whined.

'You want a beer, you earn it.'

'Can I have one too?' Adam asked.

'Let's see how well you clean up first.'

Simon and I retreated to the sofas while a terrible clattering and clanging occurred, as seemingly every dish was dropped on the floor and broken.

'Hey, take it easy out there,' Simon called after one particularly loud clang. 'We break anything, we have to pay for it.'

'It's all right, Dad. Don't fuss.'

'Thank you,' I said quietly when a more subdued clattering resumed.

'You've gotta get on their case if you want anything done at all. That was one of the first things I learned after Myra left.'

I didn't want to admit that I was so desperate for his kids to like me, I didn't dare ask them to do anything at all.

'It's going to be hard for both of us . . .'

We were interrupted by raised voices.

'I'm washing.'

'No, I am.'

'No, you're drying.'

'You're hopeless at washing.'

'You're putting away.'

'No, I'm washing.'

'Hey, guys, that's enough. The oldest can wash, the youngest puts away and the other two can dry.'

'But, Da-aad . . .'

'Come on, it's not that difficult. You can swap round next time.'

There were further protests as they sorted out the pecking order, though more subdued this time; hostilities were over, for now.

I started to pick up wet towels and beach gear.

'Leave that, Penny. The kids can do it later.'

I gave him a 'yeah, right' look and he smiled.

'Yeah, really, I'll see to it.'

Pleased to be off the hook, I threw myself on the sofa with my cellphone and autodialed Stephanie's number.

'Hello?'

'Hey, it's me. I want to apologise for being so rude the other day,' I said straight off.

'Oh.' She sounded taken aback. 'Well, I suppose I asked for it.' There was a pause. 'I've been thinking, I could probably come up the week after next for a couple of days in between book signings. But I didn't feel like ringing you, you were so rude.'

'That would be terrific. Then we can talk about my great idea.'

'You've had a great idea?' she said incredulously. 'I bet it was lonely.'

'Ha ha, very funny.'

'So what is it then?'

'Well, I reckon Dad could come and stay with me. I mean, Mum won't ever know. She doesn't even know who he is half the time.'

'True. But how will you cope? You find it hard enough with the menagerie you've got already.'

'He's no trouble. Besides, it's only a little over a year since we lost the fourth member of the family. We'd be a foursome again — without all the worry that goes with a straying husband.'

'What would the kids say?'

'I've run it past them. They don't seem to mind at all. Adam said it would be cool to have someone at home after school.'

'Well, if you're sure . . .'

'No, I'm not sure. I'll have to give it a lot more thought. But think of all the money it would save if he didn't have to pay for the villa as well as the unit.'

'Typical. You're your father's daughter, Scottish to the end. You were born with gorse in your pockets.'

'Well, it's true — Dad's told us how worried he is about the cost. Just the same, he'll take a lot of persuading.'

'I can't see him leaving St Joan's without Mum.'

'If you were really serious about coming up again, we could work on him together.'

'I suppose it's worth a try. I'll slip it into my signing schedule and make a flight booking. I'll email you.'

'Thank you, Steph. I'm so glad I phoned.'

'Same. I hate it when you and I fall out.'

'Me too.'

'I have to say, you seem a lot more relaxed and easy-going now. Must be the naughty weekend with Simon.'

'Must be. I think I've been having a bit of an epiphany up here. It's good to be alive.'

'Well, yes. You of all people would know that. Good on you, Penny. Go for it.'

'I plan to,' I said suggestively.

'Too much information,' she squealed.

'You're just jealous,' I said, pleased.

The barbecue we'd planned for dinner had to come indoors — it was bucketing down by now — so I left Simon to do battle with the frypan and the griller on the old stove while I made a potato salad and a green salad and set all the food and plates out on the breakfast bar for everyone to help themselves.

'There's nothing to do, Dad,' Drew whined as we beavered away.

'Then come and help here,' he said. 'You can peel the potatoes for Penny.'

Drew rolled her eyes and returned to the lounge.

'Hey, we can play Monopoly,' Adam cried, discovering a pile of games in the corner.

'Don't be such a baby,' Drew said. 'We're not playing games.'

Adam looked stung.

'I'll play with you,' Charlotte said kindly.

By the time they'd set up the board, Drew's competitive streak compelled her to join in. However, it wasn't long before war broke out.

'That's my hotel. You owe me squillions,' Charlotte cried.

'I do not.'

'That's because you don't have it,' Zak teased his big sister.

'You stay out of it.'

'Ha ha, you'll have to go to jail,' he continued mercilessly.

'It doesn't matter,' Charlotte said loftily.

'There's no need to be such a smart-arse, Zak,' Drew retorted. 'I'll pay.' She gave a big dramatic sigh and started counting money, slapping it down in front of Charlotte. 'There, that's all I have, I'll have to owe you.'

Charlotte, a year older and a little wiser now that she'd left the bitchy gossip of the Year 13 common room, tolerated Drew's childishness through the rest of the game until dinner, but I could hear an edge to her voice. It wasn't long before the next skirmish.

Drew, waiting for her turn in the game, came over to inspect the potato salad.

'My Mum doesn't do it that way,' she pronounced.

'Oh?' I didn't know what else to say. Simon was engrossed over the hotplate dealing with sizzling sausages and chops and didn't appear to have heard.

'Hers isn't gluggy like this,' she continued as she spooned the salad server through it.

I found it hard not to laugh — she was being so obvious. I bit back a retort and started to wash the lettuce. Charlotte got up from the deteriorating game and came over to the kitchen.

'You do a *great* potato salad, Mum,' she said, with a flicker of a smirk in Drew's direction. 'Can I do anything to help?'

'Thanks, honey. You can carry this stuff over to the table.'

'Your turn, Drew,' Zak called from the couch.

Drew scowled, flounced off to the Monopoly board and scattered the pieces around the rug with a truculent swipe of her hand.

I saw the boys roll their eyes at each other and immediately retreat to their room.

'Would you please put that away, Drew, before dinner?' I asked as pleasantly as I could.

'You're not the boss of me,' she retorted, giving me a look of intense dislike.

'No, I'm not. I'm simply asking you nicely to put something away, please.'

'No. You can't make me.'

I cut her a sideways glance and raised one eyebrow, saying nothing. Then I returned to the sink and the lettuce.

'I'll put them away,' Charlotte said breezily, returning

to the Monopoly. She made a great show of picking up all the pieces and putting them back in the box, each in its right place. Drew took herself off to the bedroom, banging the door behind her loud enough to give us both the message but not so loud as to rouse the interest of her father. He was still absorbed in his culinary task, stopping only occasionally for another swig of Speight's from the can parked on the nearby bench.

The girls bickered through dinner. With her father at the table, Drew didn't dare criticise my cooking again, but she found plenty to be disagreeable about, from her father's burnt chops (not that she would deign to eat them) to the dressing on the salad (my recipe, of course). Charlotte, on the other hand, was exaggeratedly polite and cheerful, complimenting Simon on his gourmet sausages, praising the wine, and devouring my salads with gusto — even the beastly potato salad, which she would normally never have touched.

Drew continued to pout while reluctantly helping the others with the dishes, and tossed the cutlery noisily into the drawer. The boys, sensing hostilities weren't quite yet over, disappeared to their room the second the last dish was put away.

On the way up in the car, the pair had soon established a lot of common ground. They were in the same year, though at different schools, and had hung out with friends who knew each other, plus they were both into touch, watersports, rapper Scribe, some band called Evermore and, of all things, Biology. I'd always felt inadequate in not showing much interest in Adam's favourite subject — neither Steve nor I had been able to come to grips with the finer points of the alimentary canal of a rat — but Adam and Zak shared a passion for the dissection and analysis of vermin and other undesirable creatures that only Simon could understand.

Hostilities between the girls were suspended when one of the young people from a nearby holiday home knocked at the back door to ask them round. They were having a party, she said. She seemed to know Drew from town. So it was with considerable relief that I gave them ginger beer and a packet of crisps and sent them on their way, looking forward to the ensuing peace.

The minute they left, however, the boys returned to the lounge and put something loud and tuneless on the CD player then started dancing round imitating the explosive sounds the hip hop artists were amplifying on the mike. It was awful.

'Hey guys, that's unbelievably loud.'

'Would you like me to make it believably loud then, Dad?'

'Ha ha, very funny. Now please turn it down.'

'Let's leave them to it and go for a walk,' I suggested, keen to escape the teenage testosterone.

'In the rain?'

'Why not? We've got jackets. Besides, it's only drizzling now, it might not be too bad.'

It wasn't, as it turned out. We wandered companionably, hand in hand, through the tiny seaside settlement, marvelling at the amount of money some people had to spend on a second home and all the accoutrements — boats, jetskis, tractors to pull their water toys across the beach and all manner of canoes, sailboards, wakeboards, fishing gear and some of the biggest barbecues I've ever seen.

Down at the deserted beach, the waves rolled slowly across the flat sand, arriving eerily out of the mist. We walked down to the water's edge and stood there staring out to the rain-shrouded sea.

'I've been thinking,' Simon said as he threaded his fingers through mine. He turned to face me. 'I'd very much like to see more of you.'

'More of me?'

'Yes, spend more time with you.'

'That would be nice. If we can find the time,' I laughed.

'Yes, well, that's the trouble, finding the time. So that's what I was thinking.'

'Oh?' I couldn't see what he was getting at.

'Well, you see, if we were together more of the time . . .' He looked away, as if trying to find the words hanging in the mist.

'Yes?'

'If we were living together, for example . . .'

'Oh!' I let his hand go and took a step back.

'It's all right, Penny, if you don't want to . . .'

'It's not that . . . I mean, I don't know. I hadn't thought about it!'

'Neither did I until today. It just seemed like a good idea. We get on so well together.'

'But what about the kids?'

'They'll work it out. But it's not about the kids, it's about us. If we're motivated enough to want to do it, we'll get them on side.'

'You reckon?'

'Forget about the kids, Penny, it's you I want to spend the rest of my life with.'

'You do? Goodness.' I felt breathless. I hadn't been expecting this at all. 'Don't you think it's early days yet?'

He turned back and looked into my eyes.

'No. I know exactly what I want. The question is, do you?'

'Er, well, I don't know. Maybe. I certainly like you a lot,' I said lamely.

'And I like you a lot too,' he said, still fixed on my eyes.

'Let me think about it,' I said, finally looking away after a long pause. 'It's a bit sudden, that's all. And there are so many implications. Like where would we live? We'd need a gazillion bedrooms and bathrooms — you should see how long Charlotte takes in the shower each morning. And Lord only knows what she'd say if we did move in. She's bad enough criticising her father for running off with Jacinta, and *she* doesn't have any kids at all. And Adam has been going through a difficult phase, he's been withdrawn at school, not at all like he used to be . . .' I realised I was burbling and stopped myself.

'Adam's getting on so well with Zak. He's not at all withdrawn with him.'

'Yes, they're certainly good together,' I conceded. 'But look at Charlotte and Drew. They've been getting on each other's nerves all evening.'

'True. But they'll get over it. Heavens, this is just the beginning. I'm sure they'll all settle down if we work on it.'

'Let's think about it,' I reiterated. 'Like you said, this is just the beginning.'

The girls were still out when we got home and we retreated to bed with our books, just like a couple who had been together for years. I was about to drift off to sleep when my mobile rang beside the bed.

'Oh no,' I groaned. 'I bet something's happened to Mum.'

But it was Steve.

'Ish that you, Penny?' His voice was slurred; he'd obviously been drinking.

'Yes, why? What on earth do you want at this hour?'

'You, old girl. I want you.'

'Steve, you've been drinking. You don't know what you're saying.'

'Yesh I do, I know purfickly well what I'm shaying. I want you, Penny. I always have.' He hiccupped loudly. 'Pardies.'

'It's the middle of the night. Go to bed.'

'With you? That would be very nice indeed. I'll be right over.'

'No, Steve, don't. I'm not at home.'

'You're not? Where are you then? Not with that dushty ol' profeshor, I hope?'

'None of your business. Now go away.'

'But Penny, I need you. I'shd never have left you.'

'Really?'

Not all that long ago, I would have given everything I owned to have him come back to me, to say he needed me. But now, I didn't feel a thing.

'Yes, it's true. I want to come home,' he said quietly. There was a sort of gasping sound. Surely he wasn't about to cry?

'Where's Jacinta?'

'I don't know. But that'sh not the point.'

'I suspect it's very much the point, Steve. Look, I've got to go.'

'No, Penny, don't go, don't . . .'

I hung up on him without a moment's guilt.

'Sounds like your ex is having a troubled time,' Simon said sleepily.

'He's off his tree. It sounds like Jacinta has left him. Or at least run off for the weekend without him.'

'But isn't he staying at her place?'

'Indeed. Wouldn't it be sad if she kicked him out!'

'He might want to move back with you.'

'Well, he can forget that. He'll have to find his own apartment, because he's not coming back home.'

• • •

On Easter Sunday I treated Simon to breakfast in bed, or at least a cup of coffee and an Easter egg — one of those hollow ones containing more chocolates inside. He demolished the contents then started on the shell.

'You're lucky you don't have to worry about your waistline,' I teased as he chomped his way through it.

'Never have,' he laughed, patting his flat tummy.

I'd brought Easter eggs for all the kids too — a tradition since they were little. The boys devoured theirs in no time. The girls, however, didn't surface until near midday after coming in late from the party.

'Thanks, Mum,' Charlotte said when I presented her with her usual marshmallow egg. 'Happy Easter to you too.' She gave me a kiss and took her egg off to the sofa where she unwrapped it slowly, smoothing out the foil like she'd always done.

'No thanks,' said Drew, turning aside when I proffered hers. 'I never eat chocolate. And Mum doesn't believe in all that commercial rubbish.'

'Double helpings for someone then,' I said cheerfully, unfazed by the snub, and put the egg in the fruit bowl where I had no doubt it would soon be snaffled.

I was in the bathroom washing my hands and staring at myself in the mirror, wondering what on earth I might be letting myself in for, when I heard my mobile ring again.

'Do you want me to get that for you?' Simon called through.

'No, leave it, I'm on holiday,' I called back.

I tugged at my temples, pulling my cheeks and eyes up so that I looked ten years younger. 'Who are you kidding?' I said to my reflection. 'You can't even cope with your own kids, let alone someone else's.'

A return to good weather emptied the house of kids and noise and Simon and I spent a pleasant few hours reading then chatting over a cup of tea. The peace was broken abruptly with the return of Drew, complaining to her father about some misdemeanour of Charlotte's. It sounded like some boy that Drew fancied had tried to attach himself to Charlotte and, according to Drew, it was all her fault for leading him on.

I retreated to the kitchen to prepare a roast meal — an Easter tradition of mine we'd agreed to follow.

'What's that for?' Drew said, wrinkling up her nose.

'We're having roast chicken for dinner,' I said.

'Eewww. Mum never makes roasts. They're too fatty. Mum says . . .'

'Oh quit it, Drew,' Simon chipped in. 'Penny and I want to celebrate Easter in the traditional way.'

'Well, you can count me out,' she said and flounced off to the bathroom for the longest shower in human history.

'Sorry, Penny, she's being a little miss today. She gets like this sometimes.'

'Don't worry about it,' I shrugged. 'After the dramas of the last few weeks, it pales into insignificance. I'd never have thought it possible, but I really don't care.' I smiled and reached out to touch his arm. 'There's nothing like a brush with death to give you a better steer on the unimportant things in life.'

Drew saw to it that the meal was a disaster, whining that there was nothing for her to eat as soon as I served the roast, then getting up from the table and making a great show of getting herself a salad. Simon rolled his eyes at me and whispered, 'Sorry.' I grinned in response and shrugged.

The fresh fruit summer pudding I'd made for dessert wasn't to her liking either.

'I don't like marshmallows,' she said, pushing her plate away.

'Well, don't eat them,' Simon said crossly. 'Really, Drew, you're not being at all fair to Penny.'

'It's great thanks, Penny,' Zak said, shovelling his down almost as quickly as Adam.

'Yeah, gnnnh,' Adam mumbled with his mouth full.

I suspect Simon twisted her arm because Drew actually offered to do the dishes and didn't argue with Charlotte once. Afterwards, when Simon was out of the room, she came to me and said she was sorry for criticising my cooking.

'That's okay, Drew. I can understand you're upset with me being here with your Dad.'

Her eyes widened in surprise, as if she hadn't expected me to be so frank.

The kids took off down to the beach soon afterwards, leaving Simon and me alone. We made coffee and sat on the terrace in companionable silence. It felt very comfortable.

All the depressing thoughts that had swirled around in my head in the days after the operation had vanished. From now on, I thought, I'm going to live my life to make the most of every day — for my kids, my family, my friends, my clients, and for me. No more would I take tomorrow for granted. Tomorrow was for living. Tomorrow was for me, myself and I.

'So, have you had any thoughts about how things might be for us?' Simon asked after some time.

'In a way,' I hedged.

'What do you mean?'

I sipped my coffee. I didn't know what to say. Or rather, I knew what I wanted to say, I just didn't know how to say it.

'Well.' I paused again, gathering words. 'I think you and I have definitely got something going between us, something that's pretty special, something I never thought I'd find.' I gulped, willing myself to go on. 'I love being with you. This weekend has been terrific and has shown me that we could live together, just the two of us, pretty happily.' I sipped my coffee again.

'But the thing is, I'm not ready for that yet.' I was gaining momentum now. 'I'm not ready for such a major commitment and most of all I'm not ready to cope with four teenagers under one roof. It's just too soon, Simon. I'm sorry.'

He didn't say anything for a while; he just stared into his coffee.

'I don't blame you,' he said eventually. 'We've only known each other for a few months. But I feel so comfortable with you, as if we were meant to be together.'

'I feel comfortable with you too. But I'm not ready for such a big commitment as moving in together. I need some time to live with myself now, after all this trauma. I need some time for me.'

'Sure.' He looked up from his coffee cup and smiled that lazy, wonderful smile. 'I understand.'

We didn't discuss it again while we were there, but the relationship, to my relief, wasn't affected by my rejection of his idea. The rest of the holiday flew by in a blur of sun, sea, sand and even sex, while the kids seemed to have reached détente. They spent the rest of Sunday night on the beach with other teenagers and came back late and slightly tipsy from more than the can each of beer we'd given them.

On Monday morning, Simon reminded the boys we were leaving after lunch. They'd not long stumbled out of bed and into the lounge.

'Do we have to?' Zak said. 'Adam and I want to take the board out.'

'But the weather's still rotten,' Simon reasoned.

'Doesn't matter. It's stopped raining and there's a bit of wind.'

They took the windsurfer down to the beach one last time while we packed up and cleaned the house. As soon as she'd shoved all her stuff into her bag and rolled up her sleeping bag, Drew was off after them. Charlotte stayed behind and helped.

'You can go down too, you know. Simon and I can do this. It'll be nice and cosy,' I joked.

'Why? You're not planning to move in with them are you?'

'Good Lord, what ever gave you that idea?'

'Nothing. You seem really keen on him though.'

'Do I? Well, I do like him a lot. But no, honey, you don't have to worry. I'm not living with anyone except you and Adam — and maybe Grandpa — for quite some time.'

'So you might move in with Simon one day?'

'Maybe one day. But you'll be long gone by then. So don't give it another thought.'

'I wouldn't want to live with Drew, you know, she's . . .'

Simon came back inside at that moment and Charlotte broke off.

'I know what you mean,' I said lightly and resumed packing the leftover food into the chillybin. 'I don't think the time is right either.'

Chapter 18

On the way home, Simon put Split Enz into the car CD player. For once, there were no protests from the back seat.

Charlotte listened to her iPod, dozing occasionally. The boys intermittently chatted and texted their friends. Drew stared out the window and started to nod off. Then her phone rang. Over the noise of 'I See Red', I heard her say, 'Yeah, it was good. We had a great time. Those kids from . . .' The rest was obscured as the song rose to one of its many crescendos. I figured she was talking about the friends she'd met down at the beach.

'Penny for your thoughts, if you'll pardon the pun?' Simon brought me back to the present with a jolt.

'Oh, nothing much.' I smiled at him. 'I was just thinking about what a great weekend it's been.'

'It's been very special for me.' He gave me one of his

trademark smiles and I felt my insides do somersaults.

'Me too.' I smiled back.

'And I promise not to hassle you again about moving in together. I can see it makes perfect sense to wait until our kids leave home. I want to give you the space you need.'

'At the rate time flies, it won't seem very long.'

'And we can have a lot more good times like this weekend.'

'Maybe we could do something in the winter?

'Have you ever tried skiing?'

I shook my head no.

'Well, maybe we could buy learners' packages and take the kids. I've always wanted to give it a go.' He paused. 'Or we could take one of those cheap packages to somewhere warm, like the Gold Coast or Fiji.'

'They all sound nice,' I laughed. 'I've always hankered after learning to ski, actually. And I love beach holidays. From now on, I'm not going to put things off.'

'I don't blame you. Besides, that *Twenty Good Summers* book tells people our age we haven't got long left. We should make the most of them.'

I nodded agreement. Only a few weeks ago, I'd been thinking I was fresh out of good summers; now it felt like there was a much better chance of seeing them out. I settled back to listen to the music.

During a quiet bit I heard Drew's voice, still on the phone to her friend: '. . . Dad's new girlfriend. . . . Yeah, she's okay.'

I smiled. I was happy with that. I looked at Simon. He grinned back. He'd heard too.

'You've passed the Drew Wakefield test. That's quite something,' he said quietly just as the music gathered more volume.

The journey passed quickly despite the mounting traffic the closer we got to home. I suspect I slept quite a bit of the way, hopefully without dribbling or snoring. Before I knew it, we were pulling into our driveway.

Drew and Zak jumped out with Charlotte and Adam to help unload the car.

'Here, Mum, I'll take your bag for you.' Charlotte grabbed my sports bag full of clothes and whisked it inside along with a pile of other stuff. I turned around and noticed the boot was now empty of all our gear — Adam had ferried the rest inside while I was talking. He came back out and said goodbye to Zak with much arm slapping and humour.

Charlotte returned to say her goodbyes too, thanking Simon for a cool weekend; Drew promised they could both go riding the following weekend, and she'd be able to teach her, since there were no events over the winter.

I farewelled Simon with a reasonably chaste kiss and a less chaste embrace.

'Would you like to meet up next Friday after work?' he asked. I nodded agreement. 'I'll pick you up at seven,' he said smiling, then jumped in the car and the three of them were gone.

Adam turned to me. 'Can we have takeaways now Mum?'

'Eeew, Adam, you're so gross. No wonder you're getting fat.' Charlotte prodded him in his slightly pudgy tummy.

'I am not. You're the one that's fat.' He prodded her backside — he knew her weak points.

'That's so not fair. All the McDonald's you tuck away, you should be twice the size you are now.'

'Yeah, well, some of us can take it better than others.' He prodded her tummy this time.

'Adam, that's enough,' I said. 'Besides Charlotte's quite right. You eat far too many burgers and fries for your own good.'

'Well I'm not eating tofu and that awful green wheatgrass horse fodder that Charlotte likes so much.'

'Come on guys, let's go inside and see what's in the freezer.'

'Awwwww!' Adam wasn't giving up his fries without a fight.

I nearly tripped over all the bags in the hall. The kids had kindly brought them in but that was the extent of it.

'Come on, give us a hand here,' I called them back from their sprint upstairs away from the reality of cleaning up. 'Charlotte, you can take the bags into the laundry and empty out all the washing and get it on. Adam, you can empty out the chillybin then carry the bags upstairs when Charlotte's finished with them. There's going to be a new regime around here. We all do our bit.'

I smiled at myself. How many times had I said this before? Still, things *were* different now. I'd sifted through all the theories about what might cause breast cancer and most had been discarded in the trash folder where they belonged. I knew for sure genes had something to do with it, except none of my closer rellies had ever had it. The only other possibility, I reckoned, was stress. What better excuse then for ridding my overly complicated life of some of its complications?

Reluctantly at first, but with gathering enthusiasm, Charlotte and Adam set about their tasks. In no time, the washing machine was humming away, the chillybin was emptied and back in the garage and the kitchen was cleared of the holiday chattels.

While they were preoccupied, I checked the messages on

the blinking answerphone. There were eighteen. I gave up before I started — that was way too many to cope with right now.

I opened the freezer. There was nothing. The frozen dinners had all gone. Even the pile of casseroles everyone had brought round after my operation had been cleaned out. If I was going to get dinner out of the freezer tonight, I'd have to defrost some meat and cook it. Damn!

'Adam,' I called up the stairs, 'you can have McDonald's after all. How about you bike down the road and get it?'

'Can't I drive?'

'No, not 'til you get your licence.'

'Awww!'

'No. It's just down the road. You've got a perfectly good bicycle.'

'But it's so naff. I can't be seen there on a bicycle.'

'Well you can walk then.'

'But they'll get cold.'

'Mu-uum, there's something wrong with the washing machine,' Charlotte called from the laundry.

Sure enough, there was a ghastly noise emanating from the bowels of the machine and it was juddering and jumping all over the place as its spin cycle spun out of control. Damn!

I dived over to the control panel and turned it off. There were a few final shakes and a large clunk and it stopped.

I started to laugh. Charlotte looked at me as if I'd lost it.

'Life goes on and thank God for that,' I said, clutching Charlotte's shoulder, shaking with laughter. 'Welcome back to the real world, Penny Rushmore.'

Acknowledgements

There are many friends and colleagues who have helped me on the journey to publication to whom I am most grateful. In particular, I'd like to thank Ross Gumbley for his highly humorous thoughts on humour; Isabel Mitchell for explaining the letter of the law; Amy McDermott for administering first aid; Harriet Allan for unfailingly cheerful editorial advice and confidence; Sarah Ell for fixing the glitches; and Paddy, Chris and Christine for answering bizarre questions about unexpected topics of editorial significance without questioning my sanity — at least, not to my face!